Buzz Killer

TOM STRAW

BUZZ KILLER
Copyright © 2017 by Tom Straw

Cover by Steve Cooley
Interior Design by QA Productions
Author photo © Jill Krementz

For Jennifer.
It's still a lovely ride.

"To live well is to live unnoticed."

— Ovid

"We're no longer in the Cold War.
Eavesdropping on friends is unacceptable."

— Vladimir Putin

C H A P T E R · 1

Text message and e-mail exchange, 7:12 p.m. – 12:06 a.m.:

Michael Jerome

Macie, where are you right now? V imp

Macie Wild

UnionSq. Just deposed Ivry cab drvr who picked
client from robbery lineup. PS dude's vizn so bad
couldn't find sig line on sworn stmt. Haha. Zup?

Michael Jerome

Caught a case here in night court. Def says
knows you. Jackson Hall. He's coming up for
arraignment but wants to talk with you first.

Macie Wild

I rcll. Sorry he's back in the system. Told
me all done w burglary last time.

Michael Jerome

He's down for homicide. How
fast can you get here?

Macie Wild

!!… Near sub now. I'll hop a train and be there in 10.

Macie Wild

T—Chng pln. Cncl my lect at John Jay
tnt. Seeing Jackson Hall at arrgmt now.

Tiger Foley

Will do. I'll tee-up your docs. Watch your e-mail.

To: Macie Wild
Re: Jackson Hall / attchs
[Client/JH046/parole_compliance_docs.pdf (225.4kb)]

Macie, for your ref, attaching pdf of Mr. Hall's parole files
from his prior convictions, including job history, community
service, etc., for his Criminal Justice Agency bail docs.

Tiger Foley, Certified Paralegal
Office of Macie Wild, Attorney at Law
Manhattan Center for Public Defense
New York, NY 10007

This e-mail and attachments contain legally privileged information. If you are
not the intended recipient, you are hereby notified that any disclosure or use
of this information is prohibited. - Manhattan Center for Public Defense Inc.

Text message exchange, 12:06 a.m.:

Michael Jerome
Len, sorry for the late hour. Macie and I
are at impasse and need a referee.

Len Asher
Colbert's a rerun, anyway. What going on?

Michael Jerome
We're pre-arraignment, w clock ticking,
so briefly: Client about to eat a Murder-1.
I spent all night hammering out a dispo
offer w DA. M-2, 25yrs, no parole.

Macie Wild
For the recd, not much into
determining life/dth in txt msgs.

Michael Jerome
We're crunched. And It's a fair deal.

Macie Wild

I know this def. Says he's innocent. I believe him.

                                        Michael Jerome

                                    He's boned. If this goes to trial and

                                        craters—it's a life sentence.

Macie Wild

We're bargaining years of a man's life. We're
supposed 2B lawyers, not auctioneers.

                                        Michael Jerome

                                    Or gamblers. BTW, odds are better

                                    at Foxwoods. –Shit. We're up soon.

                                        Need a Yoda moment, boss.

Len Asher

As always, it's up to the client. It may be the last
time for years his opinion matters on anything.
Go back in, make your cases, then may God
help him. . . .And whomever he chooses.

CHAPTER · 2

Macie Wild froze in place beside her '08 Corolla on the scarred blacktop of the Rikers Island parking lot and stared, fixated, at pure beauty. On the near bank of the East River, on the freedom side of the chain-link and concertina, a great blue heron stood motionless, spindles-deep in the estuary, waiting, patient, staring into the murk lapping the rocks behind it. A light morning breeze rustled a few showgirl wing feathers but the bird's focus never left the shallows. Looking every bit to her like a regal visitor from prehistory, the bill at the end of the long neck remained inches above the surface, poised to strike as if time itself paused before a lightning move would let fly the yellow dagger. Until then the hunter would see and not be seen.

It was Macie who blinked. She popped the trunk and leaned inside to ditch anything sharp, metal, or controversial. It took five seconds. She had learned years ago to start carrying her keys, fountain pen, Shuffle, L-shaped metal ruler, and telescoping pointer in a nylon zippered file, a Levenger special. She plucked it from her briefcase, added her cell phone, then, out of habit, gripped the bare finger of her left hand for the diamond ring that was no longer a security concern. After patting herself down, Macie zipped the case and shut the trunk.

When it slammed, a sudden spread of wide, blue-gray plumage took flight with two glistening streams dotting the water beneath dangling legs. She watched it flap above the tanks of the waste treatment plant on the opposite shore and then continue west, becoming an eye test the closer it got to Wards Island. She lost sight of the bird when it bisected the only Manhattan skyscraper visible from where she stood, the controversial new condominium tower recently built on West Fifty-Seventh. Between the coils of razor wire, Macie could make out the top ten of its eighty-eight floors. She turned toward the jail complex and wondered if the inmates had a view of the tallest residential building in the Western Hemisphere, with a penthouse that went for ninety-five-mil, something even Manhattan's own wealthiest couldn't afford. Maybe, she thought, people had it wrong. Maybe New York was actually a Tale of Three Cities.

Inside the Otis Bantum center the sensation of entering another world gripped her, same as always. Not just the assault of raw human noise, of stadium-decibel chatter of hundreds of voices echoing off linoleum and brick. Or even the smell of disinfectant, institutional cooking, and stale sweat. It was the soul X-ray. All the eyes that found hers and wouldn't let go. The passing inmates gazing through the ballistic glass with curiosity, or worse. And the corrections officers, tracking her, either in smug dismissal or unmasked contempt. Because she was a defense lawyer, a coddler of the lowlifes who fucked each other up and fucked up their days. Even the COs she had regular dealings with—otherwise nice guys, professionals making the most of a hard job—held a line of brisk cordiality behind an invisible, but palpable, shield. It made her wonder who was really imprisoned here.

Signed in, searched, wanded, and hand stamped, Wild affixed her visitor badge. The officer gave her the silent four-finger beckon and she stepped alone into the security pass-through. As the metal lock of the door behind her shot closed and she waited for the one ahead of her to roll open, Macie did what she always did in this suspension of time: She paused to quiet her brain and remind herself why she was here. For justice. Justice for her client. And, yes, justice for the victim.

When they brought Jackson Hall to her, he looked the same as he did on the outside. Like whatever he wore was too big for him. Five seven and 130 made everything swim on his small frame, even the orange jumpsuit that had now become a cultural meme for everyone except the McDonald's Hamburglar, who still did stripes. Hall settled quickly into his chair opposite her with a nod and the half smile he always sported, as if he just remembered a dirty joke and was deciding whether to share it.

But that morning it didn't seem so much amusement as a prison face, a dash of cockiness to give the bigger inmates reason to think twice before challenging him. They picked up their phones and began.

"Any word on bail yet? I don't think I can do this." No hello, no thanks for coming. Just a get me out.

"We're on it. Unfortunately this time it's a murder case, and—"

"'Cept I didn't do it. And it don't help the fucking *Post's* put my picture on page one and gave me that goddamn nickname." The New York tabloids had tagged Jackson Hall with some nasty ones back in 2010 when he got busted for a string of apartment B&Es on the Lower East Side. His MO was to hit lobbies, pretending to be delivering Chinese takeout, and rob units that didn't answer his buzz. Headline punsters ran his mug shot under banners like "Buzzer Bandit," "Buzz-ted," and one gold-medal groaner, "The Embuzzler." This new charge for murdering his burglary partner earned Hall a headline upgrade, and, on a slow news day, every newsstand screamed it: "Buzz Killer!"

"After the grand jury meets, I'll try again at your arraignment on the indictment." Macie knew even a lenient judge would choke on his record of two prior bail skips and three failures to appear. But no sense picking that scab just then. She tried her most consoling smile and asked, "They treating you all right so far?"

"This morning in commissary lineup one of the bangers came at me with a box cutter. Some kid trying to make a name, slashing me." He traced a line from his ear to his cheek. His face wasn't cut but raw skin curled off his knuckles and his fingers were fat with swelling from defending himself.

"That can't happen."

"Did happen. Some other fool sucker punched me from behind last night. Check it out." He turned away from the window and parted hairs at the back of his head to show her a goose egg with a nasty cut. "See what headlines get you?" When he sat back down, Macie studied the specks of gray dusting the forty-six-year-old's sideburns. She would still bet on him, even up against someone half his age. "It's not just the headline. I'm the cocksucker who broke The Code and offed his partner. I'm a walking target in here."

Wild shook her head. "Not gonna be. Deputy Warden Bohannon is supposed to be in charge of security in this unit. I'm going to spoil his day, soon as we finish."

"Go ahead, but they're already on it. The COs said they're going to transfer my ass to West Complex. That's where they isolate guys with diseases. Oh, and that old French dude who banged the hotel maid." Then he realized his audience. "My bad." And then he smiled in full for the first time. "Thanks for coming in like this."

In fact Macie could have done a video conference from Manhattan but didn't for good reasons. First, vid-confs are limited to thirty minutes; an in-person guaranteed them two hours. And second, ever since the Nassau County prosecutor attempted in vain to introduce his recording of a privileged jailhouse phone conversation between a prisoner and his lawyer, she had been wary about electronic privacy. Of course, out of practicality, she still used phones and video, but sparingly, and never for an initial debrief. The night before she'd only had five minutes with Hall in the glass conference booth in Arraignment Part Three. For something this critical, this in-depth, Macie wanted proximity and direct eye contact—even through a bulletproof partition on a jail phone that also gave her pause about privacy. Wild opened his file and took out one of her DOC-compliant pencils—no metal, no eraser. "I want you to tell me what happened, Mr. Hall. Everything."

"I didn't kill him's what happened. I might cop to some break-ins, but I didn't kill anybody."

She had to wonder how many times over the decades those exact words had been spoken over that very phone from that side of the window. But all she said was, "Walk me through it."

"Rúben and me worked some gigs here and there together. Made us some good money and all was rufus between us, you understand? Then I hear he's dead, and I get popped. It's bullshit." He finished with a strong nod, like that would be that. She looked over her list of questions, knowing that couldn't be that.

"You always worked alone before. When did you start working with this other man, Rúben Pinto?"

The thief's eyes darted away from hers and he shifted in his chair.

Macie knew her visual cues, and a whiff of evasiveness had slipped by Jackson Hall's jailhouse swagger. "We really have to get into all this?"

"Jackson, you know I do. And you know why." Macie held her pencil over a blank page and waited until resignation overtook reticence.

"Met Pinto a couple months ago fishing up at the East Harlem pier. We'd see each other and just nod, but I could tell from his vibe he'd stacked time. So over weeks we get talking and, sure enough, Rúben did a stretch at Fishkill, and when I told him I did my bit upstate at Bare Hill, he said he figured. One thing leads to another, and one day he shows up without a pole and wants to take a walk. Says he's been working a gig with a guy that's looking for a third man, and if I wanted in."

Macie jotted key words, listening without judgment as her client described how, not even a year out of prison, he'd bought his ticket back. "You know, I've been running clean since my release," he said, as if reading her mind. "But life costing what it costs and a new girlfriend costing what she costs . . ." He chuckled but she held her listening pose. "Anyway, six days a week raking up turds at the doggy drop-off wasn't cutting it for me, so I said, yeah, let's talk. So done and done."

But not for the attorney. "When you say crew. Banks? Retail? Jewelry stores?"

"Who you talking to?" That chuckle again. Raspy, just like his speaking voice, it betrayed cigarettes and cheap wine. "You'll never see me do a stickup. This gig was my thing, housebreaking. But varsity level, an elite operation. Pinto was right. Said his crew chief knew his shit. Did he ever. Man had skills. Not sure where he got them, he's not much of a talker. Strange dude, in fact. But he knows where to hit and when to hit. And no buzzing to get in. These were luxury pads, man. Doorman, concierge, perfumy hallways, and best of all, boss always knew what apartments would be empty."

"Once again," she said, "your thing."

"No people, no confrontation, no mess. You got it."

"OK, I have to ask. This step-up for you." She found the word on her notepad. "This 'elite' crew. Tell me more about the elite part."

"I just did."

"But sounds like somebody had information."

"Uh-huh. And skills, like I said. The know-how and the tools to get into these places—and out again—like ghosts."

"Undetected?"

"Still undetected. Even now."

"I'd like the name of this crew chief."

"No."

"He's involved. He could be a suspect."

Hall shook his head emphatically. "Not going there." Then he held the phone away and swiveled, shouting to the rest of the prisoners in the conference cubicles and to the hallway behind him, "Hear that, y'all? You listening? Man honors The Code here! Not giving up my crime bros!"

While he continued his loud talk, Macie decided to come back to this when he wasn't new to the fight. "Just tell me this. Was there anyone else on your crew?"

"No. Just me, Pinto, and the chief."

"And I assume it was lucrative?"

"Like it made my other jobs look amateur."

Still looking to explore the motives inside the crew, she asked, "And how did the split go?"

"Fifty-fifty. Chief got half and Pinto and me split the other. Cool with me. It was a good take. Plus, like the chief told us, it was his gear and his expertise. No complaints here."

"What about Rúben?" He hesitated. Another tell. She used a technique that worked a lot. She ignored the silence and repeated the question as if for the first time. "What about Rúben?"

Jackson Hall wagged his head side to side. "Rú was all right with it," he lied.

"Fair enough," she lied. Something more for her to come back to next time. "I want a list of the places you broke into."

"You think I'm nuts?"

"I think you're innocent of a murder. Let me do what I need to do to build your case."

He averted his gaze again. Macie had experienced this twice now and waited him out, letting the silence do its work. His eyes darted back to hers, but for only a lick. "Ai'ght. I'll tell you one. The Barksdale. And I'll tell you only because the police already know that one. They connected me and Pinto to that job, don't ask me how. Which is why I think they bagged me for his murder."

"Why?"

"Laziness. Pure and simple. Easier to go after me because I knew him and I'm this career breaker. Why give yourself a hernia when you can just bust me?"

It wasn't a defense she would ever mount, but Wild had to admit to the grain of truth. "OK, The Barksdale, got it. Why won't you tell me the others?"

"Two reasons. I won't set up my crew chief to get pinched. And second, most of the apartment owners don't even know they were robbed yet. I say, let it be."

"Jackson, look at me." She waited until he did. "We have to be a team, understand? I can't help you if you don't share everything. You're holding back."

He scoffed. "Everybody holds something back."

"Don't. Not with me."

"'K," he said. Then he tore a sheet from his notepad and blew his nose in it, another way to disconnect from her. Impatient, she waited him out while he turned away to pick his nostrils.

As often happened in that room, her thoughts drifted back to visiting her brother there when he was arrested in one of the Occupy protests. Unlike Jackson Hall and most of her other clients, Walter hadn't asked how soon he'd get out. Instead he asked her to check on his parishioners. Mrs. Montez had a broken hip and needed a meal delivered. Juan Regades was kicking and needed a ride to the clinic for his Suboxone. Five years ago, young Father Walt had gazed at his lawyer-sister from behind that glass, exhilarated—a radical priest fulfilling his destiny of civil disobedience. Justice was also his pursuit. It got him killed.

When Hall finally settled, Macie shifted gears to the murder victim, figuring he'd be less protective of a dead man. "Did Pinto have any enemies that you know of?"

"Enemies is kind of strong. He did just go through an ugly breakup with a girlfriend. What else . . . ?" Hall scanned the top of the window frame that separated them. "There was a guy he did time with up at Fishkill. Wouldn't call him an enemy though. They had this sibling rivalry thing, for sure. Lots of bickering. Under it all I think the dude was pissed because Pinto asked me to join the crew instead of him."

Of course he wouldn't give up the names of the girlfriend or the cellmate either. "And what about you? Did Pinto get under your skin too?"

Again, that hesitation. "Hey, I roll with it, ya know?"

"Just so I have it, when was the last time you saw Rúben Pinto?"

His reply came sharply. "Jeez, woman, what are you, a cop? Two days ago. We had breakfast."

"And do you have anyone who can vouch for your whereabouts when he was killed?"

"Kinda tough," he said. "Since nobody told me when that happened. Or where. Or how." Because the DA hadn't released a coroner's report with time of death, Macie asked him to start with a list of places he'd been the twenty-four hours before his arrest plus the names of anyone who could vouch. It included an off-the-books gambling parlor, his fishing pier on the Harlem River, a movie theater, a supermarket on East 101st, and a bodega in his neighborhood.

"Tell me about your arrest."

"Came late yesterday afternoon. I'm walking from my place to get smokes and a scratcher, and four cop cars roll up on me and they come out all 'get the fuck down' with guns drawn."

"Did they say how they found you?"

"Didn't tell me shit. Just under arrest for the murder of my man— Didn't even know Rúben was dead till I had my nose on the sidewalk. Then they went up to my place and made my girlfriend stand outside while they went through it."

Macie got a new pencil and said, "What's her name? I'd like to ask her some questions."

Somewhere inside him a primal switch flipped and he snapped at Wild. "No, she's out of this." Of course Macie would find the girlfriend on her own. He switched the phone to his other ear and said, "Can you tell me? How'd he die and where?"

"I heard he was killed in his apartment. Beaten and stabbed."

"The cops tell you all that?"

Macie had to make a difficult admission of the truth to a man about to go on trial for murder. The police had shut her out. So had the DA. "I got it from the TV news," she said.

He quieted himself, then his eyes met hers, melting her through the ballistic glass when he asked, "We did the right thing, turning down that plea deal, right? Ms. Wild . . . right?"

This time, it was Macie who averted her gaze.

CHAPTER · 3

The elevator ride to the seventh-floor offices of the Manhattan Center for Public Defense took forever. The doors couldn't part fast enough and Macie slammed into one on her charge out of the box and into the lobby. At the sound of the collision, a half-dozen clients all turned from where they waited in a corner grouping of worn leatherette chairs. Lenard, the receptionist, gauged Macie's hurry and pressed the automatic door release to the inside offices before her palm reached the handle. The hard snap of the steel deadbolt behind her carried a Rikers echo. Behind bars, or places people go to stay outside them, sturdy locks were simply facts.

After a quick pit stop to wash the jail off her hands, she extracted her notes, ditched her briefcase on her desk, and strode across the secretarial bull pen to the small conference room. Macie had called ahead from the RFK bridge with the thirty-minute warning, and her team sat waiting around the maple laminated conference table, ready to dive in. The room carried a tang of whiteboard cleaner thanks to her paralegal, Tiger Foley, who had just wiped the Dry Erase ghosts off the new Case Board at the head of the table. The young Australian, named not for the golfer but his own famous aboriginal ancestor from an 1860s cricket team, may have been the most perfectly suited Macie Wild had seen in the role. Intelligent, well trained, and detail oriented, her paralegal possessed the greatest talent of all: anticipation. If she could just get him to slow down so she could weed through the Melbourne accent, he'd be perfect.

She exchanged quick greetings with him and the other three: her friend and social worker, Soledad Esteves Torres; Jonathan Monheit, her team investigator; and, at the far end of the table, Chip Ross, the summer intern from Louisiana State University Law.

Macie pumped coffee from the thermal pot on the sideboard. Stirring in her Equal, she began her briefing on the jailhouse interview with their client. As the team took notes, she rose from time to time, logging key points on the whiteboard. "I think it's especially notable that Jackson Hall got himself involved in this so-called elite B&E crew. He's not exactly a sophisticated thief, and reading Rúben Pinto's file from when we represented him years ago, his CV is on the scruffy side: Juvenile delinquencies growing up in Fall River, in and out of prison for home burglaries, larceny, receiving stolen goods, trafficking in stolen property, et cetera, et cetera. It makes you wonder if these two got in over their heads breaking into multimillion-dollar condos with a serious pro. That much money is tinder for infighting. Especially with a lopsided split."

The social worker, as usual, asked the first question. And as usual, it was about the well-being of the client. "How's Mr. Hall doing in there?"

The lawyer waggled a hand. "Dicey, Sol. Last night he took a blind-side punch to the back of his head. This morning somebody tried to cut him."

Soledad traced an imaginary diagonal down her cheek, same as Hall had done an hour before. When Macie affirmed her educated guess, Soledad said, "It's gladiator school in there. Some kid's going to make a name off a target like him."

"I already spoke to the DW about expediting his turf to the West Complex."

"Deputy Warden Bohannon? I'd better follow up with Population Management just to make another wheel squeak."

"Jonathan, is that case-related?" asked Macie with a gaze down the table to the team's investigator. Busted for texting, verboten during a homicide briefing, Monheit dropped his grin and pocketed the iPhone he'd been concealing under the table.

To Wild this was one more reason to be pissed about her boss's new hiring profile for investigators. Historically the Manhattan Center had employed retired NYPD detectives who, still only in their forties, brought a couple decades of case-hardened experience to the job. Unfortunately, some of them—especially the ex-Internal Affairs cops—also radiated a harsh 'tude toward clients and palpable disdain for the more liberal-minded attorneys in the office. Recently the executive director swapped out what he called "the Popeye Doyles" in favor of new college grads with an investigative bent. So into Macie's world came Jonathan

Monheit: Twenty-four, a business major who minored in human rights, with a master's in forensic accounting from the University of Washington, and a learn-as-you-go approach to street work. "Question about the crime scene," he said, either out of curiosity or to act like he was focused. "Any progress securing permission to go in?"

"That would be a no."

Chip Ross got a puzzled look and raised one finger to be called on. "Sorry, but I've just gotta ask." The Chattanooga native turned to the investigator, merely two years his senior. "Y'all haven't been to the crime scene yet?" When Monheit answered with a grimace, the L-1 intern turned up table. "I'm not dissing anyone's performance. Truly. It's just . . ."

As he let it hang there, Macie finished for him. "Kind of insane we haven't been to the crime scene by now?"

"Mad as a cut snake," blurted Tiger with a laugh that Macie and Soledad both joined. "Welcome to Big Apple justice, southern man."

The intern waited out their chuckles. "Guess I'm missing the joke."

"No, Chip, you're good. In fact," explained Macie, "it's no joke. You see, the DA here in New York City is legendarily hard-line. They typically stonewall all defense attempts to do discovery. They shut us completely out of our own cases."

He eyed them warily. "Seriously, this is a joke, right?"

"I wish," said Macie. "The law states the district attorney's office only needs to share its evidence with defense counsel 'prior to trial.' Prior means as little as one hour before we go to court."

Foley, the paralegal, picked it up from there. "That means the prosecutor has all the goodies. All the witness interviews, all the crime scene photos, all the forensics, all the ballistics, all the surveillance video—everything we need to mount a defense."

"Doesn't get more hardball," said Macie. "I will file a request for discovery . . ." Without even looking, she held out her hand and the paralegal slipped the formal request into it, everything already completed by him, flagged for her signature. As she inked it in with the cherished Parker 75 that her father had used in law school, Wild said, "I'm sitting down with the prosecutor later. I'll see what I can worm out of her. And after the grand jury meets and we have the arraignment on the indictment, I'll file a motion for a pretrial statement hearing to suppress any comments our client might have made to the police, citing violation of the Sixth Amendment's right to counsel."

"A stall?" asked Chip.

Tiger jumped in. "No, to force them to call in the detective who's handling the case, which allows Ms. Wild to examine him under oath to learn what he or she knows and to have the right to subpoena the case files and notes the DA's wowsers won't give up."

"Sweet."

Macie smiled. "It'll be crumbs and peels at best, but anything we can get, we get."

"I'm stuck on the whole bludgeoning and stabbing part of this," said Soledad. "You and I both know Jackson Hall. He's all about no confrontation and no weapons."

"There's a first for everything," said Monheit.

"You speaking from your years of vast street experience?" asked Tiger. The paralegal had a short fuse for this rookie investigator and his hipster sense of entitlement.

Monheit walked it back. "I'm just saying what the DA will. He and the victim had a beef, and he snapped."

"All right, first of all, the victim has a name." Macie got up and wrote "Rúben Pinto" in block letters in the top left corner of the Case Board then posted a print of his latest mug shot under it. "We're doing this for him too." She directed Monheit to go to the precinct that took Hall into custody. "See what you can find out there. A line on the arresting officers would be nice. Also—"

"Hang on, let me catch up," said Monheit. While he scribbled furiously, Tiger caught her eye and shook his head. Her investigator nodded. "Ready."

"Also dig into Rúben Pinto." Wild shared what little Hall had given up about him then continued, "I hear he had a broken romance. Find out whatever else you can. Other enemies, vices, money problems, do an X-ray." Wild slowed down and watched Monheit's head bob as he jotted.

"I've got all this, constable." The paralegal indicated his laptop on which he not only keyed in the minutes, but also kept a Pear Note audio record, in case he needed to go back for transcript-level accuracy. "I'll AirDrop it after I make it all pretty."

Assistant District Attorney Theresa Fontanelli had agreed to meet Macie Wild in Foley Square at four forty-five. At ten minutes after five p.m., there was still no sign of the ADA. When the exodus of attorneys, defendants, and trial buffs streaming down the steps of the New York Supreme Court slowed to a trickle, the attorney checked her phone again for the late e-mail or missed phone message she knew wouldn't be there. Macie needed this meeting more than the prosecutor, so she waited, knowing that was the power balance. And so began the game.

It was June but the humidity was low. Nonetheless Macie's blouse clung to her skin when she leaned forward off the back of the park bench to stretch. Peering across Centre Street over a rack of Citi Bikes, she reflected, as she often did, on George Washington's quotation chiseled into the granite frieze: "The True Administration of Justice is the Firmest Pillar of Good Government." Then a lone figure in a navy-blue power suit appeared from behind one of the Corinthian colonnades under the Founding Father's inscription. Macie regarded Theresa Fontanelli and wondered if the ADA ever noticed it.

"You're sweating through your blouse," was the opener from the prosecutor. "Let's get into some AC." Without seeking agreement, without apology for being late, the assistant district attorney set a course across the square to a deli. "I missed lunch stuck in chambers with a dickhead judge who likes to hold court."

"As if court isn't court enough," joked Macie. If ADA Fontanelli caught it, she didn't let on, just pushed through the door and strode into the café ahead of her.

Wild, who had no appetite, sat across the linoleum table from the government lawyer, watching her excavate unwanted tomatoes out of her Caesar wrap with a plastic fork as she spoke. "You must have time to burn if you're meeting with me to push for discovery."

"I came for the atmosphere. And the shoulder I knew I could lean on." The ADA's eyes lifted slowly from the tabletop carnage to her. Most defense lawyers and DAs had cordial relationships. But Theresa Fontanelli, whose initials were said to be short for "WTF," lived combat ready. She also bore a special hardness toward Wild because Fontanelli had been rejected by the Park Avenue law firm that had accepted Macie. Fontanelli went on to join the district attorney's office, and, even though the recession forced Levine & Isaacs to downsize and platoon Wild to the public defender's office on a fellowship, WTF always felt obliged to prove herself better than the lawyer who got the job she didn't.

Macie had her own issue, slightly larger: Fontanelli had botched her brother's murder case. As lead prosecutor, her foot dragging and ineptitude caused so many trial delays that the murderer himself was killed in a jail escape before critical questions could be answered about the motive behind the crime. The power nature of their relationship forced Macie to swallow her resentment, but there was a jumbo elephant's trunk draped across their table.

"Tell you what." The ADA rerolled her wrap and took a bite, forcing Macie to wait while she chewed. After she eventually swallowed, Fontanelli set the thing down and napkinned before continuing. "I'm going to do you a favor, this once, and share." She must have read something on Macie's face because she did smile a little before adding, "What? I'm not allowed to be collegial?"

"No, collegial is good," said Wild. "I'm listening."

The ADA withdrew a file from her briefcase and fanned it open like a menu so only she could see its contents. "I have here select photos the Crime Scene Unit took of the decedent, Mr. Pinto, at the crime scene." She knew she had Macie's attention and milked the moment. "Oh, you'd like to see? Fine. I hope you have a strong gag reflex." Fontanelli doled out the digital prints one by one on the table in front of her like a casino dealer. Each color five-by-seven was more shocking and ghastly than the one before. Wild swallowed hard as she studied the images of a grisly, violent death with blood spray, protruding bones, and unfurled intestines. In the final shot—of the victim's head—his face was a meaty pulp, unrecognizable as Rúben Pinto. Even though Macie made no move to touch them, the ADA scooped them up and put them back in her file.

"No, you can't keep these. Nor can you have a coroner's report yet." Fontanelli winked. Actually winked. WTF?

"Is this what you call sharing?"

"I am sharing. And you know why? To give you a sneak preview of the horror show. So I can save you embarrassment and the taxpayers a lengthy trial that's a lock from the git-go."

Not terribly surprised at getting baited like this by a lawyer who talked more about winning than justice, Macie said, "Well, that is collegial of you. And here I was afraid you'd just try to spook me into jumping at a plea deal."

"Mike Jerome was going to take it."

"Mike Jerome is off the case." Wild fixed her with a determined gaze. "Guess we'll see each other in court." Macie's rebuff came wrapped in acrimony. The elephant had spoken.

The assistant district attorney paused. "What do you want, counselor?"

"A fair shot, that's all. I want discovery so I can mount the defense my client is entitled to."

The prosecutor sucked her teeth while she considered. At last she nodded to herself and said, "All right. Here's what I'm willing to do. I'll sweeten the plea down. Twenty years, add parole after fifteen—but I need an answer. ASAP."

Ever the lawyer, Wild held her ground, speaking confidently. "Jackson Hall didn't murder anyone. Much less his friend. And unless you want to rack up yet another botched prosecution, I suggest you stop playing hardball with me and go after the real killer."

Macie had landed a punch, but the ADA never blinked. She barely paused and said, "That's odd. Then why do we have an eyewitness to an altercation between your client and his friend just prior to the killing?"

"That's a bluff to get me to jump at your deal." Even as she said the words, Macie doubted them.

"A witness who heard your client threaten Mr. Pinto's life, yelling, 'I'm looking at a dead man,' quote, unquote."

"Give me the name of this witness."

"Oh, you'll get it. At trial, if you don't get your head out of your ass."

"We're into a Brady violation here, and I'll file. The Supreme Court ruled—"

" '—Prosecutors or their agents cannot withhold from the defense,' blahdy, blahdy, blah. You PDs don't live in the real world. You act like this is moot court at NYU where you can invoke Brady v. Maryland and get me to wet my pants." Fontanelli stood again and grabbed her briefcase. "You are obligated to present this deal to your client, so I'll cut you a favor and give you some time. Not much, so don't be stupid." Instead of leaving, Fontanelli quickly sat back down. "I have a picture of your client's head, documenting a wound at the base of his skull consistent with a fist fight." She slid the police photo out of the folder, held it out to Macie, then set it face up on the tabletop.

"That only supports Mr. Hall's depiction of having been blindsided at Rikers last night."

"Really. Then ask yourself this: How could Mr. Hall have been blindsided at Rikers when this was taken by EMTs at the precinct before he even went out to Fantasy Island?" She tapped the photo with a manicured finger and grinned. "This one, you can keep." The ADA dumped the picture with her food garbage on the table and walked out leaving Macie stunned by one prevailing thought: WTF?

CHAPTER 4

Shortly after eight the next morning, armed with a go cup from the lobby canteen, Macie Wild parked herself on an ass-worn oak bench in a hallway of the Criminal Courts Building to set about managing her day and deploying her team. The New York County Courthouse had opened only ten minutes before, and, by setting up shop in the frenzied corridor outside Arraignment Part One, she had been able to meet with three public defenders from the Manhattan Center, who, like her, were waiting for prisoners to finish getting docketed after overnight arrests. All three lawyers were happy to cover Macie's bail hearings for two misdemeanor clients plus another who had an order of protection violation so she could get a toehold on her Jackson Hall defense. It was common practice for the PDs to handle each other's cases when pressing circumstances called for it, and nobody disputed—or envied—the uphill road with Wild's tabloid client, the Buzz Killer himself.

Tiger Foley arrived, dreadlocks rocking, with two cups of coffee: his cream-and-sugar and a black, one Equal, for Macie. She slid it with a whoosh into her empty then accepted hard copies of the court packages her paralegal had obtained: forms consolidating each defendant's arrest report, complaint, rap sheet, and the bail recommendation compiled by the Criminal Justice Agency. These packages routinely went to the judge, prosecutor, and defense counsel of each case just before arraignment, and were seldom uplifting. She gave them a scan for accuracy then had Tiger distribute them to the various lawyers who would be covering her three clients.

Wild glanced up at the wall clock above the court cashier windows which, for reasons unknown, was the same ninety-one minutes off it had been since 2013. She didn't need a tuned clock to know her team investigator was late. Checking her iPhone for the apology text that also was absent, Macie started naming the old-school investigators, the Popeye

Doyles with beer guts and untucked shirts, who had been axed by her boss. "I miss McElhinney. I miss Felz. Even Whittinghill."

"Speaking as a gay black man who believed they fantasized about back-shooting me for the sport of it, they were, at least, punctual."

"They'd never get you, T. You're much too quick."

"How a brother man reaches thirty."

"Sorry to be a little late," called Jonathan Monheit as he arrived, casting a puzzled double take at the errant wall clock.

Wild came at him crisply. "I need to make it to a conference with Jackson Hall at Rikers at four p.m., with miles to go in-between. Every minute's taken, understood?"

"The garage said, 'lot full.' It's never 'lot full,' and I—" A woman flew past Monheit and landed on the bench on top of Tiger. A teenage girl followed, pouncing on the woman in full Jerry Springer mode, hurling a flurry of punches, gouges, and "fuckin' bitches." Tiger got pinned under the action, so Macie tried to pull the teenager away. Three court officers, an attorney, and two of the woman's sons (one dressed for his arraignment) waded in to separate the pair, a mother and daughter, as it turned out. Spitting and shouting curses that echoed in the marble hall, they got wrestled away, leaving Macie with an empty cup, one shoe full of warm coffee, and a paralegal with a torn shirt. As she helped Tiger to his feet, she spied Monheit way across the corridor with his jaw slack.

This small incident called out her central worry: If her lead investigator couldn't even work around a 'lot full' sign, and cowered instead of helping a team member in trouble, how could she trust him with the fate of Jackson Hall? Wild made a snap decision and turned to her paralegal. "Change of plan, T. Clear my calendar for the day. I'm heading out into the field."

A picture of millennial entitlement under siege, Monheit's head turreted from Tiger to her. "You're going in the field? To do what?"

"To help you with the investigation." What she really meant was to run it.

Pretty much painting dance steps on the floor for him, Macie directed Monheit to hook up with Rúben Pinto's parole officer. She recited a bullet list of things for him to ask about—like his recent straight jobs, if any, and if there were reports of coworker conflicts that could be murder motives. Wild also wanted him to have Pinto's probation case worker give up a list of his late client's friends and known associates, hopefully scoring a lead on the crew chief of his burglary team. From there, he should seek out and interview them about Pinto's recent activities and what was going on in his life. "Cast a wide net. See if they'll talk about any suspicious visitors or phone calls he might have mentioned, expressions of worry or high emotion, recent changes in habits or behavior, money changes either up or down, pissed-off husbands of lovers, alcohol or drug concerns. Basically, whatever kicks out that could be a lead. Mr. Hall said Pinto had a breakup recently. Find the ex, if you can."

For her part, she would head to the crime scene to try to gain unofficial entry through the super and to question neighbors in the apartment building. Macie especially wanted to sniff out anyone who saw the altercation with Jackson Hall that Fontanelli claimed.

Her newbie gumshoe couldn't leave well enough alone. "Wouldn't our efforts be better spent building his mitigation case?" he asked.

Wild hated thinking loss strategy, and gave herself a cleansing three count before she spoke calmly but firmly. "Jonathan, get one thing straight. Just because we're the defense doesn't mean we sit back and play defense. We need to become the detectives. Because the only way to clear our client is to solve this ourselves. The police will not help. Therefore we need to think like cops and act like cops to find out who the real killer is."

A pause and a slight head bobble. "I can support that," said Monheit. Behind him, Tiger gave Monheit the finger.

Rúben Pinto had been murdered in his fourth-floor apartment in a Chelsea walk-up that, so far, had survived the neighborhood's forced morph from gritty ruggedness into gentrified coolness epitomized by an Equinox gym, the new Whitney, and the stunning IAC tower. Even celebrity contrarian Anthony Bourdain was taking over Pier 57 to construct his international gourmet food experience. Pinto's murder had been a brutal one, and, as Macie stood across West Sixteenth Street from his haggard building, she was reminded that, tony chefs and glass sky-scrapers notwithstanding, the letting of blood kept it all real. Creeping hipness offered zero immunity from chill reality.

She mounted the three concrete steps from the sidewalk to the front door, and as Macie reached for the handle, a sharp glare reflected off the glass. Wild looked across Sixteenth and caught a shimmer of sun flare kicking off the lens of a video camera resting on a man's shoulder. Pinto's building front had been in the papers and on TV news for days. Looking at the cameraman, she thought, unfortunately for her client, the Buzz Killer story still had legs.

The vestibule was all Wild's when she entered. She made a quick survey through the inner security door in hopes of spotting the superintendent or a resident who could help her find him, but there was no activity. For yucks she gave it a rattle, but it was locked. It crossed her mind to employ Jackson Hall's MO and start buzzing apartment buttons on the panel until someone let her in, but that wouldn't guarantee access to the crime scene. So she scanned the directory for the super's listing and pressed that one. After a pause the voice of an accented older woman cut through the crackle. "Who is there?"

"Uh, hi . . . it's Macie Wild. I'm an attorney, here to see the building superintendent."

After a beat of static came a curt, "I page him." And a click.

As she waited in the airless vestibule, Macie occupied herself by examining the directory to locate Pinto's name, which was still there. After some more dead time she kicked a toe on the unsightly pile of takeout menus on the floor under the "No Menus" sign. When they were loosely corralled, she occupied herself with another look outside. Some nagging memory grit pestered her: kind of unusual to see a cameraman but no news van. Wild gave the block a once-over but the video shooter was gone.

The security door opened behind her and an old man in matching gray Carhartt pants and a crisp tucked-in work shirt stepped through from the inside. The musical jangle of keys on his belt would be the singular festive part of their meeting. A bony strongman in his late sixties, the super's hawk-like expression said, "go away," before he had barely set foot in the room. "You ask for me?" he said more than asked.

Macie handed him a business card. "I'm associated with the case concerning the homicide that took place here." Experience had long ago taught her not to say outright that she was defending an accused killer.

"You are not with the police, not the district attorney?" He handed the card back to her. "You have to move along, miss." He spoke sharply and packed some no-nonsense, Eastern European backbone in the order.

"All I want to do is see Mr. Pinto's apartment. I won't disturb anything. In fact, you can come with me."

"No, you can come with me." He brushed past her. His wad of keys clacked against the front door when he opened it to indicate the way out.

"Can we at least have a conversation about this?"

"The police told me no entry. And I have tenants—oh, are they pissed. All the disrupting and reporters and—no. *Już nie.* My boss, the landlord, say he want no more attention drawn here. So go now, or I call cops for trespassing." He thrust his nose, which had four—exactly four—wiry hairs sprouting on its surface, toward West Sixteenth.

Truth be known, it was far from the first time she had been ejected from private property. That's the plight of the defense lawyer, operating without the police power of a search warrant. As she moved on, her only solace was that Jonathan Monheit hadn't been there to witness it.

She phone-checked Tiger to get the address of the gambling speakeasy Jackson Hall had given her to alibi his whereabouts the afternoon of the murder. While Tiger looked it up, the paralegal shared that Jonathan Monheit had returned to the MCPD offices for the day with "bugger all" to show for his efforts with Rúben Pinto's parole officer. The indignity of her own crime scene expulsion tempered Macie's reaction, and she had Tiger transfer her to the investigator, who whined that the "parole prick" was unwilling to release names of Pinto's associates, and only came forth with a very short list of straight jobs Pinto had reported. Wild could picture that meeting: an oversubscribed DOC transitional assistance caseworker confronted by a self-empowered college grad expecting him to spit out information on demand as if he'd clicked onto a search engine.

"OK, good, Jonathan, you got the list of jobs. What did you learn there?"

"Nil. Pinto's coworkers didn't even remember him until I showed his mug shot. He worked two different places but only came in to get his paycheck."

Macie waited at a red light and urged herself patience. "What you learned is that Mr. Pinto had paper jobs to buff his parole jacket. It's a common favor from one con to another. They hire them and pay them. Then they take the money back under the counter, usually with vig."

"I know vig. That's like interest!" said the business major. Wild told him to try again with the parole worker the next day and to have Tiger go along. Then she ended the call before her head exploded.

Inside the Stealer's Wheel, a dive bar hunkered under the elevated Metro-North tracks near Harlem-125th, Macie stood a full minute listening to Curtis Mayfield while her eyes adjusted to the darkness. Daytime drinkers sat along the bar, spaced by solitude gaps resembling meth mouth. Brooding chins hung over their drinks until they spotted Wild. Half of them turned and fixed her with hungry leers. When she asked the bartender for the manager, a few of the patrons cockroached away, abandoning their shots and brews for the randomness of Martin Luther King Boulevard. Sometimes a woman in a suit gave off a cop stink.

Jumbo Crouch made her stand before him at a back table where he was eating a sausage and peppers on a roll. On a mild late-spring day, he had a pink polo collar showing under a lime green sweatshirt. Why? Because it was not only dark in the Stealer's Wheel, the AC was blasting. Macie felt warmer on trips to the morgue. Her receptions there were cozier too. "What you got?" the manager said, chewing around a wad of his lunch.

"I'd like to ask about one of your regulars. Jackson Hall."

His expression gave nothing away at the mention of the name. He only sucked a tendril of onion from his top front teeth. It got stubborn so he plucked it out with his thumb and forefinger, examined it, then licked it down. "I don't talk about my customers. Policy." Wild put a hand on a chair back to pull it out. "No, we're done."

"I'm his public defender. He's up on a murder charge and needs help verifying his movements over the past few days." Crouch had both hands on the sandwich so she set her card on the table next to his plate.

He broke into a smile, exposing short stubs of teeth. "Jackson's lawyer, huh? Pull on up." Jumbo set down his food and gestured her to sit. "How's he doing?"

"Been better. He said you have a secret casino downstairs, and he was here playing cards."

"Not much of a secret, then, is it? Not if you're here asking about it." A chorus of raucous whoops bled through the closed door behind him. Somebody in the basement must have won big. He ignored it. "Jackson's mellow. Even when he loses. Want to hear his nickname at the poker table? The ATM. Know why?"

"Because . . . he dispenses money?"

"He told?"

"Lucky guess."

"Don't tell him I said." He surveyed his plate like it called out his name but he shoved it an inch away and used a terry bar towel to clean his fingers. "Whatever I can do for him, just say."

Wild poised her pen above her notebook. "Can you help me verify his story that he was here?"

"You got it. Tell me whatever, and I'll swear to it."

"Thank you for that. But, you see, I only need verification of what actually happened." He showed his row of stubby teeth and nodded. Macie wanted to be careful not to derail his cooperation so she proceeded with caution. "Great. Mr. Hall says he was here playing Hold 'Em and Midnight Baseball in your game room for three hours."

"Sure. Sounds good. I'll go six hours, if you want. Anything for Jackson." A man in black slacks and a long-sleeved black shirt slipped out of the basement door and whispered in his boss's ear. Crouch shook his head. "Fuck no. You tell him nothing until he pays back the last advance. Which is a week late, and I'm thinking of fucking him up. You tell him that." The visitor returned to the gaming room and the manager shrugged. "They're like kids, you know?"

"I'm sure. Jackson Hall. Think. Can you tell me when he was here last?"

"This works better if you tell me, doesn't it?"

"Actually, sir, it doesn't." Wild had many experiences like this over the years, and they weren't good. Sometimes a witness like this was worse than getting iced out. Unless he spoke the truth, Theresa Fontanelli would smell it and shred him on the stand. She tried another approach.

"Tell you what. Can you and someone else corroborate Mr. Hall's presence here for a three-hour period two afternoons ago?"

He called out to the bartender. "Freestyle, you down with helping out J-Hall?"

Freestyle shrugged. "You say so."

"We're down," said Crouch, turning back to her. "And listen, Miss . . . Wild. Sorry for the bitch slap when you first got here. I like to protect my people, you understand?"

"We have something in common."

"And after that reporter came nosing around, I kinda had my back up."

Macie had started to put away her notebook, but paused. Hall was already in the news, but covered from the distance of his mug shot and a perp walk. The idea of a reporter circling so close to the case gave her stomach a twinge. "There was a reporter here asking about Jackson Hall?"

"Trying to. Maybe not a reporter. Making a documentary, he said. Called himself a digital journalist or some shit. Whatever. If you ask me, he looked more like a cop. That's why I shut him down."

"Did he leave a name?"

"Let me see if I still got his card." Crouch reached around to the back pocket of his jeans, exposing the grip of a revolver in his belt. "Here we go." He angled the card toward the jukebox so he could read it. "Gunnar Cody, RunAndGunn-dot-com." He tossed it her way. "The fuck is that?"

Macie Wild had no idea. But she was going to find out.

The business card put the offices of RunAndGunn.com—"Down and Digital," whatever the hell that meant—in NoLIta, which was in the exact opposite direction that she needed to go for her jailhouse meeting in Queens. Wild considered waiting or covering this base with a call, but her curiosity ran way too hot for that. Why was a documentary film-maker trying to interview one of her alibi witnesses about Jackson Hall? She needed to talk to this Gunnar Cody in person—now—and not risk getting sucked into some infinite loop of voice mail tag. So she would just show up. If he wasn't there, she could at least get face time with a receptionist and pick up a firsthand feel for the operation.

As ever, good luck finding street parking south of Houston. Macie surrendered to a gouger garage on Kenmare and circled around toward the address up Mott Street. On a spring day, there were fewer places better to hoof it in Manhattan. The architecture froze storybook New York in time: plenty of brick and stone, more old wood than brushed steel, and fire escapes unabashedly zigzagged the fronts of buildings instead of being hidden on the side. First-floor retail kept the area vibrant and young with upper stories devoted to funky apartments and commercial loft space. In just one block she passed two art galleries, a farm-to-table diner sharing a wall with a coal-oven pizzeria, and a vintage clothing boutique marketing irony. Wild stepped through a nondescript door beside a pop-up vegan chocolatier and, for the second time that day, found herself searching a directory in a vestibule.

It showed a Cody, G., but no business listing. She pressed the call button. After a brief pause, the speaker filled with the tinny background sounds of a TV or, perhaps, a radio talk show, followed by a man's voice. "Not today, thank you." Click. Silence.

Macie buzzed again. Once more came the distorted noise and the voice. A little more strident. "Look, Watchtower, Greenpeace, whatever, save it. Not interested."

Macie leaned toward the speaker, trying to sound pleasant, like the kind of stranger you'd want to talk to. "My name's Macie Wild. I'm a criminal defense attorney, and I was hoping I could ask you a few questions about a case I'm wor—"

"Top floor." The speaker clicked off and the release on the access door purred. Macie pushed through.

The elevator car, a groaning, whirring freight-style cage, let her out in a small alcove with worn hardwood flooring. Green and blue recycling bins lined the wall to her left. In front of her, there was only one door. It had a number six on it. Wild reached out to knock but it opened, startling her.

"Oh . . . hi." She caught her breath and continued, "I'm looking for Gunnar Cody."

The barefoot man in torn jeans, and showing a sliver of bare chest behind a half-zipped hoodie, appraised her quickly but without the mental TSA pat down she had endured in the bar uptown. He did give her a rapid scan though—matching the same one she was giving him. "I'm Gunnar," he said, bringing his attention to her face and leaving it there. Gunnar Cody had alert eyes. And something kind was going on in there under those soft lashes, she thought. He had an unchallenging gaze that made it easy to hold contact. A few years older than she, Macie guessed him to be the other side of thirty-five. He stroked his three days of stubble and said, "I apologize for my appearance. I was not anticipating any callers." The tongue-in-cheek formality, something out of Tennessee Williams, made her laugh, and she watched his starter set of smile creases deepen when she did.

An awkward pause followed. She had come prepared to challenge the snot out of this guy. But now, as their spontaneous little moment faded, it left Macie at a loss for where to go next. So she reverted to the playbook, albeit less stridently than she'd planned. "I want to know why you're following me."

"Following you . . ."

Wild stepped a foot closer to face him. "Please. This is too big a city to cross paths accidentally with someone twice in one day." He didn't answer, just gave her a bemused look that almost made her doubt herself. Almost. Holding up his card, she said, "I got this from the manager at the Stealer's Wheel a half hour ago. I couldn't see your whole face this morning in Chelsea. You were holding up a camera." Cody seemed completely unfazed by her. He continued to observe her, unperturbed, even when she pointed to the Panasonic 130 slung on the coatrack inside the door. "Like that one. Only bigger."

"Look, you're making a nothing coincidence into something."

"I don't believe in coincidences. I'm a lawyer."

Cody took a step back and held the door wide. "Would you like to come in?" Macie hesitated. A stranger whom she'd caught tailing her was inviting her inside his loft. Tiger Foley knew where she was, but really, what good would that do? He read her and added, "If you'd rather just talk here, it's OK." She found his gaze again, made a gut check, and stepped in past him.

His loft appeared to take up the entire sixth floor of the townhouse. Macie came to that reckoning through stolen glances from the kitchen table where they sat to talk off to the side of what architects would call the great room. Clearly a mixture of home and workplace, the space was tidy enough without being fussy. It had a definitely male vibe—super large flat screen, free weights beside the exercise bike in the den section, and an acceptable amount of clutter you get from living life. When Cody went to the fridge to get them a bottle of Saratoga sparkling, Macie stole another glance, this time at his ring finger, which was empty. She then craned to peer around a freestanding bookcase across the den where she heard the low-volume whine of what sounded like a Formula One car race. Behind that partition Wild spotted racks and tables of electronic gear: more video cameras, hard drives, and LED monitors. One screen played video embedded with time code of an expensive foreign sports car zooming around Columbus Circle at night. Cody pulled a drape across the opening, obscuring her view of his little studio, and flipped on his Sirius XM to mask the beehive droning of the racing car with some Don Henley.

"I barged in on your workday."

He settled across the table from her and shrugged. "What's a work-day?" She warmed under his amused gaze. "I'd be going at it twenty-five/seven if I could rig it."

Handed the opening she said, "Going at what, may I ask? Exactly what is RunAndGunn?"

"Don't you forget the dot-com," he said with mock seriousness. "Very proud of that here. Those domains are hard-won." As "Heart of the Matter" faded out, a sloshy-mouthed DJ, direct from the Alan Freed Studios at the Rock and Roll Hall of Fame, came on and reminisced about an Eagles concert she attended thirty years ago and how Glenn Frey had been taken too soon. "Hate it when they talk," said Cody. "Jeez."

Wild brought it back. "So. RunAndGunn—dot-com . . ."

"A little start-up of mine," he began. " 'Run and gun' being news videographer jargon for shooting whatever you can on the fly. Gunnar, Gunn; it kinda works."

"Clever."

"Manly too."

Again his self-mocking tone cracked her up. "And you do all this . . . here?"

The sweep of her hand to his home studio brought him forward in his seat. "As I said, it's a start-up. But I've got all my own gear and I'm doing just fine in a very competitive landscape. Since you're curious, I do stringer gigs, you know, freelance video for local news stations who've cut back on the number of crews they carry. They either assign me to cover events or I pick up what I can off my scanners and sell what I can. There's a lot of overnight stuff, bodega stickups, car crashes—hamburger on the highway—you get the idea."

"Twenty-five/seven."

His turn to laugh. "Exactly, exactly. But I've managed to score some coups for being new. A ride-along I did with ATF on a stinger missile raid in Jersey went viral and, next thing, one of the networks flew me to Paris after the November attacks. From there I ended up embedded on a Belgian *politie* raid in Molenbeek." Was this guy bragging, selling, or just pumped? She couldn't tell. "See, my business plan is to develop a rep for cutting-edge street journalism that's credible and impactful—hey, I should write that down. That's dangerously close to sounding like a mission statement."

Wild studied him, and things didn't add up. Oh, she bought the freelancing and the viability of his enterprise. Gunnar Cody seemed like a smart, capable, and driven guy. But something wasn't getting said. Something was buried in omission. Why, she wondered, was a shit-together guy like this doing a start-up at his age? Macie sized up his strength and bearing and came up with an educated guess. "Were you in the military before this, or something?"

But her question, however gently presented, forced a shadow over his brow. She had poked a sore spot. "Listen, if this is none of my business . . ."

"No, it's cool." He half-masted his lids as he conjured a reply. "Flat out? I was a cop." That made sense of the nightstick in the umbrella stand inside his front door. "NYPD, if you want to know. Spent most of my years on TARU. You know TARU?"

Macie did, and the mention of it renewed her unease. The NYPD's Technical Assistance Response Unit was an elite, and ultimately, secretive investigative branch responsible for a grab bag of all things electronic. The detectives from TARU did everything from photographing mobsters outside funerals, to setting up court-warranted phone taps, to planting bugs in offices, homes, and social clubs of organized crime or terror suspects. To Wild that was all fine, even necessary, within its legal limits. However, as an advocate for the civil liberties of her clients, she frequently butted legal heads over the tactics of the surveillance unit. To her, TARU had a dangerous appetite for shooting crowd video at protests and rallies. She saw them as spies who played fast and loose with the Handschu court ruling that restricted the police from gathering files on law-abiding dissidents. Cody had probably invoked TARU for street cred but it had the opposite effect on Macie. It only made her imagine him as one of the cops hosing video at Occupy, the Eric Garner marches, and the immigration protests. She must have worn it on her face. He added, "I'm definitely ex-TARU though."

"Ex how?" Studying him, she did not detect any crisis of conscience over civil liberties.

"Wow, you are a lawyer, aren't you."

"You said you were TARU, now you're ex-TARU. I'm curious."

"Let's say that I departed under less than happy circumstances. Why don't we leave it there?"

"Sure, no problem." So, fired. But the association with spying had cooled her to him and worried her. "I'd like to know what your interest is in a case I'm working on."

"Not sure I know what you mean."

"I represent a defendant accused of a recent homicide. Today I tried to get into my crime scene, and while I was there, I made you, Mr. Surveillance. Then up at the Stealer's Wheel, I discover you'd also been there. That's what I'd call interest."

Cody said nothing. In the pause, Classic Vinyl filled the space with The James Gang. "I'm not sure what you want," he said at last.

"I want to know why."

"As a lawyer . . . especially a public defender . . . you know all about the First Amendment. So, if you recognize that I am a credentialed member of the press working on a documentary, you should understand that's something I'm not required to share." The gentleness of his delivery did nothing to take the sting off his answer.

"Oh, please. We are so not at the freedom of the press stage here, Mr. Cody. I have an innocent man going on trial for a murder. I just want to know all I can about anything related to my case."

"I hear you. I'd be doing the same thing."

"Then help me here."

"Sorry, I can't say more right now."

"That's not acceptable."

"To me it is." Now he started getting heated too. "Look, Ms. Wild, I am in the midst of shooting an investigative piece of major importance to my business. It's my very first commissioned project from VICE Media." He tilted his head and cocked one brow to punctuate the significance.

"And this is related to my case? Does it connect to a man named Jackson Hall?"

"Not going to go there. And if the First Amendment isn't enough,

I've signed a nondisclosure with VICE. As an attorney, you know what that means."

"I demand to know what other witnesses of mine you have met with, if any."

"Apparently you know what that means, and don't care."

She pushed her Saratoga away and stood. "This lost its sparkle."

"Right there with you." He rose too.

Cody followed her as she strode to the door. She opened it herself and pivoted back to face him. "We'll be talking again if I find you shadowing my investigation."

"Actually, to shadow you, I'd have to be a step behind. I believe that would make you the shadow. With all respect."

Feeling the foundation crumbling under her feet, Wild had no alternative but leave it there. She stalked to the elevator and pressed the down button. As Gunnar Cody's door closed behind her, Macie could hear Joe Walsh singing "Walk Away."

Her pal the blue heron was back on the rocky bank across the C-wire from the Rikers visitors lot at three forty-five that afternoon when Wild stood at the trunk of her gray-pearl Corolla performing her ritual security jettison of jewelry, electronics, and sharps. Macie was glad to ditch her phone, weary of the flood of tweets and Instagrams hounding her, bolstering her, or offering advice about the Buzz Killer case. There were numerous attempts to book interviews with him, even a jailhouse bride proposal. Gusts out of the south kicked up some chop in the East River, but the stately bird held position, focus riveted on the broken surface, waiting to strike at the first flash of movement. Instead of slamming the trunk, Macie pressed it closed this time, leaning on it until the latch clicked, and when she glanced back from the first security gate, the heron was still on duty.

In the visitors' intake hall, she took the short line reserved for attorneys, showed the officer at the window her Unified Court System security pass, signed in, and stated her appointment to see her client, Jackson Hall. By rote, Wild held out her hand to get it stamped. When that didn't happen, she looked up. The guard mumbled, "One moment, miss," and swiveled away in his chair while he picked up his phone.

A sergeant named Fong, whom Wild had dealings with before, and liked, slipped out from a side door a moment later and gestured her to a quiet corner of the room. Macie's legs weakened on the short walk to join him because Sergeant Fong had come to meet her and he was seeking privacy. "We just placed a call to your office a few minutes ago, Ms. Wild," he said as she approached.

"Why, what's going on?"

"There's been an incident involving Mr. Hall," he said somberly.

"Incident, what kind of incident? Tell me what happened."

The sergeant stepped closer and lowered his voice. "He went missing at some point today. After a search, your client was found in the shower area, hanging."

CHAPTER 6

Guards found Jackson Hall unconscious, but alive, and Wild drove herself in a fog of disbelief to Bellevue where the ambulance had rushed
her client. She called ahead to Soledad Esteves Torres, and her team's
social worker was waiting for her in the center of the huge glass atrium
that formed the modern entrance where IM Pei had encased the old
hospital in a *St. Elsewhere* snow globe of grief and miracles. "How the
hell did this happen?" she asked on Macie's walk-up. Her question was
only partly rhetorical, so Wild shared Sergeant Fong's version. When a
corrections officer went to round up Hall for her conference, he wasn't
in his cell. They put out an alert, and a few minutes later, one of the
COs found him in an alcove near a janitorial closet with a garbage bag
cinched around his neck. It had been rolled into the thickness of a rope
and looped onto a wall pipe. Apparently there was enough stretch in
the plastic to lower his feet onto the floor, subtracting just enough body
weight from the ligature to save his life—they hoped.

"Jesus . . . A thousand bulls in there, a gazillion security cameras,
and nobody saw anything?" The firewall between Macie and her feelings was tenuous and her friend was eroding it further. "Goddamned
Rikers." Soledad had spent nearly two decades dealing with The Oven,
and every incident like this tested her shock threshold. "Department of
Corrections should either get their shit together in that place or change
the name to what it really is, Devil's Island."

Wild shook her head. "It's an epic fail."

"And their version of this? Total bullshit!" Soledad's voice echoed in
the cavernous lobby, turning heads.

Macie draped a comforting arm around Soledad. "What's wrong
with this picture? I'm calming down a social worker."

Bright light flooded the glass wall across the atrium near First Avenue. TV vans were setting up live shots for breaking news on the Buzz

Killer. The two defenders took that as a sign to go inside and check on the condition of their client.

"Unfortunately the survival prognosis for this is so individualized, I can't give you a definitive answer." But Dr. Edda, who met Wild and Soledad in the second-floor prison ward, did give them something to cling to, adding, "The good news is that they found him when they did."

Still trying to keep a lid on her emotions, which was plenty hard with the slack form of Jackson Hall stretched out and tubed-up in the room behind the doc, Macie diverted herself by latching on to the job she pledged to do on his behalf. She tried to construct a medical timeline. "Let me ask you about that. What would you say was the duration from the initial time of his . . . suspension . . . to his discovery."

"Oh, you're going to put me on the spot. OK, let's see . . ." The doctor tapped her lips with a forefinger then said, "Given his small frame, and that his was what we call an incomplete hanging—meaning a portion of his body touched the ground—I'm going on a limb for you and say two to three minutes."

Soledad chimed in, "Wouldn't he have suffocated by then?"

"Actually, his airway was never compromised. The way the ligature was placed caused a vascular restriction, meaning of his carotid, not the trachea. What does that mean? It means he was still able to breathe, but blood flow to the brain was cut off. It's not uncommon. You see this a lot in manual strangulations, especially in martial arts. After thirty seconds the victim loses consciousness. Death usually comes in one to three minutes. Again, individualized. I'm saying high end of that window based on Mr. Hall's size and the fact that the ligature wasn't bearing his full weight."

"When you examined him, did you see any signs of a struggle?"

"He's got a contusion on the back of his head which appears a few days old, from the coloration. There are also marks on his knuckles and arms."

"He got in a fight yesterday," offered Wild. "Some inmates came after him."

"Could be residual from that. Some of them appear older. Same as the head wound."

Once more Macie fretted that Hall actually got that goose egg fighting Pinto. She tabled that to ask the hard question. "You said his prognosis is individualized. But what's your guess? I won't hold you to it."

"All right, let's talk it through. He's comatose, and I have put him on hypothermia therapy. That's a cooling helmet he's got on," she said, hitching a thumb toward the bed. "And he's also under a chilling blanket. We keep him down to ninety-four degrees, which reduces the production of neurotransmitters and free radicals—the bad boys who can cause damage to the brain when it's been oxygen deprived."

"You think he'll live?" asked Soledad.

"It so varies. I'm sorry I can't be more definite. I've seen them come out in days or weeks. I've seen them shut down and slip away."

"And what about if he lives?"

"You mean brain function? What's our theme here?"

Macie nodded and said, "It varies," then swiped the wetness off her cheek. Before she left, the lawyer cast a look at her comatose client and tried to convince herself that advising him to turn down the plea deal had nothing to do with this.

After a brooding night of Google and Chipotle, learning all she could about cerebral hypoxia and ischemic neuron death, Wild began the next day holding two things in her bleeding heart: that Jackson Hall would survive, and that by doing so, he would live to see her clear him of his murder charge. After all, if he could fight for his life, Macie would do no less.

Substituting activity for pessimism over Glasgow Coma Scores and functional disability, she drove across the Queensboro Bridge to interview Rúben Pinto's ex-girlfriend. It wasn't Wild's investigator who had located her, but her Aussie paralegal. Tiger had burned midnight oil poring over the murder victim's old case files from when he had been a prior Manhattan Center client. A 2015 Criminal Justice Agency bail intake form, the questionnaire the CJA uses to assess flight risk by itemizing a defendant's roots in the community, listed his address then as a shared residence in Astoria with Cilla Dougherty, a performance artist.

Macie found a parking spot two blocks away near the Kaufman movie studios and backtracked through a neighborhood of immaculately
kept three-story row houses sitting atop one-car garages. The composition of the area was Greek with some Middle Eastern, and, judging from
the busy Sarajevo Café, Bosnian and Herzegovinian too. Dougherty's
apartment was on the first floor of a duplex wedged between a tan stucco warehouse and a driving school. When she mounted the front steps,
Wild heard broken glass being swept. It stopped as soon as she knocked.
In her periphery, drapes moved in the window beside her, followed by
a young woman's voice through the closed door. "Who's there?" Macie
announced herself, locks snapped, and the door opened. Cilla Dougherty's eyes were red from crying. In her free hand, she held a dustpan full
of shattered coffee mugs. She tried to smile but didn't quite make it and
asked to see some ID to confirm Wild was the lawyer Tiger had called
about.

For a split second, when she entered the place, Macie wondered if
all the breakage and disarray she saw might have been some extreme
performance art project. But the shelves, violently cleared of dishes, the
desk drawers upended onto the floor, and the sofa cushions slashed and
leaking stuffing, could only mean one thing. "I called the police. They left
just before you got here," said Cilla, emptying her dustpan with a crash
into the kitchen garbage can she had moved to the living room. "I'd offer
you coffee, but . . ." Her sentence choked into a sob, and she fanned the
air, signaling, "just a sec."

In her kitchen, she righted two chairs and they sat. Dougherty seemed
relieved to have the company, and wanted—or needed—to talk. She said
she had come home late after a friend's gallery opening and after-party
over in Park Slope to find her front door gaping and her home trashed.
The police said things like this were usually revenge from an old boy-
friend or somebody looking for something. Or a bit of both, thought
Wild, given Pinto's career choice. And then, as if reading her, Cilla gave
voice to it. "I thought the craziness would stop when Rú and I split."

Wild had years of experience talking to people at their worst moments, so she wasn't shy about making the segue, albeit gently. "My

paralegal said when he called you this morning that you had heard about Rúben."

Cilla nodded, strong but grim. "So sad. He and I were over. Guess we broke up, what, six months ago. Officially. But it crashed and burned before that. Still . . ." She let out a long breath.

After a respectful interval, Macie asked, "What can you tell me about him?"

"Oh, God."

"Listen if this is too hard for you . . ." Wild touched her forearm.

"No, it's just, where to start."

"How about with how you met?" Macie really wanted specifics, especially about enemies, jobs he'd pulled, all that. But first she wanted to keep things open-ended to make Cilla comfortable, to see what came out on its own.

"We met at Nightcap, down on the Lower East Side. He had me on sight. Cute, funny, worked out. Danced. Kind of rough around the edges. You know, the fixer-upper who gets you hot? The chemistry was amazing. I brought him here that night. Saw a lot of each other over two months, and then he spent more and more time here. Before we both knew it, he had sorta moved in."

"How long was he here?"

"A month too long. I was so ready."

"May I ask why? Is that too personal?"

After a contemplative beat, she said, "It's all personal. But I'll tell you. I couldn't deal with his 'lifestyle.' He told me he was in estate liquidation." The young woman laughed for the first time. "Actually not so far from the truth when you think about it. Anyway, that was good enough for me. But then it became more clear. The hours he kept, the people he dealt with. He never went to work-work. But the sex was good, the mystery of it was kind of a turn-on. You know?"

"Sure."

"But then he started bringing stuff to stash here. I called him on it. I said, 'No way I'm getting busted for stolen property.' So he got it all out. Eventually."

Wild gestured to the ruin. "Did he get it all out? Was there some-thing here somebody wanted?"

"The fuck I know." Cilla surveyed the chaos and added, "If anything was here, those assholes sure would have gotten it."

Time to slide into notes. Macie got out her pen. "Do you remember any of the items Rúben brought to stash here?"

"Of what I saw that wasn't boxed or in a duffel? Artwork—expensive stuff too. Originals—and I'm an art major, I'd know. Jewelry, small stat-ues, rare coins, stuff like that."

All portable and all high-end. Right in keeping with Hall's descrip-tion of the elite crew working luxury apartments. "Can you tell me about any people in his 'lifestyle' who may have been a problem? Anyone he had hassles with or threatened him?"

"No threats that I know of. But, fuck me. The people. That was an-other issue. Rú started partying here and having some of his pals hang out when I came home. Not savory types either." Macie began to get the picture of Cilla Dougherty as a young woman who enjoyed toying with the dangerous side until the fantasy got too real. She didn't figure her to be involved in his killing, but she may have met someone who was.

"Any stand out as somebody who gave you a bad feeling?"

"I don't even have to think. Spatone."

"Is that a first or last?"

"Never knew. Rúben always just called him by the one name. Like Adele, right?" Macie spelled it phonetically to check later and asked how Pinto knew him. "They were cellmates for a while up in Fishkill."

"Did they get along?"

"I mean they bitched at each other, then made up a lot. But Rúben and Spatone had an ugly fight. A blowout that kind of tore it."

"What was it about?"

"About Rú not getting him aboard the new crew he was working. Spatone said he was ungrateful and an asshole."

"What about that crew? Did you ever meet the leader, or did Rúben ever mention his name?"

"No. He didn't like to talk about him. Rú said he was a shit. Control freak. 'Do this, do that, follow my rules.'"

"Did he ever mention Jackson Hall?"

"Him, I liked. Rúben said he was the only one he could trust." Then added, "Which would be too weird if he killed him."

Cilla looked used up, so Macie thanked her for her time. At the door she paused, though, as another question came to her. "When was the last time you saw Rúben?"

"Four days ago. I asked him to spend the night." When she saw Macie's reaction she said, "What can I say? Chemistry."

The time crunch resigned her to skip lunch and feast on whatever random nut block Nature Valley offered in the break room, but Wild arrived back at the MCPD to find that Tiger had anticipated all that. Her default California Club from Pret a Manger sat on a napkin beside a cold can of Diet Coke at the head of the conference table. The paralegal shrugged it off. "It's what happens when you hire someone with a background in the hospitality industry."

"Hospitality happens," she said, snapping open her soda.

He volleyed back, "Do remember this at review time."

The rest of her team entered with takeout and took their usual places in the bull pen. With two quick bites to fuel her for now, Macie jumped right in while the others ate. "First off, what's the latest on Jackson Hall's condition?"

"Same," said Soledad. She gestured down the table to the summer intern. "Chip's on phone duty to Bellevue, checking in every two hours. Mr. Hall is still comatose, still on targeted temperature therapy. No improvement, but no complications or setbacks either."

"The ICU duty nurse is good people," added Chip, his accent sounding more Mayberry than Manhattan. "She promised to call if there's any change and told me not to worry about being a pest."

"Be a pest," said Wild, who then turned back to the social worker. "Please tell me you ripped DOC a new one."

"Oh, yes. I threatened filing for a DOJ civil rights investigation, and that got Deputy Warden Bohannon called in to give up a few more details. Like a shiv attempt yesterday. A CO intercepted an inmate coming up behind Mr. Hall holding a wooden crucifix with a nail duct-taped to the end."

"No blasphemy there," said Tiger. Nobody laughed, including him.

"What about the hanging?" asked Macie. "How'd it go unseen?"

"The DW says he's mystified. I said, 'What about cams?' He said it all happened in a blind spot."

Macie gave a slow shake of her head. "Doesn't pass the smell test for me." Conspiracy theories were as common as bedbugs but she couldn't call herself thorough and ignore the possibility that a guard or guards— for whatever reason—looked the other way and let this happen. Or did it themselves. If that were the case, finding out who—and why—could open up a lead to Pinto's real killer. She turned to Tiger. "Let's move forward and get DOJ in on this. Draw the papers for me, and we'll file to formally request an investigation."

"You go," said Soledad.

And then Wild shared the shitty truth of her urgency. "The fact is, this case dies if Jackson Hall does. We have to push to stay ahead of that. We do whatever it takes. Is everyone here with me on that?" They all nodded assent. "Good. Because we have plenty of obstacles." That led her to tell them about the brick wall she'd hit trying to get inside Pinto's building, then describe her alibi interview with the manager of the Stealer's Wheel. "Good alibi, poor witness." For reasons she couldn't express, even to herself, she decided not to share her overlap with the VICE Media documentarian, Gunnar Cody. Maybe later. Maybe not.

Wild moved on to Pinto's ex, Cilla Dougherty, with her break-in, and its timing, not lost on anyone. Unsure whether to spell Pinto's ex-con pal Spatone or Spetone, she printed it up on the Case Board both ways with a slash. Chip Ross raised a polite finger and she gave him a go-ahead nod. "Can't we just check DOC records to find out Rúben Pinto's cell-mates at Fishkill?"

"Don't you hate it when the interns start thinking?" said Macie with a grin. "Do that. Jonathan will show you how."

Monheit startled at the sound of his name. But, mark the date and time, within the hour Jonathan Monheit finally coughed up a lead. He and the L-1 intern got a hit from the Department of Corrections on an Amador James Spatone, who did two years at the medium security prison at Fishkill, New York, concurrent with a stretch done by Rúben Pinto. The team investigator contacted Spatone's parole caseworker, who said the ex-con was operating his own business as a personal trainer on the Upper West Side.

That's how Macie ended up parking in the lucky spot she found on Columbus Avenue after work that evening. Not to grab a nice meal on the sidewalk patio of Isabella's. Maybe later. She was in the neighborhood for an up-close interview with the owner-operator of Tone with Spatone.

New York is a city sculpted by sound as much as sight, and the whisper of a jet far above the clouds was the only intrusion except for fading taxi horns as she left Columbus Avenue behind. With each step into the residential block of West Seventy-Eighth Street, Macie progressed into a refuge of calm. It was as if every sycamore growing out of its sidewalk planter marked another buffer against urban noise. Toward the Amsterdam end of the block, Wild arrived at the address Monheit scored from DOC. A laminated sign, the kind made at Staples, was attached by twisty ties to an iron railing. It announced the name of the business in some ornate font above a smiling picture of Amador Spatone. Wild took out her cell, snapped a documentary photo, then descended the steps to the sublevel patio. There was another plastic sign on the wooden door in the archway beneath the stoop. This was definitely a small operation. Spatone had converted his apartment into his business. She had decided not to call ahead but the lights were on inside and she could hear music. She gave the illuminated button a solid push.

She waited, listening, hearing only the mega bass thump of a Drake-Rihanna track. Unsure of the bell, she gave the door some sharp knocks. While she waited some more, Wild noticed an index card with small handwriting on it thumbtacked to the door frame. It was dark under the arch so she tapped her flashlight app and bent forward to read the note. It said, "If I don't answer I'm with a client. Please call ba—" An arm came from behind Macie and locked around her neck.

CHAPTER 7

The grab was as powerful as it was sudden, jerking her backward against the man's body. Wild tried to scream but his choke hold smothered her voice. She dropped her phone and brought both hands up to pry at his arm. Strong as Macie was, her clawing was useless against the hard muscle and iron lock he had on her. Unable to move her head to either side, she couldn't even bite, and all the exertion did was rob her of more oxygen.

He walked Macie rearward, dragging her in the darkness across the little subterranean porch, unfazed by her flailing, even when she kicked over a trash can, scattering debris with a crash onto the flagstones. He firmed his grip on her with a monstrous grunt then backed her up the steps to the sidewalk. She bucked and twisted uselessly. At the top step, he shifted weight to make the turn and she managed to get a tiny gulp of air, enough to smell body odor and stale tobacco before he brute-clamped the crook of his arm to her throat again. In a panic, powerless against him, losing consciousness, Wild searched the street for help. She spotted a couple, hand in hand, silhouetted by lights and traffic on Amsterdam. But they had their backs to her and were too far to hear her even if she could cry out. But she tried anyway. Her scream died in her throat.

But wait. She heard an engine. A few yards away a car idled, double parked. She tried to see around the tree trunk, hoping the driver was inside. The car was empty. Then, as her attacker moved her toward it, a wave of ice water flooded her gut.

The trunk of the car was open.

Shit. This guy was going to put her inside the trunk.

She tried to find the strength to keep that from happening but he was powerful enough to arch her backward. Her feet left the pavement and bicycled at the air. Somewhere in a high window blocked by the leaves of the tree, a woman called out, "What's going on down there?"

The man chuckled to himself. The brazen calm of that sent another shudder through Macie. Like the struggle meant nothing to him. Like her life meant nothing to him.

As he brought her across the sidewalk Wild gave up trying to pry his arm and reached up for his face, going for his eyes. She managed to claw his cheek. He groaned and his hold loosened just enough for her to drop her chin, closing his access to her throat. While he struggled to regain his choke hold, Macie brought her knees up to her chest then lashed the soles of both feet out at the trunk of the tree. The force of her kick knocked them both backward. Still clutching her, he fell onto the side-walk, crashing hard on his back with a sharp moan. The impact of her landing on top of him knocked the wind out of the guy. Macie twisted, broke his armlock, screamed for help, and got up to run.

But he swept one of his legs in a UFC move against the backs of her knees and took Wild down before she gained a yard. She landed on all fours and screamed for help again, clamoring to get away even as the man sprung to his feet and bent to grab her around the waist. She side rolled to keep that from happening, and, as he stutter-stepped to stay with her, a voice up the street yelled, "NYPD, freeze."

Her attacker turned in the direction of the cop, and when he did, Macie bolted up and threw a kick into his groin. With a guttural "oof," the big man doubled, then lurched to his car in a hobble.

As the cop ran up, he yelled to halt, but the door slammed and the car burned rubber up the street with its open trunk waving bye. In seconds it fishtailed around the corner at Columbus, and was gone. Bent at the waist with her hands on her knees, gasping and fighting back nausea, Macie turned to the cop as he approached her. But he wasn't a cop after all.

He was an ex-cop named Gunnar Cody.

"You OK?"

"Yeah, I think so. He just . . . I never heard him . . ." Bringing herself upright she drew a deep shuddering inhale, filling her starved lungs. Shaken, but slightly more collected, Wild felt her brow thicken into a frown as she regarded her rescuer standing there, assessing her. Whatever relief she felt crumbled to confusion followed by disbelief. "What are you doing here?"

"Oh, I dunno. Kinda keeping you from getting stuffed in that trunk, it looks like."

Was it the wisecrack or the laugh? Whichever it was, everything that was weighing on Macie gave way in a mudslide into anger. "What the fuck is this?" His cool demeanor didn't break but she did see him blink. The smirk disappeared too. "You're making a joke out of this? And really. Why are you here? And don't bullshit me. Are you stalking me?"

"No, not at all."

He moved to comfort her, and she recoiled a step. "You can kiss my ass."

Sirens burped at both ends of the one-way street and the quiet block, the refuge, became flooded with flashing lights and patrol cars.

When she arrived at her apartment nearly three hours later there was a blue-and-white from the Thirteenth Precinct idling near her front steps. The pair of uniforms inside greeted her by name without getting out and said the precinct commander of the Twentieth had made a courtesy call asking their PC to make sure Ms. Wild had "a safe home." Macie had taken an immediate liking to the captain up at the Twentieth, who was a warm woman who could easily work undercover as a fashion model. She had assured her they'd do everything to get the guy, which she expected. What Wild never expected was this kind of compassion to a victim.

After a soaking in a warm tub to ease the body aches from her struggle, Macie stepped out of her bathroom to a vibrating phone. "Please tell me you're all right," said her father. Macie hesitated, not just to figure out how to answer that without freaking him more, but to wonder how he knew.

"I'm fine, Dad."

"Don't BS your old man. I just got a disturbing call from Len Asher." Wild's boss had called her while she was on her way home from the precinct to ask how the case was progressing, and she had told him about the attack. The executive director was friends with her father, so it didn't take long for word to reach him. Macie would have preferred to leave this until the morning, but gave her dad the PG-13 version just to get off the damned subject. Good luck with that. "You know how I worry about you doing this level of work," he said, leaving out the term lowlifes for once. Jansen Wild's legal clientele usually arrived at his office in black town cars, not Rikers vans. "Do you have any idea who it was?"

"No. I gave a description to the police though. They're on it."

"Do you have any idea why someone would do this? Was he stalking you? Think a minute. Could this be related to some case? What about this one you're working on, the one who tried to hang himself?" She tried to talk him down from his tree as best she could, saying it was all fine, voicing her confidence in the police captain, but he wasn't mollified, and they hung up without either of them feeling better for the call.

Macie tried to shut out the trauma noise with some tube. She uncapped a Sam Adams and watched *Iron Chef Gauntlet* on the Food Network. Alton Brown was challenging contestants to find the sweet and savory taste combo that packed a one-two punch. When the tournament finished, she killed the TV and sat numbly, reflecting on the very thing she was trying to avoid thinking about, at least until morning. But trouble had a mind of its own and she wrestled with the visual flashbacks of the assault, trying to shut those one-twos away in hopes they wouldn't come back to bully their way into her nightmares.

The ration of shit she gave Gunnar Cody on the sidewalk pretty much ended their conversation for the night. Even though the two had shared the back seat of a patrol unit to the precinct to file their accounts, his brief "How you doing now?" overture was met with a hard glance, and he took the hint.

When they made their statements at the police station Macie sensed deference to him because he was ex-NYPD. Cops shared a bond and spoke a common language. Wild had seen it before among the retired detectives with whom she had worked. Cody guessed their Sixty-One Report would be an exercise, thanks to the plateless vehicle, and the intake officer couldn't disagree. It came time for her to give her account of the attack, and she said she was unsure whether her assailant had been waiting in the alcove or had followed her as a victim of opportunity. Macie had never seen the man before, and neither heard him, nor sensed his presence, until the choke hold. Cody did most of the talking when it came to describing the guy. Even though she had seen him, Cody had a more complete view, and, again, spoke the language of The Job.

"Male cauc, thirty-eight to forty-two. Five ten to six feet, 210 to 215, muscular build. Lean. Mean and powerful like a CrossFit rat. Close, thinning hair. Brown, maybe red, in that light. Short-cropped goatee. Black or navy sweatshirt over jeans and white athletic shoes. He'll also have a superficial facial wound." Cody indicated the smear of blood on Macie's shirt collar.

"That's right," she said. "He'll have a mark on his cheek. I scratched him."

"And gave a helluva kick into that tree to bust up his plan," said Cody. "Well done. Probably saved your life." No wisecrack, no deflection, pure sincerity. Replaying that station-house moment, Wild considered the warmth and trueness of his compliment. And something else along with it. What . . . his relief?

Macie sat a few minutes pondering in the night's solitude then polished off her beer. She leaned forward, triggering a whiplash twinge in her back, and picked up her cell phone that the police had retrieved from the scene of her assault. It awakened revealing a spider web of cracked glass, but the thing still worked. She found the number she wanted. "Hi, Gunnar Cody? Hope I didn't wake you. It's Macie Wild."

The host at Felice 15 hugged two menus to his chest and waited for her answer. It didn't come quickly. Macie stood in the entry and surveyed her seating choices. The Financial District feed wouldn't start for fifteen minutes so she basically had her pick, which was precisely why she had arrived so early for her noon lunch meeting with Gunnar Cody. The banquette looked appealing, comfortable and not too intimate. But soon those empty surrounding tables would be filled and there would be too many ears in tight proximity. That deuce off in the corner would work, but with those surrounding wall mirrors, he would be staring at her from every angle for the whole meal. "If you are looking for privacy," said the maître d', "our booth is unreserved today. I would be happy to give you that."

A booth. Yes. But Macie tracked his gesture and hesitated. It was private enough. In fact, too much so. A wood-paneled nook framed by floor-to-ceiling privacy drapes? No, it fell into cozy, and cozy was the opposite of what she wanted out of this.

"A booth? Perfect." Macie's breath caught at the sound of Cody's voice. She spun to find him right beside her. "Sorry, didn't mean to startle you."

"No, it's just . . . Hi." She shook his hand. "Guess I didn't hear you come in."

"Years of tailing perps, I guess. I had a girlfriend in college who said she wanted to put a bell around my neck. Cat lady. Less said the better." By then they were at the booth and he was standing aside so she could slide in and face the restaurant. "Better view for you," he said. Then, as he sat on the outside of the padded L, Cody added, "Plus I've got this thing about not being hemmed in."

"Another cop habit?" she asked.

"Small bladder." He leaned toward her and nodded confessionally, then laughed. "Uh-oh, I'd better watch it. Someone who believes whatever I tell her."

She smiled. "No, I'd better watch it. Someone who flatters himself." When he grinned at that, she turned away to study a herd of noisy diners as they rolled in.

"Relax, no one will see you here," he said. And when she furrowed her brow, Cody spread his palms wide. "You work, what, ten blocks away, up near the courthouse? Plenty of places to eat around there. You invite me to this particular spot—very nice; glad I wore the sport jacket—but—just far enough off your turf not to risk being caught by your discerning lawyer pals, sitting knee-to-knee with an ex-cop. Tell me I'm wrong."

Macie busied herself with the menu. "I only chose this place because I heard it was good," she lied into the list of daily specials.

"Still. Kills a slice of your day coming down here."

"I spent all morning in court, and freed up my afternoon for paperwork and research. I'm pretty capable of working out my own day, Mr. Cody."

"Gunnar. And if this is the thank-you lunch you promised after telling me I could kiss your ass, it's everything I dreamed it would be." If anyone else had said that, she would be planning her exit. What was it about this guy? Somehow his swagger and self-assuredness came off as fun and naughty instead of conceited and spiteful. Like the actually-cute-when-you-get-to-know-him bad boy she was always warned about. Maybe it was the smile that invited her in on the joke. Or the kindness in his quick eyes. Macie realized he was speaking to her.

"He wants to know if you want wine." Then she noticed the waiter standing there and chided herself for losing focus. Even though this lunch was her olive branch, she really wanted to get Cody to give up why he kept popping up in her murder case. But this guy was smart, and to get him to spill, she needed to keep a clear head.

"No. No wine. Iced tea for me." Wild dipped her head to him, urging, "But you go ahead. Probably a relief not to have to abstain anymore because you're on duty."

"You kidding? I kept a cooler of Sam Adams in the stakeout van at all times." He gave her a stage wink. "The trick is to know your limit."

"OK, I can't tell if you're serious or not."

Cody steepled one brow playfully. "Like I said, one of us better watch it." He went for Pellegrino then shared the bottle, slowly filling her stem glass only halfway, showing both manners and finesse. She couldn't decide on a starter because they all looked so good. He suggested they make a meal of appetizers.

While they sampled and picked, Macie said, "You did want this, right? I just never knew a man who was happy going tapas mode."

He chuckled. "Sounds like an eighties Eurotrash hair band. 'Hello, Reykjavik, vee are Tapas Mode!' But with those two funny dots over the O in mode."

"An umlaut."

"You shame me. I scarf down all three Stieg Larssons, and did I even once look that up?" Wild caught him studying her face and she shifted away to give him another inch of DMZ. "I could sit at another table, and we could text." And when she blushed, he said, "I don't mean to make you uneasy. It's just I'm getting this push-pull vibe off you. It's OK. I get it."

She tilted her head to one side. "Get what?"

He speared an artichoke. "You're very nice, offering to take me here, but it has to be conflicting. Given what you do, and what I represent. But I'm not a cop anymore. I'm an ex-cop."

"I have absolutely no problem with cops." Then she added, "As long as they don't indiscriminately video protesters at legal rallies." And since that didn't seem to faze him, she continued, "Or, let's say, infiltrate and wiretap ethnic or religious groups without due cause."

"What, nothing about the flawed trade-off Americans have made, swapping constitutional protections for the hazy promise of better security?" She watched him fork the carciofi in his mouth and chew, forcing her to fill the silence.

"OK, that too. And, all right, I will admit my experience with law enforcement, especially pretrial, isn't so stellar. I respect them, definitely honor their service and sacrifice—but I also know they are out to stop me at all times and in all ways." He swallowed but still waited her out. It occurred to her that Gunnar Cody worked silences like a skilled interrogator. "But cops—ex or otherwise—no issues here."

"Good," he said at last. "I can't say the same for lawyers." He lofted his Pellegrino and smiled. "But let's not look for trouble." After she toasted him back, Cody added, "Especially not after that spinning groin kick I saw you land on your man last night."

She smiled self-effacingly. "I take a class."

"From who, Jason Bourne?"

Macie eased open the door to her agenda. "Now that you fear my superpowers, maybe I can get you to tell me about your big documentary project."

"Seriously? Isn't that the exact topic that made you freeze me out the other day?"

"Correction: I was the one frozen out. After asking you the legitimate question of why you were stalking my homicide case."

"Stalking. So pejorative—"

"—Three times. Once in Chelsea. Second, trying to interview my alibi witness. And third . . ." She folded a hand around three fingers, bundling them. ". . . just happening by last night when I was attacked."

"And lucky for you I did."

"How is that lucky? I smashed his nuts, and you let him get away."

"Best thank-you lunch ever." Without a beat he said, "Hey, I saw on Channel Four that the Buzz Killer's in a coma at Bellevue. What happened? I mean really."

Even though he had flipped this interview, she was glad he was engaged and answered his question. "Unclear. They found him in an alcove hanging by a trash bag from a pipe."

"How is that unclear?"

"Meaning nobody saw what happened. An inmate tried to slash him the other day, another tried to shiv him. But with no witnesses, I can't rule out staff involvement."

He set down his fork. "Um, hold up. Doesn't suicide figure into this, or are you so blindly invested in your client that you've gone, default, to conspiracy theories?"

"I am invested, Mr. Cody, in serving the legal rights of a man who is innocent of a crime and has been incarcerated without adequate protection for his safety. And please don't call him the Buzz Killer."

He raised both palms in surrender. "Bad form on my part. And bad manners. I'm sorry."

His apology seemed heartfelt so she let it slide. As they resumed passing plates, Wild circled back. "I'm still waiting. Why the stalk that's not a stalk?"

Cody reflected a moment. "All right. I'll share this much: The story I'm working for VICE has a lot of threads, one of which seems to have put me in overlap with you. But I wouldn't read too much into it."

"You expect me to be satisfied with that?"

"It'll have to do."

She rotated toward him in full cross-exam posture. "What were you doing in that neighborhood last night?"

"Helping you. Your turn."

There he was, flipping it again. There she was, sucked in again. "I was trying to interview a known associate of the murder victim. These are the straws you grasp at when you can't access the police report, the autopsy report, or even get into the damn crime scene."

"That blows. You know, I always thought it was kind of unfair how the DA locks you guys out. Not the most level playing field."

"Don't need to tell me."

"Just offering sympathy. Along with my suggestion to, perhaps, lighten up."

"I'll think about that," she said, not thinking about it at all. "Now you."

"I need to gather a little more information before I can share. I don't like to come off half-assed. It's what I hate about journalism, especially new-school. Nobody double sources or fact checks anymore."

"Are you serious?"

"I take my work very seriously. It's a mission. We have that much in common. That and tapas mode. By the way, that diacritical mark over the O. Umlaut, was it?"

Macie signaled for the check. While she got out her wallet, she wondered what just happened. How did some guy—some ex-detective—shut her down like that? She was the go-to in the public defender's office for her ability to handle witness interviews, depositions, cross-examinations, negotiations, name it. Macie put her credit card on the tray and looked back at Cody. What. Just. Happened?

"I don't want us to part mad like this," he said. "Not again."

"That's fine, don't worry. It was a chance to thank you for being there last night. And to pretend to get to know each other."

He laughed. "Look at you, lightening up." Then he read her frosty response and said, "Let me make it up to you."

"It's not necessary. Really." She signed the bill and put away her card.

"Really-really? Because I was going to get you inside your crime scene."

Yanked once more in the opposite direction, she tried to gauge his sincerity. "How?"

"How's the easy part. You did say you cleared your afternoon, right?" He rose from the booth and waited for her. Every bit of experience, instinct, and judgment told her to move on. But intrigue cast its vote.

Wild slid out and stood beside him. "I have some time," she said.

Fewer than twenty minutes later, back at Pinto's building in Chelsea, Wild followed Cody into the same vestibule where she had been turned away two days before. "You do know the super here is a tyrant. He will call the police. So unless you plan to kick in that door . . ."

"Entirely too much work. Besides, why go all Ronda Rousey when you have one of these?" Cody held up a gleaming key pinched between his thumb and forefinger. Without hesitation, he opened the security door and held it for her. Unsure how he managed this, she hesitated. Then stepped through.

He led, she followed. They climbed the stairwell to the fourth floor. Mindful of the acoustics of the tile hallway, Macie tiptoed. Cody did nothing to conceal his presence, leading with at-home strides, even clearing his throat loudly a few times. He only slowed once, passing an apartment door behind which the TV sound cut off suddenly. He caught her eye and fired a finger pistol at it but kept on, stopping at the next unit, number 412.

The posting warned, "No Entry. NYPD Crime Scene." The door was also crisscrossed with caution tape. Over six years Wild had seen plenty of these notices; every time they intimidated her. That was the idea. Quite unintimidated, Cody simply ripped down the tape. "Hey," she whispered.

"Hate that stuff," he said in full voice. She shot a glance up the corridor in fear someone would hear him. While she was turned away, the lock snapped open. And then he was standing inside, holding the door wide for her. Macie didn't budge. "Aw, you're not stopping now, are you?"

In fact, she already had. The thrill of going along on a naughty little adventure got dwarfed by a lifetime of common sense, not to mention adherence to law. Wild stared at the yellow coil of do-not-cross an inch from her toes and said, "I can't."

"You want to see your crime scene, don't you?" She didn't answer. "Tell you what. How's this? I broke in, not you. See? I just left a door ajar, and you came by and said, 'What's this?' Then, as a concerned citizen . . ."

"I am an officer of the court."

"Even better. A sworn upholder of justice who heard a cry for help and came inside to make sure everything was all right."

"But that's not what happened."

Cody signaled a pause with his forefinger, closed the door all but three inches, and moaned a feeble, "Help, help." He waited, and then stepped out with her again. "Some Samaritan."

She glanced around him through the foyer to the living room, which seemed dusky, almost lunar. Not two feet across that threshold, it vibed death scene. The funereal atmosphere and utter stillness of the place immediately stripped away any exhilaration of rolling in tandem with Cody and delivered Wild back to sober reality. "I want to know what's going on here. Starting with that key. I want to know how you got it."

"Simple enough. It's a copy of the one I borrowed from the building super this morning. 'Borrowed' being a loose term, since he didn't know I did it. But what Czcibor doesn't know won't hurt him."

"Czcibor?"

"Your Polish tyrant. But let's cut him some slack. I'd have a 'tude my-self if I had a nose covered in pubic hair."

Once more, Cody had knocked her off balance. She wagged her head in disbelief that not only had he stolen the super's key, but at the liberty he had taken encroaching into her case. As implications swirled in her head, she hit him with the bonus question. "Why are you helping me?"

"Would it be enough to say that I like you and I sympathize with your situation?"

"What do you think?"

"It's true, you know." Not seeing the thank-you face he expected, he continued anyway. "The fact is, we're here, and I figure we have about twenty minutes before someone whistles the game. Do you want to have a panel discussion or search?" Macie stayed put. "OK, well, riddle me this, Macie Wild. Wouldn't you love to know what the police and the DA know—and are keeping from you?" This guy truly was the devil on her shoulder. He watched Macie agonize for a beat and added some-thing to tip the scales. "Play this right, and you won't even have to go to trial."

"Let's turn on some lights," she said, then strode by him into the crime scene.

CHAPTER · 9

Wild liked to work methodically. She always began a site survey in the living room because it stood as the idealized version of the lives lived in a home. Spending a first-impression moment there offered her an opportunity to get a sense of the victim. A maxim her boss and mentor had drilled into her was, "In the absence of evidence, seek impressions."

That is why Macie centered herself in the toffee-colored rectangle of hardwood where a rug had once lived. She revolved a slow three-sixty, letting her eye land wherever it was drawn. Her main perception was of clutter. And what else . . . ? Transience. Even allowing for the fact that the Crime Scene Unit had probably carted away some items (as with the rug, the couch cushions were gone), the place felt like a sad void, any-thing but homey. The glass coffee table, a thrift-store castoff, was a hoard of skin mags and fast-food wrappers. Random popcorn puffs and Froot Loops, adrift under the sofa, had been cocooned by hairy dust bunnies. There was a lone plastic spork and a worn tennis ball under the bookless bookcase. On the wall a very new, quite expensive, big screen had been tagged as NYPD property; no doubt it was stolen. The Dude abided from the room's only artwork, a *Big Lebowski* poster, stuck to a wall by four tabs of duct tape. Rúben Pinto's file said he was thirty-two. He lived like a teenager. Macie's impression was of rootlessness. No center, no home, no rules.

Cody sidled up and held out a pair of nitrile gloves from his mes-senger bag. "CSU's already done their sweep," he said, "but whatever we gather on our own, we'll want to avoid contaminating." He placed a gloved hand on her forearm. "Plus, you won't leave prints, so when you hop down off that ethical high horse, you can deny you were here." He started for the rear of the apartment, calling back to her, "Let's get to the main event."

She caught up, following Cody's long strides to the bedroom. The door was shut, but unlocked. He entered like the owner, and they stepped into bright sunlight streaming through parted drapes—then stopped. Wild had been in numerous killing cribs before, but this one made her gasp. Congealed blood covered every possible surface—the floors, the walls, windows, even the ceiling—in spatters, drips, sprays, and pools, turning the place into a Jackson Pollack nightmare in 3-D. After a moment of wretched awe, Cody said, "So. This just might be the crime scene."

He took a knee and pulled a forensic swab kit out of his Timbuk2 and began to collect a floor sample from a reddish-brown stain the shape of a major continent. "A piece of advice? Just in case the detectives haven't already hit your client's closet, I'd clear it out in the event he has any inconvenient plasma residue on his clothes."

Trying to ignore the insinuation, Wild opened her Moleskine and sketched a primitive layout of the crime scene. The room was your basic rectangle with a row of windows comprising one wall, and, to the left, a closet with pocket doors also flocked with blood spray. After marking telltale spatters, Macie paused near the entry door and placed her cheek against the wall to site its contour.

"What ya got?" asked Cody.

"This." Wild dialed the air above a small crater in the plaster. "A depression and some hair. Looks to me like somebody's head hit here and slid down." The light was excellent, thanks to all the sunshine, so she got out her iPhone to snap off some documentaries. Heedful of that bump on the back of Jackson Hall's skull and the assistant DA's photo that indicated he had the wound before he got to Rikers, she was hating the implications. Macie also brought out an L-shaped ruler with both metric and inch graduations. She held it against the wall for reference and took another shot.

"Now you're just showing off," said Cody.

"Old habit," she said as she continued to fire off different sizes and angles. "Nothing impresses a jury like a PowerPoint that sends the message that the DA isn't the only one who knows the crime scene firsthand."

Cody joined her to DNA-swab that area, and while he sampled, Macie snapped wide views of the room. Then she went in for closer shots of the blood residue, also using her CSU-grade ruler. Opening the closet doors revealed three wrinkled shirts on hangers, moguls of dirty laundry on the floor, and a pair of dumbbells mixed in with a jumble of shoes. She picked up the twenty-five-pound weights one at a time and examined them.

"If you're looking for a weapon of convenience, I doubt you'll find it there," said Cody. "It's such a no-brainer that CSU would have gone for that too. If any hair, skin, or DNA was on one of those, they'd be sitting in the forensic lab out in Jamaica."

"I bet it's unlikely we'll find the murder weapon here. Either CSU bagged it or it left with our unknown assailant."

Cody paused. "Sure." She didn't like the pause. Or the tone. Not agreeing with the "unknown" part. In one syllable Macie perceived a cop's career suspicion—or, perhaps, cynicism—about a criminal's bullshit story. Same as his not-so-subtle advice to check Hall's wardrobe for blood spatter. Maybe he was right at lunch. Maybe she did have a problem with cops. Or maybe just this one.

All from one syllable.

Damn.

Cody packed the swab containers in the stash pockets of his messenger bag then came out with a GoPro. Bracing his back against the door frame, he recorded a slow, steady-handed pan of the entire room. Macie hurried to get out of his shot. "You may want to do that again with me on the outside."

"Don't worry, I'll just have you sign the standard release form for my VICE doc. Maybe you know a good lawyer who can look it over." After he recorded his panorama, he said, "Let's do the bathroom next. Never know what you'll find in a medicine cabinet or toilet tank." She let him lead again, and when he reached the doorway Cody stopped short, and she collided into him. "Whoa . . ." was all he said. Or needed to.

When he slid inside, she got a view of more blood. Even more than the bedroom. Here, too, it had splattered prolifically—high and wide. Cody said, "This dude got turned into fajitas before he passed." Macie flashed back on the gruesome photo array of Pinto that Fontanelli had teased her with. "I'd say somebody could use some anger management."

A joke, but no laugh. Wild knew enough cops to understand gallows humor as a coping mechanism.

The room was too cramped for them both, especially with the commode kicked over. It lay in chunks on the floor next to the medicine cabinet, which had been pried from the wall. So she left it to Cody to collect samples and shoot the digital record while she gave the kitchen a look. Typical of a New York one-bedroom, it was not much bigger than a Gap changing booth. Nothing controversial there. About as tidily kept as the rest of the place. Macie noticed how the residue of fingerprint powder blended with the grime on the cabinet pulls and stove knobs. Wild moved back to the living room to find Gunnar Cody at the tiny desk in one of the corners. "The computer must have been here," he said, indicating a rectangle on the desktop showing a dust ghost of its footprint. "Safe bet forensics took that too." He got on both knees in front of the open file drawer. "Join me at the altar of reality."

When she knelt beside him, Cody gestured to the mess. As with the rest of Rúben's place, the dorm mentality ruled. No Pendaflexes, just loose papers tossed in there, not unlike the moguls of soiled clothing on the closet floor. Cody began to paw through the mound. Wild rocked back to sit on her heels. "You know there's kind of a creep factor, prying into private lives like this."

"There is?" This time she didn't wonder if he was kidding or not. For once Gunnar Cody could be taken at face value. For a man like him there was no problem, let alone a creep factor.

"Let me ask you a question. Speaking as a veteran detective, why didn't they take these?"

"You mean CSU? They're coming back. See the TV property tag?" He started gathering papers out of the drawer.

"What are you doing?"

"A more thorough job than CSU, that's for sure."

"We can't take these."

"Why not?"

"It's evidence."

"Um . . . which is exactly why we should take them." Cody ignored her and got busy with his cell phone, which was vibrating. He pressed the screen to stop the alarm and rose. "Time to break camp."

"What's going on?"

"Czcibor's on the move. I GPS'd his car. We're good for about fifteen minutes, but why call it close?"

Floored, astonished—the best she could muster was, "You what . . . ?"

"No biggie. I slapped a transponder under his rear bumper. Want to see?" Cody held out his phone. On the screen map, a small blue dot pulsed on the West Side Highway. "It's basically the same way you know how close your Uber is." He picked up the stack of files. "Do me a favor, I saw one of those Urban Luggage grocery bags in the kitchen."

"Look. Mr. Cody. I can kinda sorta rationalize the unauthorized visit. Removing physical evidence? That is a line I have to draw."

He saw the resolve in her eyes. "You really are a straight shooter, aren't you?"

"My executive director once called me the Annie Oakley of moral codes."

"As a compliment or a dig?" All he got back was her resolute stare. "OK. All right . . ." He chucked the files back in the drawer then closed it with an elegant hand flourish straight from *The Price Is Right*. "Happy?"

"Ecstatic."

Out in the hallway, she peeled off her gloves and enjoyed the cool air on her hands. "Shit," he said. "Left my coat in there. BRB." He disappeared inside, and, just when he seemed to be gone a tad long, the door opened again and he stepped out with his sport coat hooked on a finger. As Cody locked up, Macie noticed the sudden bulk of his messenger bag as he restuck the crime scene tape.

"What did you do?"

He smiled. "Just keeping your aim true, Annie Oakley." Before she could react, he strode up the corridor with the paper-laden Timbuk2 bouncing off his ass. Wild tried to ignore that fact that it was a very nice ass while she caught up beside him and put her hand on his elbow.

"I want you to put those back." Before he could respond they heard a floorboard creak. It came from behind the apartment door beside them—the same place the blaring TV got muted on their way in. Cody unslung the messenger bag and handed it to Macie. Its weight jarred her. She held it while he put on his jacket. She was just about to thank him when he turned and knocked on 413. "What are you doing?"

"Feel free to sit this one out." He gave her a sympathetic face. "Really. I understand."

Macie was backing away when a woman's "Who is it?" came from inside.

"Ex-Detective Cody, NYPD." Wild noted how deftly he swallowed the "ex," and bet it was from plenty of practice. The former policeman presented himself confidently to the peephole. Two deadbolts later, the door opened.

The aluminum walker emerged, tennis balls first. "Sorry," said the old woman. "You have to be careful. Especially after the murder."

"Understood," said Cody.

"I'm happy to help, but I already told the other detectives everything I know."

Macie caught the gloat in the slight narrowing of Cody's eyes. His assumption had paid off. He scored a witness. "Well, you know how it is, check and double-check. That's how we get the bad guys."

A bingo wing on the octogenarian's arm waggled as she beckoned him inside. Worried about loitering in the hallway with a bag full of stolen evidence, Macie followed. When she closed the door, the woman turned to scrutinize her. "You don't look like a cop. Well, a pretty cop. Like on a TV show. You have very nice teeth."

Not sure what else to say, Macie smiled. "Thank you."

They baby-stepped behind the metallic clicks of the walker into the living room where the Home Shopping Network was conducting a big sale on Char-Broil cookers. At a glance her layout was the mirror reverse of Rúben Pinto's apartment, but clean and in Danish Modern, circa 1962. "We appreciate your assistance, Dr. McBlaine." Macie's head whipped toward Cody. He subtly angled a brow toward the wall of dental diplomas and professional honors for Thea McBlaine, DDS.

They declined decaf Keurigs and took seats in the airless, overheated room. Ad-libbing, ex-Detective Cody dove into an interview. He went right for the timeline, a cop's best friend: how and when McBlaine was first alerted to something out of the ordinary the day of her neighbor's murder. Macie took notes as the former dentist told the former cop about the shouting she heard in the hallway—two men—and how she couldn't see them through her peephole, but when she opened her door to spy out, she saw a slender black man yelling at her neighbor.

"Rúben Pinto?" asked Cody.

"Yes."

"And do you remember what was being said?"

"Oh, I'll never forget. The man in the hall was hollering at the top of his lungs. He yelled, 'I'm looking at a dead man, you fucking son of a bitch.' I must have made a noise then because he turned my way, and I shut my door. And locked it."

"Was that when you called the police?"

"No, that was later, because things got quiet until a few minutes later. Then I heard loud banging and screams. Lots of screams." Macie's flesh prickled in the warm apartment. She understood the banging. And the screams. "I went back to my peephole and saw a man run up the hallway toward the stairs. I didn't dare open my door, and just kept watch for the police."

"Was that the same man you saw go into the apartment earlier?"

"No. I told this to the detectives exactly like I told you. Don't you cops talk to each other?"

"Did you see the first man leave?" Cody quoted her without notes. "The . . . 'slender black man?'"

"No. I don't really know what became of him."

Cody asked her for a description of the other man. "White. A blur."

"Did you notice anything distinctive about him, even if it's trivial? Height, weight, hair color, whiskers, clothing, anything?"

Dr. McBlaine shook her head. "No."

Macie recognized the vibration pattern of the GPS alert in Cody's pocket, and both rose to leave.

◊ ◊ ◊

They stood near the tapas place next door to Pinto's building and watched Czcibor's old Volvo wagon cruise West Sixteenth for an open spot. "You did all right in there," said Cody. "I was worried you'd go all 'Ms. Full Disclosure' on me after I flushed out the only witness you have so far." An uncomfortable pause hung there. He broke the silence, speaking an ugly truth. "Doesn't look good that your client was there voicing a death threat."

"True, except for that other man. Whom the DA has chosen to ignore in favor of my client for some reason." They watched the Volvo pass again. "What I'd like to do is get a line on that white guy."

"Could he be Pinto and Hall's crew chief?"

"Love to know."

"Have you been to Hall's place yet?" He read her expression and said, "Seriously?—No?" He pulled his cuff back to check his watch. "You said you cleared your afternoon, right? You up for a little ride-along?"

Macie sized him up. Glad for some help for once, but still wondering why. "Sure."

He patted his messenger bag full of the files. "You forgot to have me put these back."

It was her turn to smirk. "Did I?"

Climbing the stairwell of any New York City apartment building is pretty much like taking an olfactory core sample. You know what was for lunch and what's for dinner, who's cleaning and who needs to take out the garbage. Macie Wild scaled the cracked steps of the walk-up in Spanish Harlem, picking up the ghost specimens: onions, cumin, fried fish, old fish. A Dr. Seuss take on lives being lived in dense proximity. Macie trudged upward while getting a cell phone briefing on her client from the team's social worker. Jackson Hall was still at Bellevue, still in ICU, still comatose. "Soledad, would you please ask the duty nurse to let us know immediately if Pilar Fuentes shows up for a visit?"

"Absolutely. Fuentes is the girlfriend, right?"

"Correct. She's not answering repeated calls. I'd like to ask her about a guy who might be connected to Mr. Hall. Don't let her know that. Just have the hospital alert us if she shows."

"I can swing by her apartment, if you want. I live, like, three blocks from there."

"I'm already here. About to meet up with Jonathan. I don't feel optimistic."

"About Jonathan, or locating the girlfriend?"

Macie cast a look up the stairwell to see how close she was to five and her investigator's earshot. "A self-answering question, smart ass." Wild left it there and hung up as she gained the fifth-floor landing. Jonathan Monheit waited, midhall, outside one of the apartments, looking not just alone but adrift.

"I've been at this since you called," he began, just this side of a whine. "No Pilar Fuentes. No nothing."

"I'm sure you covered all the bases. You covered all the bases, right?" But his attention was over her shoulder. Macie turned to find Gunner Cody topping the stairs. He told her he would wait outside. He didn't.

"Hi," said the ex-cop.

She introduced Cody by name only, leaving off any background or explanation for his presence. And her colleague didn't ask for any, but just said, "Jonathan Monheit, lead investigator," in his reedy, NPR voice as the two men shook hands. To Macie they smacked of a pairing for an action-comedy-buddy movie about a veteran cop stuck with a reject from the Geek Squad. Cody treated her associate politely. Even discreetly taking a step back to give Wild some space while Monheit recapped his fruitless door knocks, beginning with the apartment they stood in front of that was shared by Pilar Fuentes and Jackson Hall. Then he moved on to neighbors, who variously claimed not to know Fuentes or to simply say that they hadn't seen her in days. As Monheit recited a list of his thwarted attempts, Macie balanced her frustration at his unimaginative task work with her low-grade embarrassment at having the NYPD veteran witness her exchange.

However, gaining further points for discretion, Cody had quietly slipped away, obviously to give her more privacy during this excruciating professional moment. Wild interrupted Monheit's tedious litany of dead-end encounters to brief him on the crime scene and her interview with Dr. McBlaine. When she got to the part about the old woman reporting she saw another man running in Pinto's hallway, Monheit took out a spiral notebook. "Did she give you a description?"

Macie searched to find a way to phrase "white, and a blur" that wouldn't sound as feeble as the report she just endured from him. During her pause, a muffled thump came from inside the Fuentes apartment. Startled, Jonathan stared at her, frozen. The deadbolt clicked. They both retreated a yard closer to the stairs. Then the door swung open, and Gunnar Cody filled the frame, holding a fistful of mail.

"This was in Pilar's mailbox downstairs. Don't ask. I'd say she's been gone for days." Behind him, a curtain billowed at the window leading to the fire escape. "Well, you're not just going to stand out there, are you?"

Resigned to trespass for the second time in her life, excluding the usual teenage dares, Wild stepped inside. "I'm starting to understand why you are ex-NYPD."

After riffling through the ads and catalogues, Cody set them back on the counter. "It's complicated."

Monheit, who had gone from fear to confusion, transitioned to alarm. "He's a cop?"

"Ex," said Wild and Cody in unison.

"Still . . ." Monheit's gaze bounced from Cody to land on Macie. "What are you doing with an ex-cop?"

"It's complicated," she said, poaching Cody's own words, but he was too busy walking through the apartment to notice.

"Hall told you CSU gave this place a once-over, right?"

"Yes."

Monheit's voice rose an octave and cracked. "You told him about our client interview? Isn't that privileged?"

Cody smiled. "It's OK, ace. I'm sort of helping out. Fresh eyes, and all that."

Sympathetic to Monheit's spot in this accidental triangle, Macie said, "You know, Mr. Cody, this is a little awkward."

Cody disappeared into the bedroom for only a few seconds then came back out. "Awkward, how?" Then he regarded Jonathan Monheit. "Oh, I get it. No dick measuring here, *amigo*, honest." He moved to the galley kitchen and said, "Interesting." Macie showed up next to him, and he picked up a fishing pole that was parked beside the fridge. "What do you make of this?"

"Jackson Hall fished. In fact, he said he went fishing the day of the murder."

He cocked his head. "What. You mean like having a cigarette after sex?"

"No, no . . . That's one of his unconfirmed alibis." Monheit snorted his exasperation, and Cody turned to him.

"Jonathan, this is your party. As lead investigator, let's get your take." Which only served to startle the rookie.

"Well, it's pretty obvious . . . Hall, um, got back from fishing. Left the rod here." He searched their faces for feedback, got none, then blundered on. "So. That's how it got there."

"Great," said Cody. "Thanks." He crossed to the open curtain, and it looked like he was going to exit by the fire escape. Instead he pulled the window closed and moved to the door. "I got what I needed. All yours," he said nonchalantly. Then left.

The lead investigator began to retrace Cody's steps, clearly wondering what the ex-detective got that he hadn't.

When Macie burst out of the apartment building onto the sidewalk, Cody was jaywalking 103rd toward where he had double-parked. She called his name, but he didn't turn, although he halted for an ambulette crossing Lexington, which let her catch up. "You didn't have to leave."

"I know," he said. Halfway up the street the lights blinked on his cargo van as it unlocked.

She fell into step with him. "Then what's your hurry?"

"No hurry. You just don't need a third wheel. Not when you've got Jonny Midnight." Macie laughed out loud at the perfectly catty nickname he had coined for Jonathan Monheit. That seemed to please him, and he crossed his arms next to his driver door. "I have this feeling I overreached. Like I'm dragging you where you don't want to go. It's all right." He pulled the handle.

"Wait." He did, and she continued, "When you said you got what you needed up there, what was it?"

"Back to the push-pull. I keep getting these mixed signals from you, Macie."

He wasn't wrong, of course. She bobbed her head to acknowledge that. "I . . . apologize. Well, sort of. You need to understand this is all sudden and new for me."

"You mean conducting a viable investigation?" He saw her blink and walked it back. "That was shitty. Sorry. I just get a little . . . directive when I'm working. 'Get 'er done,' know what I mean?"

"So I'm learning, yes."

They stood in silence, waiting out the thunder of a passing cement mixer. When the street quieted again, he said. "It was the fishing pole."

"I'm sorry?"

"It's the *Sesame Street* theory." That got her attention. What cop invokes *Sesame Street*? "You've heard it. Sing along, if you like: 'One of these things is not like the others.'" He looked across Lex in the direction of the fifth-floor walk-up. "Every bit of that apartment was impeccably kept. Except—who keeps a fishing pole in the kitchen? I can answer that. Someone who planned to go fishing and got interrupted, or who just came back, and suddenly got distracted before he could stow it away in storage or a closet, what have you."

"That's the same thing Jonathan said."

"Except, for me, it pings my alarms. I don't give a rat's ass how the pole got there. I want to know who Jackson Hall went fishing with. Not just to set his alibi, which, by the way, wouldn't suck. But more importantly, is one of his fellow anglers a nondescript white guy? It's all about noticing what you're noticing. Thanks again to my yellow-feathered friend. That would be—"

"—Big Bird, I get it. So your alarm pings. What do you do about it?"

"What Jonny Midnight didn't. I'm going fishing. Baitin' up for alibi buddies."

"All from a fishing pole."

"In the absence of better, yes." He popped his door and added, "By proximity, I'm guessing he fished the river. Did Hall happen to tell you where?"

Wild tried to slow the cadence and get her legs under her. She wasn't sure yet where all this was leading but, thanks to this ex-detective, new pieces of the jigsaw, however small and disconnected, were suddenly on the table. Among the most puzzling to her was the interest of Gunnar Cody, a puzzle piece in itself. Why was this video-doc renegade doing all this? Was he connected to her case in a way that went beyond a project overlap? It couldn't be that he had simply taken a liking to her. The sensible Macie Wild would have applied the brakes. Hard. But her curiosity, his magnetism, and a new sense of hope had seized her. Making another break from prudence, Macie said, "I'll show you," and opened the door on the passenger side, wondering if she had just taken bait herself.

◊ ◊ ◊

Gunnar Cody improvised a parking spot on East 102nd near the pedestrian bridge he and Macie used to cross over the FDR to Bobby Wagner Walk. Joggers huffed by now and then as they strode the blacktop path alongside the Harlem River where it flowed into Hell Gate, the channel where it joined the East River. A windless afternoon, the water to their right lay flat, with the only disturbance created upstream by an asphalt barge getting a tug push south. Just a few blocks to its stern, the vessel's wake slapped against the piles of the East Harlem Fishing Pier. But Wild and Cody weren't watching waves; they were looking for signs of life on the wharf.

The walk heated Macie inside her linen blazer so she slid out of it, draping it over a forearm without breaking stride. Ahead she began to make out figures on the pier. When she turned aside to Cody to see if he had registered them, too, she caught him stealing a glance at her bare shoulders. He diverted, saying, "Think I'll lose mine too," then slipped off his sport coat. Both continued on with eyes front.

They found surprisingly few visitors taking advantage of the sunlit day on the water. "Sparse," said Macie as they surveyed the prospects. Ahead of them on the concrete outcropping, a disabled person reclined in his therapeutic wheelchair. A caregiver in nursing pastels adjusted his nasal cannula, then went back to her *People* magazine. Off to the left, across the deck, a young man leaning on a delivery bike blazed nonstop venom in Spanish into a cell phone. Breakups. They sounded the same in any language.

"Possibles." Cody's attention locked on the end of the pier, nearly the length of a football field away. Three black men stood clustered around fishing poles bungee-corded to the metal rail. When Wild and Cody got halfway there, the trio changed attitudes, two of them getting busyish checking their lines, while the third pulled a porgy from a white PVC bucket and plunked it on one of the cleaning stations attached to the fence.

"Looks like somebody caught one," said Cody on their approach. Macie watched the man in the silver tracksuit slice open the fish's belly, releasing innards and blood onto the metal tray. He didn't acknowledge Cody's cheerful greeting, just set about gutting his catch, flinging the entrails into the river with his knife to the excitement of the gulls. His pals became more engaged with their tackle, not acting with hostility, but presenting their backs to avoid conversation.

"My name's Macie Wild," she said, bypassing ice breakers. "I'm the attorney representing a man who likes to fish here. Jackson Hall." Her pause for reaction yielded nothing, so she continued even more directly. "Do any of you know him? Jackson Hall? I have a picture." She went to each, showing the fractured screen of her cell phone. They barely looked but shook no. "He's in trouble, and I'm trying to help him." She went for her notebook, found the page she wanted from Hall's debrief at Rikers, and asked, "Is one of you named Sammy, Sammy Goins? Fabio Mir? Pete Loomis?"

"Feel free to sing out," said Cody. "Like she said, we're just looking to get a brother out of a jam." He waited, then pointed to each one in succession. "Let's start with Sammy. You Sammy? Are you? What about you?"

The man in the silver tracksuit answered, but to his companions. "Sammy . . . ? No, man, my name's Otis. Otis Redding." Then he laughed, singing a few lines of "The Dock of the Bay." "You said sing out."

Macie waited for their chuckling to subside. "You see, I'm trying to find out who killed a friend of his, Rúben Pinto. He fishes here too. You know Rúben?" She held out his picture, sweeping it in an arc before them. Nobody looked. "Just in case one of you wants to help Mr. Hall, let me ask you a question. He had another friend, a white man that he . . ." —she searched for the best way to frame it— ". . . may have worked with sometimes. Do any of you know who that might be?"

"You a cop?" asked one of the two working the poles, a stocky guy in a denim shirt who'd cut off the sleeves to make it a vest. "Cause you're not asking questions like a fucking lawyer."

"I'm a public defender. I'm not with the police." Wild handed her business card to each. They gave it a glance, but their attention went to Cody. He picked up on that.

"I'm not a cop either."

"Sure, homes, ten-four," said The Vest. "By the way, thank you for your service." He turned away to check his line and the others disengaged as well.

Wild made one more attempt. "You have my card. If you change your mind and want to help, even if it's in a small way . . ." All she got were the backs of heads. ". . . Right."

They retreated in silence, Macie trying to jump-start hopes about finding a lead. Of course it occurred to her that perhaps these men did not know Hall or Pinto, and that she should return in the morning, the time of day he usually fished there. She also tried in vain not to feel the vise crush of responsibility to her client, whom she had lobbied not to take his plea deal. These were the sober places her thoughts ran as she retraced her steps down Bobby Wagner Walk when she realized she was alone.

Cody sat behind her on the retaining wall of a planter, hidden by a shrub, staring out at the end of the pier. "You in some kind of hurry?" he asked when she joined him. "No offense, but this is where you people fall short."

"Tell me what you mean, and I'll let you know if I'm offended."

"You can't accept pushback from a dickhead. That's just the opening move." He took out a pair of compact binocs and trained them on the fishermen. While he watched, he continued, "Tell me. Do you make me out as a cop? Do I really put that out there?"

No fan of profiling, Macie gave Cody a head-to-toe anyway. His face carried authority, but she also had seen it morph in a blink to playfulness. He was certainly fit, athletic even, and wore his clothes well—especially those skinny jeans he had on.

"Tell you one thing, if I was a cop, they'd goddamn know it. I'd brace their asses down at the precinct and we'd have some answers. Usually the threat of that is enough to shake the tree."

"Or you could take them for a ride." Wild laughed, but when he nodded as if that was buried in the dark pages of the playbook, she stopped. "As a cop, what did you make of Hall showing up at Pinto's door like he did?"

"As an ex-cop . . . Don't hate me, but I'd say he might look good for being partners on a cowboy hit. Two-on-one. You saw the blood and the damage."

"I do not believe he killed Rúben Pinto."

He pulled his Steiner glasses away to regard her. "I didn't say he did. I'm saying he looks good for it." Cody went back to his pier watch. "So. Do you hate me?"

"Such a strong word," she said. "Let's go with acute degree of wariness."

"A high-water mark for me in relationships." He handed the binoculars to her. "Check out Otis Redding." Macie saw only the other two. She searched left and eventually spotted the man in the silver tracksuit standing under the pier's pavilion, speaking on his cell phone. He pocketed it and called something to the others as he walked away.

"He's leaving."

Cody took the glasses back and smiled. "Otis Redding's headin' uptown. We visit. We go. He makes a call. He leaves the dock of the bay. Coincidence?"

"What now?"

"We follow." He wound the cord around the binocs. "You up for that?"

"Uh, sure."

"Good. Cause it's all we got." Wild got up to join Cody but he held up a palm. "He might have a car or get a cab." He handed her his keys. "I'll tail on foot. You meet me with my van. Give me your phone." His instructions were so softly given and matter-of-fact, she complied without feeling pushed around. He tapped in some digits and soon his phone vibrated. He pressed end and handed her cell back. "Just press redial when you reach the van. I'll tell you where to meet me." And he was off.

Macie went the opposite way at double time, and then began jogging, struck by how this day had turned since a simple payback lunch.

"This thing drives like a tank," said Wild as she pulled up to the corner on First Avenue. Cody got in the passenger seat.

"Yep, she runs heavy." He rapped some knuckles on the fiberglass partition behind them. "I keep all my gear back there."

"You mean for your video production?"

Smile lines creased the corners of his eyes before he answered. ". . . Yeah. Exactly." Then he jabbed a finger at his side window. Across 116th Street the man in the silver tracksuit was stepping out of a cigar store specializing in Dominican handmades. "Stay on him."

"You sure you wouldn't rather drive?"

"Let's go, don't lose him." Macie checked the side mirror, eased into traffic, then signaled a left to follow Otis Redding at his walking speed west on Pascale Place. Cody instructed her to wait at the corner when they reached Second Avenue, and she nosed forward so they could keep their target in view as he crossed at the light. "Thought so. He's headed to the bus stop. How you holding up?"

"I've never tailed a suspect before."

"Subject. He's not a suspect unless he is implicated in a crime. Jeez, what kind of lawyer are you anyway, Macie Wild?" That made her laugh and loosen her white-knuckle grip on the wheel.

Their man boarded the M15 Southbound, which made tailing easier, on one hand, since a bus was fairly easy to keep track of, but more challenging on the other because they had to eyeball every stop not to lose him in a crowd of passengers getting off. She grew inured to the horns protesting her slow speed, but when they came into Midtown and she got caught at a red and the bus continued on, Cody said, "You might want to tighten up."

Macie indicated the lane markings. "It says buses only."

"Nothing bad will happen. Keep it close." Battling a lifetime of respect for the law, she took a spot in the forbidden lane, giving her clear access to her M15 SBS. A police siren double chirped, and an NYPD blue-and-white pulled alongside. The cop riding shotgun signaled her to pull over.

"Crap," she said. "See?" Cody reached across her and flashed his wallet at the officer. The uniform gave a two-finger salute and the police car broke away. "I thought you said you weren't a cop anymore."

He said, "I'm not," and left it there.

The stop at Houston Street is designated for passenger exit only so it made it easier to spot the man in the tracksuit when he filed off. Maintaining the tail became trickier in the Lower East Side congestion, and they lost him once, only to regain him when he turned onto Avenue A. He rounded the corner at Third Street and breezed into a storefront offering back rubs and tension relief. "Who are they kidding?" said Cody. "It's a massage parlor."

"In the same block as the Upright Citizens Brigade," said Macie, tilting her head toward the improv group's theater. "Ironic."

"Or fitting." They shared a chuckle, and he pointed, "See the plumbing truck leaving? Grab his space." After she took an appalling number of maneuvers to park, Cody opened his door and said, "Come with me."

"Where?"

"To book a couple's massage."

Wild came around to the back of the van as Cody finished extracting the stack of Pinto's boosted crime scene papers from his messenger bag. He shut the cargo door and slung the satchel. He read her expression. "You don't really think I mean we're going to . . . you know."

"No." And then she added with emphasis, "No!"

"I said book, not get." He lagged for a cab to pass and crossed the street. She fell in step. "I want you to pretend you're a first timer and monopolize the manager with a bunch of dumbshit questions while I do my thing." Macie came to a halt on the sidewalk, and he stopped too. "Problem?"

"So you know, it would be a first. So you know." Point made, she scanned the parlor's storefront. "And what do you mean by 'do your thing?'"

"You won't need to stall too much. I hope not anyway. Depends how long it takes me to get access to his massage room."

"For what?"

"First of all, I want to see an ID from his wallet, so we have a name. An address would make it all nice."

She gestured at the Timbuk2 hanging on his shoulder. "Why do you need that? You going to slip a GPS in his pants?"

"Oh, please. He'd notice that. But I like the way you think. Almost un-lawyerly. Is that a word?" He didn't wait for an answer but opened the door for her to go inside.

The lobby might have once belonged to a tanning salon or shoe repair shop. At four p.m., it was faux midnight in the tiny reception area thanks to the window, which was tinted the fifty-first shade of gray. The odor was industrial-strength disinfectant mixed with the scent of patchouli curling off a lone stick of incense on a shelf near the manager. She was in her late fifties, with what would be called a practical haircut that went with her squared face and blocky physique. "Welcome to Bliss on Demand," she recited in a monotone, then cleared some gravel from her throat.

"*Jai Bhagwan*," replied Cody with a bow as they approached the counter.

Stage fright pecked at Macie. The reality set in that she was going to have to pull off a performance. "We were wondering if you do couples."

The woman slid on a pair of glasses from her neck chain and clapped a release form onto a clipboard. "You each want a relaxation massage?"

"Together!" Macie blurted.

"We can do that. You may have a wait. I only have one girl working now and she's with a client. Another's gal's coming in a half hour."

Cody gave Wild's foot a subtle nudge and she began her diversion. "Hm. Two women . . . is there any way to arrange a mix? Male and female?—Oh. And pricing. Is there an up-charge for doubles? I'd like to see your price list for comparison."

The manager dropped her head to peer at Wild over the top of her glasses. Cody asked if they had a restroom. She pointed toward an archway of hanging beads to the side. "Price list, huh . . . ?"

Six minutes seemed like an eternity to Macie, who had resorted to asking if they accepted health insurance when Cody parted the beads and emerged from the back, giving no sign of success or failure. "It's cash only. Seventy dollars," reported Wild.

"Each?" he asked, so sharply that Macie apologized to the manager.

Citing the price point, they thanked the woman for her time and left. On the walk back to their parking spot, he said, "His name is Fabio Mir."

"One of the names Mr. Hall gave me."

"Right. For the record, I never bought Otis Redding. Not for a second."

"Did you get an address?"

"It's a Florida license, so no help there today."

"You were gone forever."

"Five minutes, thirty-eight seconds." He flashed his runner's watch. "Fabio's cell phone took longer than I thought."

"To do what?"

"Tap it." They stopped at the rear of the van. He placed a hand on each of her upper arms and gently adjusted her position so he could keep an eye on the massage parlor. "You may have read about some of the technological advances that let police, government agencies, black hats, state actors, Fancy Bears, and certain unscrupulous journalists hack cell phones? For instance, decryption devices and radio interceptors that spoof cell towers and induce your target's calls to relay through your gear."

She gave him a skeptical look and tugged the strap of his messenger bag. "You have all that in here?"

"None of it." He reached in and pulled out a battle-scarred electronic box the size of a TV remote. "What I did instead was pair his Bluetooth to this. So now, as long as we keep in range, we can listen to all his calls. I only have one set of earbuds, so we'll have to do it in here." He unlocked the van and opened both rear doors. Seeing inside the back for the first time, Macie's jaw dropped.

The entire cargo hold of Gunnar Cody's E-350 Super Duty had been custom converted into a state-of-the-art mobile surveillance lab.

While she absorbed all this, Cody leaned over the bumper and gathered up the stack of Pinto's papers he had left earlier. He stowed the heap in a plastic milk crate, then turned to her. "You said your afternoon was clear. What about tonight? You up for seeing where this goes?"

Macie didn't need to consult her calendar to know what she had on deck. Counseling with her ex-fiancé. She mulled her choices: rehashing the breakup in Paris or the next leg of her spontaneous adventure.

Two hours later, parked outside a flophouse in the Bowery, they sat at the console in the rear of Cody's van listening to Fabio Mir place a cell phone bet from his room. In a pause while the bookie looked up the over-under, they made out the unmistakable sound of their subject urinating in the toilet. "Hear that? That's why I insist on Bose speakers," said Cody from his seat in the folding chair beside Macie's. He arched his back in a stretch and then returned his attention to the monitor in front of him that displayed a quad split—two angles of the sidewalk and two of the front of the hotel—all fed from cams on the roof of his E-350. "The sad part is, when our man hangs up, it's back to watching paint dry." Cody canted his head her way. "You bored?"

"I'm new at this. So not yet." Gunnar Cody entered such a zone staring at the monitor he reminded her of that heron she had observed near Rikers: the hunter who sees but is unseen. Same focus. Same patience. Same stillness. Macie didn't believe in omens. But watching Cody, she thought maybe she should reconsider that.

"It's not like TV cop shows," he said. "Ten years doing surveillance on TARU, I can tell you that. We had some of these go on weeks, a month. Often no payoff." The hours of isolation must have been long, she thought as she checked out the stack of books on the shelf under the monitors. She spotted the Stieg Larssons he'd mentioned at lunch along with an eclectic mix of literary fiction, travel essays, history, and classics. As he worked a camera joystick to check out some movement up the block, which turned out to be nothing, he continued his thought. "You really get to know your partners though. It's like being locked in a submarine."

That felt like her opening. "So what should I know about you?"

"You're pretty much seeing it." He smiled to himself. "Form your own judgment, but do be kind."

That sudden impishness made her smile. Again. "Can I ask a question?"

"Is this like cross-examination?"

"Let's find out. How did you get into this work?"

Fabio Mir ended his bookie call, and, by habit, Cody logged the time on a spiral pad. "Not so unique a story. 9/11 did it. I was a J-school major at Saint John's. Destined to be the next Anderson Cooper. The twin towers came down; I signed up for the cops instead. Enrolled at the academy while The Pile was still smoldering."

"How did you end up in TARU—and surveillance?"

"OK, can you kind of take the stink off that? And don't deny, I caught it." He gave her a quick glance then went back to his monitor. "To be fair, the Technical Assistance Response Unit is not exclusively about surveillance. Talk about Ground Zero, who do you think set up the landlines down there when all the cellular went out? And when there's a hostage situation, it's TARU cops who climb the telephone poles in the line of fire to set up the Bat Phone for the negotiators."

She rested a hand on his. "I'm not trying to badger the witness, honestly. Just trying to understand."

That siphoned off some tension, and he sounded more relaxed as he continued. "To answer your question, TARU found me. I guess because I was built for it. In high school, my buds and I were this combo plate of *Big Bang* geeks making all kinds of electronics shit and pulling these ballsy pranks. You know, like using a video cam to see the road while we ducked down to make it look like our car was driving itself? Crazy stuff I'd arrest myself for now. Anyway, it got around I was pretty good with a camera and had an almost-journalism degree, and that got me recruited for the tech unit. It was a blast too. Great guys, important work . . . Got to use my skills too." He gestured to the cargo interior, which looked every bit like an actual TV news minivan. "Like most of what's in here, I custom made my own snoop devices at the TARU workshop. You know, stuff for concealment. Cameras, mics, heat and motion sensors . . ."

"Bugs and secret wiretaps?"

"Come on, counselor, you have to admit, in today's world, somebody's got to do it. What did Orwell say about rough men who keep vigilance so that the innocent may sleep at night?"

"You do realize you're quoting the guy who wrote *1984* from inside a surveillance van."

"I can tell you firsthand, at TARU we stopped terror plots before they left their basements. A few mob guys had their days spoiled too." He opened his cooler and pulled out two waters, handing her one. "Fact is, people are all paranoid about police surveillance when retailers are using facial recognition at store displays to track their buying habits. Amazon, Netflix, and your phone's weather app know more about you than the police ever will."

She took a pull off her water and said, "You're kind of making my point. Not just about surveillance, but what is private anymore? Not our homes, our neighborhoods, our mistakes, our intimate moments—our secrets. Nothing is sacred. And when nothing is sacred, what happens to us?"

"*Now* who's the Buzz Killer," he said. Macie found herself laughing along with him, and how could she not? Cody had turned a despised nickname into a term of endearment.

The speakers came alive as Fabio Mir placed a call from inside the building. A man with a Russian accent answered brusquely. "Bad time. Call you back." That was that.

"So much for our entertainment portion," said Cody, sweeping his cams again with the joystick. "I think it's your turn, Macie Wild. You learned all about me—"

"Oh, I'm far from done. You don't know my appetite for the truth." Cody waited. Wild relented, not particularly enjoying the reversal. "Let's see. I grew up in a happy home of what you'd call high achievers. My dad was a state senator and is now back in private law practice."

"Where?"

"Manhattan and DC. Mom's in Doctors Without Borders."

"I'd call this high achieving. What the hell happened to you?"

"I know, sad, isn't it? My father said we were cursed with the Kennedy gene of public service."

"Is that why you became a public defender?"

"More like why I stayed one. I did NYU Law and got into a prestige firm right when the recession hit. Instead of cutting me, they offered to farm my services out on a pro bono fellowship for a year. Next thing I know, I'm at the Manhattan Center for Public Defense. Talk about getting thrown into the deep end. But I really, really loved it. It's like feeding a meal to someone who's hungry. Providing assistance to indigent clients, who are so grateful, and need it the most, is very rewarding. So here I am, still there six years later."

"Maybe you do have that Kennedy gene."

"I'm good with that. As long as it's Caroline's." Macie studied him, feeling a bit of contact rush from being part of his experience, noticing how work intensity made his face more handsome. "So what happened? At TARU. The cops. You left?"

"Not by choice." He dropped his gaze, forming the answer he didn't owe her. "I did a wrong thing for the right reason. Can we leave it there?"

"Sure."

Except Cody couldn't leave it there. "You know why the statue of Lady Justice is blind? So she doesn't have to see all the crap I pulled on her behalf." In a way that seemed important that she know, he added, "Same circumstances, I would do it all again."

The silence between them got broken by the ring of Mir's cell phone. Fabio answered, "Lazy Eight Whorehouse, when can I fit you in?" and then chortled. So did the caller, who, by his accent, sounded like the same man who couldn't speak earlier.

"Hey, dog dick, how's it going?"

"You know, the usual."

"I owe you for that heads-up call. What the fuck was that about?"

"Beats me. Thought I'd warn you off coming to the pier, just in case, ya know?"

"Cool, brother. Hey, you up for a pie? Thinking maybe I'd bring one over."

Macie got a jolt of adrenaline. This was what it felt like, she thought. Not exactly the same as bagging bin Laden, but close enough. She gave Cody a thumbs-up, but he had his eyes closed, listening, concentrating, not his first training day.

"I'm in Three-oh-six. Oh, and I got you some of those Dominicans you like. Handmade."

"See you in about a half hour. Open the window, air out the farts."

When the call ended, Cody calmly logged the time and the room number, then swiveled to her. "I've got to get a bug in there before he shows up."

Cody knelt on the rug—thick pile, he had told her earlier, to absorb sound; dark brown to absorb light. As he opened and closed drawers of a tool cabinet containing neatly organized wires and electronic parts, he explained that, even though they had Fabio's phone tapped, it wouldn't give them ears in the room to pick up conversation when his guest got there. "And as long as I'm going in to plant audio, I might as well give us video too." He plucked a tiny piece from a drawer and held it up. "Ever see a cam this small? I modified it from a dental probe. Not the highest rez, but it'll do for this."

While he assembled his rig, connecting plugs and snapping in a fresh Ni-Cad, Macie asked, "Why don't we just wait for the guy to show up, and talk to him?"

"I would urge you to look at all the precautions these two took to avoid us and ask yourself if this is a guy who's going to open up just because you have a friendly face." He reached for a black plastic box the size and shape of a jumbo pack of chewing gum and seated his A/V bug inside it, carefully inserting the dental lens and the mini microphone in the holes that had been drilled in one end. "Besides, don't you think he's going to be especially tweaked when he wonders how the hell you found him?" Cody toggled a switch within the black box and suddenly the interior of the cargo hold appeared on the second monitor. Holding the device to his face, he appeared full screen, and said, "Houston: We are go."

Still grappling, Macie said, "All true. But bugging a room . . ." She regarded his spy cam with trepidation. "We could always just set fire to the Constitution, and smoke him out."

"You went along with bugging his phone."

"Sure. After you already did it. This is proactive. It flies in the face of all I believe about privacy and . . . well, you heard me earlier. You get it."

"I do. Tell you what. We just unplug now." He clicked the toggle on his bug and the screen went dark. "You can have Jonny Midnight take it from here. But remember this moment ten years from now when you're on your monthly guilt trip to see Jackson Hall on visitors' day up in Dannemora. Assuming he lives."

Macie's mouth went dry. This was not the first time since lunch that he had brought her to a moral crossroads. Slipping through the apartment vestibule, entering the crime scene, boosting those papers. Every moment presented a threshold, and she had crossed them all. The result was that, in just hours with Gunnar Cody, she had made more headway on this case than in days with Jonathan Monheit. But this step felt different, defining. Because it was. Planting this bug involved premeditation and ethical, if not legal, trespass. Teetering at a door that would slam shut in minutes if she didn't act, Wild pondered her responsibility to a client who had put his life in her hands. By playing the Dannemora prison card, Cody had unwittingly done something bigger. He sparked in Macie an epiphany. A revelation that all those thresholds she crossed were not mere thrill seeking or, worse, some latent girlie infatuation with a danger boy. Seeing it all now from the brink, each of those moves had been incremental acts of rebellion—toes in the water—testing out her latent anger at a justice system that had cratered in the wake of her brother's murder. Macie always knew that DA politics had failed her family. But tonight, confronting a moral Rubicon made Wild recognize her own obedience to that broken system and how her acquiescence had made her complicit. Today's baby steps of defiance had delivered her to this tipping point—either to retreat or to sing that take-back-her-life song. Decision made, Macie said, "How are we getting it in there? Pull the fire alarm and plant the bug when he comes out?"

"Amateurs." Cody's mock derision was his winkless wink, an unspoken acknowledgment of the courageous leap she was making. He pulled a yellow d-CON box out of a bin on the wall. "I'm going in. I'll be Ron from maintenance setting a rat trap." He wagged an imaginary Groucho cigar, and added, "Which, I guess, I kind of will be." He took the rodent trap out of the package and substituted his own look-alike black box.

"That's brilliant. And unsettling." Then she added, "But wait, Fabio knows you from the pier."

Cody smiled a sly grin, then opened a footlocker and routed through a tangle of hats, shirts, and wigs. After quick selections and rejections, he presented himself to her in a stained sweatshirt, mustache, dork glasses, and a greasy baseball cap with collar-length hair attached to it. Macie was struck by how much he had transformed. Not just cosmetically. He had taken on a full persona, adopting the attitude and physicality of a different person. She bet herself that Saint John's University had a drama club. "You've done this before, haven't you."

He nodded. "You're not lying if you're acting."

Minutes later, alone in the van, she thought of the Native American proverb, "When you come to a great chasm, jump. It's not as far as you think." Maybe consequences would rain down on her, but Wild had made the leap, and, for now, empowerment had set her free. Macie listened to Cody's mic'd footfalls on the stairs of the seedy hotel then picked up the sounds of blaring music, an argument, and an epic orgasm as he passed doorways en route to Room 306.

His knock was followed by a muffled, "That better be pizza." The door opened, and Fabio Mir's "Help you?" carried a stink of annoyance.

"Hotel maintenance. Sorry, dude. Rat trouble. Gotta lay out some traps."

"Now?"

"I hear ya. Can I just get done and be done? Alls I got to do is put them down. They're already baited and set." Next she heard rustling, and then the monitor filled with light as the spy cam came out of the d-CON box, revealing the little room in all its squalor. The video jostled as Cody hunted for the best location, and it came to rest with the widest angle of the place while Mir looked on passively.

"I put it right on top of the AC," he said when he got back in the van. Cody studied the shot, declared it short of broadcast quality, but fine for the job.

A knock brought both of their eyes to the monitor and the spy cam in Fabio's room. Mir went to the door. "That better be pizza."

"And it's getting cold, dipshit," came a man's voice. It was the Russian's.

"Must have gotten by us while I was hustling back here." Cody's words were laced with self-reproach, and Wild started to tell him to let it go. But when Fabio opened his door she found herself unable to speak. Because stepping in from the hallway, holding a pizza box, was a white guy who was no blur at all.

He was muscular with thinning brown hair and a short goatee. The red scrapes on his cheek came from Macie's fingernails.

Wild couldn't take her eyes off the man. Seeing him on the video monitor only made the whole experience more surreal, as if her attacker, who already had wandered from real life into her nightmares, was now appearing as the surprise guest star on some low-budget TV cop show. As he set the pizza carton on the bed and accepted the cigars from his pal, a sense memory shuddered through her: the whiff of stale tobacco she got while he locked her head in a clinch against his body. Macie chanced a quick side glance to Cody. Other than the low curse he'd muttered, his face betrayed nothing, and he remained in fixed concentration on the screen action. But when she picked up her cell phone, he said, "No, don't."

"We need to call the police."

"That," said Cody, "is exactly what we do not want to do."

Her screen was night-blinding both of them in the dimness of the van, and she clicked it off. "But he's right there. They can get him."

"While we are performing a not-strictly-legal surveillance." Cody kept his attention on the screen while the visitor ran one of the hand rolls under his nose with approval. "Do you want to explain that to the arresting officers? To the district attorney? To the bar association?"

He was right, she couldn't expose herself to that scrutiny. Wild quickly fanned through her range of options, every single one less favorable than another. At last she decided to stick with the choice she already had made. In for a penny, and all that. She set her iPhone on her lap, shattered glass down.

"Besides, why stop now when it just got interesting?"

They watched the visitor file the three Hondurans in the pocket of his coat before he carefully draped it across the bed pillows. "Smells like a donkey's asshole in here. What you been doing?"

Fabio Mir shrugged. "Ass-fucking a donkey, what do you think?"

Cody turned to Wild. "Welcome to the Bowery chapter meeting of Mensa."

Mir sat on the bed, deferring to the Russian, who pulled the only chair up and opened the lid on the pizza. Both dug in joylessly. Fabio shoved half a congealed slice into his mouth and talked around it as he chewed. "Hey, Luchik, want to hear my new hustle?"

"Got a feeling I'm going to anyway."

Wild made a note— "Lou-chick?" —while Mir continued. "OK, see, I hang out near the parking lots at the Broadway theaters waiting for the suburban dumbshits to show up. I go, 'Pardon me, ma'am or sir. I'm your prepay parking-ticket agent.'"

"Seriously?" said Luchik, taking another slice.

"God's truth. I go, 'Prepay discount price is eighteen fifty-seven.' Who has change ready like that? So they always give me twenty. I say, 'I'll be right back with the validation and change.'"

"*Adios!*"

"You know it. Hundred-sixty bucks, yesterday alone." He studied his guest. "Come on, man, be impressed. At least fake it. I know it's not close to your paydays. How much did your man grease you just this week? Make me jealous. Four Gs, maybe fi—" The visitor stopped chewing and fastened a look on Fabio that petrified Macie even through a bleary lens three floors down. Mir had his back to the camera but she saw him lean back, withering under the stare. "Hey, man, just wondering . . ."

"Don't. Ever." His foreign accent made two simple words deadly.

Mir held up his palms. "It's cool, it's cool." And just as quickly, the Russian smiled and went back to eating, his menace turning on a dime.

"Just think," said Cody. "You were twenty feet from a trunk ride with this character from Grand Theft Auto."

She nodded. "Don't think I haven't—"

"Whoa, whoa, hold on. This is us." Cody goosed the volume.

Mir was asking, "You hear about Jackson?" And there it was. The link to Jackson Hall, confirmed. But exactly what was it to? Macie leaned into the screen with an amping pulse rate as Fabio continued. "Found him strung up. His ass is in a coma now."

"No shit." The visitor's reaction gave nothing away, as if he'd just heard

a second-string quarterback from the Browns got a DUI. He picked
up another slice, then lobbed it back in the box. "Fucking Rikers, man.
That's why you'll never see my *zhopa* in there."

An uncomfortable quiet passed until Fabio spoke again, this time
more tentatively. "Mind if I ask?" His companion grunted the OK, so
Mir took a pause and did ask. "What happened with Pinto?"

"Pinto got fucked up's what happened." He lasered Mir again and
that ended discussion on that subject.

"There it is," said Cody.

"Not quite. Not a confession," she said. "And even if it was, not ad-
missible. Not under these circumstances."

"More than you had ten minutes ago. Like my training instructor
at the academy always said, 'You start with shit and use it to get better
shit.'"

Up in bedbug central, the pair cracked open a couple of Fabio's Pabsts
and turned on the Yankees. "Baseball is bullshit," complained the Russian. "Is nothing else?"

"You mean like Larry King on Russia Today? Cable in this dive is
crap."

Cody threw his wig at the video screen and shouted, "Come on, you
Brighton Beach lowlife, back to Pinto, let's go," which made her laugh.
"Welcome to my world, Macie Wild. A lot of waiting for a lot of noth-
ing."

As the two of them sat there watching two guys watch baseball Macie was engaged in what she felt was America's other pastime, eavesdropping. It only took an inning for their scratching, beer belching, and
heckling the plate ump for the size of the strike zone to send her back
to digging the hole she had been shoveling since the Russian walked in.
"I'm having a really hard time just sitting here watching this and not
calling the police."

"Once again, welcome to my world."

"Fine, but at what point can we do something about this guy?"

Cody waited to make sure there was still nothing happening onscreen before he answered. "You see, that's the ballbuster part of surveillance. It takes awhile to sink in—even for experienced cops I knew on

TARU—but these assholes don't just dance for us because they're on our camera. Gathering intel is a waiting game with no guarantees. Sure, you could call the police. Want to call them? Fine. And maybe—maybe—this guy would take a hit for attacking you." He rapped a knuckle on the monitor. "But the thing is, that would probably screw you out of gathering hard evidence that he's the one who killed Pinto. And isn't that what you really want? To get your client off?"

She knew he was right but that didn't make her like it. "So the answer is to just sit here with our thumbs up our asses?"

"Well," he said with that half grin, "whatever makes you most comfortable."

At the half-inning commercial, Luchik reached for one of his cigars and got out a disposable lighter. Mir said, "Hey, man, you can't fire up that thing in here."

"What, you going all PC now?"

"Personally, I could give a shit. But they made a BFD at check-in. It's house rules."

"Who's going to know?" When Fabio answered by pointing up to the smoke detector, his guest smoothed down his short goatee and gave a rascally half smile. "Oh, I can fix that." He reached back into his coat where it lay across the pillows. This time, instead of a cigar, he came out with the biggest handgun Macie had ever seen. Her eyes sprung to Cody.

"Forty-four Anaconda," said Cody in tandem with the man holding the revolver onscreen.

"The fuck?" said Mir, rising to his feet in alarm.

The visitor hefted the Colt. "She a beauty or what? Eight-inch barrel. Double action. Mag loads. Put a hole in you the size of a hooker's pudenda." He extended his arm toward the ceiling and sighted on the smoke alarm.

"Ayyy-hey-hey!" called Mir. His buddy chuckled then whipped his arm around, eyes blazing, leveling the massive weapon at Fabio's gut. Mir held out his palms as if they could stop bullets. It's what people did.

The gunman snapped, "You done asking me questions about Pinto?"

"Yeah, yeah, promise."

"Any more stupid fucking questions?"

"No. No more. . . .Don't!"

"My business is my business, got it?"

"Yeah, got it. Totally." Mir took a half step back. But then, as quickly as he had lashed out, the other lowered the cannon to his side and gave Fabio a reassuring nod. Macie realized she had stopped breathing and resumed.

The visitor spread his arms wide and smiled, "Come on, Fabby, bring it in." Mir hesitated, then moved closer, tentatively, and accepted his friend's hug. "It's cool, brother. We all have questions, right?"

". . . Yeah."

"See, I have questions too." He snatched Mir by the hair behind his head and jerked it backward, bringing the muzzle of the Anaconda under his chin. "Like, you know my question."

"What? I don't. What question?" His eyes flashed wide to the side. He wanted to move, but he knew better. And, in case he didn't, the Russian dug the gunsight deeper into the flesh of his neck.

"Don't you bullshit me. You know what I want to know."

"This is crazy, I told you, they never said. I have no idea. Please."

"Last chance. One, two . . ."

"Holy . . ." muttered Cody. Macie squinted and turned away.

"Bam!" shouted the visitor. Driven by instinct, Mir backpedaled clumsily, sense abandoned, trying to outrun the bullet that never came. "Bam!" What's funny once is funny twice, and the gunman cackled as Mir's feet got tangled in the droop of the bedspread and he stumbled rearward, the back of his silver tracksuit racing at the camera. He slammed into the air conditioner with a crash that thundered the inside of the surveillance van and made Wild flinch. The camera flew off its perch showing them a tilt-a-whirl blur of the hotel room before it landed on the rug, listing and facing the wall.

Wild and Cody had lost their view but still had audio, so now their surveillance became a twisted podcast of *This American Life*. The Russian's laugh decayed into a cough, and, even after he settled, there came an "Oh, man . . ." followed by a renewed chuckle. "Wish I had a picture of your face, Fabby."

"Scared the crap out of me."

"Here, give me your hand. On three. One, two—"

A sea-lion groan from Fabio. "Man, I think I dislocated my elbow."

"Next time, maybe you'll let me light up." They heard that laugh and the cough again. "You OK?"

Mir said he was but his heart wasn't in it. The game had gotten too rough. Then the camera jerked and moved as Cody's d-CON trap got picked up and replaced on top of the AC unit, albeit upside-down and badly aimed, cutting off half the room now. "What's that?" asked Luchik from outside the frame.

Cody whispered the "uh-oh" Macie was feeling.

"Rat trap," said Fabio, moving away to the nightstand to toss back the rest of his Blue Ribbon.

"Since when are you the hotel maid?"

"No biggie. Guy who put it in was some retard. Don't want him to get in trouble." Mir worked his sore arm.

The voice from across the room took a different tone. All amusement was gone. "When was this? I thought you just got here."

"I dunno exactly. Maintenance guy came by after you called. So that's . . . what? 'Bout five minutes before you."

"Maintenance? In this shit hole? At night?" The Russian entered the frame, approaching the camera with his head tilted forward, peering at the unit as he drew closer. The d-CON trap rose to his face. He found the lens port and put the hole to his eye until it completely filled their screen. "Fuck me," he said. Then the video turned vertigo-swirly again as the box sailed through the air. It hit the wall across the room and dropped, this time wedging in some dark place on the floor.

Cody got to his feet. "Made."

Following some well-rehearsed mental checklist, Cody quickly snapped three toggle switches and twisted a fat dial clockwise until it clicked. The hum of servo motors filled the van as the side cams winged-in and the RF snorkel lowered. He tossed his keys to Wild and said, "Fire it up," then popped the rear door and vaulted out. She hesitated. This day had gone nowhere Macie had been in her life. And now the night had become even more volatile. How far should she take it? The last clack-clack of the antenna mast telescoping into place left her with only the silence of the acoustically deadened van and her thoughts. Bouncing the keys once in her palm, Wild decided she could at least start the engine for him.

Cody darted up to the driver's side door just as she opened it. "Never mind, I got it," he said, sounding hurried, for sure, but controlled. "You're shotgun." He took the keys from her and turned it over before his ass settled in the seat. Macie was still pulling the passenger door closed behind her while the van lurched from the curb.

"Our man was already downstairs and on the fly when I got out. See him ahead?"

"No."

"Not on foot. Up there. He's in the same car from last night."

Three cars ahead, the white sedan passed a skinny kid humping his halal cart up Chrystie Street. "Got it." The post-dinner flow out of Chinatown locked their subject in the middle of a convoy, same as them. "Did he see you?"

"I don't think so. But you gotta know he's got his head on a swivel, looking for something."

Like maybe a van? she thought, but decided it best not to say, being new at this. "Mind if I ask what the plan is?"

"We keep a loose tail," he said without a blink. They inched along for half a block when the white car jerked a sudden right, climbing up over the curb. People scattered. The sedan's shocks settled, and the Russian floored it across the pedestrian pathway into Sara Roosevelt Park. "New plan," said Cody.

Cody sounded his horn twice and flashed his brights to clear foot traffic as he rode up a service driveway and followed at a slightly slower speed. Not much on swearing, Macie groaned another curse. "You OK?" he asked.

"My whole life in this city, I've never actually driven on a sidewalk."

"Shit. He's busting a move." Cody pointed to the taillights ahead. The car had crossed the narrow strip of greenbelt and was making a left to go north—the wrong way on a one-way street.

"This guy's crazy," she hollered. Wild's heart sank a little bit at the thought that they were about to lose him. Then, just as crazily, Cody made a left to follow him. "Ummmm?" she said.

"Relax, we have the easy part. As long as I stay in his wake, he's the tip of the spear, doing all the clearing." Oncoming cars were blasting horns and swerving to the side to avoid head-ons. Unruffled, Cody worked the wheel easily and drew closer. "He's put a plate on that since last night. Probably stolen, but memorize it." He made an abrupt slalom dodge of a motorcycle and said, "Got it yet?"

"Yeah."

"Call 911. Tell them there's a drunk driver going the wrong way northbound on Forsyth near Grand. Give the color, make, and plate, then hang up." He gave the directions as calmly as if sharing a recipe. "Use this." He reached into his door pocket and pulled out a cell phone. "It's a burner. Do not give your name."

She did as instructed, even hanging up on the emergency operator, another first in a day with a spinning compass. Wild made a pact with herself not to gasp or say one more "Oh, God," and to just hang on and trust Cody with the circus ride. They nearly sheared off a man's car door, and he pegged his frozen yogurt at her side window as they blew past, leaving a pink smear. "I could be at my couples counseling now," she said.

At Grand the white car lurched east, going with traffic at last. The driver hit the gas for a clear stretch until a trash truck blocking the way put him in a last-second turn up Allen Street. "Looks like he's working his way to the Williamsburg Bridge." Cody glanced at his dash. "Fine with me, I've got a full tank."

Up ahead, a box truck made a sudden lane change for a right onto Delancey then brake checked for a couple pushing a stroller in the crosswalk. Tires squealed and the white sedan rear-ended the truck. With Cody closing in, their perp abandoned his car and raced off around the corner. Cody pulled into the driveway of a loading dock and hopped out. He must have heard Macie's footfalls behind him because he chirped the lock on the van without turning.

Cody ran fast but so did Wild. He stopped, raised his arm across her as a caution barrier, then made a one-eyed peek around the front of a seafood restaurant on the corner. "We're good," he said, then bolted off. She caught up, pacing him again. Cody seemed to know exactly where he was going but it took Macie half a block before she could pick out the back of the balding head weaving through the night crowd filling the sidewalk on Delancey Street.

The man looked back and must have spotted them, too, because he turned a hairpin off the curb and shoved a passing cyclist to the pavement. He fell onto her and the two struggled. Macie couldn't tell if the cyclist was fighting him off or he was just tangled in the bike. Losing time as Cody and Wild closed the gap, he gave up on jacking the Cannondale and charged out into Delancey, nearly getting taken down by a beer truck. The Russian continued across the street, busting through the greenery of the center divider, and disappeared from view. Car horns marked him, though, as he played dodge 'em on the other side in the westbound lanes. Cody lofted both his arms to signal traffic and followed him with Macie keeping stride.

"Subway." Again, the ex-cop's eye put him way ahead of hers. Up the sidewalk, their target flicked a quick check back, making eye contact this time as he pushed through the crowd streaming up from the Essex Station. Wild and Cody picked up their speed, but, as they approached the head of the stairs, they heard shouts and a scream. A logjam of toppled bodies littered the steps beneath them. Their perp was gone but not before he had bowled over a half-dozen commuters.

It killed Macie not to give assistance, but when Cody pressed on, rapidly picking his way through the Lincoln Logs of arms and legs, she followed, with every "fucking asshole" a stinging lash to her heart. They heard the subway's warning chimes and the recorded voice announcing, "Stand clear of the closing doors, please." Racking up another lifetime first, she leaped the turnstile behind Cody and sprinted with him down to the platform where the doors had just closed on an M train. As it pulled out Cody tore off, keeping up with the last car, searching through the windows for a glimpse of their man among the departing passengers. When it gained speed and became just two red taillights disappearing into the grimy tunnel, he turned to her, thirty yards distant, and said it all with a headshake. But Wild was windmilling her arm, and he jogged back to join her.

"Whatcha got?" He was breathing rapidly, but still controlled. She indicated a trio of college students at the opposite end of the platform, acting like they just spotted the Yeti across the tracks. "Good eye," he said, and they started toward them, picking up bits of their conversation on the way.

"You think we should call someone?" said one of the girls.

A guy in a straw fedora said, "Dude's off his meds, or something."

"Hi. Train Safety," said Cody with authority. "You see a guy go that way?"

All three pointed across the rails where a curtain of beige tarps running the full length of the station hung like sooty bed sheets from a wire cable. There was one gap where the drapes had been parted. It was just the size of a man, and it was fluttering.

Cody descended the emergency rungs as if they were no more than a swimming pool ladder. Wild traced a wary side look for train headlights in the dark tunnel and followed. "Third rail," he said pointing. She made an exaggerated step over it and they proceeded at a walk toward the gap. Cody held a shush finger to his lips then made a fast peek through the tarp opening then ducked back. He gave a nod and they both went inside.

He squatted behind a low concrete wall and drew her down beside him while he got his bearings, listening and looking off into the dingy gloom of the subway's vast underworld. Wild maintained her silence but knew exactly where they were. This was the abandoned Williamsburg Bridge trolley station. She knew because her ex-fiancé had taken her to a fund-raising event for a group trying to convert this defunct subterranean acre into an underground park called the Low Line, their pun on the famous High Line. It had a long way to go. Sprawling before them in murky light, a ghost forest of rusty girders sprouted up from hundred-year-old cobblestones and a bayou of rain runoff. The water surfaces rippled, the ground shook, and soon a train pulled into the station behind them, filling the curtain with a *Close Encounters* glow, and illuminating enough graffiti tags to rival the Berlin Wall.

Camouflaged by the noise of the idling train, Cody put his lips to her ear and whispered, "Watch out for that light, it'll make you a silhouette target." Which made her think, and not for the first time, about that .44 magnum she saw getting waved around the flophouse.

She turned to his ear, feeling oddly comfortable with the intimacy of that. "You haven't told me. What do we do if we catch him?"

"Stay behind me," was all he said. The train pulled out, darkness fell once more, and she followed him into the sprawling urban underbelly. He walked patiently and expertly, stepping around pools of water, discarded aluminum cans, snapped battens from wooden pallets, and ramen containers—anything that could trip them or make a sound. As her eyes adjusted to the darkness she saw twenty feet ahead of them a hulking structure like the conning tower of a submarine. Another train squealed into the station, spreading new light, and they ducked behind a steel column. From there both regarded the looming building, a stationmaster's tower from the last century.

"I'll clear it," he whispered and then held a palm out signaling her to stay put. Cody used the din of the exiting train to cover the sound of his movement as he inched forward in a crouch to the metal stairs leading to the old station house. Barely making him out as he tiptoed up the steps, she waited, listening, casting paranoid looks behind her. A forever minute later she saw Cody's form waving her ahead at the bottom of the stairs. Just feet away from him a giant rat, big as a bread loaf, scurried past, right where she was about to step. Macie kept her balance but set her foot down on a shard of broken glass. In that cavernous space, the crunch against the cobblestone might as well have been a firecracker. She froze. He crouched and yanked her down beside him. They squatted there, listening, searching the shadows.

The gunshot cracked like thunder. In a blink, Cody leaped on Macie, covering her with his body. The reverb was still rolling when he reached down near his foot and she saw something dark in his hand, then heard a snick as he chambered a round. They waited there like that, the weight of him shielding her until he gophered up. Cody extended his right hand, panning in tandem with wherever he looked.

In the far reaches came another bang, but not from a gun, more like a door. He followed the sound, gun at the ready as he proceeded, sweeping all sides and angles, alert for a trick. Cody reached the far wall of the ghost space, paused, then turned to call to her. But Wild was already there behind him.

An old emergency exit gaped wide open. The chain that had kept it sealed for more than sixty-five years dangled beside it, shot through with a .44 mag. Cody pressed against the wall beside the door jamb, holding his pistol in a double-handed grip. Macie put her back against the cold cement next to him and waited. After a few seconds, he squatted, picked up a chip of gravel, and tossed it into the opening. The stone bounced with echoing ticks. Cody listened, braced to return fire. Macie marked time with one long inhale/exhale.

An acre away, across the dank jungle of rusting beams and shattered bottles another M train rattled out of the station. The instant the tunnel swallowed the headlight, Cody again used the rail clatter as aural cover and spun through the doorway following the V of his arms behind his gun.

The underground fell again to silence.

Either a lot of time had passed or her breathing had become too rapid to clock it, and Macie's freak escalated. What was going on? Unsure whether to wait, follow, or get the hell out of there, she chose the option that didn't leave her all alone, and slipped through the doorway herself.

Inside was blackness and half a century of mildew. Macie focused her ears but could hear nothing and got no sense of the place or Cody's whereabouts until the next M pulled in spilling weak light in the door-way. It was just enough for Wild to orient herself. She had entered a narrow brick stairwell of concrete steps that she traced upward to find that Cody had reached the landing above her without making a sound. In the feeble glow, she tiptoed up to meet him where he had crouched at the turn of the staircase. He rested a palm on her arm, to hold her back, she guessed. But when the train left the platform, Macie realized it was to keep tabs on her in the dark.

How many flights did this zigzag upward? Since it had been an emer-gency exit at one time, it must have led to the street, or maybe an al-ley. Unless it had been forgotten over the years and bricked over, which meant the violent man with the scary handgun would need to reverse course and come their way. If so, Macie wondered who was cornered, him or them? And if they did come head to head, everything she had seen of this guy told her that he would not go quietly. As fear factors went, this was right up there. All it needed was bats.

Cody must have sensed her mounting tension and firmed his grip on her. Then, yards upshaft, came one scrape of a sole on grit. Cody removed his hand, and she envisioned it returning to cup the grip of his pistol.

Bam.

Another cannon blast, this time with a reflected burst of orange muz-zle flash. Wild's ears rang, then cleared to the sound of hard kicks against metal. One kick, then three more in rapid succession. Cody sprung up the blackened stairs calling, "Drop your weapon. Now." Then another boom from the Anaconda and the smack of a metal door bouncing off brick.

Macie froze, unsure whether to bolt or stay. Then Cody whispered, "He's gone." His voice still lived in that measured zone of cop calm. In the darkness, she followed the scent of fresh air up the flight until she found Cody crouching beside the open exit door.

"Stay put," he said. "You hear shots, haul ass the way we came." He didn't wait for her answer, but log rolled out on the ground into the al-ley. The ambient glow of the Lower East Side gave off enough light for her to watch him make his caution checks before he rose from behind a stack of discarded air conditioners and then disappeared from view.

He returned a moment later, gave her the all clear, and she followed him, crabbing sideways in the tight squeeze between a pockmarked cinder-block wall and a demolition Dumpster, their only path to the street.

"You all right?" he asked. Macie nodded, completely devoid of conviction. "Good. Know what sucks? Now you'll never know what would've happened if we'd caught him." He chuckled, but as they walked back toward Delancey, she noticed he didn't holster his gun and held it down at his thigh. Wild cast a wary glance over one shoulder then the other, haunted by the man who had brutally tried to kidnap her. He may have escaped, but, to Macie, this monster was anything but gone.

CHAPTER 14

The rear-ended box truck still sat at the corner with its emergency flashers going when they got back to Allen and Delancey. But the white sedan had *adiosed*, and when Cody asked the truck driver about it he said the guy had some brass balls. "Just came walking back all casual like he'd parked it just to run in for a lottery ticket, backed it up, and wailed out of here." He pointed to a skid patch beside some headlight glass as a visual aid. "Cops are on the way though. And I got his plate."

"Yeah, that'll help." Cody hitched Macie by the elbow and drew her to the van before they got mired in witness statements that would document them at the scene. Besides, they had a mission back at the flophouse. They both wanted to brace Fabio Mir about his camera-shy buddy. But, no surprise, he was long gone. Cody retrieved his d-CON cam and insisted Macie hop a ride with him back to her car, which she'd left at a pay lot near their lunch. "Anyway, it's on my way to the Battery Tunnel," he said, finishing up a text. "Just got a gig from Channel 2. A private plane hit the drink off Staten Island. Who you gonna call? RunAndGunn." After tapping send he slid the phone in the cup holder and added, "Dot-com."

They traveled in a bubble of silent letdown after the adrenaline of the chase. Cody stopped at a red near the lighthouse marking the entrance to South Street Seaport and watched the crowd that had gathered around a trio of urban drummers beating on inverted hotel pans and five-gallon food tubs. He rolled down his window and the van filled with the complex beat, an amazingly tight call-and-response straight out of *Drumline*. A green light came a little too soon, and half a block later, the rhythm of the city's found music faded behind them.

But there was a thrumming that beat on inside Wild. "You didn't tell me," she said.

"Tell you what?"

"That you were armed."

Cody sniffed. "I'm not stupid. That ass-hat had a forty-four mag. Forget the chain he shot clean through, did you see the size of the holes that thing put in the upstairs door?" When they pulled up outside Felice 15, her Corolla was alone on the lot. The night attendant lounged beside it on a commandeered executive office chair, the CEO of easy in-out. Cody pulled the cargo van across the driveway. "By the way," he said, "I am permitted."

"For concealed carry?"

"Am I on the stand, counselor?"

"Are you evading, Mr. Cody?"

"I don't know. Am I? Nothing wrong with a little mystery to shake things up, is there?"

One dismissive wisecrack was all it took to churn up Wild's garbage swirl of jagged feelings about the danger she'd been in, her anger over the moral lines she not only crossed but had all but pissed on, her frustration over the fragments of evidence she couldn't use, his loose hold on legality—everything. Macie searched for words and couldn't find them. So she crossed another line. She slugged him.

"What the—?" He looked at her in disbelief and rubbed his upper arm.

She shook the bee swarm out of her hand, muttering a low "Fuck-fuck-fuck . . ."

"What the hell was that for?"

"For . . ." Still at a loss, she settled on, ". . . not knowing what the hell it was for."

"You never hit anybody before, did you. Here, let me see, can you flex your fingers?" He reached for her hand, and she pulled away.

"I'm fine. I'm . . ." She opened the door and got out. "Sorry. About the punch."

"Forgotten."

"It's just, this has all been . . . I'm spent."

"I understand. And trust me, I won't let the fact that you physically attacked me spoil an otherwise perfect evening."

That time she did laugh. "OK. . . .Yeah. We don't need to work my stuff out here. You've got a plane waiting for you."

"I do."

"So . . ." She rested a hand on the door, hesitating.

". . . So."

As Wild watched him speed off, she began to calm and tried to create order out of the swirl. Not just what she had experienced since lunch, but what she had learned about the case. Taking her keys from the attendant, she felt a twinge, wondering, in spite of the ethical morass she had waded into, how she could keep up that kind of progress. Yeah, she told herself, that's what the twinge was.

Lenard wasn't at reception when Wild got off the elevator at the Manhattan Center for Public Defense the next morning, so she plopped her briefcase on a lobby guest chair to dig for her swipe card and cursed. Why had getting through locked doors suddenly become the theme of her life? Even though it wasn't Lenard's fault that she couldn't sleep and came in early, it felt damn good to release some pent-up irritation. Macie swore again when she gave up on one compartment and unzipped another. Then luck broke her way. The office door opened and two maintenance workers stepped through, one holding a ladder, the other a tool bag. "Hold that, please!" She raced to them, offering thanks. They didn't acknowledge her, except for the one with the ladder who took a dead-eyed measure of her from under a thicket of eyebrows as she scooted by.

Coffeed-up, she hit her desk, clearing yesterday's backlog of paperwork and her endless cascade of e-mails, enjoying the uninterrupted solitude of having the seventh floor to herself. A text chimed from her ex-fiancé. "Disappointed you blew off counseling so last minute. Let's re-sked ASAP." Macie hovered her thumbs over the screen, waiting for some response to Ouija. Something that wouldn't inflame, but wouldn't offer false hope either. Then she saw Paris. Dinner in Saint-Germain-des-Prés. Then the shocker. Then his tearful apology. Then her numb flight home alone. "Let's not," she said to her empty office, and set her phone aside.

Tiger appeared just before eight with a Peanut Butter Split he got her from Juice Generation and an armful of dockets and motions to execute. Macie reimbursed him then inked and dated each signature line as her paralegal fed the flagged pages to her. "Let's set a Jackson Hall team meeting for eight fifteen," she said as she scrawled. "And have Lenard call the maintenance supervisor. Look at this." Wild tapped her pen on pale waffle footprints, one on her desk and another on the cover of a deposition file.

"Primitive, for sure," said Tiger. "I hear they're cleaning overhead AC ducts. On the plus side, that means summer's coming."

"They had a ladder, did they have to stand on my paperwork too?"

"Ooh, somebody's cranky this morning. Was it last night's counseling or has the whey protein not kicked in yet from the smoothie?"

Instead of answering, she busied herself mindlessly signing the docs, unsure how much to tell Tiger or her other colleagues about the prior evening's foray into legal gray areas. In an odd way, Macie felt like a superhero, out to do good but leading a dual life. But did superheroes ever wonder if they were doing the right thing? Wonder if it was wrong to keep dark secrets? Wonder if leading two lives actually subtracted from the whole? Maybe, she decided, wondering was how Wonder Woman got her name.

Her desk phone rang. It was Lenard. "There's a Gunnar Cody here to see you."

Cody was seated in a guest chair next to a half-dozen clients filling out intakes and waiting to meet their lawyers. When she stepped out, he rose and grinned. "Hey, counselor."

Wild didn't return the smile. Instead she drew him away from the waiting area and spoke in a low voice. "I have a phone, you know. You can't just show up unannounced at my place of business."

"Interesting. Since isn't that exactly what you did at my place of business?" He'd done it again. Tossing her own stuff back in her face, but with that half smile that made it kind of OK. Macie noticed that he was in the same clothes as the day before, which meant he had probably been up all night and come directly from his assignment on Staten Island. When she had turned on the Channel 2 news at five thirty that morning, anxious about any reports of gunshots at the Essex Station, the newscast led with video of the Cessna crash a quarter mile off the Edgewater docks, including a close view of police divers plunging into The Narrows from a Harbor Unit vessel.

"Your pants are wet," she said, filling in the blank on how they got that close shot of the victim search.

"From covering the ditched plane. Turns out there's a Jet Ski business near the docks, and I borrowed a Sea-Doo to get out there for the close shots." The way he said "borrowed" told her it was just another day at the office for him, unspoiled by any obsession with rules of trespass. "I came by to give you this. In all the excitement of your exit last night, you left it in my van." He picked up a plastic milk crate from beside one of the guest chairs. "These are those files we stole from the crime scene." Heads of the waiting clients turned toward them. Macie whisked him farther across the lobby, near the elevators.

"I am not going to accept those here."

"Really? After all the trouble you went through to get them?"

She checked to make sure they weren't being heard, but lowered her voice anyway. "This is a law office. I don't want to accept or store anything of a . . . questionable nature."

He bobbled his head. "I get that. But I'd think you'd want to examine these files. There could be a lead in there, you never know. Tell you what. I'll keep them safe with me. Come by my place after work, and we'll have a sorting and sifting party." After Wild made a quick mental scan of her calendar, she agreed and pressed the down button for him.

"This is good. I'll order in." As he stepped into the elevator, he couldn't resist a parting shot. "Call first!" Cody was still laughing when the doors closed.

To be honest, Macie found the confines of the office tame after the night she'd had. As her MCPD team gathered in their little war room she felt a mix of comfort and captivity. Wild convened the session by reporting she had just made a call to the Twentieth Precinct, inquiring about new information about her attacker. Detectives had a BOLO on him, but no hits. She had nearly mentioned to the sergeant that she "happened to be out" on the Lower East Side the night before and believed she saw the man. Neither the detective nor her team would buy that. Uncapping a marker, she circled "At Large" on the whiteboard and left it at that.

Jonathan Monheit led off, asking about her cop companion at Jackson Hall's apartment. Anticipating this, Macie made it clear, mostly for the others, that Gunnar Cody was an ex-cop, now a freelance journalist, working another angle of the case. "We crisscrossed, and it happened to be at Mr. Hall's apartment." Tiger, of course, knew there was more overlap than that, but was too tactful to do anything but listen. To keep Jonny Midnight from pressing further, she questioned him. "Did you find anything in the apartment after I left?"

"I went through Hall's clothes, like you said. Nothing with visible bloodstains. Although one of the dresser drawers was completely empty. Probably the crime scene unit cleared it."

"One theory," said Macie. "We'll come back to that."

"Mind if I ask why you're keen on finding blood on our client's wardrobe?" said Tiger.

"Not at all." Here, too, she parsed her answer, leaving out the gory crime scene she and Cody had broken into. Wild didn't like lying by omission but this was a high-wire act for her: needing to share enough information so they could do their jobs, but not sharing the parts that would make them accessories to her transgressions or compromise the case. "Theresa Fontanelli flashed me some crime scene photos of Pinto. Very bloody. I also managed to speak to one of her witnesses, a retired dentist who is—was—one of Rúben Pinto's neighbors. She confirmed hearing Mr. Hall threaten Mr. Pinto's life. Checking for residue is strictly prudent." Macie wrote Dr. McBlaine's name on the Case Board and turned to the intern. "Chip, what's the latest from Bellevue?"

"Still comatose. The only change is they've gradually brought him off the hypothermia therapy and discontinued potassium infusions."

"What about visitors?" Macie was asking both Chip and Soledad. "Anyone coming to ask for him? I'm thinking about Pilar Fuentes."

The social worker shook no. "And you'd think his girlfriend would at least inquire."

"Definite red flag. This brings me back to the empty dresser drawer, Jonathan. What if CSU hadn't taken those clothes?"

Chip called out, "They could be hers. She could be hiding somewhere."

"The question would be why?" said Macie. "Soledad, you've been working up Hall's mitigation file, right? Follow up with any of Pilar Fuentes's relatives in the area. And wherever she works. Pay a visit. See if you can get a line on her. Jonathan, what's your progress on locating Pinto and Hall's crew chief?"

"NG."

"NG?"

"That means no good."

"We all know what it means," she said. "I want to know why."

Jonny Midnight's face pinked. "Because it's a dead end."

Wild struggled to keep the exasperation out of her voice. "Jonathan. We are so far from a dead end on anything. We're just getting started. Here's what I want you to do. Go back to your parole board pals. Get cozy with them. Get some names. Because names are funny. They lead to other names." She scanned the board and saw one: Pinto's former cellmate, the man she was going to visit when she got attacked. "Like Amador Spatone."

"I keep leaving him messages. And when I dropped by, he wasn't there."

"Then we repeat as needed." Macie consulted the Case Board again for unresolved items and came to the one apartment building Jackson Hall would admit burglarizing. "I'm going to assume you still haven't interviewed the victim in The Barksdale."

"Correct!" Monheit announced as if the firmness of his reply made up for a trail littered with excuses. "But we now have a name. Gregory Eichenthal."

Taken aback, Macie said, "Well . . . that's . . ."

"Different?" muttered Tiger.

"Good for you, Jonathan. Did you get hold of the police report?"

"The police won't tell me shit. It was in *Page Six* this morning." He slid his copy of the *Post* to Soledad, who passed it to Macie. Midcolumn there was a blurb about the recent theft of priceless artworks from The Barksdale penthouse of the CEO of pharmaceutical giant EichenAll. Not exactly the result of ace detection, but she'd take it. She posted Eichenthal's name on the Case Board then directed the business major to run a financial workup on EichenAll. "And Tiger, I want you to book a meeting with this CEO."

"Right. And if he doesn't want to meet with you?"

Maybe a bit of Gunnar Cody had rubbed off on her. Macie smiled and said, "Ask him if he wants to see his paintings again."

CHAPTER 15

Macie Wild and Jonathan Monheit stood on East Fifty-Third across from The Barksdale. The pre-war gem was a sight to savor: beige stone ornamented by sculpted grotesques and scrollworks of vines and grapes topping the window frames on each of its fifteen floors. A muted residential low-rise that might have been called stately when it was constructed, it rested in serene contrast to the surrounding structures that were newer, taller, more modern, and, to Macie's taste, character-devoid. Its neighbors reflected a dormitory sensibility that New York embraced in various development booms of the mid- to late-twentieth century and now seemed dated like blazers with shoulder pads. The Barksdale, an exclusive luxury address off Sutton Place South, sat dwarfed yet dignified, a quiet piece of art framed between precast brick facing on the left and tempered glass stacked twenty-five and thirty stories skyward on the right. To her it held fast as a lonely sentinel against the changes surrounding it. And an inviting target for thieves.

After they were announced, a plainclothes security man met Wild and Monheit in the lobby and rode up in the elevator with them. For fourteen chimes the bodyguard took their measure with a disinterested air. She did the same, noting he gave off the same violent potential as the thug who attacked her, although with better grooming and a custom suit cut to almost hide the bulge on his hip.

Instead of opening into a hallway, the elevator doors parted in the foyer of the penthouse. Gregory Eichenthal stood in his vast living room, far enough away that he had to shout—or, more likely, he just wanted to. "Where are my fucking paintings?"

Wild approached him across an expanse of glossy hardwood to where he waited in stocking feet on the edge of a thick oriental. At forty-two, Eichenthal not only looked younger than his corporate photo, he looked like he should be working his way out of the mailroom, not running one of the country's major pharmaceutical companies. "Thank you for seeing us. I'm Macie Wild and this is Jonathan Monheit, my lead investigator."

The CEO gave Monheit a fast appraisal and returned his attention to her. "I'm here because you said your client stole my paintings. I don't see them. If this is a shakedown, I want you to know I'm recording this."

"This is not a shakedown," she said, "and I have no problem speaking with you on or off the record. Further, I never said that I had the paintings or even know where they are."

"Then what the fuck?" He spread his arms in appeal to his bodyguard, who had taken position on Macie's blind side, holding both hands relaxed at the middle button of his open coat—the textbook draw-ready stance. Eichenthal's shirtsleeves smacked against his sides and he said, "You have thirty seconds to tell me why I should continue this meeting before I have Henry throw you out."

Monheit cleared his throat. "Sir, I don't think threats are necess—"

"Twenty seconds."

Without being asked, Macie took a seat on the nearest chair. "I may need a full minute," she said. Eichenthal processed a beat, then blinked. He sat on a sofa opposite her. "My client got involved in a burglary crew, and he admits breaking in here."

"Into my home."

"But I'm not concerned about the burglary charge, not right now. My priority is clearing him of a homicide he didn't commit."

" 'Not concerned about the burglary . . .' You're definitely not in sales. This isn't helping me get my art back."

"Getting to that. There were three men on this burglary crew. I need to identify the leader, who may be the one who committed the murder, I'm not sure. But—finding him may locate your paintings."

"Ask your client."

"He's in a coma."

"Ask the other guy."

"He's the one my client is accused of killing. So, Mr. Eichenthal, I can help you if you help me, starting with what was stolen."

"A Chagall, a Sargent, and a Wyeth." He swept an arm to a wall across the room where bare hooks formed exclamation points in gaps between numerous other paintings. "These assholes knew just what to go for. They skipped the showy stuff and cherry-picked my most valuable. Cocksuckers."

"Were you here when the theft took place? Or did anyone else see the three men?"

"If that was the case, they wouldn't have made it out of here." The threat broke on him as easy as sweat. Macie had misjudged him as a petulant millionaire. The street in him was real and not to be screwed with. "But to answer your question, my family and I were at our house in Vail. Except when I'm here on business, we're either there or Amelia Island between Thanksgiving and June."

"What about security video of them?" Wild's gaze tracked up to the small camera bracketed in the corner that she assumed he was using to record the meeting.

Her question knocked him of balance. "That . . . ? That's a new installation." The implication being, after the cow had departed.

"Do you have any photo documentation of the stolen works?" Wild's minute was up, but the victim was now engaged. He came to her with his cell phone and swiped across three images. "Beautiful," she said, and asked him to text her copies. "I assume the police art theft unit also has these?"

"Screw them. I've got private security on this. We have some technology that will light up a trail. And where technology doesn't do the job . . ." He paused for a knowing glance to Henry. "Well, we don't have the same rules of engagement the police do, if you know what I mean." His boyish face took on a sinister cast and he aged twenty years before her eyes.

"May I ask who wrote the insurance on these?" asked Monheit, who was still standing beside the security man.

Eichenthal snarled at him. "What the fuck kind of question is that? What business of yours is my insurance?"

Monheit took a step back and blanched. "Listen, I, ah . . . I'm just assuming they have a recovery team working this, too, and maybe we could, you know . . ."

Inarticulate as that was, it mollified Eichenthal, who said to

Wild—not Monheit—that he'd have his secretary forward that to her along with the screenshots. Without a handshake or good-bye, the CEO turned and started to walk off to the back of the apartment.

Macie called after him. "If you get a lead on this burglary crew chief, would you mind sharing him?"

"Not at all," he said with a grin. "What piece of him would you like?" It sounded like anything but a joke.

Wild parted ways with Monheit and gave Cody a heads-up call. "Our stolen files beckon." When Cody met her at the door to his loft he was showered, smooth shaven, and in fresh clothes, including a dress shirt that still bore geometric hints of a dry cleaner's fold. "See what happens when you call first?"

"I hardly know you."

"That's the nap. And did I need it. Forty-plus hours of wake time take a toll. I even had this bizarre hallucination that you slugged me."

"Man, you really were delirious."

It was nearly six, beer time, he said, so she accepted a Sierra Nevada and sipped it while he disappeared into his editing studio. "You're early," he called out over the freestanding bookcase that partitioned the work space from his great room. "No complaints. It's just you caught me in the middle of rendering some video. With you in a sec."

He suddenly sounded uptight to her, so Macie asked if he could work and listen. He said he could, and she tipped another swig then gave him bullets from the team meeting: Hall's coma; Pilar's missing clothes; the missing Pilar; and Monheit's lead to Gregory Eichenthal as The Barksdale theft victim.

"Lead? Wasn't that in the *Post* this morning?" he said returning from his editing bay, seeming less crispy with her.

"The power of Jonny Midnight."

"If you can't be a good detective, be a lucky one," he said, clicking necks with her bottle.

Cody called in their order for a pizza and salads, then they sat on the living room floor where he had left the milk crate of loose papers from Rúben Pinto's desk. "So, time for the personality test," he said.

"You never mentioned this."

"Don't worry, it's multiple choice. Ready?" He gestured to the jumble of papers. "Sort or slog?"

"Slog," she said without hesitation.

"You surprise me, Macie Wild. I would have figured you as a sorter."

"The case against police profiling," she said, making sure it carried a light touch. "I want to approach this in the same order Pinto put it in the drawer, kind of like a timeline. Unless you shuffled it when you tossed it into your bag."

"Now who's profiling? You go first." Macie drew from the top, an unopened cable bill. Cody left then returned with a pair of steak knives, and she used hers to slit the envelope.

"Unpaid, past due," she said. "He didn't bundle his phone, so there's no record of his calls."

"Sharp eye," he said, going for the next document, a parking ticket. "I have a feeling we're going to see a number of these. Let's start a pile and see if there's a pattern to where he's been."

As they continued, one document at a time, he asked her about her visit to The Barksdale. She gave him the rundown, from Henry, the bodyguard, to Eichenthal's abusiveness and out-for-blood revenge lust. "Afterward Jonathan wondered if Eichenthal's whole over-the-top reaction to this is protesting too much."

"Jonny Midnight said that? He may not be as useless as he looks."

"Eichenthal is bypassing the police. He says he's hunting for his paintings with private security. And not-so-veiled threats of violence. Jonathan even wondered if—"

"—Eichenthal or his goons did Pinto trying to get him to give up where the paintings are?"

She shrugged. "Just his theory."

"And not a bad one. Don't tell him I said that."

"MetroCard."

"Put it with the parking tickets. We may be able to run the magnetic strip for a history of his subway swipes. See? We are sorting. Sorta . . ."

"Question for you, gadget man. Eichenthal alluded to using technology to track the paintings? How?"

Cody crossed his arms and leaned back against the sofa. "Could be a number of things. Watermarks or embedded fibers like you see in money. But that's mainly for verification once they're found. My guess is maybe he has RFID chips either embedded in the frames or woven into the canvas edging."

"Explain RFID."

"Radio Frequency Identification. You use it every day. It's a miniature chip, a transponder that emits a signal. The bigger ones are in your E-ZPass to tell the toll booth it's you. Smaller ones are showing up in credit cards and in hotel keys that you touch to the door. I'm sure they make small-enough ones to attach to valuables like art. I'll check it out. I have a guy."

"You have a guy?"

"Come on." He gave a theatrical eye roll. "Gotta have a guy."

They continued their slog, finding a few more parking summonses, some more MetroCards, and even an empty Butterfinger wrapper. "Hello," said Cody. "Could this be a thing? Because I think it's a thing." He held up a printed form on white paper with some of the fields shaded in pink. It was a receipt made out to Rúben Pinto from Flamingo Jewelry and Pawn for an item marked "Statue" with a declared value of $300. His wall speaker buzzed a short burst. Cody hauled himself to his feet. "Know what goes with beer. Besides more beer? Pizza."

Macie examined the pawn ticket and said, "Definitely a thing," then placed it on the coffee table, not on the floor with the other pieces.

They dined picnic style on the living room rug, ostensibly so they could keep sorting as they ate. But they fell into too much conversation, too much laughter, tacitly postponing the file quest in favor of letting down and being human for a decent interval. He commanded Alexa to play Soul from Spotify and the Echo across the room delivered "Grapevine" by Marvin Gaye. Macie wanted to hear some TARU stories, and on his second beer, he obliged.

There was the day he and his partner set up surveillance from inside the first-floor window of a Midtown office to snap photos of a city councilman who was supposed to take an envelope of cash at the Gregory's Coffee across the street. "It was a perfect hide, we thought, because our window was that glass that's all blue mirrored on the outside so we couldn't be seen. And it was perfect until this homeless gent wanders up and starts taking a leak on our window. Let's just say it was a view I could live without."

Macie laughed. "And probably can't shake."

"Call it indelible. Let's see, what else?" He picked up a pepperoni that had strayed onto the cardboard and chewed it, searching for another anecdote. "There was this one guy in our unit, Sam, really knew his shit. So he says to me when I get a gig bugging a Mafia social club, 'Hide a surveillance camera behind a two-way mirror in the vestibule.' Why? Because Sam had figured out that every single hood in the world stops to groom his hair before he steps out the door. And know what? He was right. Easiest way in the world to update the Insta-Goon database."

"Sounds like you're stereotyping. Every single one?"

He stood. "All right, smart-ass, come on."

She took his extended hand for a boost and he led her around the bookcase into his studio. Video editing is computerized, so the cubicle consisted of two Macs, each connected to a pair of Thunderbolt displays. Wild took a place standing at the nearer tower, whose light was blinking energetically, even though its screen was dark. "You'll want to ignore that one. It's in sleep mode, rendering a cut I've been building." She moved over beside Cody at the other stand-up desk as he tapped the space bar on a keyboard that woke up the monitor of that unit. Its screen filled with a menu of files on the hard drive. "This is a gag reel I put together for one of the TARU Christmas parties. Here we go." He found the one he wanted and double clicked the trackpad. The display came to life with color bars, followed by a film title in bold font: "**HAIR CLUB FOR MADE MEN.**" Then, to a jaunty soundtrack of Mama Corleone and a dapper old Italian singing "Luna Mezz O' Mare" from *The Godfather* wedding scene, a quick succession of clips played of mobsters, dons, and hoods facing Cody's hidden mirror cam as they primped their hair in restaurant vestibules and apartment foyers.

"Oh, my God, you weren't kidding."

"Just wait."

Young, old, middle-aged, Italian, African American, Irish, Latino, Russian, Asian—one after another they stepped into the entrance halls, and either patted down, combed, primped, or simply admired their hair before stepping outside. For comic variety, one stopped for a booger check. Another exited the door then immediately came back in and groomed his hair a second time before he left again. That was followed by the capper. A young enforcer whose face came full screen—while he used the mirror to squeeze a zit. "Nooo. Too gross. Enough, enough." Macie groaned, recoiling from the image as she melodramatically shielded her eyes and backed away, bumping her elbow on the space bar of the keyboard behind her. She saw Cody's eyes widen in alarm as the screen of the other computer awakened. "Oh, sorry, sorry. Did I wreck something?"

Cody made a lunge for the console, but it was too late. He had been rendering video while the screen slept and now that it was awake, she saw why Cody had been so alarmed. The monitor was rolling nighttime surveillance footage of Macie's attacker—the same man from the fleabag with the Colt Anaconda—the same Russian they had chased into the subway. In this, Luchik was in a shoving match with a bouncer outside a strip club. With cold anxiety blossoming, Wild noticed the time stamp. The digits said that this had been shot two weeks ago. She regarded Cody. His expression, illuminated by the pale reflection of the monitor, looked exactly like chiseled marble. A new commotion drew her attention back to the video. The bouncer had landed on the sidewalk and the Russian began to stomp him viciously. Macie couldn't watch it. She looked away to the Finder window and her stomach twinged anew as she read the file menu: "Luka Fyodor Borodin. Raw Surveillance Vids 1 thru 9."

While the video beatdown continued, she turned back to Cody. Nothing could dam the tsunami of hurt and betrayal washing over her. "All this time, you knew who he was?—You knew his goddamned name?"

CHAPTER 16

Cody stared at Wild. He was speechless for the first time since she'd met him. His surveillance footage still rolled in the background, and Macie could hear the sounds of body blows, and felt as if each one was being delivered to her. She watched him fumbling for words, nothing like the smooth dude tossing her witty asides while driving the wrong way on a one-way street. The room began to tilt for her as implications of this two-week-old video of her attacker—and the other eight Cody had apparently filmed just like it—broke over her with a suffocating crash. Feeling his floor pitching under her like a jungle footbridge, Macie left his edit bay, left his loft, left him behind.

He followed, imploring, "Please, don't go," and "Come back. Sit down and hear me out." Wild rolled the elevator's scissor door shut and descended, watching him watch her until he became only torso then legs then shoes and then there were only the lateral CT scans of lower floors as she passed by. The whine of machinery quieted as the lift settled on the ground floor and, in the stillness, Cody's voice, calm and soft spoken, traveled down the shaft and visited her as if he were right there speaking lowly into her ear. "Is this what you do when things get tough? You either walk out or lash out?" The aural effect was so eerie, so near, so confidential, that his question might have been her own inner voice.

Macie left her hand resting on the brass door handle, which was bright as gold from wear. His words had struck home. Not just because it had been her pattern with him. But also with her ex. It's what had put her in a center seat on Air France and was Topic A in couples counseling. Wild hesitated. Then she pressed six and rode back up.

How many times over the years had Macie wished for a chance to pause the Life DVR and rewind the scene? Returning for this do over seemed exactly like that, rising into her exit in reverse sequence: Cody's shoes, his legs, his torso, his face. However, this wasn't a wish granted but a pain confronted, instead of bolted from.

When Cody reached to open the gate, she said, "Don't," and he withdrew his hand as if he'd get zapped. She stayed in her cage. "I want you to tell me why. No. I want you to tell me all the whys. Why you knew about this man for two weeks—at least two weeks—before he attacked me. Why you were following him. Why you were following me. Why you gave the police his description but not his name. Why you were able to sit there—right beside me in your van last night . . . after shaming me to go along with planting your rat trap . . ." Wild took a swallow, working to keep civil. "We both sat watching that thug up in that room—and you never told me that you not only knew him, you'd shot video of him!"

He watched her a moment fuming through the bars. "I'll tell you," he said solemnly. No charming twinkle or playful smirk. But when he reached for the latch, she stopped him again.

"Not good enough."

"I said I'd answer your questions. What more do you want?"

"I want," she said, "to know everything."

Cody didn't need to think too long, and nodded. "Deal."

"Good answer." She rolled open the gate and stepped out.

Beer gave way to coffee; the kitchen counter replaced the living room floor. Wild perched on a barstool, both hands swaddling a mug of French Roast, and hearing Cody out. "I'll need to walk it back to my piece for VICE Media."

"I have nothing but time, as long as you tell me the truth."

"I promise. No bull, no smoke—"

"No First Amendment crap?"

He filled his own cup and began. "A month ago I was down at McSorley's, catching up with some of the old crew. Everyone's swapping tales, and this sarge from the West Village starts in about some rich foreign kid in his precinct who's a one-man quality-of-life violation. The kid's blasting hip hop out his windows at four a.m., or he's drunk and pissing on somebody's car—from his balcony. I'm thinking, so what, that's your garden-variety pain-in-the-ass college kid. Maybe a little more interesting because this twenty-year-old delinquent claims he's royalty—an actual prince from Angola. Most people swallowed that, but he's not really a prince. Just a rich shit, whose even-richer mommy sent him off to Columbia University, thinking he's in school instead of living his own personal twenty-four/seven spring break. But then it gets big. One of the detectives from Special Vics says he knows about this kid. Says this prince was named in a hooker battery complaint that disappeared when the woman in question gets a new Mercedes G, and suddenly claims it was mistaken identity."

"So your sense of justice kicked in?"

"No, my sense of a hot story." Cody opened his palms to her. "I promised no bull, right? I had an opening to pitch at VICE but I needed a story that would get them excited. I dug into this prince, and it all tumbled into place. A short documentary about a spoiled, foreign, faux-royal snot nose coming to our country, kicking the crap out of it, and buying his way out of all his troubles. It had twin barrels: outrageous misbehavior and a crazy-opulent lifestyle. Hookers, fast cars, parties, clubs, all the while flipping the bird to his host city. They bought the pitch for *The Devil Prince* before I even finished. My cop pals were more than happy to slip me his arrest records and a list of eyewitnesses plus one or two victims who'd talk in shadow. I just needed to get some footage of the bad boy in action." He smiled. "Kinda my wheelhouse."

Macie already was sorting it out. "So when I came here before and you were screening that car racing laps around Columbus Circle like the Monaco Grand Prix . . ."

"The *Príncipe do Diabo* himself, in his Lamborghini Aventador. By the way, he clocked ninety-six in Central Park. Almost turned a horsie into hamburger. I have it, if you want to see it."

"Not if it'll slow down your confession."

"Getting to your man Luka Borodin now." He took a sip of coffee and leaned against the sink, facing her across the countertop. "So after a few days of following our prince—"

"Does he have a name?"

"Indeed. It is Jerónimo Teixeira. It's Portuguese derivation. Angola was once a colony of Portugal, did you know that?"

"Remind me not to interrupt."

"I keep eyes on him, day and night. He's going everywhere but to class. It's clubs down in Meat Packing, it's drag racing some fool on the West Side Highway, and along and along, right? Then just before dawn two weeks ago outside a strip club off the Deegan, I'm ready to pack it in when Teixeira, who's underage, but c'mon, he's a prince, gets his Angolan hinder tossed out into the street by a bouncer. I found out later from the club's night manager that our testosterone-infused *príncipe* had forced a lap dancer into unwanted oral sex. I roll video while the lad is getting shoved against a wall by some failed defensive tackle when up walks this guy, who pulls the bouncer away from the kid and starts delivering the beatdown you just saw on that video."

"And that was the first time you saw Borodin?"

He affirmed with a nod. "Tell you the truth, I didn't know who the hell he was. What, some random citizen at that hour, in the Bronx, looking for a bouncer who telegraphs his punches? Then, after the stomping, it's clear this guy knows Teixeira because he gives the kid his own handkerchief and drives off in the Lamborghini with the prince riding shotgun and holding his head back from his bloody nose. You don't need a gold shield to detect that this guy is private protection, AKA: muscle. Which only juiced me up, because my VICE project had just gotten kicked to a whole new level."

He'd become animated by his own story and started pacing the kitchen. "So grabbing at the chance to give my documentary more investigative teeth, I e-mail a still frame of Teixeira's chaperone to my SVU buddy from McSorley's, who runs the face through the Real Time Crime Center's recognition db. Out pops a name—Luka Fyodor Borodin, Russian immigrant with a repo business on Long Island (give me a fucking break). Mr. Borodin also has a police record. But there's a wrinkle. After a decade in the US, only one arrest, five years ago, for assault and battery—he put a competitor in the hospital. Charges got dismissed with no explanation or documentation. You're a criminal attorney. How often do you see a violent offender walk like that? And don't be PC. How often?"

He had her there.

"Exactly. And also? No current address. No contacts, no more repo business, no nearest living relatives, none of that. So with only a name, I made it my project to get my own line on Luchik." Macie thought back to how Mir greeted him in the fleabag the night before. "I looked it up. Nickname means luck in Russian. Cute, huh? Don't you love criminals?" She gave him a look that said on with it. "Once I'd made him, I began to spot him on the fringe of my prince's activities. I got good footage of Borodin, but I never managed to track him to an address. He's a slippery one. But I kept on him. The other morning when you spotted me outside the crime scene in Chelsea? It's because I was watching Borodin, not you. I didn't know why he went to the crime scene, but there he was. And Borodin had been to the Stealer's Wheel, too, which is why I checked it out. And that night you were attacked? It was no coincidence I was there, you already know that. But I wasn't following you. I was keeping tabs on Luchik. Thank God."

"We were right there in the precinct, and you never told the police?"

"Not with you there. Too much splainin'—and not the optimal moment to drop this on you. But as soon as we split up that night, I put him out there to my NYPD boys and girls. Trust me, Luka Fyodor Borodin's name is now in all the Be On the Look Out advisories."

"You could have told me last night when he was in that flophouse and I wanted to call it in. Or how about when we were chasing him all over the Lower East Side, including the sewer?"

"Let's not embellish. It was exciting enough."

"Stop it. Give me a straight answer. Why didn't you tell me?"

"I started to last night. Afterward. Then things got pissy."

"Pissy?!"

"You went over the top. Remember? Someone, could be you, slugged me." He moved closer to face her across the counter. "But it's been tearing me up since. That's why I came to your office first thing this morning. But you killed that, so I invited you here."

"To go through Pinto's files."

"To get you alone. But then I didn't know how to broach it." Wild recalled the unusual tension she'd heard in his voice when she got there that she had ascribed to work stress. "I was afraid of how you'd react. And you can't deny I was kind of right." She couldn't. "At least you didn't slug me again."

"Don't even," said Macie. "So not there yet."

He came around and sat on the stool beside her. "I admit it. I screwed this up. But, truly, I need you to believe me, I meant to be righteous here, Macie. I kept it a secret at first because I needed to protect my project. When you showed up here, I didn't know you. So I held my cards. But I've grown to . . . respect you. And like you. Unexpectedly. And that left me in a deep hole I had to dig out of. I guess I still am." He paused and tried to read her. "And I hope I have."

Wild believed him. Maybe because she wanted to. Maybe because he had given her a viable story and a convincing apology. In fact, he had been more than just convincing. Cody had made himself vulnerable in a way she found touching.

She stood and started for the editing bay. "Show me everything you've got on this Borodin. Now that I know why you were following him, I want to know why he was following me. And how he connects to Jackson Hall."

The remainder of the strip club footage played out just as Cody had described it, right down to the unintentionally comic exit of the thug motoring away in a Lamborghini with the prince nursing a nosebleed in the passenger seat. After that Cody loaded up a series of other shots he'd hosed on consecutive late nights outside clubs. His lens found Borodin lurking at the perimeters but always within striking distance. Waiting limo drivers occasionally tried to engage him in small talk but always retreated after a frosty look or something he said. The video dimmed and glowed green for the next setup: night-vision surveillance of Jerónimo Teixeira making a cocaine buy uptown in Saint Nicholas Park. A sure sign of a rip-off, a figure worked his way up behind the Angolan prince.

Only to be taken down by one forearm hammer and a single kick by Borodin, whose limbs streaked phosphorescent trails with each blow.

Cody's video from Chelsea looked familiar to Wild, however not the perspective. From West Sixteenth, across from the Pinto crime scene, Macie saw herself pass through the shot. But the lens didn't react to her, lending credence to Cody's assertion that she wasn't the subject of his attention. The Russian smoking a cigar at the corner, watching her, was. The same man who, in the subsequent shots, came and went from the Stealer's Wheel in Harlem the same day that Cody went in to ask some questions and leave his card.

Next up in the queue, a certain evening on West Seventy-Eighth. Macie felt her throat constrict as the camera shadowed Borodin, who was walking the sycamore-lined sidewalk past the brownstones. Out of caution or because he heard something, the man stopped. The camera tilted and yawed as Cody sought cover behind a parked car. The footage dipped to black for a second then resumed, with the perspective now from a low crouch, pointing toward Amsterdam. But Borodin was nowhere to be seen. Then Wild heard her own distant shouts. The shot pitched down to Cody's running feet, jostling as he called, "NYPD, freeze," before it all went black.

"All right," said Macie turning from the monitor. "We know why you were following Borodin. The question is . . ." She left it hanging, an invitation for him to engage, and he picked it right up.

"Why was Borodin following you?" Cody flipped off a few switches and they sat a moment in silence but for the cooling fans on the equipment.

"Ever since that," Wild indicated the dormant monitor that had just replayed her assault, "I've been tossing old cases I've handled, racking my brain for clients with an ax to grind. Even my dad asked me about that as a possible motive."

"That's fine, you know, Detective 101 stuff."

She studied him. "You don't sound convinced."

"Because if you felt a genuine threat from an old client, you wouldn't be wondering. I'm old school about these things. I subscribe to a scientific rule known as Occam's Razor."

"Purporting that convoluted theories should be set aside in favor of the simplest one." She raised a brow at him. "Detectives aren't the only crime solvers, Mr. Cody."

He gave her a warm look, a mute appreciation of the easing tensions. "So if we're so smart, let's burn some brain cells. Let's examine why my thing with Borodin brought me to you."

"Right. We're looking for a nexus. Something—whatever it is—connects, and Borodin is the glue."

"There ya go." He began to pace again. "Let's try this. Leave you in the mix—after all, he did stalk and attack you—but let's shift you from the center of this. Put Borodin there instead. And, except for providing muscle for the prince, where else have we tracked him?"

"There's the strip club. The drug deal . . ."

"Outliers. The things that connect are all about your client, Jackson Hall." He counted each off on a finger. "Pinto's crime scene: Jackson Hall. Stealer's Wheel: Jackson Hall. Your assault: Jackson Hall. He and Fabio talked about him last night. So that's all tight. But why? Why does Borodin care about Jackson Hall?"

"He killed Pinto?"

"Little doubt," said the ex-detective. "But there's more to this. Like why?"

Wild reflected. "Could Borodin be the burglary crew chief?"

"Mm, not bad. *Très* Occam of you. But you know what else is even a more direct A-to-B? Jackson Hall, Rúben Pinto, and the elusive crew chief did what? Burglarized high-end apartments. What does our naughty prince have? A high-end apartment."

"So you're theorizing Hall and his crew ripped off the prince, and, assuming he is not the crew chief, Borodin, his goon, is now dealing out payback?"

"Or trying to retrieve Teixeira's stolen goods, who knows?"

Macie thought back to her interview with Hall at Rikers, and how he wouldn't specify the places they'd hit, except for The Barksdale. "I want to know if Teixeira's apartment was hit."

"Why don't we find out?"

Now Macie paced. "Great. Do you have somebody at NYPD you can call?" Then she saw his wheels turning. "I've only known you, what, three days? But I know that look. . . . What?"

"I need to reserve my IOUs." He checked his watch. "Screw calling. Let's pay a royal visit."

CHAPTER 17

Cody followed his GPS to the transponder he had planted weeks before under the prince's Lamborghini. It led them to Pier 40, the sprawling recreational complex built out over the Hudson River on top of a former marine terminal. At that hour, just after ten p.m., the parking lot was sparsely occupied as they cruised it, scouting for his sports car. They found it angled piggishly across two spaces near the Village Boathouse. Cody got out and went to the rail to survey the dock. Finding it empty, he drove across the concrete to the rugby pitch, backed into a space, and killed the engine.

They sat in silence as he got out his Steiners, first to scan the area for Borodin, then to scan the river. From across the field they could hear diehards at the trapeze school squeezing in their last few skinners before it closed. "All right to talk?"

"You are go to talk," he said, binocs fixed on the water.

"Now that we have video of this Luka Fyodor Borodin, we should see if Rúben Pinto's neighbor can ID him as the man she saw running up the hall."

"Great idea. So great that I already did it this morning." He lowered the glasses. "Well, it's a logical lead to follow, and I wasn't going to lose time waiting for you. I stopped by to see Dr. McBlaine right after you shooed me out of your office."

"And?"

"She even used a lighted magnifier. You know, like old folks use to blind you across restaurants?"

"Once more. And?"

"Said she couldn't be sure. In court, a cutthroat defense lawyer like you would reduce the poor woman to a Depends fail." He resumed his surveillance, but this time panning his binoculars along the parking lot and the river walk behind them, still keeping watch for Borodin. The roar of an approaching speedboat brought their attention back to the Hudson. A quarter mile out, one green and one red running light pinpointed a vessel as it bounced in the chop. "That'll be his X-35," said Cody, handing her the Steiners. She gave a look and picked out its lurching silhouette in the surface reflection of the Jersey City skyline.

Wild lowered the sun visor to check her reflection in the mirror. "You know, I think blonde's an option you should consider permanently," he said as she fussed with the wig they agreed she'd wear when they formulated their plan. "And relax, you're going to do fine. Nothing to worry about." Then he slid his Beretta Jetfire into its ankle holster. "Ready?"

They waited at the bottom of the gangway for the boat to arrive. Macie strained to see if Borodin was aboard, but he wasn't. It came in at a reckless speed that made Wild brace for a collision, but Jerónimo Teixeira, standing at the controls in ironic surf jams and a neoprene vest, laughed at the screams of the three young women with him, reversed thrust, and the MasterCraft sat down in its own wake, barely nudging the dock. One of his companions hopped out and cleated the bowline while the prince sized up the strangers approaching him across the float.

"Nice boat, Mr. Teixeira," said Macie. Hearing her use his name threw him off, as Cody said it would. They both watched him scan the parking area above for some kind of trouble. Or maybe for his Russian babysitter. Cody angled himself behind the prince so he could keep an eye on both him and the gangway, which seemed to unnerve Teixeira even more, which wasn't a bad thing. He already seemed off. Either drunk or high or both.

"I know you?" he said, forced to turn to face him. "If not, take a walk."

"No need to be testy, sir. Here, let me help." Cody tied off the stern line and held on to the slack end in case their man got any ideas about a water exit. "In fact, helping is why we're here."

One of the women, who was lounging on a padded bench, moaned. "I think I should go to the ER."

"She all right?" asked Wild.

"Not your deal, bitch." This prince didn't seem regal at all. In decades past, he'd be called a punk, and it would fit.

Macie addressed the young woman directly. "You hurt?"

"My leg. We were waterboarding, and I hit something."

"Waveboarding," corrected Teixeira. "Fuck me."

"Waveboarding at night?" Cody shook his head. "On the Hudson?"

"I've got plenty of situation here, doucher. So why don't you just be the fuck gone." He spoke with a slight accent. A little bit of Portuguese that might have sounded charming from someone else.

"Not looking to hassle you, seriously." Cody stepped forward and handed a fake business card over the gunwale to him. "I'm Jim Cagney and this is my associate, Beth Lacey. Reliant Insurance."

"This about the guy with the Audi? Fucker cut me off, man."

"No, we're not involved in that, Mr. Teixeira." Now that he'd bought the role, Macie played it. "We're investigators looking into a series of burglaries in your neighborhood. I understand from a neighbor of yours on Bethune Street that you were also a victim?" His face puzzled, giving him a naive look. For the first time, the twenty-year-old kid looked his age.

One of the other women called, "Jerónimo, she might need some ice."

"Yeah, we'll get some ice. Later, later." Then he said to Macie, "Look, I don't know shit about any burglary. I'm not missing anything. 'Less I got popped tonight."

"No, this would have been within the last month."

"Not me." He flipped the card into the drink. "We done?"

"Almost." Cody took out some photos. One of Jackson Hall, one of Rúben Pinto. "These might be the burglars. Take a look and see if you've seen them before."

He gave the pics a look and handed them back with a shake of his head.

"Just one more, and we're done."

Teixeira studied that one a bit longer than the others, then gave Cody a smirk. "No, not this one either. But tell you what. I'd do her, for sure." Then he handed back the photo of Macie. He obviously didn't recognize her, either as a target or as the woman standing six feet away in the blonde wig and the oversized smart glasses.

"Nimo . . ." whined the injured woman.

"Hold, skank." The prince wasn't just rude. He was distracted, struggling the way drunks do when they're trying to summon a loose thought. "Now I got a question for you. If you're checking out a robbery at my crib, what are you doing here?" He made another paranoid glance along the railing of the parking lot above. "How'd you find me?"

Macie felt herself tighten. But Cody took a confident step toward him. "We're Reliant. We're everywhere."

The prince gave him an unsettled look. "Listen to me, dickhole. You got anything more to ask you ask my lawyer, understand?"

"No problem, sir. Who'd that be?"

"Name's Orem Diner. You talk to him, and be the fuck out of my sight."

"Be certain we will," said Macie. Then she led Cody up the ramp, telling him all she knew about Orem Diner, attorney at law.

They met the next morning for a stand-up breakfast at the Café Europa on Lex then walked to Park Avenue for their appointment with the Angolan stud's attorney. Macie found herself taken with Gunnar Cody in a skinny suit and tie. She couldn't help it, and snuck glances at the crosswalk reds. He joked that it was all in keeping with surveillance; that he had dressed to fit in. The wide sidewalk was typically immaculate and ablaze with the end of the season's red tulips and a border of blue Dutch hyacinths. As they passed the Waldorf-Astoria, recently bought by a Chinese conglomerate for almost $2 billion, Cody mentioned that, in the years before it shut down for renovations, United States presidents quit staying there due to concerns that its new owners included spying along with room service and Wi-Fi. That set her to reflect once more about sacred spaces. She was already paranoid that Amazon knew whether or not she'd finished her e-books; now even a former leader of the free world had to wonder if that crunchy thing in his Waldorf salad was a walnut or a microphone. Then Wild got jarred out of her conspiracy daydream. The revolving door to the law building jerked to a sudden stop with her trapped inside.

She twisted toward Cody, who was still outside, squinting through the glass to see what the trouble was. Macie then peered into the outbound side of the rotary where a well-dressed man had stumbled and was hauling himself back up to his feet. He made eye contact with her and mouthed an apology through quivering lips. The guy looked ashen and his forehead gleamed with sweat. He removed a pocket square from his suit jacket to hold to his mouth. It almost got there before the man vomited against the glass. Wild looked away, in revulsion as much as to give him privacy. The door started to rotate again and she baby-stepped through to the lobby followed by Cody. "Should we help him?" she asked.

"We've got it, folks." A pair of security guards stepped out to aid the sick man.

Ten minutes later they sat alone on a sofa in the conversation area of Orem Diner's corner suite, sipping coffee and looking down at the dome of Saint Bart's while he finished a meeting. "Check out who he's with," said Cody. She turned from the skyline to the glass wall that gave onto the partners' offices. A cluster of attorneys filed out of the conference room with a future Hall of Fame quarterback who was taking the NFL to court over a suspension resulting from some controversial body part Tweets. The athlete towered over a slender patrician in crisp shirtsleeves and his trademark bow tie. But the QB's body language was classically deferential to the attorney, who sawed a handshake with both hands, and laughed at something the athlete called out to him as he glided off toward Wild and Cody.

Orem Diner shed years the closer he got. Up the hallway, he could have been seventy but when he extended a hand and shared his relaxed smile he became sixty. With his hard-parted graying hair, rimless glasses, and lanky frame, he resembled a genial Norman Rockwell subject instead of the formidable attorney who brought so many opponents to settle with the mere mention of his name.

"Thank you for seeing us on such short notice," she said as they settled back onto the sofa. He took the love seat across the coffee table.

"Nonsense. You caught me at a good time, and I'm curious about your interest in my client." An assistant delivered him a hot tea and left. He dunked the stainless infuser but kept his attention on Wild. "Plus I confess I was curious to see how the daughter of my old classmate grew up.

Last time we saw each other, you were coloring unicorns in your dad's office. By the way, you're much better looking than he."

"Smarter too." She laughed and he joined her. Macie's father not only had gone to law school with Orem Diner, they also had clerked for the same US District Court judge before building lucrative careers at separate practices. Wild still heard his name from time to time from her dad when the Yalies would work together, or sometimes against each other, on legal actions. Although Diner was resolutely low profile (you'd never see him as a talking head on CNN or Fox News), his big cases thrust him into the spotlight enough that Jansen Wild would reminisce about his fellow Bulldog whenever he reluctantly appeared on the evening news.

Age lines formed parentheses around the attorney's mouth. "Condolences about your brother. I can't imagine." She thanked him simply. What else was there to say without pitching herself down the dark hole of that conversation? Attuned to that, Diner shifted the topic to Cody. "I thought Len Asher gave the boot to all the ex-cops in his investigative team. You must be very good at what you do."

"You've got a sharp eye," said Cody.

"About you being an ex-cop or good at what you do?"

"Why quibble?" Cody shrugged, staying pleasant enough, but reserved.

"Mr. Cody isn't with the Manhattan Center. He's assisting me on a case."

"Which, I am betting, will bring us to the reason for your visit." The attorney blew across his tea and a pleasant scent of bergamot drifted Macie's way. He took a sip, set the china cup in its saucer. "What has Jerónimo Teixeira done this time?"

At their breakfast premeeting, Wild and Cody had agreed not to give up what they had observed, so Macie phrased a response that kept their cards close and might help them learn a few things they otherwise wouldn't have. "I take it from your question that he keeps you pretty busy."

Looking every bit the long-suffering parent, Diner spread his arms as if beseeching the heavens. "You know the saying 'not worth the money?'"

Well, there's a lot of money, so I won't lie. He's worth it. But barely. I ask myself every single day his name comes up, 'What now?' So. What now?"

"It's not anything he has done," she said. "I'm looking into some burglaries of luxury apartments and condos related to one of my cases. We approached him to ask if his place had been hit, too, and he said we should talk to you. Here we are."

The attorney lounged back and laced the fingers of both hands around one knee as he considered. The pause was long enough to make her wonder what he was weighing, his answer or her question. "Did he say he'd been burglarized?"

"No. He just seemed to want to get rid of us."

"He had female company," added Cody, shading it with meaning. "And we didn't have his full attention."

"Oh, yes, I've had those conversations with him. But I can attest to his answer. If Nimo had been robbed, he certainly would have called me. Probably at three thirty a.m." He leaned forward again, and turned one click of the knob from hospitality toward business. "You went to a lot of logistics for something you could have handled by phone. What else were you hoping to ask me?" His unwavering scrutiny of her reminded Wild of her father's observation that, beneath that Rockwell persona, lived Rocky.

Here again Wild and Cody had figured out what to (and what not to) say. She tag-teamed to her companion. "We were wondering if you've ever heard the name Borodin. Luka Fyodor Borodin."

"No, doesn't mean anything. But hearing a detective say all three names like that makes him sound bad. Is he?"

Instead of answering, Cody took out a two-by-three still frame of Borodin and placed it next to the tea service. "Have you ever seen him?"

Diner gave it a look and shook no. "You're asking a lot of boxy questions here. I know the technique, I've used it. Mind just laying it all out so I can be helpful—assuming I can be? Who is this fellow, and what does he have to do with Jerónimo Teixeira?" He winked. "See, that's how you cut through it."

"He is one of Mr. Teixeira's associates," said Macie.

"Associates?" He scoffed. "You make Nimo sound respectable."

Cody said, "Trust me, this guy is anything but. We were just wondering if you knew of him so we could get a handle on locating him."

"And this is for a case of yours, Ms. Wild? The Buzz Killer perhaps? I'm embarrassed to admit my shoeshine reading is the *Daily News*."

"So you don't know him?" Cody wedged into the conversation ahead of Macie.

"Asked and answered." The attorney gave him an irritated look then turned a softer side to her. "If you'll pardon the understatement, my client runs a bit out of control. There's a lot I don't know unless he goes afoul of the law or causes damage." He tapped the photo. "How do you know this Borodin is connected to my prince?"

Cody jumped in ahead of her again. "We know," was all he said. And would say.

At that, Diner rose to signal the end of the interview and picked up the photo. "Mind if I keep this? I promise to be discreet, but I do want to look into it for you."

"Please."

"And if I learn anything, I can reach you at the MCPD?" He took her card and examined it. "You know, Ms. Wild, given your lineage and experience, we should have a further conversation about your career."

"That's very kind. Maybe sometime. Later. Thank you for the meeting."

"Something's not right," said Cody as they waited for the express elevator. "I wear the new suit, and you get the job offer."

They set out for Queens to visit the pawn shop where Rúben Pinto had been a customer. Cody drove Macie's Corolla so she could use the travel time for a hands-free office check-in. When she finished, they were midspan on the Queensboro Bridge. "Jonathan Monheit just gave me some interesting news."

"That, in itself, is a headline. Jonny Midnight has news?"

"Be nice. He pulled an all-nighter digging into Hall and Pinto's burglary victim from The Barksdale."

"That would be the pharma CEO."

"Right. Gregory Eichenthal. According to Monheit's research, his company, EichenAll, has troubles with the FDA. There have been allegations about rigged testing for one of their BP meds that has had a higher-than-acceptable incidence of fatalities."

"You know, you hear the announcer rattle off all that stuff at the end of those commercials. 'Side effects may include bleeding from the eyes, ulcerated rashes, or sudden loss of life. Discontinue use if you feel like you are dying.'"

"Funny to you, not so much to the victims. Or the CEO. He's getting throttled by a massive devaluation of company stock. Monheit says that would make him desperate for liquidity. He's already got his Amelia Island estate up for sale."

"Poor baby." Cody drummed his fingers on the wheel when they stopped for the usual gridlock at Northern Boulevard. "Gee, is it possible Mr. Eichenthal staged the robbery to collect insurance?"

"That's exactly what Monheit said."

He cocked his head to one side as if listening to unheard voices. "I sense a disturbance in The Force. Jonny Midnight's starting to think like an investigator."

Flamingo Pawn was hard to miss. The flashing neon bird in the window was electric pink and extremely bright, even with the morning sun angled against the storefront. While Cody squeezed into a no-parking spot on Steinway and fished out an NYPD courtesy card for the dash, Wild observed that this shop would be a logical go-to for Pinto—walking distance from where he had flopped with his ex-girlfriend. Bracketed by a hipster alternative to Starbucks on one side and a dress shop with clothes that looked like they could catch on fire on the other, the broad strokes of yellow and orange paint on the pawn window promised easy cash: "New York's Fairest Appraisals of Gold and Jewelry!" —in four languages.

Inside the store was clean but had the sad yet welcoming odor of an attic. Nothing was in reach of the customer, but behind the counters the walls brimmed with musical instruments, fitness equipment, china and crystal, samurai swords, even a saddle with a Stetson racked on the horn. The glass cases held finer items, grouped by category. Jewelry and watches in one, another with electronics like dated laptops and iPods, circa 2009. The center case displayed collectibles: autographed baseballs, soccer balls, pennants, and jerseys on the right; on the left, signed Broadway playbills, glossy photos of Sinatra, Yanni, the Ramones, plus hardbacks from Bukowski, Jacqueline Susann, and Doris Day, "personally inscribed by the author," according to the handwritten index card. An engraved sign above the firearms read, "No Loans for Guns, per NY Law."

They waited while a bored girl who couldn't have been a year out of high school counted out greenbacks to the only customer, an old man who licked his fingers for his recount, then caned out past them. "Help you today?" she asked, not sounding like it was a mission.

"We're here to redeem an item," said Macie. She placed the pawn ticket on the glass. Beside it Cody set the $300 he told Wild that he'd put on his VICE budget.

The girl read the printout, gave them a once-over, then disappeared into the back, saying, "Daaad?" as she rounded the corner.

A moment later a middle-aged man came out to deal with them. He was her spitting image but with a thick head of hair fastidiously sprayed back like a doo-wop singer on a PBS reunion concert. He scanned the chit, gave them the same look his daughter had, and folded his arms, leaving the cash where it was. "You have some ID?"

Wild didn't expect that and turned to Cody, hoping he'd know how to handle this. He did. "You have paper that says you ran a check this wasn't stolen?"

The man took a half-step back, uncrossing then recrossing his arms. "Not looking to get shitty here, friend."

"Too late." Cody gestured to the counter. "Simple transaction." The pawnbroker hesitated, so Cody added, "Nice gun collection. When was the last time somebody dropped by to run an ATF check? I can make that happen. I assume you're FFL 02-compliant."

After one full second the man picked up the pawn ticket and said, "I think we're square here."

"Good. While we're talking." He took out pictures of Jackson Hall, Rúben Pinto, and Luka Borodin. "Know any of these?"

"Middle one. This is his ticket."

"Not the other two?" Another look for show, and the man shook his head.

Macie asked, "Do you have anything else Mr. Pinto pawned here?"

"You can just answer," said Cody. "Warrants are such a pain, am I right?"

"No, just the statue. Hang on." He went to the back room with the pawn ticket. Cody slid by the keep-out sign and moved behind the counter so he could keep an eye on him. "Private area," said the man on his way back. Cody complied and joined Macie. The pawnbroker opened a brown grocery bag and placed the item on the counter. It wasn't just a statue.

It was a Grammy Award.

Macie bent over to read the inscription. Cody asked. "And the winner is . . . ?"

CHAPTER 18

Woody Nash became a teen music sensation in the mid-1960s with his own rowdy take on the California surf scene. If the Beach Boys were the Beatles, his band, the Woodies, were the Rolling Stones. The Beach Boys got haircuts; the Woodies got laid. Unlike Brian Wilson and his ho-dad crew, Woody's band actually surfed. And they were the ruffians who didn't leave the beach at sundown. Their first big hit told the tale with its title. "Get a Woody" sold a million, launched a platinum LP, and silenced critics who said they were only riding in the more famous band's wake.

Except, that is, for the National Academy of Recording Arts and Sciences, which never voted a Grammy to the Woodies in their breakout era. Not even with their legions of swooning fans, dominance of Boss Radio airplay, sold-out concerts, and a gazillion in record sales. That oversight got corrected three years ago when a music blogger revived interest in the genius songwriter and performer behind the so-called Vandals in Sandals, leading to a Lifetime Achievement Grammy for Woody Nash.

With the paper bag holding that gramophone statuette tucked football-style in the crook of her arm, Wild and Cody entered the polished marble lobby of the Crystal Court Luxury Residences on the Upper East Side. Earlier in the week, Jackson Hall had refused to give up a list of the upscale apartments his crew had burglarized, and now, thanks to a dead man's pawn ticket, Macie might have found one. The uniformed concierge greeted them from behind an opaque frosted glass counter. "Good morning, may I help you?"

"Thank you, Martin, yes," said Wild after a glance at the embroidery on his tunic. "We have something for one of your residents. Woody Nash?" A limo driver Macie had recently cleared of a bogus hit-and-run charge had driven just about every VIP in Manhattan. He had returned her voice mail within ten minutes with the address of the musician.

"Is Mr. Nash expecting you?" Martin's Irish brogue sounded friendly enough, but there was skepticism in his appraisal of them. Nash was famously reclusive, at least outdoing Brian Wilson on that score.

"No, sir," said Cody. "But you can announce us. We have something for him." He gave both their names, which Martin wrote down, making Gunnar Cody spell his.

The concierge set down his pen and opened his hands. "Why don't you give it to me. I'll see he gets it and be sure to tell him you came by."

Macie hugged the brown paper bag. "It's personal."

"May I at least ask what it is?"

"Not much," she said. "Only his Grammy Award."

Martin verified the contents of the shopping bag then personally escorted them to the thirty-second floor. Partly as security protocol, but mainly because he would need to unlock Woody's door to let them in. His discretion was exemplary when he explained that odd wrinkle to his job. No doubt service to affluent Manhattan was no less full of idiosyncratic demands than at Downton Abbey. But they soon learned idiosyncrasies are one thing. Some shit is just crazy.

After a card key swipe, the concierge pushed open the door, called, "Your visitors," and sped off as if he were barefoot on hot coals. Left on their own, Wild and Cody stepped inside, greeted by a mixed fragrance: Nursing home meets locker room. Windows, sealed tight at this altitude, had created a greenhouse of funk. No one met them. They stood in the foyer, waiting. Macie sang out a hello up the short hall to a dim living room lit by the light bleed around blackout drapes. No answer. The only sound was trickling water like you hear from those kitschy fountains in Thai restaurants. Perhaps the eccentric musician was into Eastern meditation. If so, a few incense sticks would only improve the place. The pair moved ahead.

The sunken living room was divided in two. On their right, the part visible from the foyer had been done up lavishly in California Modern. Decorated in whites with curved ceramic bookcases, authentic Eames chairs, a circular white Formica coffee table orbited by round cushions in red, blue, and yellow leatherette. That half of the room re-created a Sputnik decade when technology's streamlined promise cast America's gaze west to a utopian future. In the dusky light, they made out a Fender Stratocaster mounted with a black-and-white of Buddy Holly playing it. That priceless artifact hung beside Elvis Presley's crimson-accented karate gi, autographed "To Big Woody" by the king. The left side of the room was a different world entirely.

First, the trickle. The source was anything but a meditation font. A thin stream of water dripped from one nostril of a morbidly obese man—naked but for his immense boxers. Meet Woody Nash. Head canted, the genius musician was pouring saline from a neti pot into his nose while standing over a catch basin positioned between his flip-flops. To complete the bizarre picture, he was behind glass. That half of the living room had been walled off, floor-to ceiling, behind an immense window. Woody had created an isolation bubble complete with an oversized therapeutic bed, a mashed-down futon, a dining table, even a kitchenette on the far side. The effect was of an exhibit at a zoo. Or mental hospital.

The water stopped flowing and he held up a forefinger, signaling them to hang on. He set the pot on an end table, squared himself over the basin, snorted out the remaining saline, and blew his nose into a man-sized tissue. He then used it to dab neti spatter off his exposed Sumo gut. "Let me see my Grammy."

"I have it right here, Mr. Nash. I'm Macie Wild and this is—"

"The Grammy! You said you had my fucking Grammy, let me see it, goddamn it." He threw the balled tissue at the window and advanced toward them, his naked belly becoming a giant white amoeba where it pressed against the glass. By reflex, both she and Cody retreated a step.

"You got it, ace," said Cody. Wild held the sack for him and he lifted the statue out and presented it, engraving forward, with both hands. Woody finger combed back his oily gray hair, slipped on a pair of thick glasses, and leaned forward, leaving breath fog on the window as he squinted to read the inscription.

"Fuckin'-A, great. Thanks. Just leave it there on the coffee table." He turned away, buck-snorted something disagreeable, and paced his room, humming scales as if testing his voice after the sinus work. Walking a full circle, he seemed surprised to see them still there. "What.—Oh, right." He opened a pantry cabinet in the kitchenette. Even in the muted track lighting the contents of the shelves were startling. Cash. Stacks and stacks of cash. He waddled back to a sliding drawer cut into the window and pushed it through. It held two one-hundred-dollar bills. "You can touch them. I'm not sick or anything, I just need the oxygen in here."

"No, thanks," said Macie, and slid the drawer inside to him.

"What the fuck. I'm taking back my stolen Grammy, no police, no questions asked, and you're, what, gonna shake me down for more?"

"We don't want money, Woody." Cody set the award down on the coffee table to show good faith. "We want to ask you a few questions."

The recluse's face tautened and his eyes widened. The panicked darting of irises echoed his viral on-camera meltdown three years before at the Grammy satellite ceremony for which he made a rare outside journey—a twitchy, medicated, thirteen-block limo ride to Radio City Music Hall—where his acceptance was beamed live to the Staples Center in Los Angeles. He'd worn a slouch hat to hide his eyes, had to be escorted onstage from the wings by two handlers, and bolted halfway into his mumbled speech because reading the teleprompter made him look up too much. "—What questions? You're those assholes from *Rolling Stone*, aren't you? I said no interviews. Is that what this is?"

Cody dismissed that one. "Reporters? No, not at all." But then the VICE freelancer felt Macie's death stare of truth, and amended, "*Rolling Stone*? no way."

"I'm the attorney for one of the burglars who stole this, Mr. Nash. We went to a lot of trouble to track down your property so we could return it to you. I just want to ask you about the break-in so I can gather some facts to help my client, who's been accused of a crime he didn't commit."

"Why should I help you?"

"Because we helped you," said Cody. "I'm sure a Lifetime Achievement Award means something."

"Wanna know what this Lifetime Achievement Award means? It's the consolation prize because they gave all the real awards to the Beach Boys." He began stomping about his room, grabbing a fistful of red vines from a glass canister, biting one off like jerky and ranting, "Where was the fucking Grammy for 'Get a Woody'? Where was the Grammy for

'Gnarly Wood'? The Beatles give Brian fucking Wilson hand jobs for *Pet Sounds* and 'Good Vibrations.' What about *Pound Sand*, huh? Or 'Hangin' Eleven'?" He was panting. By his third licorice, red vine juice dripped down his front, mingling with rusty stains around the fly of his boxers.

Cody nodded. "Beach Boys. Bunch of posers." That slowed Woody down, but he viewed him with a wary eye. "No, seriously. Wilson drops in some goofy, electro-Theremin sci-fi effect he heard on *My Favorite Martian*, and he's a genius. It's not genius, it's novelty."

"It's novelty," repeated Woody.

"You want cutting edge? *Hangin' Eleven* was truly subversive. Gettin' high and surfin' naked, am I right?" The man behind the glass was a picture of agreement—and astonishment. Macie held her own sense of surprise, wondering where that arcane knowledge came from. Who was this Gunnar Cody, really?

Whether mollified by Cody's support or merely medicated by the stunning array of prescription bottles lining the bedside table, Woody came down off his harangue. He eyed Cody. "So you're a detective?"

"Sort of."

"You have a gun? Can I see it?"

"Maybe," said Wild. She was starting to understand how good-cop, bad-cop hadn't become a trope for nothing, and assumed her role. "First a couple of questions. Was the Grammy the only thing stolen from you?"

"Uh, yuh. Cause I surprised the shit out of them, and they ran."

The glance between Wild and Cody signaled their shared recognition of the anomaly. Jackson Hall had said the crew chief knew all the places that were vacant—borne out by the CEO's hit at The Barksdale, at least. "So you walked in on them?" she asked.

"Walk in?" Woody frowned at her like she had just said the dumbest thing in the world. "From out there? Hell, no, I was asleep. And they sure didn't expect to see me." Understatement, thought Macie, given what they had just been greeted by.

"You saw them then?" Cody took out a pad. Woody seemed to like that. "How many were there?"

"Three."

Wild swallowed hard. Coming over, they weren't sure what they would get from this victim, maybe a line on other stolen property they could trace, if they were lucky. Now they were talking to an eyewitness who might be able to give them a description of the elusive crew chief. If Woody saw him, and if he continued to cooperate. If, if, if. "Woody," said Cody to his new best bud, "can you describe them? Think carefully."

"Don't have to." He lumbered away to his nightstand and returned with something neither of them had seen in years—a Polaroid photo. "It's kind of messed up. The flash went off when I took it, but you can sorta make them out, can't you?" He slapped the picture against the glass. Yes, it was glared-out, streaky, and the framing was at a steep tilt, but there were three discernible forms in the shot: Jackson Hall, Rúben Pinto, and, in the foreground, a third man holding a canvas carpenter's bag. Disappointingly, the flash kick against the window obscured part of his bald head. But on his forearm, above where his gloved hands gripped the leather handles of the tool bag, part of a tattoo showed under his sleeve.

A furrow appeared between Cody's eyebrows as he looked from the Polaroid to Wild and back. "You did call the police after the theft, right?" Woody nodded. "And the detectives came here to interview you."

"Of course."

"As a detective myself, Woody, I have to say I'm confused as to why they never took that picture as evidence. Was there another one maybe?"

"No, just this." He fanned himself with it.

"Did you show it to them?"

"Nope."

"Did you tell them about it?"

"No."

"Why not?"

"Because they were assholes."

Cody put away his pad and smiled at the big man. "Want to see my gun now?" The old surfer's face broke into sunshine.

Back at the Manhattan Center for Public Defense, Wild made the rounds to brief her team members individually on her latest while she made status checks on their case work. Her client's medical condition stayed on the top of her mind. So far Jackson Hall remained in his coma. She convinced herself that no change was, at least, hopeful. Soledad Esteves Torres and Chip Ross had been on the hunt for Hall's girlfriend. Pilar Fuentes had not only been absent from visiting her lover in jail or the hospital, she was also MIA from her job. Relatives hadn't heard from her either. Wild told them to keep tracking. Meanwhile she'd be paying extra attention to the news for found female remains—a caution informed by experience. Jonathan Monheit had been pressing forward with his investigation of Gregory Eichenthal's financials. Without police power to get search warrants, he had to rely on public records, but he was making the most of them. Also a reputable Wall Street blogger had recently posted rumors that a friendly takeover bid that was being put together by one of the pharma giants was in jeopardy as a result of EichenAll's FDA troubles. Macie told him to go make friends with experts at Christie's and Sotheby's for a primer on stolen art. "You also might want to start watching *Antiques Roadshow* to see if anyone shows up with a Sargent or a Wyeth."

He made a face and said, "A joke, right?" So damned literal, she thought. Just when he showed signs of getting his sea legs, he reset to Jonny Midnight. When asked about reaching Pinto's old cellmate Amador Spatone, he shrugged and gave her what she now called The Midnight Look.

Tiger wove in and out of her meetings with docs to sign and motions to initiate on her other cases. Her paralegal also had news on their filing with Justice on Hall's incident at Rikers. The matter was being turned over immediately to the US Attorney for the Southern District of New York. In other words, they took it seriously. That wouldn't bring him out of his coma, but it was a step toward justice for others, and might rattle the Corrections stonewall enough to crack it.

Lenard called from reception as Macie came back from her restroom break, "Got one holding for you, Ms. Wild. Somebody Dinner."

Macie double-timed to her office and stretched over her desk to grab the blinking line. "This is Macie Wild."

"Macie, it's Orem Diner."

She lifted the cord over her computer screen as she came around to sit. "I hope you haven't been on hold long."

"Can I tell you? It's actually refreshing to call a law office where they don't know who I am." He laughed and said, "I was happy to see you face-to-face this morning, although I wish the occasion had been about other than my punk prince."

"Likewise."

"I wanted to let you know that Jerónimo Teixeira's home has not been burglarized. Unfortunately I still haven't turned up anything on this Luka Fyodor Borodin you mentioned. But it wouldn't be the first time Nimo hooked up with some rough trade."

"Well, I sure appreciate the courtesy of the personal callback."

"I'll keep you posted, should I learn anything, but that's not really why I called." By reflex, ever the student, Wild grabbed a pen. "I wanted you to know my feeler was serious about joining the firm. More so after you left and I spoke to your dad. He tells me all the great things you've been doing." He paused for emphasis. "Practically for free."

"Well, it's not just about the money, you must know that."

"Actually I don't. I'd be lying if I said otherwise. I'm not about saving the world, but I do like winning. And someone with your smarts and your background would be a super acquisition here. And, if you twist my arm, I'll certainly let you do all the pro bono you want. Will you at least think about it?"

Wild set her pen down and aligned it between blank lines. "Sure."

"So it's a no." He chuckled and said, "Your father called it. But it was worth a shot."

"And I thank you for that, Mr. Diner. If I ever change my mind . . ."

"You won't. But if you do . . ."

"I'll let you know."

"Another thing," he said. "As someone who cares about Jansen Wild's kid, I wanted to offer you some advice. It's free, mind you. See? I can do pro bono too." His words were lighthearted but his tone wasn't.

"Advice about what, may I ask?"

"Frankly, it's about that fellow you came in with today. Gunnar Cody. I'm familiar with him through his involvement in one or two of our prior cases. Not directly with me, but through partners in the firm. I'll be blunt. He's no Boy Scout. Far from it. I'll stop short of slander, and stick to facts. Last year the district attorney had to pull him as the key witness in a trial because of some nefarious activity he was involved in. As a favor to your dad, I'm giving you a heads-up. You may want to steer clear."

Macie found herself pressing the phone hard against her ear and released it. "Oh, well, thanks, I guess. Thanks."

"Your reputation is pristine, Macie. Keep it that way. I'll leave it at that."

Whatever good she felt at having one of New York's preeminent attorneys court her was offset by an imbalance that nagged her all day. It made no sense to Wild that Orem Diner could get inside her head about Gunnar Cody. Macie tried to shrug it off while she went about her work, but the residue of the lawyer's caution about her ad hoc investigative partner hovered in the background, a spirit dragging a chain.

It played out for Wild by unconsciously distancing herself. Instead of calling to give Cody an update on her team's progress, she took the coward's route: e-mail. Macie told herself she wasn't creating space because she didn't trust him. But when he called late that afternoon, she hesitated before tapping accept because she was afraid he would hear something in her voice. Something wary. "Heyyyy," she answered, pushing brightness.

"I know he's your guy, and all, but I am officially done waiting for Jonny Midnight to get his thumb out of his crack about Spatone. I mean, come on, we have an address—you were there yourself—and, instead of door-stepping the dude, your lead investigator is waiting to be called back like the date for the prom he probably also never got. Sorry to unload, but Rúben Pinto's cellmate is a potential lead that's dying on the vine or could skip. I say we drop by now and brace his ass." She hadn't heard him go off like that before, and wondered what was up. What happened to the usual soft batting of dry Cody humor?

"Sure. Ah, I'm totally up for that. Now's not the best time though. I'm at Starbucks, just about to start a meeting."

"Right, of course. I'm just . . . I'm wanting to get some traction is all." Wild said she understood, and they made arrangements to meet near Amador Spatone's personal training studio later.

When she hung up, Rick Whittinghill, one of the Popeye Doyles who got the broom from the Manhattan Center, returned from the barista with two coffees. The retired Internal Affairs detective sat down at Macie's table and asked, "So who's this ex-cop you want me to check out?"

CHAPTER 19

Cody was right where he said he'd be, sitting outside the Irving Roasters at Seventy-Ninth and Broadway when Wild came up from the subway. He ditched his empty espresso cup and said, "I'd offer you a latte, but I think we should just get there and do this."

"Me too. Besides, I'm kind of caffeinated."

"Right, Starbucks. How was your meeting?"

Trying not to put out any guilt tells, she sloughed it off. "Eh. A meeting." The walk sign had four seconds left and she darted ahead across Amsterdam. He sped up to keep pace. "Any luck with the tattoo database?" she asked, lobbing out a subject change.

"Shit, I don't know what the delay is." There it was again. The edge she had heard over the phone. "Maybe it's the crappy Polaroid. Or because it's only a partial. Hopefully they'll work it out, and we'll get something." They reached the corner at West Seventy-Eighth. "That's why I want to quiz this joker, since he may have a name, and we can tell the RTCC to suck it."

A middle-aged man with a crimson face from his private workout trudged up the cement steps to the sidewalk from the Tone With Spatone studio. Below, the door under the stoop was open and the personal trainer, a good match to his Department of Corrections mug shot, called out, "Keep pounding back that water, Norris, you got that?" Norris, too wasted to speak, lofted his refillable sports bottle in reply. That's when Cody squeezed past him, skipping steps down to the little patio. "Sorry, boss, we're appointment only, and I'm done for the night." Cody continued toward the door anyway, and when Wild descended behind him, Spatone sized up both and code-switched from small businessman to ex-con. "S-up."

"A little conversation, Amador. You can make time."

"You proby? You look it, but I don't know you."

Cody spoke before Wild could disabuse Spatone of his parole officer assumption. "Time to get acquainted. Inside or outside, your call." Spatone clocked the sidewalk where his client pretended to hydrate, while eavesdropping. The trainer stepped back to let them inside.

"Nice," said Cody, scanning Spatone's converted apartment. The dining room had become a reception area with plastic chairs and a water cooler. Instead of a sofa and coffee table, the living room was furnished with racks of free weights, Swedish balls, incline benches, and a resistance station with chinning bars. Hardly Equinox, but it covered the basics.

"I'm guessing you're not here for a tour. You gonna make me piss in a cup, what?"

Wild said, "We're not with the Probation Department, Mr. Spatone." Frustration showed all over Cody. He would have to live with that; her default wasn't duplicity.

"What, then? NYPD? I wanna see credentials." When nobody moved, Spatone snagged Cody to give him the boot. The instant he put a hand on him, Cody twisted, locked the ex-con's arm in a hold, hooked a leg around the back of his knee, and dropped him face-first onto the rubberized tiles. It all happened so lightning quick, Spatone had no time to do anything but curse as Cody goosenecked his wrist back by the thumb in a power restraint.

"These are my credentials, asshole."

"Cody . . ." Wild implored him with a look to let him go, which he ignored.

Spatone spit a loose hair he'd picked up off the floor and said, "It's cool, OK? You break my thumb, how'm I gonna work?"

"Do we have an understanding that you're not going to get stupid?"

"Yeah, yeah."

"Promise, Amador? Because I refuse to wrinkle my good suit over you." The man didn't answer, just let his body go slack in submission. Cody released his hold and took a step back, keeping watch as the trainer got to his feet.

"So if you're not cops, what?" He shook some feeling back to his hand. His eyes darted to a cabinet, lingered there, and came back to them.

"I'm an attorney." Pointedly, Wild stepped in front of Cody, making clear her unhappiness with the takedown.

"Guess what. You're going to fucking need one for yourself when I sue your asses."

"You're not suing anyone, know why?" Cody sidled over to the cabinet where Spatone had been stealing glances. "If I open this, I'd better find Chia Bars in here. Because if you're an ex-con with a firearm, guess where your next gym class is going to be held."

Taken down again, he flopped on one of his plastic chairs and rested his elbows on his knees. "What's this about?"

"We just want to ask you a few questions," she said.

"Whatcha got?" More docile now, Spatone gave no clue that he had done time. Sweet faced with a close-cut faux-hawk, he seemed the gym rat you'd feel comfortable asking to spot you. He had a short body and a square build, the kind you could imagine going all Pete Rose, if he let himself.

"I'm a public defender. I represent Jackson Hall." Wild assessed him for a reaction and saw the stoicism familiar to her with prisoners. "He's been charged with the murder of someone I know you are familiar with. Rúben Pinto."

"Still waiting on a question."

"I got one," said Cody. "Where were you when he got killed?"

"Not killing him's where I was. Shit man, I don't even know when he bought it." Macie gave him the date and approximate time. "Have to check my bookings, but I was probably here listening to some CPA grunt."

"Check," said Cody. "We've got time."

Spatone went to his desk beside Macie and got his cell phone. After some scrolling he said, "Yep. Was here."

"Show me. And I want the client's name and contact info." Cody stepped close enough to surf the screen. The ex-con looked at his calendar again and frowned.

"Huh. Guess I was mistaken. I didn't have a booking then."

"Bad news for you," he said.

"Why? You think I'd do my cell boy? Fuck that."

"If you could prove where you were, that would be helpful," offered Macie. "Nobody's accusing you, but I do have an account that you and Mr. Pinto had been fighting lately."

"Who told you that? Bitch who threw him out? Like she's who you should be dogging. Or Hall. I know he's your client, and everything, but there was some ugly shit there. Man."

"Ugly how? I want to know." Wild opened her notebook to signal she meant it. They'd already had corroboration about Jackson Hall's threats, maybe she could learn what was behind them.

"Your man was all up in Rú's shit, accusing him of skimming the take from a crew they worked." He paused. Not the brightest man, Spatone realized he may have carelessly outed them as thieves. He sat back down. "But I don't know anything solid about them stealing, you see."

"Relax," said Cody. "We know they weren't exactly volunteering at the food bank."

"Yeah, well, Hall, he's the type's got this stick up his ass. And he was ripshit, calling my crime boy out for disrespecting the crew by stashing on the side before the cut."

"Did he?" asked Cody.

"How'd I know? I'm an honest working man."

"I also heard you were unhappy with Mr. Pinto for getting my client on the break-in team instead of you."

"Cilla. Know what she is? Shit disturber." He wagged a forefinger in the direction of her notebook. "You write that down."

"You have a lot to say about Pinto's ex," said Wild. "If I showed your picture to her neighbors, would they ID you as the guy who tossed her apartment?"

"You could be talking Chinese, lady. I can't understand a word," replied Spatone. But he rubbed his eyes to hide them.

"Tell me about this crew." Cody hooked a chair and sat knee-to-knee with Spatone. "Names."

He was not only dumb, but a poor actor. Spatone made a meal of trying to look like he was searching deep memories. "Don't really know. Pinto and Hall, they kind of kept it tight."

Cody pretended he didn't hear that. "All right, so there's Rúben Pinto, Jackson Hall . . . Still waiting on you, Amador."

"Couldn't tell you."

"Looking for bachelor number three. Who's the crew chief? A name."

"Got me."

Wild opened the Photos app to her copy of Woody's Polaroid and handed her iPhone to Cody. "Visual aid that might help you." He held the image up. "We've got a Jackson. We've got a Rúben. Who do we have here?" Spatone gave the picture, maybe, a nanosecond of review and shrugged. Then sat back, crossing his arms.

Cody turned aside to Wild. "I've seen better acting from Yorkies pretending they didn't poo on the rug." He handed back her cell and returned his attention to Spatone. "You sticking with that?" Spatone stared at his lap. Cody took out his own phone. "One more. Recognize this guy?"

Unlike the other shot, he examined the screen grab of Borodin carefully. "Nope. Never saw this dude before. Should I know him?"

"Be glad you don't," said Cody as he stood. "If your memory unclogs, here's how to reach me." He let his business card flutter onto Spatone's lap.

"I'm sure it won't."

"Then all I can say is, enjoy your snap inspections from proby." Then he and Wild let themselves out.

Macie lit into him as soon as they reached the sidewalk. "I need to tell you right now: You pull another abusive stunt like that, I am reporting you."

Taken aback, Cody held his palms out to her. "Whoa, whoa, whoa. Stunt? Abusive?"

"And deceitful." She held back while an elderly gent ambled by leading an old miniature schnauzer with its leash fouled under a foreleg. As they shuffled on, Wild realized she was standing on the exact spot where Borodin had tried to trunk stuff her. She continued in a lower voice. "Can we, ah, talk someplace else?"

"I love it that you call this talking." When she didn't register the slightest amusement, he blurted, "Dinner! And cocktails. We should

definitely unwind and smooth off the edges. Besides, since you treated
me to a conciliatory lunch, I owe you. What do you think of Isabella's?"
he asked, suggesting the place she had intended to take herself before
she ended up getting attacked.

The evening was mild enough that all the patio seats on Columbus were
filled, so they took a table inside. Over her sidecar and his Jameson
old-fashioned, things mellowed a bit, but Macie still needed to unload.
So she did, just using her inside voice this time, taking him to task for
strong-arming Spatone in his own place, not to mention pretending first
to be a probation officer, then a cop. "If you don't get me arrested, the bar
association would sure take a dim view of continuing to license me, even
as an accessory."

When she'd had her say, he responded, "Can we talk real world here?"

"Are you seriously going to try to defend this?"

"I'll try. How serious I am depends on how soon the Jameson kicks
in. Let me begin by saying this is not my universal approach. We had a
chance at a hot lead, and he was going to shut us out if I didn't go street
with him. A firm leash jerk is a language guys like Mr. Amador Spatone
understand. May I remind you he's a criminal?"

"Cody, I work with criminals all day. And night. They have rights.
Some are even decent people."

"Oh, please." He tipped his rocks glass. "Could you do another?" She
nodded and he signaled for a fresh round.

"Want to know what it comes down to for me, more than anything
else?" she said. "I have a hard time with hotheaded behavior. Plain and
simple, it's a real red flag. And—Mr. Cody—especially upsetting because
I've never seen that as part of who you are. You're ballsy, and I kind of
like that. But you're a finesse guy. I like that even more." The new drinks
arrived. When the server left, she continued her thought. "So what I
need to ask is whether this is part of your total package, or is something
just up your butt today?"

He swirled the cubes and set the swizzle stick on the napkin beside
his glass. "All right, you want it?" He lifted his glass then set it back

down. "The reason I don't have that ID on the crew chief isn't because of the shitty Polaroid or that the tatt is only a partial. The Real Time Crime Center has done much more with far less. . . .We struck out because I struck out." This time he did go for a sip. "I called it in, and the desk detective I got was not a friendly, let's just say. No, let's call it out. I got dissed. By a guy I've known for years. Not closely, but we crossed paths often enough on the job, right? And I've even dealt with him successfully a time or two since I left the force. Today? A fucking wall of ice. He not only won't run the mystery man or his tattoo through the db, I get this lecture about abusing department resources. So you want to know what was up my butt—so far that it went up a mile and did a barrel roll? That. That is what was up my butt, counselor."

"I am so sorry." And she meant it. A couple of hours ago she was asking a former Internal Affairs detective to sniff around about Cody. Now, seeing him angry, hurt, and embarrassed, her heart went out to him. For the first time, Macie saw behind his wiseacre insouciance. Maybe Gunnar Cody had emerged from his NYPD departure more wounded than he let on.

"I don't need that." He flicked the air with his fingers, chasing away her sympathy as if fanning a gnat. "I'm just giving you a fair answer to a fair question." Cody made a study of his ice cubes like they would tell him something if he stared long enough. "You know," he said, "you spend your life thinking you're made of stronger stuff. You go through your shit storms and shake it off. Onto the next. Then, out of nowhere, some anal-retentive gatekeeper slams the door, raises the drawbridge, and then takes a piss on you from the ramparts because you're defrocked. You are outside, and outside you shall stay." The server appeared to take their food order, read the mood, and retreated. "Can I tell you something, Macie? I never thought anything could feel worse than the day I lost my badge. But today, today did." Of course, she very much wanted to know how he had lost it, but opted for patience. He was opening up to her in pieces on his own, and Macie didn't want him to feel cross-examined and shut down.

After they ordered their meals, she rested a hand on his arm. "Is this OK? You're not going to put me on the floor in a thumb lock, are you?"

"Uh, no."

"I can only imagine what all this brought back to you today, but I would say this. Don't empower those people. I see it in my office all the time. You've got to release yourself from the smalls and the unworthy."

She doubted that she had changed his life, but Macie's words came from her heart and were anything but pro forma. He had opened up to her in a way that exposed a vulnerability she never had anticipated. It was especially profound coming from a man she'd known only a few days. As they enjoyed their meal in newfound peace, he apologized for going ass-kick on Spatone. In balance, she acknowledged her hypersensitivity to cops coercing suspects. Macie even allowed that, maybe, there were a few gray areas. Back to Orwell and rough men who keep vigilance. "I just don't like to be around when it happens," she said. "Hate it, hate it."

"For the record, I am not a hothead. My approach to Spatone was calculated. Pure technique."

"Is this supposed to make me feel warm and fuzzy?"

"I mention it because you said hotheadedness was a red flag. Your words." He thought a moment and added, "I like you. I don't want red flags on my ass."

"Same," she said, hoping her smile masked the twinge about releasing Whittinghill to run a check on him. But he saw it.

"Am I hitting a nerve? Wave me off if this is too personal, but red flags come from experience."

He had shown his belly to her, but rather than confess about Whittinghill, Wild decided to share her own intimate sore spot. She told him about Paris: the engagement getaway that ended the engagement. "Second night of a romantic week in Paris. We'd spent the day wandering Luxembourg Gardens and the Musée D'Orsay. We got a perfect table at Allard."

"The Alain Ducasse spot on the Left Bank."

"So you know it. We were being treated like royals—he's William, I'm Kate. The champagne is flowing, the meals are served. He gets their signature dish, the duck with olives. It's perfectly medium rare, a shade of terra cotta set against the green olives. It's what you see on a *Bon Appétit* cover. I get out my cell phone to take a picture of his plate, and he slaps it out of my hand." Cody's eyebrows popped. She nodded, affirming. "Not a 'please, don't' or an 'I'd rather you didn't, honey.' Swatted the phone out of my hand, right onto the table beside us."

"May I say? Holy shit."

"You may. I was stunned. The whole restaurant was stunned. When I could finally talk, I said, 'What did you just do?' And he says, 'Are we here to eat or take pictures?' I left. Just walked. He followed me, but I got a taxi back to the hotel. I won't get into it all—I've probably overshared already—but he shows up with flowers, an apology, lame explanations; all of it after I'd just finished throwing up. He calls me too sensitive, I chuck his bouquet in the trash, he gives me a shove. Not a smack, mind you, but a hard shove. I got on the first plane I could book." Wild held up her hand and wiggled her fingers. "You'll note the diamond has left the building."

"How long ago?"

"Not enough."

"I'm sorry," he said, which is just about all that could be said. But then he gestured to his plate. "Listen, I'm just about done with my branzino, but if you're hot to do an Instagram . . . no prob." It was simply the perfect thing to say. Her laugh erupted so suddenly she covered her mouth with her napkin in embarrassment. She put her other hand on his arm again and, this time, left it there.

"Never thought I'd ever be able to laugh about that, Gunnar."

The sound of her calling him by his first name for the first time brought his eyes up to meet hers. The intimate stillness between them was broken by a man's voice.

"I understand you're looking for me."

They both turned to see who was speaking. There was no mistaking the man from the Polaroid, sitting at the table beside them.

CHAPTER 20

While Macie sat speechless, Gunnar hardly blinked. "I'm sorry," he said, "do we know each other?" The man didn't react. He possessed one of those neutral faces Wild usually saw on guys waiting for wheat grass shots at Liquiteria—all patience and ease and quiet confidence. Late thirties, he was lean like a competitive cyclist, but with the clean, polished head of a swimmer. But there was something off about him. Something about those deep-set blue lasers, which were so alert and assessing. Then it hit her—no eyebrows. Macie had known people in her life who suffered from alopecia, but, from his clean bearing, she took him to be a shaver.

Gunnar's forearm tensed under her hand and she tightened her grip, a silent plea not to go street in the bistro, please. He relaxed and appraised the crew chief, who had situated himself with Macie between them so Gunnar would need to climb around to reach him. Meanwhile he'd left himself a clear path to the exit. A shaver and a planner.

"This is going to be a short meeting," the man said. "Is this how you want to spend it?" His voice followed a flat line, as indifferent as his face. This was the focused temperament of a master burglar. And, reflected Macie, of a potential killer.

"How did you find us?" she asked.

"Let's talk instead about why." He laced his fingers together on the tablecloth in front of him. When he did, his eyes followed Wild's gaze to his ink, but he made no effort to conceal the tattoo, which led her to believe he wanted them to see it. "I'm here to do you a favor. I'm going to save you the trouble of spinning your wheels on me when you could be looking for Rúben Pinto's real killer."

"Oh, say no more." Gunnar bowed his head in mock gratitude. "If only OJ had been this forthright. Oh, wait, that *is* what he said." He leaned forward to direct his laugh to Macie and slid his chair back a few inches. The move wasn't lost on the visitor.

"If you're thinking of dealing a play, I'll be gone before you clear your seat."

Wild intervened. "Does this mean you know who actually killed Mr. Pinto?"

Not so much relaxed—call it tranquil—he slid his gaze off Gunnar to her. "Not my concern. Except to make clear that it's not I."

"And your concern about our wheel spinning wouldn't have anything to do with the inconvenience of us digging into your life?" Then she added, "For whatever we might find?"

"Let's not be cute." His thin lips twitched a minor smile. "You know what I do. And, damn straight, I don't like you routing around, potentially hindering my ability to do it."

"Do you have a name?" Gunnar came in bluntly, tired of playing this dude's game. "Mr. Clean?" He turned to Macie. "What was the name of the genie in *Aladdin*? Oh, right, Genie." Then, back to the crew chief. "What do we call you?"

A pause. "You don't."

"You seem smart," she said. "Enough to see we aren't being unreasonable. I have a client—Jackson Hall from your own crew—facing a murder one for a homicide he didn't commit. You factor into the equation perfectly, yet you expect us to take your denial at face value."

"Want to talk factoring in?" Gunnar waited for him to float his eyes back to him. "I hear there was trouble in paradise. Your boyee Rú was doing some skimming out of your haul. I call that a motive."

"Call it what you want."

"We know he secretly lifted a Grammy. What else did he steal from your take? Something bigger? More valuable? Or did you teach Pinto a lesson on principle? Some honor-among-thieves kind of thing?"

Rather than buckle under the taunts and questions, the man answered one that hadn't been asked yet. "I was nowhere near Pinto's apartment when it came down. In fact, I've never even been there."

Gunnar bent forward. "You have an alibi?"

"In fact, I do."

"What is it?"

"Air tight."

"What does that mean?"

The crew chief rocked his head side to side, dismissing it as a stupid question. Then he decided to dignify it. "Here's a big word for you. It means 'unassailable.'"

"How so?"

There was a clatter of wheels as the restaurant host delivered an aluminum walker up to a nearby table and helped an old woman up to her Rollator. As soon as they shuffled into the aisle, hemming in Gunnar and Macie, the crew chief glided to the exit without casting a look back. They both stood to follow, but there was no way to get to him without bowling over the senior and her party. The only sign of him was the glass door near the reception podium slowly closing in his wake.

Gunnar sat back down. "You're not going to chase him?" she asked, also taking a seat.

"And put Nana in the ER on her night out?" He slipped his phone out of his pocket. "Not that I didn't think about it. But he's vapor by now, trust me."

The aisle finally cleared. "You sure you don't want to . . ."

"Chase him? I would, if I didn't have a better idea." He held his screen up, said, "Give me a sec," and replied to a text message. When he finished, he asked, "You want to order an espresso or a tea or something? That brownie sundae looked pretty good."

"I'm not understanding how you can just sit there."

"You wanted finesse?" He gestured to himself. "This is what it looks like."

After a double espresso for him and an Earl Grey for her, they strolled two blocks to Amsterdam where Gunnar had parked his van in front of a Chirping Chicken. A pudgy young guy in his late twenties who had his long black hair tied up in a bandana was leaning against the E-350's curbside fender, forking some *arroz con pollo* from a takeout container. Even at a distance, they could see that about 20 percent of the transfer never made his mouth and had come to rest on the ledge created by the bulge of his stomach. "Remember how I said everybody needs 'a guy?' Well," said Gunnar, "this is my guy. Say hello to CyberGauchito. CyberG, this is Macie Wild."

"Yeah, so I got from your Facebook pic," he said, lightly accented in Spanish. "Oh. My bad." He transferred his plastic fork to the food container and shook. His hand was moist and kind of squishy. Wild managed to smile, and fought the urge to wipe her palm on her clothes. She thought about Purell and how it was this guy already knew about her.

Gunnar had given her a one-block briefing on the hacker she was about to meet, a Black Hat from Buenos Aires, self-nicknamed after an Argentine folk hero with magical powers, Gauchito Gil. "A lot of hacktivists come from down there," explained Gunnar. "Apparently where he grew up there are so many have-nots, that legions of young people like the CyberGauchito had no money for gaming, software, or even Wi-Fi, so they learned to hack it. Now it's grown to a gutsy subculture born out of necessity. Some of the exploit coders—hackers who expose software vulnerability to companies so they can patch it—make up to a million for writing one exploit. A lot of them have put their millions into start-ups and spawned a legit tech industry in Buenos Aires." The tubby guy with the see-through beard and granny glasses looked like anything but a budding millionaire, but magical powers can work wonders, she thought. Didn't the FBI pay someone that much to break into the San Bernardino terrorist's iPhone?

"Hey, man, you picked the right parking spot." CyberG gestured with his fork to the storefront, spilling more rice onto the sidewalk. "The food here is insane." He shoveled two more helpings into his mouth and, still munching, shit-canned the remainder in the basket on the corner. "Wanna get to it?"

His guy's girth made space too tight for all three of them to fit comfortably inside the cargo hold, so Gunnar winged open the rear doors, and they stood in a cluster while the Gauchito unloaded a black box and a printout from his backpack onto the carpeted floor. "This afternoon," Gunnar explained, "I gave CyberG Spatone's phone number, figuring, as a freelance fitness trainer, his business number was also his cell."

"It was," said CyberG.

"The idea was to monitor Spatone to see if he called anyone after we rattled his cage."

"He did." Again from the Gauchito.

Macie whipped her head to Gunnar. "You had him hacked?"

"Uh," said Gunnar's guy, speaking his mission statement, "kinda what we do."

As Wild tossed ramifications, she asked, "And you can just do that?"

CyberG cackled at the naïveté of the question. Gunnar asked what he had learned. "Well, I didn't do a voice tap. That's a bit more involved for short notice. But I did get into his carrier for outgoing calls. Ninety-three minutes ago . . . that's about right, right?"

"Right," said Gunnar.

"Ninety-three minutes ago, your man placed two calls to the same number. Don't get too excited. It's a burner." He turned to Macie. "Single-use cell phone."

"I know burners," she said.

"Then you know the bad news. Not registered to a name or an address. Minutes probably paid for by an untraceable or stolen card. But the good news—CyberGauchito always has good news, *es verdad?*"

Gunnar played their little game. "*Es muy verdad.*"

"*Absolutamente.*" He spread a printout of a Lower Manhattan street map on the brown shag. "I have a ping off a cell tower where both calls were received."

"How far apart?"

"The calls? First call was like a minute. Second call was longer. Three minutes, and it came sixteen minutes after the first call."

Gunnar ran some calculations, but Macie beat him to it. "Spatone called the crew chief right after we left. The crew chief probably told him to follow us. When he saw us go into Isabella's, he called back to report. That's how he found us."

"Macie Wild, you may have a future in detection," said Gunnar. He bent to study the map. His hacker had drawn a circle around the location of the cell tower that received Spatone's calls. "Same tower for both calls, so that means he probably wasn't in his car or on the move. Not a for-certain, but somewhere in this circle could be either his home or his office, or whatever." He angled himself to let Macie have a better look.

"Hate to be the wet blanket," she said, "but that's a two-block radius, downtown. We're talking high-rise offices, apartments. . . .What do we do, go down there and yell, 'Marco!' and wait for, 'Polo'?"

CyberG smiled. "Actually that's sort of exactly what you're going to do." He set the black box in front of Gunnar. "Signal-strength meter. Programmed with your crew chief's burner cell number. It's still a needle in a haystack, but if you drive or walk the zone I indicated on the map—and assuming he hasn't run the battery down or turned it off or pulled the SIM from his phone—you might pick up his signal. Then it's a matter of following the strength of its output on the meter to home in on him."

Gunnar looked at his watch. Wild said, "Tonight? You mean now?"

"Would you rather wait until he runs down the battery or shitcans the phone?"

Wild looked up at the darkening sky and said, "Know what I'm learning? Never have a meal with you without bringing an overnight bag."

Once again Wild found herself behind the wheel of the custom cargo van, this time driving a grid pattern of the Financial District while Gunnar rode shotgun with his nose to the black box cradled on his lap. Although cheaper rents near Wall Street had coaxed droves of millennials downtown, mostly as craigslist roommates, the streets rolled up at night after the stock markets closed and happy hour ended, which made traffic perfectly accommodating for Macie's low-speed circuit. "OK, I'm getting something," said Gunnar, but without excitement. She noted the ex-cop had slipped into his dispassionate tone again. Surveillance mode, she thought. "Can you slow it down?"

Wild took it to eight miles per hour. As they passed Hanover Square she glanced to the passenger seat and saw the blue LED numbers on the signal-strength meter getting busy. She couldn't tell whether they were going up or down, though, and Gunnar's expression gave nothing away. At the stop sign in the perplexing five-point intersection where William and South William met Beaver Street, he twirled a forefinger to say keep rolling, and she did. "Losing it."

"Sorry."

"No, that's a good thing." He directed her to circle back around until they found a parking place. It took some hunting but she snagged one half a block from South William Street. They got out and walked the neighborhood. After some trial and error, the black box led them to a Gilded Age brownstone near the five-point merge. They walked both sides of the building from end to end and got the strongest reading on the Beaver Street side. "So it's one of those," said Cody as they stood across the street taking in the facing apartments.

"Now that we know the building. What do we tell the police?" He gave her the look she had first seen outside the crime scene when he passkeyed Rúben Pinto's door. It said, "Get real." "Gunnar, he might be a material witness to a homicide. Why did we go to all this trouble if we're not going to let the police take him?"

"Because we actually want to learn something. And they might just send him underground."

"Learn something how?"

But he already was crossing the street with the black box. Macie almost followed until she saw him climb the scaffolding in front of the optician's next door to the old building. When he reached the second floor, he made a Tarzan swing off the pipe over to the fire escape of the apartments and started reading the blue glow as he ascended.

"Top floor, corner," he said, back on the sidewalk. Macie traced six floors upward to the only illuminated windows. "I see this as a two-camera job." Gunnar clamped his free hand lightly on her arm. "You up for being my best boy?" She lingered in thought, unable to ignore how much she welcomed the familiarity of his contact.

"Gee," she replied, "how can a boy refuse?"

In a single trip from the van they carried two robotic video cameras, a pair of telescoping tripods, and a duffel containing small sandbags, Wi-Fi receivers, and a couple of unidirectional shotgun mics. "Careful not to drop those cams," said Gunnar. "You're basically carrying my NYPD severance." Using his fireman's passkey, they entered the apartment lobby across the street from the crew chief's place and climbed the internal stairs to the rooftop.

At the ledge facing across the street to the target apartment, Gunnar took out his mini binocs to survey the windows where he had gotten the strongest signal. "No movement, no crew chief," he said. The drapes were open but, from Macie's vantage, all she could make out was a living room in one window and the bedroom in the other. Finished with his initial survey, the ex-TARU detective methodically went about unpacking the cams from their cases, mounting them to their tripod heads, and aiming each at a window. "Wanna sandbag those so we don't get any drift?" It only took her a beat to process what he meant, then she placed one of the small canvas saddle bags on the foot of each tripod leg. He tested both setups with a jiggle, gave her a satisfied nod, and added, "Two more for the microphones." While he knelt to train one directional mic on each room, Wild draped sandbags to fix them in place too. "For someone with a bug up her ass about bugs, you're pretty good at this," he remarked as he snapped in his Wi-Fi connections and powered up the battery.

"I also hate cleaning my bathroom, but I do it."

"You're so fancy." He tossed the last sandbag on top of the empty duffel so it wouldn't blow away and strode across the roof to the access door. "Let's invade some privacy, shall we?"

Back inside the cargo hold of the van, Gunnar Cody exercised his rituals of turning to a fresh page in his spiral notebook and logging the date and time of the surveillance start from the codes on the monitor. Next he tested the joystick governing each camera, putting them through their robotic pans and tilts, adjusting the LoLux mode for the light, then pushing in and pulling back with their 30x optical zooms. "Still no sign of life?" asked Wild, also following custom by squeezing into her familiar-ish place on the folding chair beside him.

"He's in the shower, listen." Gunnar raised the gain on the directional mic trained on the bedroom window. Even through the glass, the muted sound of water in a stall was unmistakable.

"Amazing." Then she added, "And scary."

"Here at RunAndGunn-dot-com, we do both."

Accustomed to the glacial pace of a stakeout, Wild busied herself dimming the screen of her smartphone and relaxed. She knew better than to ask what they hoped to learn, but did anyway, just to have some conversation. Patiently he reiterated that the nature of this work was to catch what you could, and that you didn't always know what it would be until it happened or got said—if it ever did. The life lesson he'd learned as a scuba diver was that the best way to meet the fish isn't to chase them but to sit on a rock and let them come to you.

A squeak, probably the shower faucet turning off, brought his hand to his phone. "I do have a plan to stimulate the action though."

"Isn't that chasing the fish?"

"Let's call it throwing out chum." He held up a pause finger and spoke to his phone. "Amador, *mi idiota*, how the fuck dumb do you think I am?" He listened, nodding, then said, "Nah-ah-ah, don't hang up, not if you know what's good for you. Do you really think I couldn't figure out that you tailed us to Isabella's so you could sic that dickless cue ball on us?" He held the phone away and Macie could hear Spatone's shrill protests through the earpiece. "Listen, dipshit, do not—Amador, do not insult my intelligence with your lame denials. Save them for the probation officer I'm sending your way. We know your pal Uncle Fester did Pinto. He denies it but his excuses are as puny as your dick. We know Pinto skimmed the Grammy from Woody Nash's. We also know all about the paintings from The Barksdale job. I'll bet that's what got him killed. I'm also betting you helped, so get your affairs in order, buddy. There's a room waiting for you upstate as accessory to murder one." Gunnar pressed end and checked his watch. "Please stand by."

He pressed a speed dial. Whoever answered did so on the first ring. "We cool?" He smiled, said, "You're the best," hung up, and turned to Macie. "My CyberGauchito was conferenced in on that call to Spatone, and when Amador picked up, CyberG ran a malware code that gave him a voice tap on his line. One of the directional mics picked up the ringer of a mobile in the apartment. As soon as the man answered, "This is Jeff," Gunnar flipped a switch on the console. Spatone's voice spilled over the van's speakers, "Hey, man we've got some bad shit happening."

On their separate pads, Macie and Gunnar jotted the first name of the crew chief as he questioned his caller in even tones. "Amador, breathe. Tell me what's got you so rattled."

Spatone barked out the call he'd just received from Gunnar, ending with, "This guy's bad news, Jeff. Says you killed Rú and he's going to hang it on me for conspiracy." They listened to his breath scratching erratically on his mouthpiece. Up on the monitor, Jeff appeared for the first time. In sweatpants and a long-sleeved tee, he crossed by the bedroom window then disappeared, only to reappear in the living room. Wild fixed her eyes on that screen as he approached the window to look down at the street. His bald head gleamed, reflecting the city lights. She concentrated her thoughts, willing him to admit that he was the killer. Like it would happen in a movie or cop show.

But this wasn't, and he didn't.

"Amador. Listen to me. You need to control your emotions. This opera of yours is why you didn't make the cut."

"Fuck that shit, man," he hollered, making Jeff's point. "I don't need this kind of trouble. Are you even hearing this?"

They watched the crew chief draw the phone away from his ear and stare at it, as if considering a hang up. Instead he resumed the conversation, still sounding unfazed. "Amador, trouble is only going to come if you don't hold it together."

"Bull shiiiit. I know how these things work. Dude's squeezing my balls cause he wants yours. And now that lawyer has me down for tossing the bitch's crib the other night."

"Then you should be glad I didn't let you come along." Gunnar nudged Macie and traced a check mark in the air. Her flyer of a question to Spatone had smoked out the crew chief as the wrecking ball at Cilla Dougherty's place. "My advice to you is pop a Xanax."

"You've got lots of advice, homes. Like now you're telling me to chill. You need to get some pulse goin', man."

"I'm chill because everything *is* chill." The crew chief turned from the window and walked a slow circle, barefoot, around his living room.

"Easy when you're protected, and I'm not." Spatone's words lit up both faces in the van. Macie jotted the word: Protected. Then drew a circle around it. Gunnar simply logged the time.

"You want protection? Shut your pie hole." The slang, delivered so dispassionately, made it sound all the more menacing. "If you're getting hassled, go take a long drive for a couple weeks."

There was a pause from the other end. Then Spatone said, "That's it, huh. Don't I even get a thanks for the heads-up?"

"Thank you for the heads-up. And good night." The crew chief ended the call and tossed his cell phone on the sofa. Macie and Gunnar watched him pass through the bedroom again and waited until they heard the sink run and the chugging of a Waterpik before they spoke.

"Protected," she said. "So what's it mean? I mean, I know what it means. I just don't know how exactly."

"Could mean lots of things. Protected could be armed. Could be connected to a mob or gang—highly likely, given the crazy access he gets to secure buildings. Plus, this guy's not going to Flamingo's to pawn a Sargent or a Chagall. Safe bet he's got some hardwired connections for that." She studied the angular cut where Gunnar's jaw met his neck, watching the almost imperceptible flex of muscles as he worked something out. "Then there's the other kind of protection."

"Police?"

"Police, pols . . . I've seen it all. Shit rolling upstream to some pretty eye-popping places over the years. Usually they cross-pollinate with the gangs and mobs. Hard to say what we have here. Haven't heard enough."

They sat in silence the better part of another hour, watching and listening. Occasionally Gunnar used his controllers to pan and zoom the windows to study the layout. Unfortunately the apartment was as spare as the tenant. No stacked boxes of stolen items on the dining table or multimillion-dollar canvases leaning against the foot of the king-sized bed. Jeff the crew chief occupied himself on the living room couch flipping between an old episode of *Dog The Bounty Hunter* and a sharpshooter competition on the History Channel. His cell rang. He picked it up but set it back down without answering. CyberG's worm was programmed to have Spatone's call infect the burner so Gunnar had a readout of the ID, but it said, "Private Caller." It rang again. The crew chief hesitated, muted the TV, and answered.

"Don't dodge my call again," said the man on the other end. Jeff didn't reply. Just waited. The caller continued. "I need a status update."

The crew chief turned off the TV. "I'd call if it turned up."

"Turned up. Sounds like you're not looking."

"I am on this."

"After what happened with your handpicked crew, confidence is low. You don't want confidence to be low." After a short pause, the voice continued, but more clipped, "Lose this phone. It's contaminated." And the caller dropped.

Jeff powered off the disposable, removed the SIM card, and sat staring at the dead TV. A low droning sound startled Macie. Their subject left the couch and crossed the room. Gunnar panned the lens with him. He took the receiver off the wall unit. Someone was buzzing from the lobby.

Minutes later the crew chief opened his front door and waited. Not long after, a woman came in and introduced herself as Dora.

"You're late."

"They shut the J train. I had to get a cab."

The man stood there, looking her over; she stood there, letting him. Gunnar zoomed to see her as best he could. She was partially blocked by a pillar at the corner of the kitchen counter. Then, as if telepathically, Jeff stepped back and beckoned her forward. She advanced into plain view. Dora had on an olive-green blazer, carefully torn jeans, and construction boots. Under the blazer, she wore a tight top with her bust spilling over and showing plenty of cleavage. "Prostitutes don't look like prostitutes anymore," said Gunnar.

"Maybe you don't know it when you meet one," Macie replied. And then added, ". . . Detective Profiler."

"Know what Dora looks like to me? Not a hooker at all. More like the hot young mom from Albuquerque who didn't get past the blind auditions on *The Voice*."

Wild laughed in spite of herself. "It's a job, like any other, as long as it's consensual."

"Construction boots?" asked the crew chief.

"I can take them off."

"Maybe . . ." As he continued to appraise her, Dora dropped her over-sized purse on the floor and pulled off the scrunchy that was holding her wavy hair back. She shook her head to free the curls, and they fell, brushing her shoulders. She smiled provocatively. He said, "No. Put it back up."

She didn't move. "Make me."

"Is that what you want?"

"Is that what *you* want?" She unbuttoned the single button of her blazer and, scissoring the scrunchy between two fingers, stuffed the elastic band deep enough into her cleavage to disappear, then traced the fingertips across her lower lip.

Gunnar said, "I think she just put the sensual in consensual."

Jeff moved a step closer to her. "You really want me to make you?"

The woman retreated a step away, countering in a semicircle, teasing him. "Do you think you can?" He took another step, and she took one of her own to the side. "Cause I'd really like you to try and make m—."

His left hand sprang out and took hold of her hair. Macie gasped. But the woman flashed teeth in a challenging grin as he clutched her. "Yeah, like that. Make me, Jeff, make me." He kept his grip, smiling only slightly in return, and drew her toward the bedroom. Just before reaching the doorway, she ducked and twisted herself free, then spun behind him pressing herself on his back so he couldn't reach her. He spun to face her, and they threw themselves into a kiss. Anything but romantic, it was feral; two animals at danger play, signaling hunger and menace. Locked in their clinch, he walked her backward. The camera lost them between rooms but the bedroom cam picked them up, still mouth-to-mouth, but he had peeled off her blazer and she let it fall to the floor as he tumbled with her onto the bed.

"You doing OK?" asked Gunnar.

Wild realized she had been holding her breath. "Ah, what's the, um protocol here?"

"Usually it's to tip her if she does a good job."

On the screen, the crew chief had his sweatpants off and had straddled her with a knee pinning down each arm. "Still want me to make you? Huh?"

"Want to know what I want? Here's what I want." She raised her head up between his thighs, her mouth open, struggling to reach him, while he teased her, playing keep-away.

Macie looked off to the side. "By protocol, I mean, do you sit and watch this?"

"Truthfully, it's all clinical to me, as many of these as I've seen." He gave her a thoughtful look. "You're uncomfortable."

"Well, it's . . . it's nothing I'm used to."

"Sure, well, let's help you out." He threw two switches and the monitors went black.

Wild waved both hands. "You don't have to do that. Doesn't that mess you up?"

He shrugged. "I've still got audio, if he happens to blurt out a confession at the money moment." Reading her, Gunnar also lowered the volume a hair.

"Thanks. I appreciate . . . Thanks."

The two of them sat side by side at the console facing blank monitors, eavesdropping on a sexual encounter. Amid the moans and bed squeaks and unintelligible mumbles dampened by a window between the couple and a microphone across the street, Macie thought back to her first time on surveillance just two nights before when she'd gotten on her soapbox to Gunnar about nothing being sacred anymore. Now she was a participant in her own cautionary tale. And as much as she tried to stave it off, she found her attention not only pulled to the audio, but attracted to it; not picturing the burglar and call girl she had seen on the spy camera but her own idealized, imaginary sex partner. When the hoarse moans fell into a rhythm, she let her gaze drift beside her. Macie was busy trying to mask the flush she felt. Gunnar sat as she always had seen him at that console, stoic and detached. But was he? she wondered. What was really going on behind that aloof coolness? He felt her gaze and turned to her and she snapped her head away, pretending to make a note. If he registered her little moment, he didn't let on. Ever stoic, ever cool.

But then, as the man's groans grew to shouts, Gunnar turned the volume all the way down.

"You don't have to do that for me."

"Not a problem. A block away, and I bet we could hear him without the mics." He got out his phone to check e-mails and texts. "We'll join the happy couple for the postcoital glow. Meanwhile, smoke 'em if you got 'em."

Ten minutes later he slid the audio back up slightly. "Still?" said Wild. The crew chief was still groaning, albeit sounding subdued, perhaps because of the low volume.

Gunner snickered. "*Que macho hombre.*"

He backed off the level so it was deep in the background. Then suddenly Jeff's moans became urgent, then a cry. "No, no, no, I don't know, I don't know . . ." Followed by other voices. Dora's, plus another man's. Gunnar jerked upright in his seat and powered up the monitors.

The pictures came on immediately to reveal Dora standing in the living room, fully dressed, looking into the bedroom where the crew chief lay naked in a bloodbath on the sheets with two powerfully built men standing over him.

CHAPTER 22

"Holy shit." Gunnar zoomed in closer on the bedroom. The goon with his back to the window shifted to lean over the crew chief and, when he moved, revealed to their camera that Jeff was not only naked, but bound at his wrists by handcuffs. Gunnar panned with the joystick to his ankles and saw he was cuffed there too.

"You going to be smart or keep bullshitting me?" said the goon.

"Not again, please." Jeff pleaded, broken, crying. "I don't know, I don't know, I d—!" The goon had a large plumber's wrench in his hand and he brought it down on the crew chief's knee. Jeff's scream split the air inside the van. An empty Poland Spring bottle on the console vibrated.

Macie's mouth had filled with gauze. She had to try twice before she could get any words out. "Don't argue. I'm calling 911."

But Gunnar was ahead of her. Keeping his eyes locked on the screen, he opened a drawer and pawed out a cell phone from a half dozen in there, burners, no doubt. "Hi, police? I heard a man screaming for help and I looked out my window and there's these two big dudes beating the crap out of a guy in the apartment across from me on Beaver Street." He paused and Wild could hear the operator's measured voice spill from the earpiece before he continued. "Hurry. Guy's bleeding pretty bad, I think they're trying to kill him." He gave the crew chief's address, floor number, and orientation, then hung up.

Up on the screen, Jeff had gone fetal, rocking on his side, whining, and holding his knee in his cuffed hands. The second goon muscled him onto his back again with a jerk of his leg irons, prepping him for another dose of pipe wrench. Dora, the hooker, drifted in from the living room. "I found his cell phone. Look, the SIM card's out."

"Why's that?" asked the man with the pipe wrench. He turned to his victim. "Why's the card out?"

"Infected!" Jeff blurted eagerly, glad to have one question he could answer. ". . . Phone's bugged." His three invaders traded looks, then started making paranoid room scans, craning their necks high and low for hidden mics or cameras. The goon with the wrench went to the window and scoped the view.

As his gaze methodically tracked the length of the street and then along the facing buildings, Wild said, "Is he . . . ?"

"Yep. He is."

"Do you think he could . . . ?"

"Dunno. Lots of ambient light around here." Macie and Gunnar leaned forward in tandem, studying the face on his monitor. The thug's eyes explored patiently, expertly. They drifted right past the lens then snapped back. "Shit," muttered Gunnar. "We're blown."

Pipe Wrench turned to his accomplices. "Get him up. Get him the fuck out of here. Now. Now!" Without hesitation the pair descended on the bed. Dora untucked the sheet and rolled Jeff in a swaddle, concealing his nakedness and restraining his protesting body at the same time. The second big man hoisted him over his shoulder like a sack of rice. It only took seconds. They had this drill down.

Gunnar sprung out of his chair and jammed a hand in his messenger bag, coming out with a Sig P220 Elite. He ejected the magazine to check his loads then slid it back in. "They're going," said Macie. Gunnar looked up from chambering a .45ACP. On the living room cam, Dora left the apartment followed by the goon hauling the crew chief. Pipe Wrench, however, reappeared in the window. He found the lens again and stared into it, cold, defiant. Macie felt a twitch at her lower back. Then the man made a pistol with his bare hand, aiming his forefinger at them. He mouthed, "Pow," stared a beat longer, then turned and left too.

Gunnar said, "Wait here," and opened the cargo door. As soon as he did, blue, white, and red flashes bounced off the storefront they were parked in front of and disco-balled the inside of the darkened van. The unmistakable deep-pitched rumble of a police car engine roared by, followed by another. Revised plan. Gunnar stayed inside, slammed the hatch, and lit up the E-350's rooftop cams. Another screen came to life; a street view of NYPD blue-and-whites responding to the call, converging up the block. "First Precinct, man," he said. "They don't dick around." Macie tried to read his tone. Was she hearing respect or disappointment?

"Were you hoping to rescue him yourself?"

"Hell, I wanted to get inside that apartment. See what's-the-what in there." He flicked on his scanner, programmed to monitor the secret tactical frequencies. The space crackled with cop talk: monosyllables and ten-codes punctuated by beeps and squelches. The uniforms were deploying. Gunnar placed another anonymous 911 call, adding his eyewitness update about the victim, kidnapped, and on the move, trussed in a bloodstained bed sheet, plus descriptions of the attackers. It all came back over the air in a monotone from the dispatcher in seconds. "And, of course, I would have rescued him," he said as an aside when he retook his seat.

"No editorial. Just wondering."

"Right. Here's a tip, counselor. Don't try to BS a cop." He tapped his nose and winked. "Highly developed fecal detector."

The two of them sat watching the street fill up with more cruisers and listened to the real-time soundtrack of the uniforms making their search. Gunnar translated the radio calls for Macie, annotating the jargon. The responders quickly located the empty apartment—that broadcast came even as they clocked the officers going through the living room and bedroom on their rooftop spy cams. TAC frequencies gave the play-by-play of the building search; clearing the elevators and stairwells. Then came the call for a chopper. "Desperation move," said Gunnar.

"You know that for a fact?"

"From odds. They're not toting this dude around downtown like a side of beef. Organized like they were, count on a waiting vehicle, maybe two. Trust me, they're history."

"So what's next? What do we do?"

"We're doing it." He extended both arms over his head and stretched, tipping his folding chair on its hind legs, then leaned forward over his console, tweaking the joysticks. Two of the flat screen's split panels zoomed in closer on the apartment windows. "If you can't visit the crime scene, counselor, visit the virtual one."

"Is this legal?"

He chuckled. "Know what I'm gonna do? I'm going to put a jar over here so you can drop a quarter in it every time you ask me that."

The helicopter arrived, lighting up alleys and the mountain ranges of plastic garbage bags on the sidewalks for the uniforms while they grid searched. Upstairs, the apartment filled with moon suits as the forensic crew checked in, strobing pictures and dipping down out of view to place yellow markers on the floor and mattress. The pair of detectives working the scene hung back, observing the lab unit and debating whether a new female sergeant on their squad was straight or gay, their conjecture broken only by speculation whether the Mets would ever spring for some gloves. Macie said, "This is like WFAN without the commercials. Or expertise."

"Know why they call surveillance being a fly on the wall? Because that's what you attract with all this bullshit." He lowered the volume by half but slid it back up a few minutes later when a CSU tech approached the detectives with a small plastic bottle.

"I found this tucked away inside this." The forensic technician displayed something in the flat of his gloved palm. Gunnar tried to zoom on the object but they huddled around it, blocking his angle. Whatever it was, the detectives agreed it was worth checking out. The lead took out his cell phone and slipped off one glove so he could dial.

He identified himself and briefed the person on the other end where he was. "The Geek Squad found a slip of paper in an empty Advil bottle with a garbled bunch of numbers and letters. Can you run it through the db?"

"He's on to the Real Time Crime Center," explained Gunnar. "They can crunch it through the database. Sometimes you get a hit on something useful like geo coordinates or a secret bank account. Sometimes it's just somebody's Powerball pick."

The lead detective held the slip of paper under a lamp and slowly read it off. "Set? 'TRDS73##RWM*BC//KIQQ.'" When he recited it a second time for verification, Macie double-checked her notes. Gunnar, on the other hand, finished keying it into an encrypted text to Cyber-Gauchito to run his own search.

While they awaited the search results, Macie and Gunnar watched a replay of the video they had blacked out. They saw the hooker slip handcuffs onto the unsuspecting sex partner as her accomplices let themselves in and commenced a brutal interrogation. By midnight, neither Cody nor the NYPD had yet scored a hit on the alphanumeric code. A supervisor showed up in the apartment to report that, following a building and neighborhood canvass, there were no eyewitnesses to the home invasion or the abduction. "What did I tell you?" said Gunnar. "History."

Wild's cell phone thrummed on the console beside her, and when she answered, she sat upright, on full alert. "When?" She checked the digital time code in the corner of the screen and nodded as she listened. "I'll be right there." She hung up and stood, bumping her head on the carpeted ceiling. If it bothered her, she didn't let on. "Jackson Hall's out of his coma."

Dr. Edda met Macie and Gunnar at the elevator when they stepped off into the jail ward at Bellevue. As they cleared security, she presented the circumstances guardedly. "When people do this on TV, they're always wide awake. Trauma to the brain isn't like that. It's not like a switch gets thrown and they light up." Caveats aside, there was no denying the joy radiating from the doctor. "We're always quantifying on a scale. On the low end, you've got no recovery. Up a notch from that is a vegetative state, and so on. Mr. Hall came back to us in what we classify as a minimally responsive state. Lots of gaps and lulls, but he knew his name and could follow simple instructions like squeezing my hand on command. Over the past few hours he's progressed to small amounts of rudimentary conversation and can pick up things on his tray and put them back where they were." The neurologist smiled. "For a little guy, he's got a lot of will."

Gunnar spoke for the first time. His question ran true to form. "How soon can we talk to him?"

In response Dr. Edda appraised Cody then said, "Cops."

They were shown a place to wait in the lounge where, through the crosshatch of security bars over the windows, they could make out a sliver of red taillights on the FDR between darkened hospital wings. Just past two a.m., Dr. Edda escorted them to Jackson Hall's room, cautioning them on the way that their visit would be brief and not to disturb or excite him. "This goes against the grain for me," she said to Wild, "but when I told him you were here, he beamed." Stopping outside his door, she regarded Gunnar again. "Nice and easy, right?" Then she stepped away to confer with a nurse.

Jackson Hall did indeed smile at her when Macie entered and stood beside his bed. Sure, it was disconcerting the way his eyes stayed locked on her for so long but Dr. Edda had prepared her for that. She took his hand, which felt dry and papery, but he gave her a firm return squeeze and his grin widened. So he wouldn't be thrown, she introduced Gunnar Cody as someone who was helping her with his investigation. But Hall's expression clouded and he swept anxious looks from him to her. Reading the moment perfectly, Gunnar spoke softly. "Glad to meet you, sir. And that you're doing better." Then he retreated to a corner chair so Wild and her client could have their own time—while he monitored.

Beginning slowly, Macie asked how he was feeling. Hall pondered that a bit and whispered, "Alive." His raspy laugh made her throat sore, but she grinned back. Gauging him to be more lucid than she'd expected, Wild eased into some questions, fearful he might relapse at any moment.

"Do you recall how this happened?"

His eyes drifted closed and the sheet slowly rose and fell on his rib cage. "Some fucks took me from behind." He drew a sharp breath of remembrance and his lids popped open. "Strung me up. Left me to die." The corners of his mouth twitched a quick grin. "Here I am."

Hall asked for some water, which she gave him from the cup and straw on his tray table. After a full minute of silence, Jackson Hall spoke again. Frailty vanquished for now, his voice came barbed with anger and resolve. "Too many killings. And, Lord, what will they do next?" He turned his head to Wild. "No more protecting anyone. Done with that shit."

Seizing the opening, Gunnar jumped right in. "Jackson, do you know this man?" He came over and showed a screen grab of Luka Borodin.

Hall nodded, but didn't seem fazed. "Some friend of Fabio's. Hung out at the pier a couple times lately. Russian, or some shit. Came and went. Why?"

"Was he ever there when Pinto was there?"

After a moment to think back, Hall said, "No. And I remember cause he was always asking for Pinto. Why wasn't Pinto around, stuff like that." He gave them a look. "You think he—?"

Dr. Edda and a nurse came through the door. "His heart rate set off an alarm at the nurses' station." She took her patient's pulse while the nurse charted his vitals off a monitor. "I really think it's best we call it a night, Ms. Wild."

Gunnar said, "But we were just starting to—"

"—I have to insist."

Gunnar made the slowest exit in history, still talking to the patient. "Do you think you could tell us some of the places you and your crew hit? I mean besides The Barksdale?"

"I am sorry. You have to leave. At least for the night." Gentle, firm, and the final authority. As Macie and Gunnar headed for the door, Jackson Hall called to them.

"Morning," he said. "You come back then." Wild gave him a small wave and left.

On limited sleep, Macie Wild stood before the judge in Arraignment Part One at eight the next morning, entering pleas for a low-echelon drug dealer, a second-time order of protection violator, and a shoplifter. She finished up by securing a reduction of bail for a young woman who went on a four-hour spending spree at Macy's with a credit card she filched from a deli. Handing off her paperwork to her paralegal for processing, she pushed through the rear door of the courtroom to find Gunnar Cody riding the oak in the hallway outside Room 132, the office with the thick metal door and a sign that read, "Police Only." He smiled as if he'd been expected and held out a cup of Starbucks. "You do the dark roast with one Equal, right? Thought you'd want to be sharp for our meeting at Bellevue this morning." She hadn't made arrangements to go there with Gunnar, but clearly, in his mind, that was a done deal.

"Uh, thanks," she said, taking the coffee.

"Just another service we offer at RunAndGunn-dot-com." He gestured to the main lobby. "Van's right out front. That courtesy dash card, man. Still works like magic. Gotta love New York."

When they reached the hospital, instead of being led to Jackson Hall's room, Dr. Edda sat down with them in the lounge where they'd killed time the night before. The low deck of oystery clouds rolling in from Jersey had dampened the morning sun and filled the alcove with a dusky gloom. "I'm afraid you can't see Mr. Hall this morning. And no, it's got nothing to do with your . . . interview . . . last night. He's had a bit of a setback." She held up a hand in caution. "Nothing to be alarmed about. I told you, brain trauma recovery is slow. It also has its ups and downs. He's in a down right now, and needs rest."

"When do you think we can see him?" asked Gunnar.

"Maybe later today. Maybe in a few days. These things take their own time. But I understand you are eager to get some information from him."

"We are," said Wild. "But, if it's not to be . . ."

"He asked me to give this to you." The doctor held up a small envelope. "After you left last night, Mr. Hall insisted I write down some things and deliver them to you. Here." She handed the envelope across Gunnar to Macie, who opened the flap and took out a sheet of lined paper. It was a short list of apartment buildings. Beside each building was a date and a last name (probably of the resident). There was only one full name on the page. It was at the bottom and it was circled: Jeffrey Stamitz.

Gunnar surfed over her shoulder and said, "For a doctor, you have lovely handwriting."

"Thank you. And you still can't go in until he's ready."

They found a bench in Bellevue's atrium where they could wait out a passing cloudburst and survey the document. They began with the circled name, both agreeing that Jeffrey Stamitz must be the burglary crew chief. He had introduced himself as Jeff to Dora the hooker and used it on the call to Spatone. Gunnar got out his cell and thumbed it into a text. "I've got a bro up in the Seventeenth Precinct who'll run the name through the system for me." He hit send and wagged the phone. "And he won't ice me like that dickwad at RTCC. Why not? Because this bro owes me after I sent him some 'anonymous' head shots of Dora and the home invaders that I pulled from our surveillance video." Gunnar must have read her surprise at that because he responded, "Hey, you think I'm not going to share material evidence on some bad guys when a life is at stake?" But then he added, "Before you think I went all kumbaya here, I'm covering my ass legally. Yours too. No charge, counselor."

With an early jump on the day, and only four addresses on Jackson Hall's burglary list, Wild called Tiger to clear her schedule and rode uptown with Gunnar, hoping to interview some wealthy crime victims. On the call, Tiger had asked if she wanted Jonathan Monheit to meet up and accompany them. When she offered a simple, "No, thank you," Macie could hear the knowing smile in Tiger's voice as he also replied simply, "Understood." The subtextual exchange left her feeling like working with Gunnar Cody was developing into her dirty secret. She glanced over at him while he checked the side mirror for his merge onto the FDR and decided she could live with that.

They agreed to visit the apartments in the order of Hall's dictation. The first one was on East Fifty-Seventh off Sutton Place, just a few blocks north of where the crew had boosted the paintings from the pharma CEO's penthouse in The Barksdale. Macie and Gunnar used the fifteen-minute drive to talk strategy. First, they wanted to get a response to their photo array of the various players. Now that they felt confident they had pinned Stamitz as the crew chief, their greatest curiosity was whether anyone had seen Luka Fyodor Borodin. Luchik not only had attacked Macie, but either he or Stamitz could have been the white blur glimpsed at Rúben Pinto's murder scene. Gunnar had shown Pinto's neighbor both photos early that morning, but Dr. McBlaine still couldn't be sure. Second, they wanted an inventory of what got stolen in case there was a common thread or a pointer to a motive—or buyer. "I also want to get a sense of the revenge impulse from any of the victims," said Macie. "Although Borodin still tops my list for killing Rúben Pinto."

Gunnar couldn't resist a taunt. "You mean, assuming your client didn't kill him."

"Pull my pigtails all you want, but the more I learn, the less I see Pinto, Hall, and Stamitz as anything but victims."

"Spoken like a true public defender."

"I think I may put my own jar right here." Wild tapped a finger on the empty cup holder under the dashboard. "So you can drop a quarter in there every time you say that."

Instead of putting them on the elevator, the concierge of the Sutton Crest escorted Macie and Gunnar from reception across polished marble the color of desert sand. They reached a secluded recess of the first-floor lobby and a corner grouping formed by two black leather sofas and a love seat around a coffee table of lacquered wood and bronze. An elderly man watched every step of their approach. He had the love seat all to himself and looked enthroned there in his long white robe and headdress. The *ghutra* flowed over his narrow shoulders in the traditional Emirati way, rather than being folded. "I am Fahad Sharif," he said after dismissing the receptionist who delivered them. "You are with the police?"

At the mention of police, the three young men lounging on the pair of sofas slowly turned to them from the flat-screen TV that was showing a cricket match from Wales. They were in their early to late twenties—younger versions of him but in designer jeans and expensive tee shirts. Wild could see herself in the reflection of the nearest one's aviators as they passively regarded her. Then the trio lost interest and returned to their match: Sri Lanka versus Pakistan, according to the graphic. She was just about to fish out one of her Manhattan Center for Public Defense cards when Gunnar seized the lead.

"I'm Cody. This is my partner, Wild." Again so adept at speaking the truth that fosters the lie. He sure sounded like a cop, and if the wealthy foreigner from Dubai would accept obfuscation over identification, who was she to correct him? "We are here about the burglary of your apartment."

"Sit, please," he said and gestured to one of the sofas. A son or nephew, whichever he was, vacated it and rounded the coffee table to flop down with the other two. While she put away her business card and took a spot next to Gunnar, Macie assessed the surroundings. An apartment lobby, even a posh one, was not her ideal interview site, but the concierge had whispered to them that, although he had an entire floor to himself, Mr. Sharif liked to spend his mornings in the public areas of the building, usually in the company of his family. They had no complaints. First stop, they had scored a hit.

"I admit to a bit of confusion," said Sharif in English with a Brit flavor that hinted at UK schooling, maybe Oxford. "You see, I did not report a burglary to the police department." His eye went to Macie as she got out a notebook and pen but he didn't object. "How is it that you came here to talk to me then?"

Keeping the lead, Gunnar answered with his own question. "But you were robbed, were you not?"

The old man considered then said something in Arabic to the others. Without hesitation all three rose from their sofa and left, going around the corner to what must have been the elevator banks. When they were alone, Fahad Sharif said in a low tone, "I am quite ill, you see. And I do not wish to involve myself in petty upsets. It is a wellness strategy promoted by my oncologists. So when I discovered the theft, I resisted the impulse to pursue or avenge it." He angled his head toward Gunnar. "I have answered your question. Now, I ask you again, how did you come to know about it when I did not make a report?"

Wild slid forward on her cushion to reply, but her "partner" broke in. He said, "One of the burglars is in custody," once again telling a truth that maintained the illusion of being with the police. "This is a repeat customer. He admitted breaking in to your place."

"If he has confessed, what do you need me for?"

"Information," said Macie. Hoping they were past the charade part. "We wanted you to look at some photographs and tell us if you recognize anyone in them."

"That is not likely. We were not in residence at the time of the robbery. I only am here when I am in New York for my treatments at Memorial Sloan Kettering."

Macie said, "It must be helpful to have such a nice place near your treatment center."

He gave her a condescending smile. "Helpful . . . Yes. Which is why I bought it. Because MSK is nearby. For the few weeks a year I am in the city, it is quite convenient."

She laid an array of four-by-sixes on the table: Borodin, Hall, Pinto, Stamitz, Spatone, the Pipe Wrench duo, and Dora. Sharif slipped on a pair of glasses and studied them methodically. While he did that, Wild imagined the staggering amount of wealth that permitted someone to buy a multimillion-dollar penthouse basically for use as a hotel for the dates he was in town for treatment.

"I do not know any of these." He took off his readers and sat back, suddenly fatigued and ashen, resembling a faded picture of himself.

"Take your time," said Gunnar. "Even if you weren't here last month, is there anyone in this grouping who may have been hanging around? Maybe pretending to be a delivery person . . . Painter, plumber . . . anything?" Sharif looked again but with impatience. Finished, he shook no.

Fearful of losing his cooperation, Wild flipped to a blank page in her Moleskine. "Could you tell us what was stolen to compare with the burglar's account?"

He closed his eyes. The pause was so long Macie and Gunnar exchanged glances. Their witness wasn't dead, was he? "Jewelry," he said at last. When they asked for a description, he closed his eyes again and recited a list, mostly *thahab*, "Gold, in Arabic," he explained.

"Belonging to your wife or daughter?" she asked, earning a smile from him for knowing that Islam forbids men from wearing gold. "What was taken?"

He recited a list of necklaces, bracelets, anklets, rings, earrings, and bangles with specific recall of gold tone and precious stones. Missing from him was his collection of wristwatches. Two Cartiers, a Louis Moinet Tourbillon, a Patek Phillippe, a Piaget, and one Ernest Borel."

Wild did her best with the spelling and tallied the items on her list. While she did, Gunnar asked, "Can you give us an estimate of the loss?"

Without hesitation, he said, "Four hundred seventy-six thousand US dollars."

After the stunned silence that followed, Gunnar asked, "And you did not report this?"

"And invite more upset? Scrutiny? Interference . . . ?" He gestured to the two of them. "My illness has educated me that, once your family is cared for, a fortune is trifling when you have limited days remaining. Any problem that is only about money is not a problem."

Gunnar Cody's check-in with his contact at the Seventeenth yielded no progress finding the kidnapped burglary crew chief, Jeff Stamitz. Their next stop brought them to the luxury condo of another wealthy target, although this one had reported her burglary to the NYPD. The victim was Holland Bridgewater, author of blockbuster horror novels and a tips-to-riches success story, having leaped from waiting tables to landing on the *Fortune* 100 Highest-Paid Celebrities list in a span of four years. Her personal assistant retrieved them and took refreshment requests on the ride up to the fifteenth floor of the majestic limestone pre-war on Fifth Avenue. They waited while sipping mineral water from Baccarat crystal tumblers in the darkly furnished living room with views of the Loeb Boathouse in Central Park and the Dakota, just beyond Strawberry Fields. While a grandfather clock tapped off the seconds with somber strokes, Gunnar went to the window to enjoy the Central Park vista. Macie took in the expensive, albeit gloomy artworks: original oil paintings of eclipsed faces peering out from shadows, a castle rook in the middle of a graveyard sheathed in fog, an oxidized copper statue of a knight who was either melting or sinking into a bog.

When the writer appeared after ten minutes, she was already halfway across the thick carpet in her slippered feet before they noticed her. Holland Bridgewater smiled, introducing herself by her first name, and sat, hooking one leg under her. She was dressed for comfort in Gap jeans and a University of Vermont sweatshirt. Oh, and a necklace that Wild guessed could have paid her rent for the coming year and a half. "Sorry to keep you waiting. You caught me writing."

"Ten minutes," said Gunnar. "That's what for you? Two more best sellers?" Her response was unamused so he tried to recover. "I don't mean any disrespect. Just the opposite. You're so prolific. Didn't the *Huffington Post* call you the female Stephen King?"

"I see you haven't read me. Stephen is a god, but our styles are utterly different. I'd like to see some identification."

"Of course," Wild handed over her business card before Gunnar could speak.

Bridgewater gave it a glance and said, "You're not with the police?" Again skating ahead of Gunnar, Macie laid out the landscape. How she was defending one of the burglars, and that Cody was an ex-detective, and that they'd teamed up. In a lie of omission, she left out his VICE Media gig, assuming an investigative media connection wouldn't be so welcome here. The author considered in silence. "So I don't have to talk to you, do I?"

In a role swap, Gunnar turned to Macie, deferring to her. After all, he had already opened the conversation by tripping on his shoelaces. "That would be purely your option, Ms. Bridgewater. But since I'm assuming the police haven't done much for you, and the fact that my client was part of the team that was in here, my colleague and I are in a unique position to work toward recovering your property and bringing other participants to justice."

Bridgewater freed her leg from under herself and leaned forward, laser intent on Wild. "You mean there was a team of them in here?" Hooked, she gave the room a once-over, and it probably wasn't the gruesome artworks that had suddenly creeped her out. "The police never told me that."

"They probably don't know," said Macie.

Gunnar added, "Or aren't saying." His cred as an ex-cop was now working in his favor.

"I'd like you to look at some photos." Taking a page from the Cody playbook, Wild got right to it without asking for a green light.

After Macie dealt out the head shots on the coffee table, the author reacted. "Hold on. Are you saying all these people were in here that night?"

"No. Three, as far as we know. The rest may be involved in other ways."

"But involved," said Gunnar with a weight that was hard to miss. As with Fahad Sharif, they asked her to review the faces in the context of minor encounters the days and weeks prior to the break-in—even negligibly—such as with a delivery person or repairman.

"Afraid I won't be much help with that. I was gone writing the three months prior to the burglary. I sequester myself either at my place in Vermont or Bermuda when I'm on deadline. The only real reason to come to New York is for meetings with my publisher or to get a decent cosmo at Balthazar." She surveyed the faces anyway. Nobody scored a hit but she asked her assistant in to view the array. No matches there either.

Holland Bridgewater had some of her own photographs to share with them: a file of pictures she had taken of the stolen property years before for insurance documentation. The folder not only held the shots but a copy of the single-spaced list she had provided the NYPD detectives working the case. On it there was some jewelry plus rare collectibles including mint first editions of books such as *Notre-Dame de Paris, The Hound of the Baskervilles,* and *The Cask of Amontillado,* the quill pen used by Edgar Allan Poe to write it, a lock of Boris Karloff's hair, a shooting screenplay from *House of Wax* autographed by Vincent Price, and an obscure Austrian technical publication from 1893 entitled *Handbuch für Untersuchungsrichter, Polizeibeamte, Gendarmen.* Bridgewater said, "Translated it means *Handbook for Coroners, Police Officials, Military Policemen.* It was a groundbreaking work in forensics and has margin notes by the criminologist who wrote it."

"And criminals stole it. I'm seeing the irony here," said Gunnar, getting his first return smile from the writer. It didn't last.

"When can I expect my stuff back?" The process of review had picked at the scab. "You said your client was in on it. Can't you get my property back to me?"

"It's not so simple. He was attacked in jail and has been in a coma. But when he's well enough, I promise I'll try to find it for you."

Bridgewater said, "I'm no detective, but I make a living studying human nature's underbelly." She floated a copy of the list of her stolen property onto Wild's lap. "These aren't iPhones or Xboxes that can be fenced anywhere."

Gunnar picked right up because he was already there. "Somebody knew what to look for. They only took what they came to find. Can you think of anyone who knew they were here, or has expressed an interest in them? A collector, maybe?"

"The thing you obviously don't know is this: I make it a point to make sure nobody knows I'm even living here. Too many fans, too many nut jobs, too many aspiring writers who show up and want me to critique their 800-page manuscripts. I'm serious. My name's not even on the deed. I bought the place through one of the privately held limited liability companies my attorney set up for me. Any mail that gets delivered comes to Creve Coeur Enterprises LLC, not to Holland Bridgewater."

◊ ◊ ◊

"This one here." The Jets all-pro wide receiver double tapped one of the photos from the spread Wild had dealt out in front of him. "Him, I know." Macie and Gunnar tried not to telegraph their excitement as they craned from opposite sides of Larry Don Henkles to see who he was pointing out.

It was Rúben Pinto.

A handler from the athletic wear company that was paying the NFL star $5 million to endorse its brand strolled up. "Waitin' on you, Knife," he said, using the nickname Henkles got from the sound-alike cutlery company—and how he sliced through cornerbacks. Without excusing himself the athlete stepped away to crouch beside a kid in a wheelchair while photographers snapped away and a Channel 7 crew rolled video.

Macie and Gunnar had found Larry Don there at the children's hospital up in Harlem thanks to the doorman at his apartment building who bought Cody's cop pose—especially when he showed him the photo array. Who asks for a badge when you're getting fanned with mug shots? After poses and high-fives, the wide receiver made his way back over to them at the side table in the corner of the room. "You sure about him?" asked Macie, holding out Pinto's pic.

"Damn straight. Fuckin' weasel's dead meat, I see him again."

The defense lawyer in her wanted to caution him, but the moment passed when Gunnar started in. "Can you remember where and when you saw him? Was he hanging around your building? And how far before the burglary was it?" Larry Don's face pulled into a knot of dismay. The handler started over but he waved him off. "Something wrong?"

The football player's lips tightened and he worked them back and forth in thought. "I'm wondering if I should have my lawyer here."

Macie and Gunnar traded glances and she chimed in, "I promise whatever you say to us will be confidential, Mr. Henkles."

Her words or, maybe, her way, reassured him. "I didn't see him before. It was after. Two days after the break-in, a messenger drops off a letter at the front desk of my building. Note says he wants to sell me back my shit and to call this number and no cops or deal's off."

"Did you keep the note?" asked Gunnar.

"Yeah, but it's just some typing on a sheet of paper. No handwriting, no name even."

He was starting to clinch up again. Gunnar said, "Keep going."

"Uh, so we talked . . . and . . . OK, here's the deal. He wasn't offering back all my stuff. Not the jewelry, the artwork, or the cash they boosted. Just one thing. Something that wasn't on the list I gave the cops." He made a privacy check then continued in a low voice. "A book. See, I do some betting. And I keep this ledger. I like to see how I'm doing, how much I'm up, you see."

Gunnar knew the answer, just as Macie did, but he asked anyway. "Sports betting?" Henkles nodded. "NFL games?" Another nod. "Let me guess. Betting on some of your own?"

"Little fucker basically shook me down. You have to understand." For a split second, Macie thought she was about to hear a murder confession. But he said, "I agree to his price of three Gs to make this go away. On the day I'm ready to do this, he calls and says, 'Now it's gonna be ten grand.' Fucker's squeezing my balls. So I end up coughing up ten large to get the book back. He told me to do it in cash, twenties, and bring it to this autograph event I had a couple of weeks ago. He wanted to do it in public. So he's in line with the other collectors, and when it's his turn at the table, I'm signing his jersey, and he gives me a peek at my ledger in his manila envelope. I slide him my envelope, he slides me his, and he's gone."

"Did you talk?" asked Macie.

"Not him. But I did. I said you try to milk this or call the league, I'm coming for your ass and you will be dead. But first, you'll wish you were."

Macie heard the athlete's stabs of breath and wondered if, maybe, he would need a lawyer.

Not exactly on a budget that allowed for posh Upper East Side dining, they hit the salad bar at Eli's Essentials on Madison and had a lap lunch on the wooden sidewalk bench outside the storefront. Between bites and appraisals of passing couture and fancy dogs they reviewed what they had, and had not, learned from their interviews. Gunnar, whose detective training had taught him to look for these things, saw no apparent connections between the victims. All they had in common were wealth and the luxury apartments it afforded them. None of them knew each other nor did they belong to the same clubs, take part in the same charities, or socialize in the same circles. "One thing I did get though—nothing against rich people," said Gunnar just as a man with a bespoke face strolled by in $1,700 made-to-measure Ballys, "but half the vics we talked to were absent from their gazillionaire condos for months around the burglaries. I mean, who buys these luxe urban palaces and leaves them sitting vacant?" Hit by a second thought, he added, "I'm not offending you, am I? I mean, your family isn't exactly shaking cups of change outside the subways."

Wild had never shared that her parents were both well off, and she gave him a puzzled frown. He chuckled. "Oh, please, it's all over you. Just watching how you hold that plastic fork is giveaway enough. The big clue, though, was the way you described the duck and olives in Paris, if you don't mind me revisiting your romantic Fukushima."

"You got that from my breakup dinner?"

Gunnar tugged at an earlobe. "I heard that and said, 'Facility with haute cuisine. Not your Dollar General shopper.' And before you accuse me of being judgmental, that's where I get my crew socks and tighty-whities. Anyway, my point is . . . well, pretty much forgotten."

"You were talking about the crime victims being gone for long stretches of time. It's really not unusual. A third of the posh apartments and condos uptown are vacant ten months a year. That's from the Census Bureau. Go ahead and hate me, I'm a research geek."

"So the cop in me is wondering whether Stamitz, the crew chief, really had inside info, or if he knew that, too, and the odds were just in favor of vacant apartments to burglarize. That would explain the boner of stumbling in on the Grammy winner." She set her salad bowl on the pavement and started a list of observations and questions on the next clean page in her Moleskine.

Wild added, "I'd like to know if the MO of this team was to sell back stolen property to its victims."

"You mean instead of fencing it?"

"Or, maybe it's a combination of the two."

"Or, maybe Rúben Pinto went rogue, working his own scam like Spatone said."

Macie grew tired of staring at the baby spinach leaf that had landed on his thigh and plucked it off, then wondered if that was too familiar. When his eyes met hers, she immediately stood. "We should get back to our victim interviews."

Since they already had visited the pharma CEO at The Barksdale and Woody Nash at the Crystal Court, they crossed them both off and set out for the last place on their roster, which was down near Columbus Circle. They continued the conversation about the burglaries on the drive, adding a few more questions, including whether the crew had shopping lists going in, who the items were fenced to, and where they were stashed pending disposition. Since Jackson Hall might have those answers, Macie chanced a call to Dr. Edda. She reluctantly agreed to allow them some time with her patient, but not for another hour when Hall got back from ambulation therapy.

The Ajax, a spire of cobalt blue glass, looked as if it hadn't so much been built up from amid the tight cluster of luxury high-rises off the southwest corner of Central Park as inserted down into it by the hand of some unseen god from another galaxy. Judging from the appraisal Macie Wild and Gunnar Cody received on their arrival in the cavernous lobby, the concierges also believed themselves to have been deposited there by celestial decree. Under their imposing stares, and surrounded by furniture and hanging fabrics that made her feel underdressed, Macie was all too happy to let Gunnar lead off. He started in full cop mode with a street, "Hey, how's it going?"

"May I help you?" was all he got. It sounded like verbal pepper spray.

"Yeah, my partner and I are here to see your resident on the fifty-sixth floor." He consulted a spiral notebook and added, "That would be your penthouse."

"And the nature of your visit today?"

"Absolutely. We're here to investigate the burglary in that residence on . . ." —another glance at his notes— ". . . the twenty-second of last month." In their periphery, a formidable man in a charcoal suit with a communication earbud quietly moved over to join them. Gunnar gave the security man a nod and turned back to the concierge. "If you'd be so kind as to announce us, we can take it from there."

"And whom would you like me to announce you to?"

Jackson Hall's list didn't include a name for this stop, so Gunnar tried to bluff it. "The resident. Tell them it's Cody and Wild. Thank you."

But the man behind the counter didn't pick up his phone. Instead he said, "I'm afraid you've been given the wrong information or address. There has been no burglary here at The Ajax."

"Trust me, we couldn't be more sure of our information or our address."

"You are with the police?" When his look traced to Wild she tried not to cave.

Avoiding a direct answer, Gunnar said, "This is a follow-up, so . . ." He mimed a visual urging, putting a phone to his ear with his thumb and pinkie.

"I would like to see your identification. Both of you, if you please."

"That wasn't mortifying or anything," said Macie when she slammed the door of the van.

Gunnar paid the parking attendant and they pulled out of the garage. "It's an odds game. Look at all the access we got today. If this were baseball we'd be in Cooperstown on the first ballot."

"I don't know what I would have done if they had called the police." And then, just to be shitty: "The real police."

"May I say your anger is kind of a turn-on?"

"No, that would qualify as exactly the wrong thing to say. Second only to calling me your partner for the second time."

"Is that my limit? Because the thing about my limit is that I never know what it is."

"You're there."

"What do you make of the company line? 'No burglaries. Not here at The Ajax.'" As was his way, Gunnar shifted the topic. She decided to hold him to it.

"Stop with the partner, OK?"

"Does that mean no burglaries, for real, or none I'll discuss with you, you fucking 99-percenter fuck?"

Wild caved and jumped over to his thread. "Hard to know what's being discreet or what's hiding the truth. One more thing to ask Mr. Hall."

"Also I want to ask why we had names for all the other victims, and not here. Put that in your little book—partner." Macie started to get pissed off. Then she looked at him and started to laugh.

Something was up with Dr. Edda. When she approached them at the jail ward nurses' station she looked like a version of herself, like her much older sister. "What is it?" asked Macie.

The neurosurgeon regarded both of them grimly. "He's gone."

Wild heard a click in her throat as she swallowed and steadied herself on the counter. "When?" And then to soften the sharpness of her reaction, "You did warn us about setbacks."

"Oh, forgive me." The doctor put a gentle hand on her forearm. "He isn't dead. He's gone. Mr. Hall escaped."

Wild entered the Manhattan Center for Public Defense in a vertigo daze. After holding sopping paper towels to her face in the restroom, Macie emerged feeling revived, but far from clearheaded. Outside the conference room door, Tiger popped a cold can of Diet Coke and handed it to her on their way into the team meeting. As if caffeine were the drug of sense.

She had nearly asked Gunnar to come with her. But then came the swarm of second thoughts. The boat-rocking his presence might create in her team—especially with her official investigator, Jonathan Monheit—wasn't worth it just when she needed all her resources ready to address the new crisis. NBC4NY made the decision for her. The assignment editor tapped him to do freelance coverage of a subway platform stabbing, and Gunnar peeled off to make his rent. Afterward, he said, he wanted to do a check-in on the naughty Angolan prince, Jerónimo Teixeira, to see what the subject of his VICE Media doc was up to. But really to see if his goon, Luka Borodin, was back in play. So she laid out to her defense team what she knew about Jackson Hall's escape from Bellevue.

It wasn't much.

Following Hall's ambulation session, which amounted to an assisted walk around the corridors, his physical therapist stopped at the nurses' station to sign him back in. When the rehab worker turned around from the clipboard, after mere seconds, no Jackson Hall. That triggered a lockdown and search, but the prisoner was nowhere to be found anywhere in the jail ward. The guard posted at the elevator was certain he did not get by her. Nonetheless, the New York Hospital Police conducted a full search of all floors of Bellevue, inside and outside the jail ward, including a survey of all taxis and transit that made pick-ups on First Avenue and the surrounding area. They came up empty. Wild concluded by saying,

"Right now, NYPD and Hospital Police are reviewing security video to track his movements after the nurses' station."

Soledad Esteves Torres shook her head. "They'll never tell us."

"How does someone get out of there?" asked Chip. "When I was doing my coma watch on him they told me Bellevue's jail ward is as secure as any state prison."

Tiger chuckled. "Unless somebody delivered him ground beef with hacksaw stuffing."

"It's normal to jump to the conclusion that he broke out," said Soledad, "but let's not overlook other possibilities, right?" The social worker gave a cautioning look around the conference table before she continued. "There can be aftereffects of brain trauma and coma. Short-term memory loss, confusion, disorientation, even reactions to overstimulation from noise and light."

Wild scoffed. "Oh, sure. So he just sort of wandered out of a high-security jail ward like Mr. Magoo?" Soledad's head snapped toward her in disbelief. "Sorry, Sol. Don't know where that came from."

"I'm guessing a shitload of pressure," said her friend.

"Driving over here 1010 WINS was saying that NYPD and PAPD have broadcast a Be On the Look Out for an accused murderer on the loose. That puts our client in the crosshairs. And considering Mr. Hall's diminished capacity," she went on, with a nod to her social worker, "there's an extra layer of danger surrounding him. So . . . danger from the cops, danger from Luka Borodin, who is still off the grid . . ." Wild paused, considering whether to share the potential danger from the Pipe Wrench Duo who went after the crew chief. That would mean explaining her night of dodgy surveillance with Gunnar, including the questionable means by which they tracked down his apartment. Taking another uncharacteristic step away from transparency, she held it back, rationalizing that nobody in that room doubted Jackson Hall's peril, and that adding that detail only would be redundant.

Raising his hand to be called on in the back of the room, the L-1 intern was anything but sheepish when he spoke. "Any of y'all consider that our client's playing us?" Chairs pivoted his way. "I'm new, but it seems to me nobody's talking about how he hasn't been straight with us from the start. Hiding facts from you, Ms. Wild. Then there's the threats he made to the murder victim. Now he's got an APB for being an accused murderer on the loose, because that's kinda exactly what he is."

"Mr. Ross, I completely agree that there is more to our client than he has disclosed," she replied. "But if this summer internship teaches you nothing else, let it be that innocent until proven guilty doesn't mean faultless. But it does mean that we advocate for justice for him. At the same time, we keep a healthy BS detector too."

From there she briefed them on her day in the field interviewing Jackson Hall's burglary victims, ending with the burglary denial at The Ajax, which they all found odd too. "Speaking of BS detection. Tiger, I know you have a full plate, but run a check of records to see who owns the penthouse at The Ajax. Don't make contact, just dig it out."

"Too right," said the Aussie.

On the opposite side of the table, Monheit flashed angry eyes at the paralegal for infringing in his territory. But Macie wasn't done with assignments. Jackson Hall's escape was a game changer, opening another flank in her investigation and reminding her how thinly her resources were spread. God, where would she be without Gunnar, she was surprised to find herself thinking. The bigger surprise was what she found herself saying. "Jonathan, I need to get you back out in the field."

"Ah . . . sure."

Wild moved to the Case Board. "See the list of Mr. Hall's regular hangouts and known associates? I want you to pay a personal visit to all of them. The bar, the fishing pier, even Amador Spatone—you never know."

"Got it." Then he said, "What am I looking for?" causing her to second guess her decision.

"A lead on our client. Barring that, agreement to notify us if he shows."

"You really think they'd bust him?"

"Tell them, it's either us or the police." Jonny F-ing Midnight, she thought. "Soledad, I didn't get much out of his doctor, she was too traumatized. Would you follow up at Bellevue and see if there's anything he may have shared with Dr. Edda that would hint at a direction he might have gone?"

"You got it. Meantime, fugitives go to ground with family and lovers. I'll make a second effort to locate Pilar Fuentes. Even go back to her apartment uptown."

"Good idea. And Chip? I'm going to give you contact info for the burglary victims I talked to today. The last one, Larry Don Henkles, said Rúben Pinto got in touch to extort money to sell back some of his property." Flagging it as privileged, Wild shared it was a betting ledger, but instructed the intern to reach out to the other victims to see if any ransom attempt was made by Pinto—or anyone else.

"You mean like Mr. Hall?"

"I mean like Mr. Anybody. I want to establish whether this whole burglary club was about extorting or if it was just Rúben Pinto."

"Because?" asked her lead investigator.

"Because, Jonathan, it could be a motive for murder."

Assistant District Attorney Theresa Fontanelli's phone call to Macie Wild was full-frontal, loud, and clear. "I am serving you official notice that, as an officer of the court, you are required to hand over your fugitive client, or face criminal prosecution as an accessory and for obstruction of justice."

"And hello to you, too, counselor." The verbal body slam had jarred Macie while she was still in a vulnerable place. But, once again, unconsciously stealing a page from Gunnar Cody, she volleyed with a wisecrack. The assistant DA was less than amused.

"Fuck hello," said WTF. "A murderer is at large. He is your client. I want him locked up."

"One: he is only accused of murder. Two: I have no idea where he is. Three: if you don't dial it back, you're going to be listening to a dial tone." The fact that Wild was on her cellular and, as such, there could be no dial tone made her worry her bravado sounded false. So she blew past it. "For the record, Theresa, I don't want him at large either. Not that I worry he will do anything; I'm more concerned a rookie cop will box him into a bad situation or some vigilante who saw his face on the news tonight will deal out some street justice."

Fontanelli did bring it down a peg, but held her ground, if more civilly. "You can worry about that. I get to worry about the safety of citizens and law enforcement. Your man's running with a banner on his BOLO that reads: 'Armed and dangerous.'"

"Based on what?"

"Counselor. He busted out of a high-security ward at Bellevue. It makes him capable of anything. Now to get back to the reason I called. If Jackson Hall makes any contact with you, you are obligated by law to urge him to surrender and to notify us immediately of his whereabouts. Clear?"

"As a sworn officer of the court, I would do nothing less." The line went dead. "Fuck good-bye, too, I guess," said Macie.

At ten forty-five that night, Wild stood before a forest of microphones in the carriage turn off First Avenue in front of Bellevue Hospital. The blaze of TV lights mutated the news reporters and crews behind them into distorted silhouettes like dancers in the Lady Gaga halftime show. She looked for Gunnar but couldn't locate him through the glare. He had counseled her on the where and when to do this presser. The "where" was to avoid the Manhattan Center for Public Defense, which screamed criminal law. Bellevue made sense because a hospital made a better visual case for spinning her client as a patient, rather than a murderer. "Like it or not," he'd said, "TV news is all about the optics." The "when" was early enough for the ten p.m. local newscasts to go live; close enough for the stations with elevens to use her video as a breaking news lead.

"Good evening," she began, introducing herself and spelling her name for the record. "I am a public defender with the Manhattan Center for Public Defense. Today my client Jackson Hall, who was a patient here at Bellevue Hospital, disappeared following ambulation therapy that was part of his rehabilitation from a coma. Mr. Hall was a patient in the jail ward and it is unknown whether he escaped or wandered out due to disorientation, which is a common condition, post-coma, or whether or not he was taken. I not only come here tonight to address the media, I also want to speak directly to my client."

Not knowing which camera to look at, Macie selected the one directly in front of her. "Mr. Hall, if you see this message, I urge you to immediately go to the nearest NYPD precinct and turn yourself in. Otherwise, I ask you to get in contact with me. You have my number. Call and I will arrange safe passage for you. But do not remain at large. Please come in. Now." In her pause, Macie glimpsed Gunnar in the crowd with his camera up, then continued. "To any friends and family of Jackson Hall: If you hear from him, call me. You are not helping him by harboring him. The greatest help you can be to him will be to assist us in bringing him in safely." Wild recited her phone number and indicated that it would be answered anytime, day or night.

Reporters called out questions to Wild but she stepped away. She had made her points, and nothing more she could say would do anything but confuse her messages. When she reached the pillar where Chip was waiting for her with a bottle of water, she twisted the cap and scanned the press line again for Gunnar. There was a gap where he had been standing and she felt an unexpected hollowness.

In her dream she was watching Gunnar but through the blinding white harshness of TV lights—and at a distance. Because he was on a video monitor. A monitor on the rack inside his van. She watched Gunnar on screen, drifting like smoke, disembodied, untethered from the planet. Here, and then not. Because he was also with her in the back of the van. Not beside her but underneath her as she straddled his lap. She was thinking, I can't, but it was also she who was driving this moment. She felt, as much as saw, his gaze locked into hers. Riveted, as she had seen it clamped on the monitors so often in the crackling seconds before scales tipped from anticipation to anxiety to violence. The thrill of watching—the excitement of knowing and being unknown, noticed and unnoticed—filled her. And warmed her.

In her dream.

Wild awoke in dampness. Perspiration at her neck and lower back chilled her as she sat up with naked skin suddenly exposed to air conditioning. By habit, she checked her iPhone for missed calls and e-mails. She found a voice mail. Macie didn't recognize the number, and listened. It was Gunnar, no doubt from one of his burner cells. "Call whenever you get this. I'm working an incident for Channel 2. They found a body." She threw off the remaining covers and stood, not shivering from the AC, but from alarm. Macie waited for him to say whose body, but the thin blue bar on her screen tracked across two seconds of silence, hit :00, and then reset.

Some cops call them floaters. Bodies discovered in water: rivers, ponds, canals. Floaters are a superset of dry floaters, which are bodies discovered high and dry in out-of-the-way places like abandoned warehouses, parking garages, and basements. Wet or dry, they are called floaters because body gases from decomposition have given them a degree of inflation. Even the dry ones look like they'd bob pretty good.

It all happens fast. When death shuts off the oxygen supply and the body's pH balance goes south, enzymes immediately get to work breaking down cells. Methane, CO_2, hydrogen sulfide, and nitrogen get released as a byproduct, inflating the cadaver in gruesome ways. Anyone who saw drifting corpses in the Katrina footage knows how the horror show plays out. Up close it's more disconcerting to the uninitiated. Even in the early stages, after just a day, when swelling disfigures the mouth, contorts eyes into a bulge, and warps the skin to a marbled, multicolored sausage casing.

Gunnar Cody had documented that and more in the series of close-ups he had taken of the remains before the homicide squad arrived at the tidal marsh near Co-op City. Now shooed away outside the yellow tape, he stood beside Macie, getting long lens shots, pictures that could be shown on broadcast TV. Against the rising sun, the gang from the Office of Chief Medical Examiner erected a fabric partition around the discovery site. Behind it, the body would be hoisted from the muck and onto a gurney for a prelim field exam.

While Gunnar uploaded his G-rated video files in time for the morning newscast, Wild surveyed the grim work of the medical examiners across the swaying reeds and wondered if this was the body dump, or if Jeff Stamitz had come in on the tide.

Macie walked back to the dirt service road under the drawbridge where Gunnar had parked on the verge. She waited, leaning against the open cargo door of his van as his fingers danced over the keyboard and trackpad. He said a toneless "Ka-ching" when his last file shipped to the news editor, then invited her in to screen the extra footage he'd shot. "No, thanks, I get it. Pretty grim stuff." But her decision was as much about avoiding the ghastly footage as the residue of her erotic dream. Best not to mix the two, she thought.

"A fave? Next time, leave a complete message. You scared me shitless it was Jackson Hall."

"Promise," he said. "Next time I call you in the middle of the night about finding a corpse ass-up in a tidal basin, I'll comply with all your personal requirements." Then he resumed his screening.

She accidentally surfed a glimpse of one angle and quickly turned away. "Are you actually going to use this in your VICE piece?"

"Not sure. Parts, probably. Depends on relevance. But I'm not screening for that, not yet. I'm doing my own little forensic on the decedent." After freezing some frames and zooming in, he shut down and pivoted in his chair toward her. "Our crew chief was tortured. Majorly."

"We saw that through his window."

"I mean after. And more than the pipe wrenching. That was the teaser. He's got split fingernails from spikings, one of his eyes looks like it got an acid wash, and burn marks on his skin are telltales of TENS wanding."

"I need help here."

"Transcutaneous Electrical Nerve Stimulation. Holistic doctors use it therapeutically. S&M practitioners crank it up and use it as a fetish. Black Ops max it out as a way to get prisoners to talk. My guess is, unless they find a bullet hole somewhere I missed, the TENS juiced him into a heart attack. Somebody wanted him to talk about something."

Wild, who had walked picket lines over waterboarding, shivered at the barbarity of what Gunnar was describing. She tried to set aside her feelings for the victim and focus professionally on what it meant, on how it related to the murder charge against her client. "Pinto. He wasn't just killed. You were with me and saw all the blood. He must have been tortured too."

"Except this is next-level. This here, this was a rendition."

"And looking less and less like Rúben Pinto was a kill over the crew's split."

"I wouldn't argue with that." His gaze raked past her and she turned. A new pair of plain-wrap undercover vehicles pulled up to the crime scene. A man and a woman, both in sharp suits, got out of each car. Gunnar picked up his still camera to snap off some shots.

"But what for then?" she asked when he set his camera back down. "Why were Mr. Hall's two associates both tortured and killed?"

"When they find your client, I sure hope he has an answer." After a ponder, Gunnar added, "Assuming whoever tried to kill him in jail doesn't have him now."

The implications of that brought Macie to a hard decision. She steeled herself and said, "I need you to do something you may not want to do."

No matter what Wild did to hold her team's attention, their noses kept swinging like weathervanes to the ex-NYPD surveillance detective lounging against the side wall of the conference room. If Gunnar Cody felt their stolen glances, he didn't let on, just rocked lightly in his task chair, coming a millimeter from brushing the glass-framed print of the Constitution while he listened to the defense attorney's briefing on the body in the Bronx.

Macie delivered her recap, omitting, by preagreement with Gunnar, the iffy surveillance they had done at the burglary crew chief's apartment. Then, taking a leap, Wild turned the floor over to him to describe the condition of Stamitz's corpse. All studied Gunnar carefully as he spoke. He was not only a curiosity in their midst—an ex-cop whose spying they believed flew in the face of the framed document hanging on the wall behind him—his cool description of the tortured body stunned them to a queasy silence. "What kind of beast does something like that?" asked Soledad when he'd finished.

Although her question was rhetorical, he replied, "A beast who's trained to get information."

"Mr. Cody also has inside information that Rúben Pinto may have been tortured, as well," added Wild, careful not to divulge that she had broken into the crime scene along with him. So many minefields in this arrangement, she reflected for the umpteenth.

"Why would they be tortured?" asked the team investigator.

"Well, Jonathan, if this were a homicide detective squad room, we'd be kicking out theories left and right about that." His tone was inclusive, not condescending, even though Macie could still see herself and Gunnar holding their sides the day he had branded his hide with a nickname. "One I'd toss on the table is the simplest: They stole something somebody wants back."

"Or maybe one of their victims is pissed and wants to send a message," offered Monheit.

"Except," said Chip. The intern looked as if he would lose nerve when they rotated toward his end of the table, but he continued. "Rúben Pinto ransomed some of the Jets player's stolen property. If they were holding something else, and if negotiations got stalled, somebody could be taking it to the limit."

"That's good," said Gunnar. "You sure you're just the summer kid?" Wild, who had been listing the theories in a boxed section of the Case Board added, "Property Negotiation," and asked Chip if he'd made contact with the other victims.

"I did. Spoke with all of them, except Larry Don Henkles. No contact from anyone trying to ransom back property." And then with a skepticism that belied his Southern ways, he added, "Unless they're lying." The look between Macie and Gunnar spoke volumes. The most instinctive investigator on her team would be going back to school at the end of August.

"There's one person you haven't interviewed," said Cody. "The owner of the apartment at The Ajax."

Monheit said, "But they said there was no burglary."

"Total stonewall," said Gunnar. "At posh digs like that, they don't like to go around advertising break-ins. What's the apartment owner got to say, that's what I want to know."

"Over to me then," said Tiger. "I got tasked with tracking the penthouse owner. It's been like sorting out a madwoman's breakfast, but I just got an answer."

Macie asked, "Who owns it?"

"Nobody." He read their faces and explained. "Nobody, as in not a person. It's deeded to a limited liability company."

Macie turned to Gunnar. "An LLC. Just like our horror novelist on Fifth Avenue."

"Where it gets really cloudy," said the paralegal, "is it's paid up. No mortgage to trace to an individual owner. And no phone listed for the apartment. What I was able to finally suss out is a deed registered to Exurb Partners LLC."

Rather than ask him to spell it, she had Tiger post the name on the whiteboard. "I want to talk to them," she said. "Does this LLC have a phone number?"

"Indeed. It dumps to an automated voice mail. Very robotic."

"OK, what about an address?"

"I Street Viewed it just before we met." Tiger showed his laptop. The screen displayed a ramshackle storefront in Queens with a neon sign: "Checks Cashed – Mailbox Rentals."

After the meeting, Macie invited Gunnar to her office to do some brainstorming on next moves. He said fine, but after a minute to use the gents. She couldn't resist. "That's the difference between your office and mine. Here, you don't have to use a milk jug."

"Crude" was all he said before he took his leave. For the first time since she got to the MCPD that morning, Macie felt her muscles unclench. Maybe it was from having him join in with the team. Maybe it was the baby step toward transparency that brightened her conscience. With a few relaxed seconds alone, Wild phoned her father and arranged a quick lunch. As she hung up, Rick Whittinghill came in without knocking and made himself at home in a guest chair. The sight of her former investigator—whom she had asked to run a check on ex-Detective Cody through some old pals from Internal Affairs—jarred her with panic. She bolted to her feet.

"Rick."

"This a bad time?"

"Uh, could be better."

He waved an envelope. "Just came by to get HR to pay out my unused vay-cay. And while I was here, I thought I'd update you on that IA check you wanted." No sooner had the retired cop said the words than Gunnar rounded the open doorway from the hall. The Popeye Doyle saw her reaction and hauled himself out of his chair. "Hey, Detective Cody." He thrust out his hand and they shook. "Rick Whittinghill."

Gunnar took his measure. "We met?"

"No doubt. I worked Burglary out of Midtown South forever."

"You say so. Rick, is it?"

Smooth as could be, Whittinghill fanned his vacation pay envelope and said, "I was just stopping by to gas about old times while I picked up a check from these cheap pinkos." He chuckled and slid by Gunnar to the hallway. "Hey, Mace, we'll be talking." With a pleasant nod to the other ex-cop, he left.

By his expression as he sat in the chair Whittinghill had just vacated, Macie couldn't be sure whether Gunnar heard the comment about the Internal Affairs background check. Or, if he had, whether he would even relate it to himself. It appeared as if she had dodged one. Or Gunnar Cody was just that good at poker.

They rehashed the meeting, starting with her appreciation for how he eased into her group. "Even though I'm the poster boy for human rights violations?" he asked.

"You flatter yourself. Nobody'd put you on a poster. A dartboard, maybe."

They agreed that the hot lead to follow was the mystery around what did-slash-did-not happen at The Ajax, including who really owned it. Macie was already on that, and told him she had booked a lunch with her father so he could take her to school on LLCs. "Oh, so I'm not invited? Not the first woman I've known who wanted to hide me from the parents." He rose. "Actually that gives me some time to do some field work on the case with *mi amigo*, the CyberGauchito."

"Field work?" It rattled her that he would be out doing something on his own. "Like what?"

He smiled. "You really wanna know? I didn't think so." He paused at the doorway. "I've got to tell you, I've never seen anyone with so many misgivings."

"Good. They're a sign I may still have some morals."

"And here I thought you just wanted some face time with your dear old dad." Jansen Wild helped himself to the bottle of Asahi on the waitress's serving tray and poured. His loving concentration on the rising head kindled a familiar heartache in Macie. "It's an old trick," he said as the server departed. "Lunch in exchange for free legal advice. At my hourly rate, I don't blame my clients for trying. Cheers."

She saluted with her iced tea; he took a long pull on his Dry. "Hourly rate? That's bull, Dad. Who do you handle that isn't on retainer?"

"The ones who take me to lunch thinking they're getting freebies. Then the monthly comes and they usually can't sign a retainer fast enough." Her father, a popular former state senator who left politics to resume his law practice full time, serially turned down important appointments to political posts and judgeships. He still did a lot of pro bono work, but threw himself into expanding his firm, already one of the most lucrative and influential in New York, by opening Seventh Street offices in Washington, DC. "Hmm, am I required to answer the question of a public defender of limited means when I'm paying for the sushi too?"

"Send me an invoice. I dare you," she said with a laugh.

"If you took Orem Diner's offer you could treat me for once." With a twinkle, he added, "By the way, I told that shyster he was wasting his time trying to recruit a true believer like you." Their miso soups arrived. He set his to the side, cued the waitress with a finger twirl over his beer glass, and said, "Why do you want to know about LLCs? Is this related to your Buzz Killer?" He enjoyed her reaction and added, "Hate the tabloids, love the headlines." She acknowledged that it was connected and gave him a thumbnail synopsis, after which he polished off his Asahi and said, "So you still don't have any idea what's what? Did it ever occur to you that your client may have snowed you, and you should cut your losses? He sure cut his, breaking out of the jail ward."

"Thank you for continuing to treat me like I'm eight years old, but I can handle this, and that does not mean cutting any losses. I don't do that. Besides, I may be onto something." Wild filled him in on The Ajax and how Jackson Hall said his crew had burglarized it but she couldn't interview the owner, who was hidden behind an LLC. Jansen Wild nodded and said, "LLCs never used to be a specialty for us. We do them now, of course, because they're becoming so prevalent. Especially here in Manhattan. You probably don't want to get back in touch with him, but the top attorney for shell corporations is sitting a block and a half from here. Orem Diner gets so much LLC business, I'm getting rich on the overflow that he tosses my way. But I could certainly give you a thumbnail."

The daughter knew the father's understatement when she heard it. Thumbnail from him would be a full course at NYU. "Just the basics will work. Starting with, why so many LLCs for residential real estate?"

"It's in the name. Limited Liability. Many of the property owners—OK, most of them on this island—are hugely wealthy. Those deep pockets spell legal exposure. Everything from personal injury suits from slips and falls to property damage actions from other tenants for water leaks, fires, noise . . . lots of noise litigation. Then there's environmental lawsuits: the building creates too much shade, the foundation settled and cracked someone's wall, the whole panorama. Residential owners are going for LLCs for the same reason celebrities form personal services corporations. Sure, there are tax and accounting advantages, but mainly, it shelters their personal wealth from lawsuits. Especially from the litigation trollers."

Macie told him about Holland Bridgewater, the horror writer. "I guess privacy is part of it too."

"I'm smiling because I set up Holland's LLC for her. That's privileged, of course."

"Hang on, I have to make a call to *Page Six*."

"Smartass." Their food came, along with his beer. His third, observed Wild, who tried not to count, but did. "Wealthy folk just can't get enough privacy," he said after a bite of toro. "It's not only the actors, sports stars, celebrity chefs, and dot-com-billionaires. There are plenty of brick-and-mortar CEOs who don't like to have their personal addresses out there for anyone to find with a visit to the City Registrar.

"Let me give you one more broad category of use for these shell corporations. A lot of these big money people, especially foreigners, operate under corporate budgets. Their accountants and lawyers handle their bills and property docs so they don't have to concern themselves with the drudgery of life's logistics. And if they don't care a whit for their hundred-foot yachts or their private islands, why should they for something as trivial as their third or fourth home—a getaway pad in Manhattan?"

Macie finished her last shrimp tempura roll and asked, "Then if it's some blah-blah LLC, how does a developer or real estate broker know who he or she is selling to?"

"Most times they don't. It's all handled through attorneys. The LLCs can be everything from subsidiary companies to paper holdings or can be listed under names of distant relatives, mistresses, even a favorite pet."

"I'm surprised hiding under a basket like that is legal."

"Perfectly."

"And don't the property sellers want to know who's buying?"

Jansen Wild dabbed his eel sushi in the ceramic bowl of soy sauce and scoffed. "Here's the only thing the brokers ever want to know. Ready?—'Do you have the cash?' Any other questions are just an obstacle to profit." He ate one more piece of sashimi, leaving the rest, and waited while she made some notes. When she finished, he was studying her gravely. "I want you to assure me you'll be careful. One street attack is enough for a lifetime, young lady. And Orem told me about this ex-cop, what's his name? Cody? I crossed paths in court with this asshole a few years back. Steer clear of him. I'm told people get hurt when he's around." Mr. Wild peered into the froth in the bottom of his glass and said, "I lost a kid already. No more, promise?"

Parking her car Midtown was an extravagance she would have to defend when she submitted her expense report to the MCPD business manager, but Wild balanced the cost of staying above ground to receive calls against strap hanging, incommunicado, on the 4 Train to the Brooklyn

Bridge-City Hall stop for nearly a half hour. That was all it took to sell herself. Now if she could only sell the bean counter in three weeks when her EXR-100 came back with a stripe of yellow highlighter and a pink "See me" Post-it attached. Macie tipped the attendant when he delivered her old Corolla between a Mercedes and a Tesla, then pulled out into traffic. She glanced at the door of Restaurant Nippon as she passed, wondering if her father had really stayed behind "just to use the loo," or was it to find a spot at the bar?

The lunch reminded her that closure is not only overrated, it's a delusion. The murder of her brother—of his son—lived as a constancy, a bruise upon every day and wakeful night. Macie coped her own way through her work, her kick boxing, and probably some unassessed behaviors that were subversively destructive. Meanwhile her dad grew remote and started drinking. Her mom took more dangerous assignments in Doctors Without Borders, preferring the hellfire of Aleppo to the living hell of her solitude. Macie always had given her dad a pass on the alcohol. She made no comment today, but came close. His need had lost its social masking and become too obvious. A conversation with her mother was definitely in the offing—whenever she got back from her field hospital in another war zone.

Wild's iPhone sounded an incoming e-mail, but she waited until the long light on Forty-Second, her last chance to check it before the FDR downtown. Macie's breath caught when she saw the sender. It was from Jackson Hall.

Nearly poking a finger through her brand-new screen, she tapped it open and read. "I need your help. I'm cribbing uptown." He gave an address in the Bronx and finished with, "Don't be pissed. Just come. Just you." A long blast of horn behind her brought Macie's head up to a green light. Wild drove but not to the FDR. She made an illegal left, heading uptown.

On the Willis Bridge, crossing the Harlem River, she relented to her instincts and called Gunnar Cody. She got voice mail and only said she'd heard from Hall, then hung up. Working with him had made her sufficiently paranoid not to commit her client's location to a phone message.

Even his. He'd hear it and be in touch. That would suffice. It would have to.

Google Maps led her under the RFK-Triboro into a mix of slender clapboard duplexes squeezed between no-frills industrials of stucco and painted brick. Rounding the corner onto East 134th Street, she went right by the address Hall had given her. The place was that nondescript: a two-story cinder-block cube with no signage sitting next to a scaffolding company. Wild found a spot up the block and got out. Even in this industrialized zone, broad daylight under puffy white clouds bleached the spare building and gave it a folksy, Edward Hopper feel. There was no traffic; the only vehicles on this road were clunkers parked in front of the various hardscrabble businesses. She saw no pedestrians either. The sole sign of life was the occasional clang of metal pipe ringing out of the scaffolding company garage entrance. If you wanted to lose yourself from a manhunt, she decided, this would be a serviceable place, at least for a while.

Macie circled around a tow truck parked on the driveway, then replied to Hall's e-mail. "I'm here." She waited. There were no windows on the ground floor, so she scanned the two on the upper, wondering if he was watching for her. A deadbolt snapped and the metal front door swung open. What someone wisely coined as the gift of fear rose in her and, instead of approaching, she took a few steps backward.

And bumped into a man who had silently come up behind her.

On her turn to him, he stifled her scream by clamping a cloth over her mouth and nose with one hand while he locked her arms to her sides with a sharp, wraparound bear hug. Then he slackened his lock on her ribs, allowing her to gulp for air. The intake tasted like a cleaning solvent, but cloyingly sweet. Her head grew light and her vision fogged. The next breath burned the back of her throat and her knees went slack. The last thing Macie remembered was the face of the man hauling her into the open door. She tried to say, "Pipe Wrench," but was unconscious before the words could form.

CHAPTER 26

A week had passed. Or maybe fifteen minutes. Who knew? Not Macie. All was timelessness and fog. Her brain felt swaddled in the same coarse woolen blanket as her tongue. The eyeballs moved, but behind putty lids too heavy to lift. A hard swallow tasted of rubbing alcohol mixed with Kool-Aid powder and burned her throat like strep. Drawing in air both hurt and helped. It carried the odor of diesel and stale motor oil but each inhale brought her around to slow consciousness with enough clarity to be scared shitless. Even though her eyes were closed a man's voice said, "She's back," and the other answered, "About fucking time." Apparently playing dead worked with bears, not so well with attack dogs.

Wild forced her lids open, and the first thing she saw was their backs while they fiddled with some gear on a workbench. Which made her wonder why they were so careless with her until she tried to wipe her mouth and couldn't move her hand. Her wrists were Velcroed to the arms of the chair. That small bit of effort taxed her and she checked out again, waking next time to Pipe Wrench giving her light slaps on the cheek. "Rise and shine." Sing-song, but his cynical voice robbed it of any cheer. A mask covered her mouth, and every breath lifted the haze. So, oxygen. She filled her lungs with deep huffs and took in her surroundings. The room had a high ceiling, narrow oblong windows where the cinder-block walls met the roof, and a concrete floor showing ancient grease and oil stains. The metal rolling garage door to her left was down, and smeary tire tracks indicated where cars and trucks had come in and out for repairs over years.

Pipe Wench took away her mask. "Time for a chat. Be smart, and it'll save a lot of trouble."

"And pain," said the other, the second man at Stamitz's apartment invasion. Wild looked around for an actual pipe wrench and didn't see one. But there were plenty of tools mounted on the walls, not a welcome sight.

"Nicely now," said Pipe. "Where is he?"

"Hall?" she asked. "I don't know. I came here looking for him, you know that."

"Not Hall. Where is the Russian?"

The last time Macie saw Borodin, she was chasing him into the Low Line. "He could be anywhere. I have no idea."

His friend was impatient, volatile. "Fucking lawyers. Let me give her a jolt just for being a bitch."

Pipe Wrench ignored him. "What did Hall tell you?"

"About what?"

Pipe Wrench persisted evenly. "What did he tell you about the take?"

"What take?"

Her tormentor leaned in close enough to smell his breath. "The take, the take, the—"

"—I don't know anything about his take. You mean from the break-ins?"

"Now we're getting there. What about the pouch?"

"Pouch? Honestly, I don't know anything about a pouch."

A silent decision passed between the pair. Pipe turned to the work-bench; his partner grabbed Macie's blouse with two hands and ripped it apart, sending the front buttons ticking in all directions across the cement. Her attempt to cover up was thwarted by the straps binding her wrists. She tried to kick him but her ankles also were fastened to the chair. She heard a click then a droning hum that reminded her of the beehive her mother had started in the garden up in Rye. Pipe Wrench turned toward her from the worktable. He was holding a silvery metal wand, the size and shape of a microphone, trailing a thick cord lead-ing to a box with lights and a dial. He approached her, then thrust the smooth metal head against her diaphragm. Immediately her skin burned and her solar plexus tightened involuntarily into an agonizing clench. Macie gasped, a moan of pain knotted in her throat. He pulled it away. While she panted, head down, Wild didn't need to ask: she knew exactly what that was. A TENS machine like this had scorched the crew chief before he got dumped into the tidal marsh. It may have even been the same one, a grim thought that Macie tried to suppress because it was a preview of coming attractions.

"You can try to hold it back," said Pipe Wrench, "but you can't fight this."

"Unless you die, trying," said the other, with a cackle.

"I'm going to explain something to you." Pipe held up his wand. "That was nothing." He reached for the TENS box on the workbench and turned the dial up a notch like a burner on a stove. Did the hum really grow louder or was that the blood rushing in Macie's ears? "At this level, there's a good chance the muscle contractions could stop your heart. You up for that, or do you want to start talking?"

"Please. Don't. You're asking me questions I can't answer."

"You mean won't answer."

"Can't. Because I don't know."

"Hmm, which is it? One way to find out." For good measure, he gave the dial another click. A noise made them turn. It was like a small pebble or a coin bouncing off the rolling garage door. Then silence. "Check it out," said Pipe Wrench.

His partner left Macie's side and tiptoed to the garage door, resting a precautionary hand on the grip of his gun. He pressed an ear to the articulated metal and listened. Satisfied, he turned and shrugged. That was his pose when an engine roared, tires squealed, and the entire garage door got ripped off its frameworks with a thunderous blast as a tow truck barged clean through it.

Gunnar Cody floored the wrecker through the space. The roaring truck detached the garage door, which stuck to its grill and turned the business end of the rig into a snowplow of angry steel. It broomed the entire area in front of Macie, scraping away Pipe Wrench, his torture device, even the workbench, slamming the lot into the wall so hard it lifted the rear tires of the fifteen-ton Freightliner.

The blitz became a ghastly slow-motion event for Macie, who gawked at her torturer, now pinned between the warped metal door enfolding the front of the wrecker and the wall of hanging tools. One of them, a long chisel, had impaled him through the back of his neck, leaving a gurgling exit wound between his Adam's apple and jaw where the blade protruded. Poetic for the man favoring a tool as weapon of choice. His accomplice's lower leg splayed out from under the engine block, a lifeless foot lacking only a ruby slipper.

Cody hustled around the rear of the truck, ducking under the tow hook. "Don't look," he said, then stood before her to block the view of the gore. He had on a pair of nitrile gloves that made it difficult to undo her restraints. After some cursing, he finally threw aside the last strap and got her to her feet. Her purse was on the floor behind her chair. He snagged it and asked, "Can you walk?"

"I think so."

"Good. Then you can run." He didn't wait for agreement but hooked an arm around her back, then ushered her past the collision to the rear of the garage. He gently set her to lean against the wall before he opened the back door, made a recon of the outside, then enfolded her again, hauling her into the narrow breezeway separating theirs from the next building. Chalking it up to her vulnerability after the trauma, Macie found his physicality powerful and comforting. At the end of the tight little alley, he planted her against the cinder blocks, boosted himself up to stand one-footed on an electric meter housing, and pulled down a cable taped to the outside of the oblong window overhead. "We're clear, let's go." But after he made his cautionary peek around the corner of the building, he held back. A few seconds later a car passed. When it was gone, he drew her out onto the sidewalk one street behind the auto repair shop. He picked up speed as they got closer to his van.

"Wait," said Wild. "My car . . ."

"Is parked far enough away that you're better off leaving it for now." Gunnar opened the passenger door and helped her up. "No sense wandering back to a crime scene. There you go, lift your knee." But Macie hesitated. She had so many questions, so much had happened so quickly. Then she heard an approaching siren, and just got in.

Macie wept. The tears came unbidden, and she sobbed as quietly as she could, facing away from him all the way out of the Bronx, hugging her blouse together but really hugging herself. Gunnar said nothing. He let her have her feelings without platitudes or diversion, although once, at a stoplight after they crossed the river into Manhattan, he did place his palm on her knee. She didn't respond to it, but felt a little sorry when the green light came and he removed it. "How did you find me?"

"Does it matter?"

"To me."

"You've got Find My iPhone toggled on. When I got your message and you didn't return my call, my Spidey-sense tingled. Plus I have my guy. You know, CyberG."

"You hacked me."

"Be grateful for that."

"You came damned close to taking me out along with those two."

Resigned to justify the grand entrance, Gunnar said, "You're familiar with TARU, that little unit I used to work with? The one you have a bug up your ass about? One of our gigs was setting up communications for hostage negotiations. What I did was straight out of training. I assessed the location then planted a mic and lipstick cam looking down from the window so I could get a visual on you and your pals." She recalled him pulling down the cable as they left and nodded that she was following so far. "With eyes and ears on that garage, I was able to do two things: one, measure distances and positions; two, I saw and heard you were in danger. Guess you didn't know one of my numerous skills is how to hotwire a truck. Which I would have proved if the keys weren't already in it."

"Why didn't you just call the police? A novel idea when someone is kidnapped."

"Timing. Or did you kinda like the pain thing? Those TENS units get used in BDSM dungeons, too, you know. So there's no shame if you did."

"I don't think I've ever known a man who could drive a truck into a steel garage door, kill two people, and joke it off. Don't you feel regret?"

"Yes. It was a perfectly fine garage door." At the next light, he turned to her with a more sober look. "Of course, there's something. Maybe not regret, I don't know . . . But don't forget they were about to turn your heart into a Hot Pocket. That's when I lost my deep sense of kinship for them." Gunnar locked eyes with hers. "You just do the job. Period, full stop."

She sat quietly for a few blocks, touching the superficial burn on her stomach. "I think we need to report this." Anticipating him, she added, "At least I do. Officer of the court, and all that."

"Not sure that's a good idea."

"Wish I could say I was surprised to hear you say that."

"Well, seeing how we still aren't sure how your Buzz Killer mysteriously disappeared from a highly secure jail ward—while under police supervision—I would suggest that the police are not your best option, counselor."

The weight of the trauma, the spreading stain of conspiracy made her blurt, "I need to go to my office!" Then Wild seemed to realize how manic that came off, and dialed it down. "I need to be busy. And I need to stay on my case. Cases," she corrected for good measure.

For his part, Gunnar said exactly the right thing. "Don't need to explain anything to me."

First she wanted to change clothes and clean up. Out of an abundance of caution and for her peace of mind, Gunnar offered to escort her to her apartment and then drive her downtown to the public defenders'. Macie accepted without a blink.

After he walked her place to clear the rooms and closets, she showered while he made them some coffee. When she appeared, it was with damp hair, a crisp blouse, and a suit right out of the dry-cleaning plastic. She drew an approving sip from her mug and tilted her head toward him. "Thank you."

"Not too strong?"

"I mean for rescuing me. In all the craziness, I realized I hadn't said that."

"Not a problem. Although this is the second time I've saved you, and the second time you've given me shit after."

She draped a hand on top of his, the make-good for the missed moment on their drive. "Next time, my turn."

"So I can give you shit?"

"You can try."

"I love a challenge," he said, laced with flirtation. Once again, Macie found herself drawn to the current of warmth flowing from him. Then he switched the subject. It felt the same as when he had taken his hand off her knee in the van. "OK, so while you've been performing your ablutions, I've been thinking about why those two fucks were drilling down on you about Jackson Hall's take." Wild withdrew her hand and pulled a frown. The sensation of her violation was still fresh. The heat of the shower had made her skin burn, and now, reliving her rendition was having the same effect on her breathing. "Oh, listen, if this is uncomfortable for you . . ."

"Maybe just now. Give me an hour." She laughed. "You're looking at the Queen of Compartmentalization."

But he studied her with those kind-sad eyes and said, "If you'd feel better not being here alone, you're welcome to crash at my place tonight."

She ran a finger around the rim of her mug, and said, "No, I think I need to cocoon in my own place." Then she looked up to him, adding, "But you can stay here." Macie felt a chest flutter and quickly tagged it with, "On the couch I mean. I don't mean . . ."

"Right. Whatever you don't mean— Yes, I'd be happy to."

Even though it was the end of her workday, Wild settled into her desk with a vengeance. The self-proclaimed Queen of Compartmentalization needed the governing of a realm to distract her, and she began with a session of docket signing with her paralegal. When she had finished, the Aussie gave her a squinting appraisal. "You doing all right? You look a bit of a cot case."

"You're going to have to translate."

"There I go again with the Melbournese. Exhausted. Fit for bed."

Macie thought about confiding her ordeal. Tiger Foley was one of those rare people with whom she could share a secret and know it wouldn't go anywhere. But this was too loaded, especially since it wasn't just about her, but also about Gunnar having killed two men. So she told the truth she could tell. "It's been stressful, Tige. Client on the loose, body turning up this morning . . ."

"Of course. Just checking." He gathered the signed documents. "Shall I assemble the troops?"

She declined. Not only was Soledad Esteves Torres off campus in Red Hook on an outreach to a coworker of Jackson Hall's girlfriend, too many meetings stalled progress. "I'll just do some office hopping."

Tiger grinned. "Then, if you'll excuse me, I'll go fossick the cubbies to make sure someone's actually in them when you 'roo around."

Jonathan Monheit was in the middle of typing up his notes from the visits he'd made to Hall's known associates. "I'll still send you the e-mail, but here's my download, going geographically. I did East Side first. The fishing pier was NG. All school kids or some day camp, whatev. No adults. I'll go back in the morning. That's when his buddies usually met. Next, the Stealer's Wheel bar on 125th. Lovely establishment. When I finally found somebody who'd talk to me, he said there was no sign of him."

"You think that's covering?"

"It occurred to me. But he also told me other people had just been in looking for him, so I figured he was being straight."

"Other people? Like what, cops?"

"I asked. He didn't know."

"Did you get descriptions?" He gave her the Jonny Midnight blush and said he'd go back and ask. "And did you make it to Spatone's?"

"My Upper West Side leg. He was there, but wouldn't open the door. Yelled through the little peep hatch that last time he talked to you, his friend Stamitz got fished out of a marsh in Baychester."

Chip Ross didn't have an office. He had a modest perch in a bull pen shared with the other summer interns. It's what the budget allows in a public defender law office. Chip had just returned from a follow-up meeting, and Macie found him taking off his blazer, revealing a powder blue oxford shirt drenched with perspiration from the humidity. "This could be something," he said, blotting his forehead with his sleeve. "Got a call a couple hours ago from one of the sons of that Arab dude."

"Mr. Sharif?" she asked, hoping respect was contagious.

"Yes, Fahad Sharif. Anyway his eldest son was there the other day when I reached out to him to ask if anyone had circled around to sell back any of his stolen property. Mr. Sharif had said no, but his son—Idris is his name—he is into college football, and we got to talking LSU. 'Geaux Tigers.' So I guess I made a connection, because when Idris called me to meet up with him just now, he told me his dad actually had been called by someone trying to sell back two wristwatches." Chip looked at his notes. "One of the Cartiers and the Patek Phillippe. At first, his father was going to buy them back, but after they agreed on a price, the guy squeezed him for $5,000 more at the last minute, just like with Henkles. Mr. Sharif walked away. Said he was too sick to deal with the stress."

"Did he say who the caller was?"

"I asked. He never knew because his father never got a name."

"You're right, this is definitely something. Nice going, Mr. Ross."

"So we have confirmation of a pattern," said Gunnar. Macie had called him as soon as she finished with Chip. "Somebody, or a couple of some-bodies, on that burglary crew was trying to extort ransom for some of the items."

"Not only of ransoming stolen goods," she added, "but exploiting the victims at the eleventh hour with a price bump. Could that be enough to give one of our burglary victims a motive to kill?"

"You mean kill Pinto? Maybe. Stamitz? Possibly. If I don't sound completely sold it's only because those two were done-up royally before they died. You don't cowboy somebody like that over a wristwatch. But it's a clue we didn't have before. Hopefully we'll figure out where it fits. Hang on a sec." In the background, Wild heard Gunnar telling someone to keep the change.

"Where did I catch you?" she asked when he had finished.

"Scene of the crime. I took a cab to the Bronx to retrieve your car. Something told me you might like it back."

"Don't you need my key?"

He chuckled. "Any other stupid questions?"

An hour later, Wild made a stop in the break room to retrieve the bottle of Sancerre she had left in the fridge, a purchase she had impul-sively ducked out to make after her phone call with Gunnar. She asked the clerk what went into an old-fashioned, and also bought a bottle of Jameson, which she had seen him order at Isabella's, and some micro-brew bitters made by some purveyor from Park Slope. Ignoring the fact that she was stocking up for something more than an evening of body-guarding, she enjoyed the tug of war between denial and anticipation. Macie slid the bottles into her canvas Whole Foods reusable and turned off the lights in her office.

In the lobby she stopped and set everything down to answer her cell phone. It was Rick Whittinghill.

Macie switched her office lights back on and waited for him. Her former MCPD investigator didn't take long; Whittinghill had called her from the Starbucks over on Worth, and brought her a coffee. "I forgot what you took in it, so I snagged pretty much the works." He set the cof-fee on her desk and, from the pocket of his sport coat, fished two each of the different sugars and sweeteners from the fix-up bar. "Milk, you're on your own." She selected an Equal and stirred it in while he took a seat. "Sheez, sorry about rolling in on you like that this morning. With him right here, and all. Christ, I'm losing my edge."

"It's all good, Whit. You sidestepped it fine. No harm done."

"So." He gestured to her Whole Foods bag with the liquor bottle necks poking up. "I see you have some plans for the night, so let's get to it." From another pocket of his jacket, he pulled out a manila envelope that had been folded in half. While the ex-cop unbent the metal butterfly clasp to open it, a twinge pulled at Wild's solar plexus, which was tender enough from the abuse it had taken. Could she call this off now? she wondered. Should she? Before Macie could decide, Whittinghill spoke, citing the front page of his report from Internal Affairs. "Gunnar Cody, Ex-Detective First Grade." He paused to scan the page and then the next. He took off his CVS bifocals and set the papers on his lap. "A couple of things. Speaking as an ex-cop myself? Up top, nothing heinous." Macie felt relief spread through her and nodded, trying to keep her smile measured. "Apparently he's got a smart mouth on him—who doesn't? Got written up a few times for insubordination. Also some citations for . . ." he put his glasses back on to recite, " '. . . repeatedly exceeding the scope of his assignments.' That would be crossing the line once too often. Again, what cop worth a shit hasn't been there? Still, kind of a dick pattern."

"Well, thank you Whit. This is very helpful. I owe you one."

"Not done yet. Something unusual."

"All right . . ."

"A portion of his IA file is under seal."

"What does that mean?"

"It means exactly what it means. There's something in there nobody—especially a snoop like me—is supposed to see." He folded the papers, slid them back in the envelope, and redid the clasp. He set the package on her desktop and patted it lightly with his wide fingers.

Wild touched the inflamed skin on her stomach. "Is that bad? I mean of course it's—probably not good, right? Sealing a personnel file?"

"Could be anything. Could be something that carries liability, legal or civil liability, to the department. Could be he had a sharp lawyer negotiate the seal as part of his exit from the force. The point is, it's sealed. So who's to know?"

In the liquor store, Macie had been toying with telling Gunnar not to bother with the couch that night. Now she found herself wondering if she should cancel the big evening. Compared to being tortured by electroshock, this emotional jolt about a past that was controversial enough to go under official seal was low grade, but still troubling. Yet by the time she came up the steps from the R train at Eighth Street, Macie had gone back and forth with this Internal Affairs news and come down on the side of taking the longer view: grown adults come with pasts, herself included. Maybe this was all best left set aside, if she could do that.

When she turned the corner off University Place, Gunnar was sitting on the stoop of her building, smiling wider the closer she got. He rose, offering her car keys, which were looped over his pinkie for the taking. "Gassed up and parked. Alternate-side's in effect; you'll have to move it in the morning."

"You had my car key?"

"I relieved you of it during my daring rescue after you insisted it would be a good idea to hang around and get your Corolla while half the Fortieth Precinct was rolling up. Considering the ordeal, your memory may be hazy about that. Thank goodness one of us had a clear head, right?" Wearing a sunny mask, Macie took the key from him and fished out her house keys to let them in. On the elevator ride, she smelled the lightness of his cologne and a small ripple ran through her. As they strode to her door, she said, "You know, I was thinking. Before I met you I had what I thought was a very colorful life. But no car chases, no kidnappings, no electric-shock torture . . ."

"You're welcome," he said.

The liquor bottles clanged as she set the Whole Foods bag on the counter. "Hey, now, whatcha got there?"

"Don't peek."

"Curiosity is my only virtue." Gunnar peered in the bag and palmed the Jameson.

"Just a little something to help the time pass for my bodyguard. I got some hipster bitters too."

He set the bottle down on the tiles and smiled. "Someone pays attention." Instead of making her feel lighthearted—the way she had envisioned this moment—his appreciation only churned up the guilt Macie thought she had tucked away. He picked up on it. "Something wrong? I forget to wipe my feet?"

Macie led him to the living room to sit on the sofa with her. A confession would be the only way she could do this night. Without a strategy, other than to speak her heart, she said, "Gunnar, I need to tell you something. I came by some information today. Information about you and your departure from TARU and the NYPD." He didn't speak, but gave her the kind of attention that matched the gravity that had suddenly befallen the party. "You told me yourself that you left on rocky terms. What I came across was . . . that whatever those circumstances were, they were serious enough to be placed under seal." He drew a lengthy audible inhale and his lips whitened as he pursed them. "I can see this is awkward for you," she continued, putting a hand on his. "It is for me, too, but we seem to be on the brink of going somewhere beyond partnering on this case, and I don't want a secret from you. It feels dishonest, and I wanted to be transparent."

"Are you hearing yourself?" he asked evenly. "You talk about transparency in the same breath you say you happened to 'come by' some information about me?"

Wild's limbs became leaden. "This was a mistake. I never should have brought this up. It's not easy to have a conscience sometimes." His neutral stare made her nervous and so she filled the void. "I guess part of me was hoping, you know, quid pro quo. Like, if I opened up to you . . ."

He withdrew his hand from hers and tapped a forefinger on his temple. "Macie, there's still a detective in here, and you are insulting his intelligence."

"I am not insulting you at all. I just don't want us to have secrets."

"You didn't 'come by' anything. Don't compound this by making it sound like it's some shiny quarter you found in the gutter. You like transparency? Here's some: The guy who saved your ass today doesn't like to be snooped."

Macie told herself not to rise to the bait, but couldn't hold back. "Ironic. From somebody who's all about snooping."

"Very glib."

"Look, let's just—let's pop that cork and have a night." After she suggested that, he stood. But not to play bartender. "Can't we at least have a conversation about this?" she asked.

"I'll tell you what I told you when we met. My exit from the force is my business. And after this, it's going to stay that way, you can count on that."

"Gunnar, don't." But he was already on his way to the door and didn't stop, even for a glance back. Wild sat alone a moment in tortured silence before she hauled herself off the couch and sauntered unsteadily to the counter. She snatched up the bottle of Jameson and pegged it across the kitchen into the sink where it shattered, spraying the walls and ceiling with Irish whiskey.

CHAPTER 28

Macie's next day became a mix of moving forward on the case while dragging the tonnage of regret for having to do so without Gunnar. Wild had adapted more than she knew to having an adroit partner in him and had to still herself from the reflex to check in or to share. The shattered Jameson and all that went down the drain—literally—with that was another matter, another ache.

The *New York Ledger*, one of the city's also-ran tabloids, was where Macie finally found the only mention of the incident she had escaped the day before. "Squeeze Play in Da Bronx" was the headline in a two-paragraph squib buried on one of the middle pages with the weekend anglers' report and a photo of a llama in somebody's yard in suburban Hicksville, Long Island. The copy was an attempt at glibness, reporting the deaths of two unidentified men crushed by a tow truck in an auto repair garage. Detectives from the Fortieth Precinct were investigating it as a potential homicide. Funny, she thought, folding the newspaper, how something so life-death for you—and death for two others—barely makes the radar in a city of millions. Or was it not getting more play for other reasons? Once again, Macie wished she could match her conspiracy paranoia with Gunnar's.

Jonathan Monheit showed up at her office door goofy with excitement. "This may be big," he said as she motioned him to sit. "Also it may not be the most legal or ethical thing I've done. In fact, now I'm . . . God, I wonder if I should even disclose to you, since it could make you an accessory."

"Got a dollar on you?" His face puzzled and he nodded. "Hand it over." When he gave the buck to her, she said, "Attorney-client privilege. Talk to me."

Jonny Midnight leaned forward and lowered his voice. "I have some contacts. All right, one, a fraternity brother, at the corporate headquarters of Rúben Pinto's bank. I asked him—discreetly—to do a snapshot of his account history. Check it out." He made a few taps on his iPad and came around her desk to show her the spreadsheet. "All pretty much what you'd expect. Low amounts coming in and going out. More going out actually. But here. See that? A $9,995 deposit. Total red flag."

"Almost $10,000, in a lump sum."

"Almost ten because ten means the bank has to report the activity under federal regs. I'm betting Pinto knew that would bring scrutiny so he kept himself under the limit. And why?"

Macie was right there, but let him enjoy his unique moment of success. "Tell me."

"Because scrutiny is what he didn't want. Because this was the extortion money he squeezed out of that football player in exchange for returning the betting ledger he stole from him."

The ramifications of Monheit's findings were support for the developing picture that at least Rúben Pinto, if not possibly the entire burglary crew, fenced its stolen goods, but ransomed back some of them too. Wild didn't need to do too much abstract analysis. All she had to do was replay the question Pipe Wrench tortured her over the day before. He wanted to know about the take. "This is terrific, Jonathan. But a first step. See if you can do the same with Jackson Hall and Jeffrey Stamitz, the crew chief." His eyes widened, and she said, "Aw, come on, you did this once, you'll find a way."

"I suppose I can," he said, rising to go. "And I don't need to worry. Attorney-client privilege, right?"

"Oh, I just made that up so you'd talk." She handed back his dollar, and he was still wondering whether she was joking or not when he left.

Her team's social worker was late getting in following a visit to Department of Corrections headquarters in the old Bulova building out near La Guardia. Soledad Esteves Torres had gone there to press for full disclosure about what happened at Rikers the day Jackson Hall was found hanging. "I also told them I don't like the smell of his escape from the Bellevue prison ward. BHPW is supposed to be state-level security, and he just wanders out?" She opened the fridge in the break room to retrieve her lunch bag and, after she closed it, she showed a weary face to Macie. "Sometimes it just feels like the system isn't working. Then I wonder. Is it working, but against us?"

The two ate together at one of the little picnic tables outside City Hall where they could see the traffic flow off the Brooklyn Bridge and watch the tourists pose with the NYPD detail on the beat around the mayor's office. Wild sidestepped Soledad's questions about how she was doing. "You look kinda spent, Macie. Is there something you need to talk about?" That's what happened when your friend was a licensed social worker. But opening up about her surveillance exploits, her torture in the Bronx, not to mention her parting with Gunnar, would only dig a hole and pull the dirt in. So Macie shifted to ask Soledad about her search for Jackson Hall's MIA girlfriend.

"First of all I can tell she's not dead. Her coworker friend hasn't opened up yet, but I'm reading from the way she talks about Pilar that she's not deeply worried about her."

"You think she's hiding her?"

"I do. And if not physically, she knows who. You know, these things take time. We want it all now, but trust has to be built. I'm visiting her again this evening." She took a forkful of her rice salad. "I wonder who she's hiding from."

Wild flashed back to her TENS session. Then the crew chief's body in the marsh. Then the Pinto crime scene. Then her near-abduction by Luka Fyodor Borodin. What Pilar Fuentes was hiding from wasn't the question. It was, is Jackson Hall hiding with her? And could they find her, or him, before somebody else did?

Gunnar Cody was leaning against the brick wall outside his apartment building with his head down, thumbing a message on his cell phone, when Wild approached. He never looked up, but when she got within speaking range, he said, "Almost finished." Macie came no closer and held her spot at about the same privacy range as an ATM line. And about as warm. "Ready," he said, pocketing his iPhone and boosting himself away from the wall. She got a reserved smile, and he didn't lead her into his vestibule. Instead, he said, "Let's take a walk."

NoLIta on a June evening is a bath of golden light and warmth. He seemed to have a destination in mind, and so she just stayed at his elbow as they wove past the window shoppers and cafés until he gestured through the gate of the little pocket of a park on Elizabeth Street. The Gothic statuary made the small patch of urban greenery a small cemetery without the bodies. They crunched over the pea gravel past an ornate stone balustrade to a granite bench that was being vacated by a couple that looked in a hurry to get to dinner or to bed.

A Jeep Wrangler paraded up Elizabeth, blasting Bruno Mars. After the mega bass faded away and muffled night sounds again filled their oasis, Gunnar said, "So what's up?"

"I'm wondering if it's time to, I dunno, to reset."

Gunnar rocked a little, an internal nod of confirmed suspicions. "I think we need to clear some air first."

"OK . . ."

"You caught me way off guard. Everything's great, and then, sproing. Like stepping on a rake and the handle hits you in the face. Anyway, I got too pissed to be—articulate—in the moment. But I still feel the way I did. About you going behind my back like that. You know, I have had to walk a very fine line lately. Doing my job—and teaming with you—has definite pluses, but it has not always been a day at the beach." He counted off on his fingers. "My job. Our job. Also feeling a need to protect you. You've been more than . . . your word: transparent . . . about how you feel about what I do. Well, I have some issues of my own. Like sending that ham and egger Rick Whitinghill to sniff around Internal Affairs. And don't insult me by trying to cover for him. Even if I weren't savvy enough to see through that charade in your office when he 'just happened to drop by' for his 'vay-cay pay,' I still have plenty of eyes and ears at One-PP who tip me off when the bloodhounds are out."

"I'll cop to that—no pun. But that was initiated before I really knew you. Before I—" He might have heard something more than he'd bargained for if he'd let her finish that sentence. But he interrupted.

"See, you're using the same rationale I did for not coming clean right off about knowing who Luka Borodin was." He paused. Then, sounding conciliatory, added, "So does that even it out?"

"It could . . . If we let it." Then, advocate that she was, Wild tempted fate with one more try. "So no chance you'll tell me why part of your personnel file is under seal?"

"Nope, sorry."

"Gunnar, don't you trust me?"

"You kidding? I totally do. But I can't talk about it." Wavering slightly, he added, "Maybe someday. Not now."

"That's trusting."

"And that's sarcasm. I'm liking that side of you, Macie Wild." He shifted to face her. "Look, remember that first time in the van, when you said that we all have our secrets and that something needs to be sacred? This is me, saying, 'amen.'"

Wild thought a beat and smiled. "Are you sure you aren't a lawyer?"

"Are you sure you aren't trying to make me pay for something that's none of your concern?"

"I'm trying to make it so we can work together. Again."

"All right . . ." He rocked his full-body nod again and stood. "We aren't getting anything done sitting here."

Unfortunately it didn't take long for Macie to brief Gunnar on her progress since they split. A short walk back and an elevator ride sufficed to cover what little headway she had made. As Gunnar pulled open the accordion gate at his floor, she ended with the spike Jonathan Monheit had found in Rúben Pinto's bank account that would have coincided with his shakedown of the NFL star. "Definitely quacks like a duck," he said.

An intense funk of fast food and unshowered maleness greeted Macie's nose when she stepped into Gunnar's place. "Honey, I'm ho-ome," sang out Gunnar, prompting his Argentinian hacker to gopher his bandana and eyeballs over the partition that separated the edit bay from the great room. "Hide the NSFWs," Gunnar teased. "We're comin' in." CyberGauchito paused his work only long enough to give Wild a shy head dip followed by a tug of his chin whiskers. Without a word, he returned to his multiple monitors and keyboard. From the archipelago of takeout garbage and coffee cups around the overflowing trash can, she surmised whatever was going on, it had been a long undertaking.

"I see you've been busy too," she said. "This about the case? Or your VICE video? Both?" Two things gnawed at her: one, the pang from her obvious exclusion, albeit self-inflicted; two, the certainty that going to the park for a chat had been a litmus test for her return to the action. She let go of both. Some things were not fruitful to spend emotional capital on.

"Like you, breaking a sweat. Wouldn't call it progress yet," he called from the kitchen, returning with pale ales for them and a cane sugar Coca-Cola for El Gauchito. Gunnar dragged in one of the kitchen chairs for her, clinked bottlenecks, and paced while he filled her in.

"Back when we got that burglary list from Jackson Hall, I gave it to an ex-TARU bro who owes me from now to when Justin Bieber is in a walker. I had him run it against any other nearby neighborhood crimes, misdemeanors, and complaints that preceded or followed each break-in. This would be a routine search any detective does when trying to be comprehensive in an investigation. The dicey part is, as I am not strictly NYPD, I needed the favor and didn't want some gatekeeper icing me again. My bro bearded for me, scored the data from RTCC, and, we shoot, we score! Foot-patrol unis from Midtown North issued a Pink Summons—that's a Quality of Life ticket—to one Rúben Pinto who was found trespassing in shrubbery on private property at 3:18 in the morning. Significantly, the planter Mr. Pinto was cited for violating is the landscaping of The Ajax luxury condos. With me? This Pink was issued in the early hours after Hall said they burglarized the place."

"The take," said Macie. "Pipe Wrench, that guy you . . ." Mindful of CyberG, she didn't finish. "When he tortured me, he wanted to know about the take. A pouch."

Gunnar toasted her. "So we both agree it's possible that Rúben Pinto skimmed from whatever the take was at The Ajax, secretly tossed it in the planter on the crew's getaway, and came back to look for it later."

"Did the summons say he had anything on him?"

"No. They just wrote him up and let him go. Why would they think to search the bushes in the dark without cause? But I think Pinto boosted something he came back for later and got. And somebody is hell-bent on recovering whatever it was."

"I'm the last one you need to convince of that," she said.

"The obvious question is still, who got ripped off in The Ajax?" she said.

He added, "And who had the clout to deny that there was a burglary?"

"We're back to that LLC."

"That's right. Whoever, or whatever, Exurb Partners LLC is, this shell corporation that bought The Ajax condo is the hot lead."

"But you were there at our defense team meeting. Exurb is a mail drop in Queens. And the way it's set up, the owner is legally masked by the LLC," she said. "With no mortgage, it's even harder to put a name to it. And the condo management probably doesn't even know. Or care. Like my dad told me, when you have a cash buyer for a $40 million place like that, the incentive to create red tape is minimal."

"Understatement of the decade."

"Thank you," she said and took a swig of her beer.

"All of which is why I have called upon my Buenos Aires black hat to help me try to identify the mystery tenant through some unorthodox means."

"It's a fucking pain in the ass," said CyberG without turning from his monitors.

"No pain, no pain, *correcto, mi amigo?*" He turned back to Wild. "What we've done is create our own facility to review security cameras in and around The Ajax to try to capture the owner of the condo in question on camera so we can ID him or her."

While CyberGauchito scrubbed through video, Gunnar gave her the quick and dirty of his footage acquisitions. "Since The Ajax's spy cams record to hard drives hooked up to off-site servers, that data flows over a secure internet connection."

"Secure," chuckled the hacker. "Riiiight."

"With limited time and resources, we narrowed our focus down to key locations at and near The Ajax." He bent beside Macie and showed her on his iPad an architectural plan with red dots indicating the cameras from which he had slurped video: "Ajax main lobby; Ajax underground parking spaces reserved for the penthouse; and the private express elevator to the penthouse tucked away between the Coach and Joseph Abboud stores in the mall under The Ajax."

"I've walked by there a hundred times," she said. "I never knew it was there."

"Kind of the whole idea of a private elevator." He set the iPad on the counter. "We've been screening pretty much nonstop since yesterday. Scooch on up." Gunnar rolled his task chair over to the other keyboard and monitor setup, leaving space for Macie to place her chair beside his. Soon his fingers flew across the keys and trackpad, rolling grainy video that she immediately recognized as from the lobby of The Ajax. He was searching at four-x speed, the only way to get through all the footage from three cameras in his lifetime, he said, only part jokingly. Whenever people appeared he would toggle down to regular speed, click a screenshot, which went into a holding file, and then move on again at quad rate. The tediousness of the work matched the dead hours she had experienced in his van, and she found herself rooting for more unpopulated stretches, just to be able to clear more video without slowing down to log one more tenant whose elevator ride ended on one of the middle floors, according to the illuminated display above each car.

After a few hours, she offered to go get some pizzas, as much to quell her hunger as to break away from the monotony. On her return, Gunnar taught her just enough of the bare basics of the editing program to spell him at the controls while he ate a slice. "Ho, check it out," said CyberG. The black hat had been scouring the underground garage where four spaces reserved for the penthouse had sat empty throughout his screening. Until then.

Gunnar paused Macie's video and both turned their attention to the other monitor where an HVAC repair van had pulled in and stopped. The hacker pointed to the embedded time code. "Night of the burglary." All eyes stared, all hoping for a glimpse of a familiar face—Hall, Pinto, or Stamitz. Instead the van rocked slightly from the motion of someone unseen getting out the far side. Seconds later, a gloved hand holding a can of spray paint shot up into view and sprayed the lens until it was covered.

"Well, that's no fun," said Cody. "Gauch, do a blitz and see if this is all she wrote." Some double-clicks on the trackpad, and time code sped to a blur as the video scanned at the fastest speed available without disengaging content. The monitor suddenly went bright again and CyberG slowed it to real time. The embedded digits established it as 08:12:24 the next morning. A cloth was being swabbed over the lens, and a maintenance worker they recognized from their past screening gave the camera one more spritz of solvent and a cursory wipe that left half of the lens still obscured by black enamel. Satisfied enough, he hopped down from whatever he'd been standing on and left. They ignored their other material and huddled around CyberGauchito's monitor, four-xing through a video that might as well have been a still: a static shot of empty parking spaces and an alcove leading to the penthouse elevator. Just before eleven a.m.—10:44:10, by the time code—activity.

The hood of a black town car nosed into the bottom of the frame and stopped. Gauch shuttled down the speed to normal view. A man got out of the back seat on the far side, which put his back to the camera. Without turning, he strode to the alcove, swiped a key card, the elevator immediately opened, and he disappeared inside, face unseen.

CyberG bumped the speed up again, and a half hour whizzed by in thirty seconds until he slowed it all down again when the light blinked on above the elevator. The same man stepped out and walked back to his waiting car, talking on his cell phone. Between holding the phone up to one side of his face and the blackout of half the lens, they never made him out. When the car backed out, Gunnar said, "Balls. This close. Not even a shot of the plate on the car. Very inconsiderate."

He and his hacker spent the next hour replaying the footage frame by frame and attempting every video enhancement the software offered. When it was clear no doctoring was going to yield an identifiable image of the man's face they sat quietly, just thinking. Macie's eyes burned, and she wasn't even the one doing the heavy lifting. "OK, new thought," said Gunnar, sounding like a man trying to bolster himself. "Play it down from his exit of the car, back-to-back with his return from the elevator." After watching that sequence twice, he said, "Export that to a file." He smiled and gave Macie an eyebrow flick. "Gonna skin this cat yet."

"What are you going to do?"

"Two things: first, endure a slew of fucks and shits from my ol' pal from TARU. Because, second, I'm going to ask him to submit this clip to the Real Time Crime Center as if it's official police business."

"Do they have more sophisticated enhancement capability?"

"Yes, but enhancement won't help. Our raw material is too corrupted to clean up digitally. What they do have is something called Gait Analysis."

"Help me out here."

"Gait Analysis. Gait, as in how we walk. Everybody's stride is unique—as individual as fingerprints. RTCC has built a database of gaits, same as they have with scars, tatts, and facial recog. It's a bit of a Hail Mary, but I've used it before, back when I was on the job, with crazy-amazing results. We got lucky here catching him on video, assuming he is the condo owner. Let's push it."

At midnight Wild sat in the stillness of her apartment in the company of a lone candle, a glass of the Sancerre that she never opened after impulsively christening her sink with the bottle of Jameson, and her own sullen thoughts about the direction of the Buzz Killer case, which had gone flat, to be charitable. Oh, yes, potential leads had surfaced. So had new victims to interview, crime scenes of promise, and no shortage of other players—of lethal capability—who were in a footrace with her. But to where? Nothing had knitted together. Her funk rose out of a dark recess within Macie that she was all too acquainted with. It incubated the plague of the apt pupil who feared she wasn't studying enough. Or, more to the point, that something was sitting right there under her nose that she was overlooking. Macie's phone made her jump when it rang. The caller ID was Gunnar's. "Hope I didn't wake you."

"Hardly. I'm just catching up on some office e-mails." She took another sip of wine.

"Live it up. Just wanted to let you know my man at the precinct did give me a ration of shit, but he ultimately submitted the video clip to RTCC."

"Oh, good. Fingers crossed. I guess pretty soon they'll have a database for fingers too."

"Wouldn't be hard. Cops see a lot of them. Middle fingers mostly." After a pause he continued, "Listen. The real reason I called? I'm glad we're back. We are back, right?"

She chuckled. "Seems so. And I'm glad too."

"Good, good. Any interest in breakfast or a coffee in the morning before you go in? I can come your way."

"I'd like that but I'm meeting my dad up at his office. Probable TMI for you, but he said he needed to have a talk with me about my mother. I'm bracing myself for divorce or separation news."

"Oh, I'm sorry."

"Hey, at least it's not more danger admonishments. If my father had his way, I'd be sequestered inside a Park Avenue law office, litigating intellectual property rights."

"Instead of consorting with reprobates like me." If he only knew, thought Wild. "Can I pick you up for lunch then? I'm kind of a bony shoulder to lean on, but I can distract you with whack theories and moral indignations."

Wild laughed and said, "Thanks, I'll just Uber it. I'll need to get right to the office." The candle wick sputtered, throwing a spark. "But I'll call you after. We could have dinner, if you like."

The next morning, she sat on the on-deck sofa outside the door of her father's law office. Taking in the familiar scent of incinerated Winstons coming off his secretary's clothing always transported Macie back to her preschool visits when Bunny Liuizzi would play big-girl work with her, guiding Macie's little hands to three-hole punch the printer paper and let her use pastel highlighters to sign make-believe dockets. Play became passion, and the public defender submersed herself in the memory as she watched the seventy-two-year-old bend to swap her commuter cross-trainers for her office cross-trainers—the only difference being the degree of patina on the outsoles. "This morning New York-One had some gal on who claims she spotted your runaway Buzz Killer in Herald Square. At a Tad's Steaks, can you believe it?" She sat up with a huff, pained by the curvature of her spine, then finger combed her practical hair behind each ear. "You hear about that?"

"I got some texts. Nothing confirmed."

"Looked to me like she was hoping to grab her fifteen minutes of fame." Casting an appraising look through the internal window, the woman who had worked loyally with her father from his early practice, then up to Albany, and back to private practice, said, "Looks like he's about to wrap his call." Bunny returned to her opinions about the questionable eyewitness, using it as a bridge to her evergreen topics: selfie mania, piercings, and what's with the body ink? Macie found it hard to feign attention. She was too busy stressing whether the family cloth was about to tear.

To her relief, Jansen Wild had not asked her there for yet another blow to the family unit. Although Macie's comfort was dampened by indications that the shoe only had been given a temporary reprieve before dropping. His agenda still bore the thorns of marital discord. "I'm worried about your mother," he said as they settled into his conversation grouping. One plus to a morning meeting was that Wild caught him before the serious drinking began. Trying not to be obvious, she studied him for the signs of maintenance tippling. But his color was good, his eyes were clear, and his movements were controlled instead of the Frankenstein monster grabs he made at pens and mugs when he was secretly sauced.

A sudden concern flicked inside Macie. "Did something happen to her over there?"

"Not directly, no. She gave me fits when she was in Syria with those barrel bombs aimed at hospitals. Christ, what is our world?" He took a sip of water, and with a steady hand. "She did just have a near miss though. Some teenage girl her colleagues were operating on had a suicide bomb sewn inside her stomach that killed everyone in the tent. Your mother was off-shift but they evacuated the unit, and she's going to Germany for a week of R and R. I e-mailed her, asking her to come home."

"Let me guess."

"You know it. I got a terse reply I'd rather not quote." He gathered himself and said, "Mace, you and I both know there's been a lot of bad stuff in the groundwater since Walt died. I don't know if this relationship can be saved, but I still have feelings for her. I don't want to go quietly."

"Dad, I'm sorry. Have you told her?"

He snapped at her. "What, in a goddamned e-mail?" Then, calming, he continued, "That was shitty of me. See what's happening? The e-mails are unsatisfying at best, brittle at worst. And our phone calls are always on the run, like she's avoiding me." He took some more water and came to his point. "I need your help. I need an intermediary."

Macie felt herself sink an inch deeper into the sofa cushion under the weight of all this. The words left her mouth kicking and screaming. "I suppose I could call her."

"No, I want you to see her. I want her to have some face time with you so I have a fighting chance at a next step. Maybe some counseling, I don't know. She's going to be in Munich for the next eight days."

"You mean now?"

"I'll cover your ticket, your hotel, everything."

"Look, Dad, any other time—"

"I was afraid so." He closed his eyes and wagged his head in resignation, then held up a palm. "I get it. I understand."

"Do you?" He stood and managed a brave smile. Macie hugged him and said, "I will call her though. Promise."

How had John Lennon put it? That life is what happens to you while you're busy making other plans? With enough on her plate to solve world hunger, Macie Wild stood on the corner of Lexington and Fifty-Fourth, wandering a circle while she talked to her mother, who was just finishing lunch in Germany. The six-hour time difference wasn't the only separation she felt. That toxicity in the groundwater had seeped across the Atlantic, and the relay of her father's overture was met with stony deflection. After a sigh, Dr. Wild assured her daughter that there was nothing wrong. "At least no more than there was before," she added, contradicting herself. Her next dig told Macie she was wasting her time with the call, and would have wasted a week with a trip. "How's his drinking?" asked her mother.

After a few minutes on safer topics: Englischer Garten, Neuschwanstein Castle, and tweens with surgically embedded IEDs, they said their "love yous" and Macie hung up to tap for an Uber.

The phone hail app displayed a pickup in six minutes, not bad for the shank end of a Midtown morning rush. Headlights flashed, pulling her focus up from her scan of e-mails to the black MKX drawing up to the curb. The app said she still had three minutes to wait, and she took the early arrival as an omen of a good time-management decision. "Foley Square, right?" asked the driver when she got in.

"Yeah, thanks. Actually it's a block off the square past the courthouse. I'll direct you when we get close."

"You got it."

In what felt like a blink, they got off the FDR at the Brooklyn Bridge exit as Wild composed her last e-mail. On send, she closed up her mobile office, looked out her side window and then the rear. "'Scuse me. I think you missed the turn for Foley Square."

"Construction," he said. "I'll have to detour. I won't charge."

But his next turn took them north. They were looping back uptown, moving farther away from her destination. Wild always trusted her instincts, and they were flashing warning signs. As they approached the underpass beneath the Manhattan Bridge, she saw the stoplight turn yellow ahead. Macie slid her fingers around the door handle and looped the strap of her bag through her wrist so she could bolt when he stopped. The door locks shot closed and, instead of stopping, the driver floored it. She called out, "Hey!" which felt stupid. It was also ineffective. The engine roared deeply and her head lightly bumped the passenger window as the driver wove back and forth across lanes, threading the needle between slow cars and oncoming traffic. "Stop. Let me out! Now!"

He ignored her completely, and whipped the steering wheel in a hairpin turn into a street she didn't know in a neighborhood she didn't recognize. He pressed a garage door opener on his sun visor and a wrought iron gate rolled aside on the driveway of a moving and storage warehouse. They took the curb cut with a bounce and flew into the opening. Macie caught a glimpse of a man in a black suit monitoring the door as they shot past.

The driver braked to a hard stop and got out without a word, leaving her locked in, then walked somewhere out of her view. The man in the dark suit was still standing inside the garage entry, just watching her through the rear window as the draw chain clanked and the rolling metal gate slammed shut. He crossed over to her and the lock buttons snapped up so he could open the door for her. He held an ID out for her. Jermaine Stack, it said, FBI.

"If you'll come with me, please, Ms. Wild." He smiled pleasantly, but in a way that left little doubt what he expected her to do.

Special Agent Stack escorted her at a respectful distance between a pair of parked moving vans to the back of the warehouse where bright fluorescent light spilled out of an open office door. Another agent, a female in a blue suit with her credentials on a lanyard, stepped aside when she got to the threshold, and when she did, Macie could see Gunnar sitting on a folding chair facing a desk. He gave her a neutral nod. He wasn't handcuffed and didn't seem harmed. The female FBI agent gestured to the empty seat beside Gunnar and Wild took it. Stack shut the office door and leaned his hips on the desktop to face them. "I want to know what right you have to kidnap and hold me without probable cause," she said.

"Let me guess. The attorney," said the female agent to her partner.

"I'd like to keep this informal, OK, counselor?" said Special Agent Stack. "We'd just like to ask a few questions, and then you both can be on your way."

"I want a lawyer," said Cody. Then he turned to her. "Oh, hi. You're already here." He shrugged to the agents. "I'm guessing she's going to advise me not to answer anything."

"You about done?" Stack waited for his point to land, then said, "We want to know what your interest is in Pyotr Trifonov."

Gunnar leaned over to Macie and stage whispered, "He spoiled my surprise. We hit pay dirt with that Gait Analysis."

"You know that comedy routine would play better if you were actually still a cop," said Stack.

Cody shrugged, "You know, it's so hard to please audiences these days."

"Special Agent Nemec and I will find our entertainment elsewhere, thanks the same. Right now we'd just like to ask you two a couple of questions."

Macie stood. "Special Agent Stack, Special Agent Nemec. This constitutes confinement without cause. Citing our legal rights under the US Constitution, we are not answering any of your questions. Gunnar?" She then made to take a step toward the door but he just sat there.

"What do you want to know?" Gunnar asked them. Macie blinked at him in disbelief. He stayed put; she sat down.

The two FBI agents traded looks and then regarded Cody with a degree of suspicion. Nemec spoke this time. "We'll ask you again," she said. "What's your interest in Pyotr Trifonov?"

Cody said, "What makes you think we have an interest in Pyotr Trifonov?"

Stack replied, "Come on, don't bullshit me. You ran a Gait Analysis on him last night. Tell us why."

"Interesting," said Cody. "An RTCC database search lit up FBI radar? How come?"

"Once again, we ask," persisted the other agent. "Why a Gait Analysis?"

"How about he had a smooth gait, and I wanted to know who that bad boy was?"

"Do you think we're fooling around here?" asked Nemec.

Stack worked his jaw muscles. "You are both interfering in a federal investigation. And we want to know why. Why Trifonov? And bear in mind, any false statements to federal investigators could result in charges of obstruction of justice."

Macie said, "And I'd like to get a statement from you on why you think you can just snatch citizens off the street and bring them in for interrogation without a warrant or probable cause." The two just stared at her. "All right, my turn. What is the FBI's interest in Jeffrey Stamitz?" That got a quick exchange of looks between the pair, so she pressed it. "I recognize you two. You were at Stamitz's body dump in the marsh near Co-op City."

Gunnar seemed to like this feisty Macie. He picked up his cell phone. "I have a visual aid if you need a memory jog. Here it is. I got your pictures. Nice suits."

Stack scrambled to regain the upper hand in his interrogation. "Once more. What is your interest in Pyotr Trifonov?"

"Growing," Cody said with a grin. "More and more, the longer you keep asking. I think we're done here." His interrogators reacted with severe looks. Gunnar stood and said, "You two are free to go." Then he quickly added, "Oh, wait! Aren't you supposed to warn us to keep our noses out of your business?"

Special Agent Stack opened his wallet and withdrew a business card for each of them. "If you change your minds and want to cooperate . . ."

Macie finished for him. ". . . Stand on any corner and wait to be kidnapped?"

Gunnar gave her a firm nod of approval. "Macie Wild, showin' me something."

Back at the Manhattan Center for Public Defense, twenty minutes later, Wild called a team meeting and invited Gunnar to attend. "The man who is likely being shielded by Exurb Partners LLC and is, therefore, the probable owner of the penthouse at The Ajax is a Russian named Pyotr Arkady Trifonov."

While Macie block printed his name on the Case Board, Tiger sung out, "Got him right here," and spun his laptop screen so the others could see the Google page he had just pulled up. He rotated it back to skim-cite from the article. " 'Oligarch,' they call him, of course. Let's see, 'Industrialist . . . Profited from the post-Glasnost era of entrepreneurial possibilities in former Soviet Bloc nation-states . . . Expanded reach to newly opening markets around the globe . . .'" Tiger smiled and looked up. "I think it's fair to say Mr. Trifonov won't have to conduct a bake sale to pay for that luxe condo."

"Mr. Cody also got that much off the Internet this morning when his source came up with Trifonov's name," added Macie.

Soledad Esteves Torres said, "That's a big break. How'd you get it?"

"From the FBI." As soon as she said it, Gunnar's eyes widened at the risky disclosure.

Soledad said, "Fine, then, don't tell us." Then she laughed. "The FBI . . . that'll be the day."

"Wherever you're getting all this," said Tiger with an approving eye on Gunnar, "keep it coming."

"Now," said Wild, drawing an oval around "Trifonov" on the board, "am I the only one here to see something I don't believe in? By that I mean coincidences." She used a red marker to draw a long arc from Trifonov's name to Borodin's and back.

"It's raining Russians," said Gunnar.

"Coincidental? Not buying it." She turned to her MBA-investigator. "I want to drill down. Jonathan, I want you to give me a workup on this man."

"You mean drop everything else?" His question carried the cardinal sin of an investigator: an absence of curiosity outweighing effort.

Gunnar must have had enough because he pushed himself off the wall and flopped forward, leaning at Monheit. "That is exactly what she means, and you know why? Because right now Pyotr Trifonov is the hot lead. And, as every detective worth his wrinkled ass knows, when all else fails, you solve cases by what? By following the hot lead." A tense stillness descended on the room. Gunnar felt it and sat back again, addressing the team's investigator with a more collegial tone. "Jonathan, we're looking at a murder beef against your client, Jackson Hall, right?

And that forms a nexus with the two deceased members of Mr. Hall's burglary crew. Which, following it all along, points to some sort of retribution, a ransom gone wrong, or a deadly attempt at property recovery after their string of burglaries. Good so far?"

"Good."

"Great. Of all the burglaries we know of, the only one that doesn't fit the pattern is The Ajax. Why?"

"Because they denied there was a burglary."

"These days we call those alternative facts. But now I have reliable sourcing that points to an actual burglary."

Monheit wagged his head, quizzing himself. "That makes no sense. Why would they claim otherwise?"

Gunnar snapped his fingers. "There you go. You have just asked the question that IDs the what?"

"The hot lead."

"The hot lead indeed. Yes to dropping everything else, brah. X-ray Trifonov. More than that. Full-cavity search. Get it while it's hot."

"On it," said Jonny Midnight.

Macie gave Monheit a two-hour deadline before dismissing him to dig while she turned her attention to a thread of her own she wanted to follow. "I also want an X-ray of the crew chief, Jeffrey Stamitz. Today. Chip, you take the lead on that." The law student's eyes widened, so she added, "And so I'm not throwing you in the deep end, your life raft is going to be Tiger."

Jackson Hall's absence continued to cast a pall over everything, so Wild directed Soledad to make another run and recontact his missing girlfriend's coworker plus anyone else who might be a connection to the runaway Buzz Killer. "The clock's working against us, Sol. The longer he's out there, the more danger he faces from whomever he's hiding from—and that includes the police."

For lunch, she and Gunnar camped in her office, feasting on expired yogurts from the break-room fridge while they tried to make some sense out of the morning's fed encounter. Macie wondered about its basic logic. "I don't even want to know how the FBI hacked my Uber app. But why Uber-nap me when they could have come here to the MCPD or summoned us both to Federal Plaza for an interview on their turf?"

"One simple reason," answered Gunnar. "Either they wanted to intimidate us or they needed to firewall us from the official records."

"That's two reasons."

"Correct me, fine. I'm filling in as I go. It's part of my process."

"And it's a beautiful thing. Talk to me about your firewall theory."

"Let's start with a premise. Every organization, whether it's the FBI, your MCPD, or . . ."—Gunnar traced an air circle with his spoon until he landed on another example— "my merry band of scruffy disrupters at VICE Media . . . They all have compartments. Little pockets of folks with hidden agendas who work their dark magic behind closed doors or at dive bars after hours. Sometimes it's as mundane as office politics; sometimes it's more than that."

"I'm with you. But I'm still stuck on why."

With an impish grin, he said, "At the risk of expanding this to three reasons, here's the best I can do. Back when I was a detective, the only time I would work a shakedown like we got was when I wanted to keep it off the books. Either because I wanted to rattle someone—you know, get them jumpy so they'd talk—or I was going against orders. Or the orders were not to leave a trail that leads back to the unit. Or the commander."

"Hold on, are you saying they could be doing this clandestinely because they're up to something illegal?"

"Not necessarily. It could be, but it could also just be something internal that they don't want the other FBI boys and girls to know about."

She gave that a careful ponder and asked, "Which was it with you when you did it?"

Ex-Detective Cody gave her a deadpan look and said, "I respectfully invoke my rights under the Fifth Amendment of the US Constitution, on the grounds that answering such questions may incriminate me." She waited for him to laugh, but he didn't.

Gunnar Cody's tough-love talk must have lit a fire under Jonny Midnight. The nerd, universally viewed as punching above his weight, called the defense team back to the conference room exactly two hours later and blew them all away. Including Gunnar Cody, his chief doubter, who later called it the Midnight Miracle.

The lead investigator, a scant year out of business school, stood before the group on the solid rock of his MBA training. "I have prepared the X-ray you asked for on Pyotr Arkady Trifonov," he began. "I confess I had a bit of a head start. Although I was no expert on Mr. Trifonov at lunchtime, for my International Business Studies courses at the University of Washington, I did extensive research into post-Glasnost Russia, so a lot of what I'll be telling you about here was top-of-mind. The material I have on him, specifically, I got through deep diving the Internet plus some long-distance calls to my old professors and what stuck from my essay on one of our class resource books, *Putin's Kleptocracy* by Dawisha. I got a ninety-eight." He took a swig from his CamelBak and turned to the portable whiteboard he had rolled in.

"OK, who is Trifonov? Years before Wikipedia called him an oligarch, he was a member of what they call in Russia, the *Nomenklatura*. That's the elite of the elite in the former Soviet Union."

"Like a Kardashian is to us?" kidded Tiger.

"Even bigger. If that's possible," replied Monheit, who enjoyed his own quip before he pushed forward. "Pyotr Trifonov ranks just slightly behind Afanasy Glebov, Bogdan Yerokhim, Ermolay Letov, and—and I can see these names mean nothing to you, but take my word, these are the tight group of Vladimir Putin's inner circle. And what makes this group so tight? Simple. They have been made very, very, very wealthy under a Russian leader whose personal slogan is, 'Reward your friends; punish your enemies.' So. Pyotr Trifonov is in the friend category. How did he and his buddies get so rich?"

Gunnar raised a lazy hand. "I'm going to guess illegally."

"Probably," said Monheit. "I only hedge because, under the system they are using, it's so easy to see, and so hard to prove. But here's the best model I can build to speculate: Putin is formerly KGB out of Saint

Petersburg. After Gorbachev and Yeltsin, he gets political. But what else went on in Russia after the Soviet breakup? The KGB gets dissolved, and is now reincarnated as the FSB. And, as it morphs, the FSB teams up with the organized-crime factions that have been taking advantage of all the economic instability of the transition." He laced his fingers together to illustrate. "So you have the ex-KGB coming together in union with the Russian mob. And who was Comrade KGB himself? Vladimir Putin. You don't have to be a genius to infer what that could mean."

Chip said, "That the head of government controls the secret police and organized crime."

"Like he said, you don't have to be a genius," said Tiger. During the laughter, Macie tried to math-out the ramifications for Jackson Hall's case and everything connected to it, but decided not to get ahead of herself. She needed an open mind to absorb it first, and went back to jotting notes from the surprise guest expert.

"All these people I told you about from that inner circle not only have longstanding relationships with the Russian president, they are either involved in finance, intelligence, drug enforcement, or military."

"Everything you need to run the table," said Macie.

"And do they ever. Yeltsin had tried to build a different economy by letting government-run companies go private. Putin came to power and wanted to get control of those pesky oligarchs who had the audacity to make a profit, so he took back the companies—like Gazprom—turning them into state-owned giants. Then he sold off the assets to his buddies. Remember? 'Reward your friends; punish your enemies.' Problem: there was allegedly so much corrupt money being siphoned, they had to get it out of the country to hide it. So what might you do if you were Putin's pals? Set up offshore companies of their own, not just to make more profit, but to stash the billions and billions in black money getting pilfered out of the Russian economy. Which now brings us to Pyotr Trifonov."

Monheit rotated the other side of his rolling whiteboard to face them. It contained the bullet points he had just made and his coming profile of Trifonov. Beside it was a photograph he had pulled off a Russian website. Macie got an odd feeling of déjà vu when she saw it, but then dismissed it. *60 Minutes* or CNN had done an exposé on Putin's supposed plunderers. Maybe she had seen him there. "Mr. Trifonov had a number of marginal fiscal enterprises as his part in this—alleged—laundering scheme," said Monheit. He pointed to the bullet on the board corresponding with each scam he enumerated. "Trifonov worked closely with an organization called Baltik-Eskort, a security entity from Putin's old stomping ground of Saint Petersburg, bodyguards now rumored to provide safe routing of all that corrupt cash."

"And I'll bet," said Gunnar, "to eliminate anything or anyone getting in the way."

Monheit resumed. "Pyotr Trifonov helped set up various 'crony banks.' Those are banks with only a handful of clients, let's assume Putin's cronies, and their sole mission is to process all that dark Russian money and funnel it throughout the globe. As you can see from the list, most of them are in Moldova, right next door to Russia. From there, Mr. Trifonov set up a few of his own companies with his share of stolen capital. An import-export company in tax-friendly Ireland, even a mining operation in Africa, where he had apparently lived as an intelligence officer for a number of years in the nineties. And not without some scandals."

"Now you have my ear," said Tiger. "Please tell me there's sex or drugs."

"The former," replied Monheit. "There was a paternity mess in the 1990s when Trifonov's African mistress, a local architect, got pregnant. The story got hushed, and the baby mama in question suddenly became one of the wealthiest women in Luanda."

"How did our burglary victim from Dubai put it?" said Wild. "'Any problem you can solve with money isn't a problem?'"

"There are more scandals, albeit less juicy. Just recently, one of Trifonov's crony banks in Moldova got hit by an audit, and Mr. Trifonov made a fast move to get out of Dodge. A number of nations, including Canada, refused to let him in because of the corruption baggage. So he ended up here in the US under a conditional visa, living somewhere in New York City."

"I think we know where," said Cody.

"Actually he has no address of record," said Monheit. "He has a leased office down near the Flatiron, but I got no answer on the calls I made to it. And the building management referred me to his attorney." He turned a page of his legal pad and read it. As he said the name, Macie immediately recalled why the picture resonated with her. She and Gunnar had both seen Trifonov before. And it was recently.

As Wild pushed her way through the revolving door to enter the ground-floor lobby of Orem Diner's law firm, she relived the morning she had done the same thing almost a week before when the turnstile had abruptly halted and she saw the sick man on the opposite side of the door wing fall ill. "It was him," Macie announced to Gunnar when he whooshed through behind her. "No doubt now. It was Trifonov."

Even though the reception area at Diner and Partners was expansive, giving them ample separation from the other cluster of visitors, voices carried on the polished parquet flooring so the two of them sat in silence. They already had done their speculation about what Stamitz and his crew might have stolen from The Ajax that night. If Trifonov dealt in that much cash, the HVAC van they saw pull up on the security cam could have handled quite a haul. Macie shivered as her mind drifted back to another vivid memory: Pipe Wrench repeating, "The take, the take, the—"

"Macie Wild, why did they plant you out here instead of in my office?" said Diner as he came up the internal winding staircase from the floor below. He was in shirtsleeves and a hand-done bow tie in a summer color. The young attorney at his side took some files from him and peeled off the opposite way from the senior partner who was hugging Wild. Cody got a firm grip and a quick release. They declined beverages and settled into their former spots in his corner suite. Diner took off his glasses and, while he cleaned them with a microfiber cloth, asked, "What can I help you with this time?" The question was for her but he took in Cody as he spoke, as if to gain some clue.

"I wanted to make a delicate request, so I'm here in person. I would like to arrange a meeting with one of your clients."

Once more he gave Cody a once-over and went back to the subject of their prior meeting. "Jerónimo Teixeira? I can save you some trouble there. First of all, he has left the country for an undetermined amount of time. But I did finally get an answer on this Borodin character you asked me about. Nimo acknowledged Luka Borodin was his bodyguard. He also said that the man flaked out and disappeared on him. So this all seems to be a lot of concern about nothing."

"Actually it's not Mr. Teixeira I want to talk to. It's someone else. This is awkward—quite the delicate part—but I think one of my clients may have robbed him." He waited, searching her, so she said the name. "Pyotr Trifonov."

Orem Diner turned to the window and stared a long five-count at the dome of Saint Bart's before his gaze swept slowly back to her. "What makes you think this Mr. Trifonov is a client of mine?"

"We passed him in your lobby last time we were here. He was leaving as we were coming in."

"And you inferred, circumstantially, that he was a client of mine."

"Mr. Diner, I didn't come here to lock horns with you. If for reasons of privilege you don't want to acknowledge whether Pyotr Trifonov is a client, that's your right."

That softened the other lawyer, and he said, "As fellow attorneys, I might consider an off-the-record conversation with you."

"I appreciate that." Reading his concern about the third party in the room, she said, "And let me assure you that confidence would extend to Mr. Cody as well." Gunnar didn't respond; he just nodded. It seemed assent enough.

"I will stipulate that Mr. Trifonov is a client on certain matters. But I don't know anything about him being robbed. You mean he was mugged by one of your . . . um, clients?"

"No, burglarized. At his condominium."

"At The Ajax," said Gunnar, speaking for the first time, and for effect. When Diner didn't react, Macie slid in.

"He owns the penthouse. Or, as you must know, he does through his LLC, Exurb Partners."

The lawyer didn't blink. Wild's father had told her that Orem Diner was where secrets went to die, and his passive courtroom face offered no information. He took his time, and quietly said, "Whatever reasons people who may or may not be my clients come here to see me, they do so under privilege, knowing that I won't divulge confidences. Not just in the content of our dealings but by the very fact of them. This is the foundation upon which I've built my firm. It's also the legal right and expectation of the client." He folded the microfiber cloth in a rectangle and closed it in his eyeglass case with a snap. "Having said that, I'll make an effort to get in touch with Mr. Trifonov." Diner licked a finger and reached for a blank note card on the coffee table. He wrote a letter T, for Trifonov, on it then said, "Satisfactory?"

"And appreciated," said Wild, not feeling like she had really gained anything.

She let Gunnar go out the door before her and lagged to have Orem Diner to herself. "You have been very kind to me, and I wanted to return the courtesy."

"All right . . ."

"It's become clear that this Mr. Trifonov runs in some dangerous circles. As a family friend and colleague, I just hope you are careful."

He draped a paternal arm around her. "From someone who's been doing this longer than you've been alive, Macie Wild, I learned early on that people who run in dangerous circles can always use a good lawyer. You ought to know that." He removed his arm and gave her a sly wink. "The difference between us is that mine pay a bit more for the trouble."

Back downstairs a light mist had begun falling from a weak front rolling across the Hudson from Jersey. Nothing menacing, just enough to make the daytime headlights of taxis and town cars shimmer on Park Avenue in the afternoon murk. Wild made a phone check and found two missed calls and two texts. One from Tiger, the other sent at the same time from Soledad. Both her team paralegal and social worker had flagged the messages urgent. Both read, "Call immediately."

"Stand by, I'm going to tie-in Soledad," said Tiger when she phoned back. He didn't just sound urgent, but pressed. "I've got Ms. Wild. You there?"

"I'm here," replied Soledad, speaking in hushed tones. "Macie."

"What's going on?"

"Ready for this? I've got a line on Jackson Hall."

The mist had thickened into a light drizzle but Macie was oblivious to it. She had just gotten the biggest glimmer of positive news since taking on this case. "Line on him how?" Wild pressed the phone to her ear and plugged the other so she could catch every word, every nuance amid the horn honks on Park Avenue.

"Through Jackson Hall's girlfriend. She's in the loo, but I'm here with her now."

"Pilar? Where?" When Macie spoke the girlfriend's name, Gunnar took a step closer, studying her intently.

"At a Panera. That coworker of hers I've been schmoozing finally caved, and she set up a meet. I've spent the last hour and a half trying to convince Pilar to trust me and to put us in touch with him."

"Then he's alive? She knows where he is?"

"Yes to both. She's teetering, but still needs a nudge. I just wanted to let you—" Soledad's exhale rustled on the mouthpiece, and when she next spoke, it was hurried. "Listen, I've got to go. She's coming back. Hang close. With any luck, next time we speak, it'll be to put you together with Jackson Hall."

Wild decided to wait for Soledad's update call at her MCPD office where she could get some work done, but was unable to focus on anything else. Gunnar asked to hang out with her, and in his van on the way downtown she mused at how half the media and all the NYPD were about to be bested by a social worker who exercised basic people sense and a finely honed art of human connection. "Yeah," he replied with a sigh. "But isn't it always kind of a letdown when there's not a little burning rubber and flying lead?"

Under the gaze of the twin lions at the New York Public Library, he made an illegal left onto Fifth Avenue and pulled a phone from the door pocket to dial the CyberGauchito on speaker. He put his *porteño* black hat on the digital trail of Pyotr Trifonov, dictating a menu of where to sniff and what to look for. Macie bristled when Gunnar said he also wanted a full anal done on Orem Diner's office server to hunt for anything related to the Russian, particularly contact info, dates of contact, payment methods, FBI summonses, the works. Yes, she chafed, but Macie didn't object this time. She wondered: Is this how it begins? A blind eye to expedient ethical breeches, until you eventually become inured, and see this as standard procedure instead of the dishonorable practices you once deplored? By the time they took the left fork onto Broadway at the Flatiron, Macie began reflecting on how she might be living the parable about how to boil a frog—in the starring role.

While Macie answered a subpoena request on another case, Gunnar announced it was past dinnertime and phoned in a pizza order for delivery. He had just hung up when Chip appeared in Wild's doorway. The intern was drenched. He was the only one who didn't seem to notice. "Haven't they heard of umbrellas in Louisiana?" asked Gunnar.

"This happened on the way to the subway. It's pouring over in Bed-Stuy."

Tiger slid in the office beside him. "This is what L-Ones are for, right? When there's footwork to be done in bad weather, send the intern."

"You asked us to do the X-ray on Jackson Hall's crew chief, right?" A drip hung on the tip of Chip's nose. He wiped it with his sleeve and continued. "Well, Stamitz's recent records, for some reason, are not available. Not anywhere. But we did find a prior burglary arrest he had from about eight years ago. So Tiger and I used the method that worked for you when you checked out Rúben Pinto by finding his old cellmate. We found Stamitz's burglary accomplice."

Tiger picked up the narrative. "The bust came after a very ballsy predawn visit to the luxury hotel suite of a Chinese industrialist who was in Manhattan and just had bought a pair of antique dueling pistols at auction." Citing from notes, he continued, "Made in 1797 by a famous London gunsmith, valued at over a hundred thousand. Stamitz and his partner went totally *Mission: Impossible*, very Ethan Hunt. Defeating sound monitors, skirting a laser beam . . . They snagged the pistols, including the wooden case, showed up to sell them to the fence, only the fence was undercover."

"Busted," said Macie.

"Except Stamitz skated," said Chip. "But his accomplice did not. He's the guy I just interviewed."

"Fuck me . . . Stamitz is a CI," muttered Gunnar.

Both Chip and Tiger deflated. Gunnar had stolen their punch line. But the intern soldiered on. "That's, um, right. His old partner, now living in Bedford-Stuyvesant, always suspected Stamitz cut a deal with the feds. The accomplice did a five-year stretch, and he believes Stamitz walked because he agreed to become a confidential informant for the FBI."

"Otherwise known as a CI," added Tiger with a thanks-pal glance at Gunnar.

"Sorry to get ahead of your story," he said, "but you're kind of in my area. In law enforcement you develop snitches lots of ways. The best ones either have axes to grind or their balls in a vise. What doesn't line up for me, though, is getting turned by the FBI. A burglary like the one you described isn't a federal crime."

"Exactly what I told his accomplice," said the law student. "But he said the FBI got jurisdiction because they drove from New York City to Hoboken to meet the fence and crossed a state line with firearms involved in commerce, which bumped it to federal level."

Gunnar nodded and added for Macie's benefit, "The FBI set him up. Stamitz would have been prime pickings because he faced hard time and had major upscale B-and-E skills. A player like him would be tapped in to high-level fences, mob operations, burglaries-to-order, name it. They probably even let him keep stealing as long as he threw them useful intel or set up busts whenever they needed them."

Before Gunnar could continue, Wild's cell phone rang. "It's Soledad."

Ever discreet, Tiger took Chip by the elbow and whisked him out into the hallway, closing her door as they left. Macie swiped to answer and tapped the speaker option. "Sol?"

"I'm here."

"I've got Gunnar Cody with me. You're on the speaker phone, is that all right?"

"Sure, if it's just you two."

"Just us. Door's closed. Whatcha got?" Wild felt a phantom TENS burn tingle, even though the mark was fading.

"It took some doing, but Pilar finally let me in."

"Sol, that's wonderful. Where is he?"

"She'd been couch flopping with her coworker in Flushing since Pinto got murdered, but when Mr. Hall got out of Bellevue, they met up and cribbed into a place up in Harlem. It's all off the books. I'm sworn to secrecy but it's in a building owned by the guy who runs that bar near the 125th Street station."

"The Stealer's Wheel?" asked Macie. She and Gunnar traded knowing nods. They had both been there, both talked to the owner. Jumbo Crouch. The man who claimed to know little about Jackson Hall's movements, but was willing to perjure himself to alibi for whatever Macie needed.

"That's the one. She called it their safe house. Pilar just phoned him from here in Forest Hills. He gave permission for you to visit him." Soledad paused. "She didn't say anything about bringing Mr. Cody though."

Wild answered without hesitation. "I need him to come with me. Especially at this hour. My client will simply have to adjust."

"Your call, honey. Ready to write this down?" Soledad recited the address and apartment number on East 121st and then had Macie repeat it back. "I'll be at my phone all night, if you need anything."

"Thanks," she said. Gunnar stood and tapped his watch. "We're leaving now. Have Pilar stay scarce. And, Soledad. Good work."

"Yeah, great work," called Gunnar as he strode out the door ahead of Macie, who was fast on his heels. They breezed through the lobby together, passing their pizza as it was being delivered.

Gunnar parked around the corner on Adam Clayton Powell Jr., walked with Macie half a block north, then they abruptly U-turned, retracing their steps, so they could notice if they were being followed. As a further precaution, Gunnar bypassed the address Soledad gave them and led Macie into a bodega. He made a career of pretending to examine the chewing gum while he scanned the security video monitor behind the counter for any sudden loiterers on the sidewalk. She kept an eye out for vehicles slowing as they passed. They made another street check before they mounted the stoop to the apartment building.

The sign out front said it was under renovation and gave a property management number for future rentals. Inside everything smelled like the welcome of Harlem's bright promise: new paint, brass polish, and freshly sawn timber. When they gained the second-story landing, the full length of the hallway floor was protected by unrolled kraft paper side tacked by blue painters' tape. Gunnar held up a forefinger to signal, and they stood and just listened to the silence. The quiet was absolute except for the air brakes of a bus on Powell Boulevard. When they proceeded, the crinkling of their footsteps on the brown construction paper announced them, which may have been the idea. Gunnar had briefed her on how to approach the door, and when they got to it, they took their places on opposite sides of the frame. He gave her the nod, and she knocked. No movement inside, no "Who is it?" Macie knocked again and said, "Hello? It's me, Macie Wild." Still no sound. No death scent either; they both sniffed for it. Gunnar tried the knob. Locked. And solidly with brand new hardware. After one more, sharper, unanswered knock, she mimed going outside to use her phone and they left.

Back at the landing a familiar voice spoke from the stairwell a floor above. "I thought you were coming alone." Gunnar drew Macie back to cover on the underside of the stairs.

Macie tilted her head up to the dark of the stairwell. "You know Gunnar Cody, Mr. Hall." Just in case he had memory gaps from the coma, she added. "From the hospital?" Macie side glanced Gunnar and threw in, "I trust him with my life."

There came a long pause and the voice asked, "What about mine?"

"That's why he's here. I wouldn't have brought him otherwise."

Jackson Hall's answer came in soft footfalls descending from the upper floor. He rounded the final turn above them and held on a stair halfway down the flight. Somehow he looked even smaller to her than usual. And weak. Like he could hardly manage the baseball bat he was gripping.

Without asking permission, Gunnar made a security walk through the apartment Jackson Hall was using as his hideout. He cleared the back rooms, closets, bathroom, and galley kitchen in short order. The place was not only small, the only furniture was a pair of mismatched lawn chairs and a sleeping bag, all in the living room. There was a silent portable radio plugged into a corner socket and a cooler whose lid looked as if it doubled as a dining table. The setup was ascetic—a campsite in a building under rehab.

Hall was explaining how he managed to slip out of the jail ward at Bellevue when Gunnar returned to the living room. "Everybody who's locked up thinks every day about how they'd make their break, I don't care what they say. It's so ingrained that you spend your days going around like The Terminator when they showed what his evil eyes were seeing. Which is everything. Close-ups of doors, asking yourself if that one's locked. Or who do those keys on the counter belong to, that sort of thing. But whoever thinks that getting put in the hospital ward is a launching pad doesn't know how tight it is there. State-max tight."

"So how did you?" asked Wild.

"Wasn't as dramatic as you'd think. I'm walking back, my therapist stops to sign something or chat up some nurse, whatever, and I keep walking, because I see a corrections officer reading the bulletin board beside the elevator she's supposed to be watching and the door next to her is wide open. So I just quietly got on and mashed the magic button and rode out of there. Keeping my head down and ears open, waiting to hear the shotgun pump." He spread his arms wide. "As you can see I succeeded in my journey without becoming ventilated."

"As your attorney, it's my duty to tell you that this . . ." —Macie gestured to the safe house, which screamed futility— ". . . this can't continue. You do know that, don't you?"

He jerked his chin toward Gunnar. "That why you brought him? To drag me back?"

"Mr. Cody is not with the police."

"Well, is it?" he insisted.

"You already know you have to call this game," said Gunnar, but with the tone of a counselor instead of the heat. "That's why you agreed to see Macie tonight. You just don't know how to do it and keep yourself safe." Jackson Hall's look was his answer: the doleful face where swagger once lived. "As I hear your story," continued Gunnar, "I'm convinced somebody inside Bellevue made sure you got outside—and for a reason. Same as somebody inside Rikers tried to kill you. Maybe for a different reason."

"But why would somebody just let me out?"

"Because the only other crew members who can lead these people— whoever they are—to whatever they're looking for are dead." Gunnar had become the bad cop not by browbeating, but by working the fear already inside Hall. He saw his body count update register on the fugitive and affirmed it. "That's right. They got Stamitz too. He died ugly."

Fearing that Gunnar's pressure may start to work against them, Macie intervened. "Mr. Hall? Let's try to be practical about this. Now is the time to keep our heads and find a path out of this mess. Agreed?"

He gave her the same plaintive look. "I keep sinking deeper. I don't know what to do."

Since both lawn chairs were taken, Gunnar slid the cooler beside him and sat. "I have a thought, but first I need you to walk me through how you got into this. And I need you to treat us both like you're in the confessional. No lies. No dodges. You fuck with us, you fuck yourself."

In quiet submission, he hung his head and muttered, "Arright . . ." The man had endured too many days and nights of fear to need much more of a push. Jackson Hall's resistance was prebroken, degraded by the force of his own terror. "What do you want to know?"

Gunnar could have taken it from there, but in a gesture of respect or, maybe, partnership, he gave the go-ahead nod to Macie. She knew right where to start. Where her torturer had left off. "I want to ask you about the take from these burglaries. You told me Stamitz, your crew chief, set up all the targets. Did he also handle fencing the take?"

"Yes, he was turnkey, that's the expression he himself used. Man said, 'I am the total package. Where to hit, when to hit, how to get in, what to score, how to dump it.' Sometimes I felt like a glorified mover: lift and load."

"A well-paid mover," commented Gunnar.

Hall shrugged. "Yeah, enough."

Wild continued her line. "What about Rúben Pinto? Did he feel undervalued?" The cross-examiner in her added, "Did he feel sold short?"

Even though Hall had once declared he was done protecting people, he now worked his jaw to contemplate an answer. Gunnar said, "Jackson, both these guys are dead. Fuck respect."

That message cut through the moral clutter. "Yeah, Rú was always pissing and moaning behind Stamitz's back. Especially since we never got the tally, you see. The chief just gave us a cut and we took it on faith." The corners of his mouth hinted at a smile. "It was good enough for me. That was some good money."

"But Pinto—" Macie paused. There was a sound from the hall. A snap. Was it the building settling or someone out there? Gunnar moved to the peephole and listened for footfalls on the kraft paper. Satisfied, he opened the door and stepped out, returning in a few minutes with a thumbs-up as he snapped the deadbolt behind him. False alarm or not, Macie felt more urgency and pressed more than she normally would have. "OK, let's say it. Pinto was pissed off and was skimming, am I right? I've heard this from his pal Spatone, so let's just say it."

"It's true."

"But he was doing more than pocketing some of the take on the sly," said Gunnar, gliding into her interview like a choreographed dance. "He went back to some of the victims to do shakedowns."

"Trying to sell them their own stuff, as ransom," she added.

Jackson Hall bobbed his head. "Pinto had his own game all figured out. Especially if he found anything the vic would rather not have seen or known . . ."

"Like extorting ten grand to sell back Larry Don Henkles his sports betting ledger? Yes, we know about that," she said. "And Mr. Sharif's wristwatches."

"What about the paintings from The Barksdale? Did Pinto skim one of them too?" asked Gunnar.

Hall shook no. "I was on lookout with Rúben the whole time. Both of those paintings left there in Stamitz's bag, I saw them."

"Both?" said Macie and Gunnar at the same time. She clarified for Hall. "The owner claims three of his paintings were stolen."

"Yeah," said Gunnar. "Two by the crew and one by the owner, Gregory Eichenthal."

"Let's get to The Ajax." Not wanting to lead him too much, Wild kept it open-ended. "Talk to me about the break-in there."

"Our last job. Little did we know. Stamitz was obsessed with it. Me and Pinto, we said it was too risky. Big, secure, some serious shit. But he was all, 'Grow a pair,' and 'Go big or go home.' And I had to trust the man. Tight-ass, but knew his shit. Weird, now that I think about it, how he always knew who to hit, who wasn't home, how to get in and out. Same with The Ajax. Rolled into the parking garage in an air-conditioning truck. Chief had a swipe card for the private elevator and a little black remote he used to defeat all the electronics and alarms. The crazy thing was, we got into that big-ass penthouse—and it was empty. I don't just mean nobody home, I mean empty-empty. This place we're sitting now has more stuff in it. You could have roller-skated in there."

"So what was there to steal?" she asked.

"Getting to that. Stamitz knows exactly where he's going—again— and beelines for the master bedroom walk-in closet. It's empty but there's these two safes." Hall demonstrated a full wingspan to indicate their sizes. "Free standers, like you see in old bank movies, except these had electronic lock systems. Stamitz brought along this remote clicker. He said it ran autodial software to do what he called a brute-force hack. I want to tell you, that thing popped both locks in under a minute. But even then he got all, 'Let's go, let's go.' The man's in a rush because he knows we only have eight minutes before rounds get made and the shit fan revs up. So it got a little chaotic. He gives very specific instructions what to take and leave, and goes to work unloading the first safe. Pinto and I do the second one."

Wild found herself echoing a word from her own interrogation. "What was the take?"

"First of all, cash. Stacks of it. That's on the Go List."

Gunnar asked, "How much?"

"Never found out. But in our safe, I'd call the stack two feet tall and another foot wide. So we got the cash, and some jewels in there too. Not like necklaces and such. More like stones. All into our duffel bag."

"Anything else?" Macie was sensing the application of brakes from her client.

"Uh, yeah, passports. A fancy shoebox full of them."

"Did they go?" she asked.

"Not on the list."

"Did they go?" A lawyer always knows what to ask. He shook no. "That was it?" Then he hesitated.

"Jackson," said Gunnar, showing impatience. "What did Pinto take?"

Hall licked his lips. "There was a canvas pouch. A zipper thing with a padlock like you see merchants use to take deposits to the bank." He moistened his mouth again but his tongue made a dry click before his admission. "He pantsed it. Checked to see that Stamitz had his head in the other safe and slipped the pouch down his pants."

"Was the pouch on the Go List?" Macie asked.

"Yes."

"Wouldn't Stamitz know it wasn't there?"

"Who the hell knows what Stamitz knew."

"And Pinto saw you watching when he secreted this pouch?" He nodded. Then, even though she knew the answer, Wild asked anyway. "And you never told Stamitz?"

"Hell, no."

"So," said Gunnar, "in and out in under eight minutes. The safes were left how?"

"Closed and locked."

"And the canvas pouch." They both knew it ended up in that planter, but Gunnar let him tell it. "What happened to that?"

"On the drive off, Pinto chucked it out the window. Chief got all paranoid after Rúben boosted a Grammy from that fat fucker's apartment and started doing random searches after gigs. So my man winged it into some bushes like a Frisbee when Stamitz was making his turn to Columbus Circle."

"Back to the job," said Gunnar. "Was there anything else in the safe or in the process that might be trouble?" Jackson Hall answered with a clean, credible no, which brought them back to Pinto's private take. "What happened to the pouch?"

"Pinto went back and got it."

"And?" said Macie.

"He tried to sell it back."

Gunnar asked, "How did he know whom to call? The condo owner is unlisted. Or did you have a name?"

"No. No clue who the owner was. Rúben did it same as with the betting ledger. He called The Ajax front desk and said he found this canvas pouch and offered to return it to the owner. He left his number and some guy calls right back, saying he wants that property, and Pinto says sure thing but then starts to negotiate." Macie and Gunnar traded a look. Both knew that Pinto had set his own murder in motion with that call. But who was the caller?

"Did this guy who called have an accent, did Rúben tell you?" she asked.

"Yeah, how'd you know? We figured Russian, because that's where a lot of the passports were from."

"Any names on the passports?"

"Yes, ma'am, and all Russian. I don't remember any of them." She asked if Pyotr Trifonov or Luka Borodin meant anything, and he just shrugged.

Ex-Detective Cody, who would not be deterred, reasked his question. "One more time. What happened to the pouch?"

"It was trouble, that's what happened. Rúben's coming up out of the subway the next day, and some dude starts smacking him around, wants the pouch, where is it, and all that. Pinto's got some prison scrap in him, drops the guy, and splits. Then comes to me and asks if I'll . . ." He paused, recognizing the leap he was making. Neither of the other two helped him fill the blanks. This had to be his own confession. "Pinto asked me to hold it for him. Which, stupidly, I did. Then I come back to my apartment and the door's wide open and the place has been tossed. This is what Pinto and I were fighting about before he got himself killed. Getting me in his fucking scam. Folks scaring my girlfriend, searching our place."

"But they didn't find it because you just had gotten it," said Gunnar. "If they had found that pouch, they wouldn't have kept at it and killed Pinto, and Stamitz, and you wouldn't have sent Pilar away to hide, and on, and on." While Hall rested his chin on his chest, Macie reflected on poor Stamitz. The contingency planner-control freak didn't know about Pinto's take. The crew chief was being truthful the whole time he was tortured to death.

"What's in it, Mr. Hall? What's worth all this killing and trouble?"

"Honestly, Ms. Wild, nothing that appears too valuable to me. Looks like somebody emptied a desk drawer of office supplies into it and zipped it closed."

She didn't care if he was being truthful or not. Macie only wanted to know one thing. Same as Gunnar. And when they asked him, it was in a surprise duet. "Where is the pouch now?"

Material evidence could be a two-edged sword. A coveted item or a smoking gun, literal or figurative, could damn the accused. Sometimes, however, it could lead to exoneration. A signed receipt that proves the defendant was out of town the day of a murder, as one example. Yet Wild's experience as a criminal defense attorney had taught her that, yes, a sword had two edges, but also a point. And that sharp tip represented the third, most useful, alternative: material evidence that revealed the actual killer. That was the sort of evidence she was hoping for as they followed Jackson Hall, disguised in a wig from the back of Cody's van, to the basement of the Spanish Harlem apartment building he and Pilar had fled. As they approached the storage closets for each apartment, Gunnar asked, "Didn't the crime scene unit go through your space?"

"With extreme prejudice," he said with a humorless chuckle. Hall flicked the broken padlock as he went by the door that still had a remnant of crime scene tape swaying on one side. At the end of the row of closets he reached up to a high shelf and retrieved a key from under a paint can. "I have a side agreement with an old lady who lives on the first floor, cash only, for some extra space. Let's just say I found it useful over the years to temporarily park some of my overflow property."

"Stolen goods," said Gunnar, not asking.

"It's this one here," said Hall, not answering.

He opened the unit next to the basement wall. Inside he pulled a dangling string and the overhead bulb revealed that the right half of the closet was filled with old, musty furniture that was stacked tall, pipe racks of winter coats from the last century, and an artificial Christmas tree. The left side was clear enough for one person to squeeze in, which Hall did, slipping past a tower of moving cartons to the back corner where some fishing rods leaned beside a net hanging by its aluminum hoop from a nail. There were three steel tackle boxes on the concrete floor. He picked up the one with the padlock and set it on one of the corrugated cardboard dish packs. After turning the barrel combination, Hall opened the lid, lifted the tackle tray of hooks and lures, and brought out the canvas zipper pouch that he had described. It bulged from whatever was inside it. Pinching the tab, he ran the slider the length of the thick brass teeth, which made a serious grating sound as it opened. Hall took a step back and Macie and Gunnar leaned forward to huddle over it, eager to see what was in there.

Wild held her iPhone flashlight over the mouth of the pouch. As advertised, it looked like a jumble of office items. Gunnar produced a single nitrile glove from his pocket. One by one, he fished out some of the items to examine. They were mainly rubber stamps, ink pads, and a few brass paper crimpers, the sort of tools notaries hand squeeze to emboss seals on documents.

They heard a pair of footsteps and froze. Gunnar quickly replaced the crimper he was holding and relayed the pouch to Macie. He peeked out the open door and relaxed. A pair of teenagers, no doubt looking for a place to do what teenagers do, froze when they saw him and ran back upstairs. "I'm thinking this may not be the best place for this," he said, taking the pouch from her and giving it a firm zip.

They weren't sure what they should do next, but whatever it was, it would be done downtown, so that's the direction Gunnar pointed his van on the FDR. It wasn't the most comfortable to have Jackson Hall perched on the divider between them, but his small build, so handy for break-ins, also made this work. As they were passing the Con Ed plant he asked Macie, "You really need to take me in?"

"There are laws and ethical obligations I have to abide by. They say, unequivocally, I am required to return you to custody and to deliver material evidence to the district attorney."

"Fuck that. I'm safer out here than in there."

"I get it, but I don't see an alternative."

They rode in silence a few moments then Gunnar asked, "Did Rúben Pinto say anything to you about what the stuff in this pouch was?" he asked.

"*Nada.* He just wanted it out of his life till things cooled."

"Cause I'm thinking, counselor," he said, leaning forward to see her around Hall.

"About?"

"About the burglary of a foreign national, that would be Trifonov. The accused, your client, spotting cash and stacks of passports. Our material evidence in hand is some kind of official-looking shit. I wonder if this could be part of some sort of ID forgery operation. Which, to me, kicks this up from city to federal."

She twisted in the seat to face him, clearly sparking to this. "Plus we have reason to believe that Stamitz was a confidential informer to the FBI."

"What the fuck?!" shouted Hall.

"Which is two-way street," said Gunnar. "How do you think Stamitz got his inside info on places to hit? Maybe not all of them—he had his own sources too—but I guarantee you his deal was to do occasional à la carte break-ins for the feds. The Ajax has that smell all over it." He leaned around Hall to address Macie. "So what I'm suggesting is, if you feel bound by your so-called ethical obligations, why don't we call our new friends at the bureau and deliver both Mr. Hall and the evidence into arguably safer custody with the FBI?"

While Macie opened her wallet to find the card they had given her, a pair of street bikes—New York's latest quality-of-life scourge—roared by her window full throttle, racing through traffic. Instinctively Gunnar checked his mirrors; they seldom traveled small. Sure enough, two more single headlights roared up, but instead of passing, they paced him on either side of his taillights. His windshield filled with red as the two bikes in front of him eased brakes to slow him down. "You buckled up?" he asked her.

"Yeah, why?"

He turned to Hall and said, "Press your palms on the roof and lock yourself down. Do it."

The instant Jackson Hall placed his hands on the ceiling the front bikers made a hard brake check on Cody. He swerved his wheel right and punched it, passing them. Immediately all four motorcycles sped after him in pursuit.

CHAPTER 34

That time of night, traffic toward downtown flowed fast, but Gunnar booked it faster, overcoming a Subaru SUV that was clogging the slow lane. When he was sure the four performance cycles were overmatching his speed, he jerked a suicide right in front of the Forester and worked a last-chance exit onto Houston. Both his passengers muttered expletives as he sidescraped the guardrail that divided the exit ramp from the FDR. Gunnar cast a side window look, hoping his maneuver had forced the motorcycles on the wrong side of the Jersey barrier. But with whining downshifts, they wove slaloms through the no-return gap between the highway and the K-rail. "They're still on us," said Wild, eyeing her side mirror.

Gunnar floored his accelerator and clicked on his high beams in case some kid or meth head wandered out of the Wald projects, then he mashed his brake, ignoring the stop sign for a rolling right onto Houston. Jackson Hall lost his balance on the sharp turn and toppled, landing against Gunnar's neck. "You got to hold on, bud."

"Shit, nothing to hold," he said, hoisting himself upright and wedging his left arm behind Gunnar's headrest for support. The small man rocked side to side as Gunnar zigzagged around westbound traffic. The four motorcycles stayed close and unshakable.

"Do you have a plan?" asked Macie.

"You mean besides trying not to find out what these gentlemen have in mind for us?" He was passing Avenue D. Taillights started popping red in front of them. Gunnar voiced a warning this time before he wrenched the van into another sudden right where Second Street made a dogleg split off Houston and ran parallel to it. Nobody followed. The four bikers blew by on the other side of the divider. Their headlights created flickers as they got eclipsed by the succession of slim tree trunks in the block-long planter between them and the speeding van. "To answer your question, the Ninth Precinct is up and over a few blocks. I'm going to try to make that."

Hall didn't like the sound of that. "You said no NYPD."

"Sue me," said Cody. "Your lawyer's right there."

"Gunnar . . ." a warning from Macie, peering ahead. One of the bikers had accelerated and split off from the pack and was pulling to a stop ahead of them in the middle of the intersection.

"Got him." Gunnar calculated just enough squeeze space between the Kawasaki and an MTA bus idling at the corner. But when the biker raised both hands up in a classic aiming stance, Gunnar steered straight for him. "Shooter. Duck down, best you can," he said calmly, then floored it. There was a muzzle flash and a crack but the shot went high as the man jumped back out of Cody's path. As he raced by, Gunnar shoved his door open. It walloped the biker with a metallic thud. His helmet smacked the window and blew it out just before the door slammed shut from the impact. The side mirror got knocked off-kilter but Gunnar could see the biker back there, flattened in the middle of Avenue C.

"Sweet," said Jackson Hall.

But Gunnar was too busy scanning for the others to respond. It didn't take him long to eyeball them. A pair had raced ahead to cut up onto Avenue B and were tearing ass toward them, roaring the wrong way on the one-way Second. They rode up off their seats, ghostly forms illuminated by each set of headlights they dodged, legs bent, shifting weight from peg to peg as they wove around traffic. Gunnar took one hand off the wheel, fished his Sig Sauer P220 Elite out of his messenger bag, and wedged it between his seat belt and his hip. He might take out one, but two of them at once, especially if they flanked him, would be a definite challenge. He quickly ran options. They all sucked. The street offered no turnoffs and the block of flat storefronts and fenced apartments gave zero cover if he stopped to take a stand or to run—all shitty options because he had companions in tow, one of whom was still frail from his coma. He drew the Beretta Jetfire from his ankle holster and held it out to Hall. "You've got one in the chamber and eight in the mag. On my command only, send them all at the dude on your right. Macie, keep your head back." Bearing down to close their fifty-yard gap, one of the bikers made a frantic swerve to avoid a cart of knockoff purses a vendor was pushing from the curb. His knee clipped the trolley's corner, bumping the wagon sideways and caroming the Husqvarna laterally across the road, sweeping the wheels from under the other bike, and launching both riders through the plate glass window of an adult day care center. Macie and Hall both cried out with noises you only hear on carnival rides. Cody gave it the gas.

At B, he took another hard turn northbound. When the van settled, Hall gave him a nudge and held out the pocket pistol. "Hang on to it for now," Gunnar said. "You never know."

Macie said, "Police station's on Fifth Street," as they passed Third.

"Yeah, but way over past First Ave.," added Hall. It wasn't lost on Wild that, for different reasons, everybody in that van knew where the cop shops were.

The zigzag of a single headlight in the side mirrors caught Gunnar's eye. "I wondered what happened to our Ducati."

"How close?" she asked.

"Intimate," he said. The motorcycle pulled up on Gunnar's side. When it came even with the van's rear tire, Gunnar swerved to see if he could thump it. The biker had quick reflexes and adjusted, dropping back and coming up on Macie's side. Gunnar tried the same maneuver, but this time, the Ducati accelerated after its dodge, coming up on her side window. "Mace, lean over onto him. Now." Wild immediately complied, folding herself across Hall's lap. Gunnar floored it. The bike matched his speed, but then Gunnar stood on the brake. The Diavel flew past. In a squeal of rubber, the van skidded into a rocking turn onto Fifth Street and charged west with no sign of the motorcycle behind them. Their relief was short-lived.

"Crap, this doesn't go through." Their block of East Fifth terminated at the Village View towers and resumed on the other side of the housing complex. Gunnar cranked a right. "We'll have to go around. Shit." Sixth ran one-way the wrong way, so he tore up to East Seventh. Just as he was making his turn, a single headlight switched on across the intersection at the far corner of Tomkins Square Park. They all saw it.

"Son of a bitch was waiting," muttered Hall.

Gunnar drove fast but the Ducati Diavel was, after all, a Ducati Diavel. And whoever was riding it had balls, driving it right up on the sidewalk. The motorcyclist paced them, even ducking under some scaffolding, then passing to get half a block ahead. The rider downshifted into a hard brake, ending in a fishtail, but expertly stopped upright. Gunnar saw the biker's hand reach inside his jacket as they went by and he punched the gas.

When the shot rang out, it was not a crack. It was a thundering boom. As Gunnar's rear tire exploded and he struggled to maintain control of the speeding van, Wild's sinking thought as she grabbed for the dashboard was that she knew the sound of that gun. It sounded like only one she had ever heard. It was imprinted on Macie after its blast filled the Low Line underground—the night she and Gunnar were chasing Luka Borodin.

The van shuddered as the rear tire shredded and slapped the wheel well with every revolution until it flew off and the rim started plowing asphalt. Forward motion gave way to lurching slippage and the vehicle lost steering but not speed. "Hang on, hang on, hang on," muttered Gunnar, sounding tight yet even. Macie braced against the dash. Gunnar poled his right arm across Hall hoping to check his forward pitch. They collided with a portable steam boiler that had been set up in a parking spot outside an apartment building, crashing into the steel housing hard enough to send everything in the passenger cab flying, including Hall, who ended up sideways on the floor at Macie's knees as the van rebounded off the structure. It hinged forty-five degrees back out into the street before they bucked to a stop.

The next blast from the Colt Anaconda came immediately, and sent a .44 magnum through the wall of the cargo hold behind them and out through the windshield, leaving a spider web of cracked glass around the exit hole. Gunnar reached for his Sig Sauer but it wasn't there. It had flown loose with everything else on impact. He made a quick scan of the floor of the cab but didn't see it. "Everybody out. Your side. Hurry. Stay against the boiler for cover. Go, go!"

But the crash had stuck Wild's door closed. "It won't budge." After two tries at pushing, she threw her body into the side and it groaned open. Macie unbuckled and slid out. Jackson Hall, still on the floor mat, had to crawl, but he made it. The driver side left Gunnar exposed to the street, so he swung his feet over the center console and ass-scooted into the passenger seat. In that instant, another round shot clean through the headrest where he had been sitting and put another hole in the windshield above the steering wheel.

He rolled out with the others, herding them to the protected end of the steel box covering the boiler. "BRB," he said, then wormed low into the van again to retrieve his backpack, which held the courier pouch from Hall's stash. Gunnar also made one last sweep for his P220, gave it up, and hurried to join Macie and Hall, who, hopefully, still had his backup pistol. "What the fuck?" said Gunnar when he got there. Macie didn't get his question until she turned and saw what he saw.

Jackson Hall was gone.

"Any chance he gave you my gun?" She shook no. On the far end of the boiler, the Ducati revved. "Run," said Gunnar, giving her a nudge west on the sidewalk. Macie was fast and he let her lead so he could keep tabs on their rear flank. Behind them, he saw the headlight of the motorcycle ease up to the driver's side of the van. Borodin took off his helmet and dismounted to open the door, either checking for bodies or the courier pouch. It bought them time, but not much.

Ahead some hipsters had braved the light drizzle and were vaping over some espressos at a sidewalk table. "Call 911," shouted Gunnar as they ran by. "Tell them officer needs help." They ran onward, Macie not feeling confident in getting an assist, judging from the couple's blank stares. Macie and Gunnar were thirty yards from First Avenue when the Ducati engine sparked to life. Borodin was on the move.

They had just passed Saint Stanislaus when Gunnar hooked a hand on Macie's elbow and drew her into a service alley, between two buildings. It was barely wide enough for them to stand side by side, a coffin-shaped plug that dead-ended, which was far from optimal, but it was unlit. She took his lead and they crouched on top of a bulkhead door in the shadows against the back wall. Heads bowed to look as formless as possible, they side glanced the mouth of their alcove and waited.

All the night noise of New York City filled their brick recess. The hiss of truck brakes, car horns, distant sirens—fading and too far away to be coming for them—the oonce-oonce-oonce of dance music. Then came the sound that made Wild's soul grow icicles: the low rumble of a slowly approaching motorcycle. The patient hum of the Testastretta engine spooked her because it signaled a hunt. And she and Gunnar were not only defenseless, they were cornered. The reflection of the approaching single headlight off the rear window of a parked car gradually grew brighter. "Head down," whispered Gunnar. Tempted as she was to look, Macie pointed her face at the blistered paint of the cellar door under her knees, knowing that the glint of an eye would give them away.

The motorcycle lingered a few eternal seconds, then the thrum of the engine began to fade. Gunnar jogged to the corner of the alcove for a peek. She joined him. There he was. Borodin sat in the saddle with his back to them, duckwalking his Ducati up the block. He stopped at First Avenue to look north then south. She felt Gunnar lean against her, getting set to run the opposite direction, but the killer heeled his Diavel backward and turned their way for another search of East Seventh. Macie stuck with Gunnar as he bolted back to their hide, fishing through his bag on the way.

Every responder carries personal duty gear, stuff not issued by the department. For firefighters, it's anything from dry socks to eight-penny nails for chocking doors. For cops—and, yes, ex-cops—the essential is a Swiss Army Knife on steroids called the Multi-tool, containing a strap cutter, spring action needle-nose, a Phillips screwdriver, even an oxygen tank wrench, all fitting in the palm of your hand. Gunnar brought out his Leatherman Multi, dropped to his knees, jammed the point end of the pliers between the hasp plate and the bulkhead door and started prying for their lives. He didn't bother with the padlock, too formidable, but the cellar door was of old plywood, years past needing paint, and soggy from the recent rain. The point of the pliers was digging wood, but not budging the hasp. "Check the street," he said in a low voice.

Macie darted to the corner for a spy and rushed back. "Three doors up. He's looking behind trash cans."

"Fuck, fuck, fuck," he whispered. Unable to lift the hasp and bust the lock, Gunnar returned to his backpack for his Mini Maglite. Laying the barrel flat under his pliers, he used it to create a fulcrum to lever against the stubborn hardware. The deep growl of the engine drew closer. Then another sound: The groaning protest of screws getting pried up. Gunnar jammed his weight down onto the lever and the latch popped, sending zinc-plated steel tinging across the concrete. He yanked the double doors wide. "You first." Macie scrambled below. The opening was dark but her feet found a metal staircase. Gunnar was in right after her, pulling both sides of the hatch closed. He didn't light his flashlight.

They waited under the steps in silence.

Then the worst. The drone of the Ducati engine filled the alcove above them and bright light sliced through the crack between the bulkhead doors. They both retreated off the stairs but Gunnar grabbed a string mop he found leaning against a water heater and climbed back up, jamming the handle through the door pulls just as Borodin tried to lift it. The mop danced in the brass grips as their pursuer gave the bulkhead a more violent try. "Go," hissed Gunnar. He gave Wild a shove just as four slugs pierced the wood above where they had been standing, projecting an LED constellation on the cellar floor.

Macie and Gunnar didn't know which way to go, except away. Macie's ears rang from the thunderous gunfire, which made her feel even more disoriented than she already was. Gunnar lit the Mag and swept the basement. His light settled on a wooden stairway in the far corner. He traced a circle with the beam for her reference and they hustled up the steps. The door was unlocked. As they raced through it, one more gunshot, then they heard the mop handle clatter onto the basement floor and the bulkhead hatch whack open. Once Macie was through the door, Gunnar locked it, both knowing it would be a delaying tactic at best.

They found themselves in a kitchen supply store. It was well after hours, and the lights were off, but there was sufficient illumination seeping through the storefront to make out the gleaming pots and pans and gourmet gadgets on the aisles of shelving. They sprinted along a line of coffeemakers and fondue pots to the front door to make their escape. It was locked. Not just locked—it was also sealed off by an accordion security gate that enclosed the front door and both display windows. The cage was padlocked to a steel bar on the floor. "Maybe a back exit," he said, and beckoned her to the rear of the shop. On the way there, they passed the basement door and heard the telltale sound of ejected brass jingling on the concrete. The back door was dead-bolted with a lock that required a key. As they heard slow footfalls creaking on the cellar stairs, Gunnar turned a quick circle. His light fell on a sign: "Professional Cutlery." They raced over and found every knife imaginable—all locked behind glass. The cellar doorknob jiggled, followed by the thump of muscle and bone against wood.

There was a demo kitchen area for culinary classes off to the side. Gunnar pointed. "Get down behind the counter and stay there." Then he scooped a marble mortar and pestle off a shelf and pegged them at the wall display, shattering it. In seconds, he crunched over the broken shards and crouched next to her behind the granite counter. He gripped a mezzaluna in each fist, demonstrating how to hold them like brass knuckles, only with cutting blades. "Just in case I don't stop him, fight like hell." For good measure, he left her a ten-inch cook's knife. Gunnar darted away just as a blast from the Anaconda sent the doorknob pinballing the length of the showroom and the basement door flew open. It shuddered as it smacked the wall.

Luka Fyodor Borodin was in.

Macie held her breath and listened to get a sense of his movement, but the Russian must have been standing still, taking stock of things. She wished she could text 911 and cursed herself for leaving her bag in the van. Wild was looking around for a landline when they heard scraping and exertion grunts. An angled mirror hung above the kitchen area so that customers could see the range top when guest chefs taught classes, and, from below the counter, Macie and Gunnar tilted their heads upward to the reflection and saw what was making all the noise. Borodin was wrestling a heavy butcher block table against the cellar door to prevent their escape.

Keeping low, Gunnar stole a quick foray to the shelves around them, gathering potential weapons. She joined in, and they quickly had accumulated a pile of everything from rolling pins to meat tenderizers to sharpening steels. Ducking into a squat next to the fondue pots and accessories, they watched the mirror. As soon as Borodin started to round the end of the aisle, Gunnar rose and chucked a marble rolling pin at him. He missed, but their attacker retreated. Only briefly. When he came around again, they both launched more cook tools, and he backed up again. But everybody in that store knew this holding action wouldn't last.

Gunnar started ripping the cellophane off a jar of pie weights sitting on a shelf beside cheesecloth and a spindle of dish towels. He whispered, "On my sign, you throw everything you can at once. Make it rain." She nodded. He scooched to the far end of their counter, snagged a chef's tunic off a hook, then pointed at her. Macie turned herself into a ball machine at the batting cage, lobbing everything she could get her hands on. Gunnar used her cover to sprint across the open space and shelter himself at the endcap of the aisle. After wadding the chef's tunic, he flung it in an arc up and behind Borodin. The gunman's shoes squeaked when he pivoted and got off a round at the flash of white cloth behind him. During the blink that his back was turned, Gunnar sprung across his aisle, bowling the open jar of pie weights toward him. The tiny ceramic peas skittered, spreading across the floor. Borodin whirled back and took a wild shot, but Gunnar had made cover behind the display shelves on the far side. The slug exploded a case of crystal stemware. Just two steps into his pursuit, Borodin slipped on the loose pie weights, lost his footing, and landed face-first with a sharp groan.

While he was down, Gunnar extended both arms and threw himself full force into the gondola shelving that separated him from Borodin's aisle. The metal display was heavy. It rocked but didn't tip; he only succeeded in showering egg beaters and kitchen twine down on the other side. Gunnar could hear the other man scrambling to get up and gave it an all-or-nothing push. The six-foot-tall rack teetered then tumbled over with a satisfying crash. A pained "Fuck me" came from under the rubble. But the top of the overturned display had landed wedged against the lower lip of the cashier's island. Borodin wasn't squashed, he was only pinned in a constricting tunnel. Gunnar could hear him struggling to crawl free as he hurried back to Macie.

"Basement," he said as she sprung to her feet. They'd get out the way they came in. But to reach that door they had to give up cover and cross Borodin's aisle. Gunnar had pictured him squeezed head-first the opposite way but signaled her to keep back behind the aisle display while he moved the butcher block.

The table was massive and heavy. Its top alone was sixteen inches deep of solid walnut, but Gunnar threw himself into it. Finding the right grip on the turned legs, he managed to hump it a few inches from the door. The noise of his effort drew attention. A muzzle flash lit up the black crawl space under the toppled display. The .44 magnum slug hit the thick block with a smack. Gunnar flinched, but this was their only chance. He grasped the table again and resumed his effort. Macie couldn't bear to stand there watching him be a target. She dashed out to push beside him. With both of them shoving, they scraped the thing a foot and a half from the door, just enough to get through. Macie yanked the door open and had one foot on the stairs when the next shot came.

Gunnar cried out and went down. She turned from the basement and came back in. He was on the floor with blood streaming from his calf.

Wild helped him to his feet, but he slipped in his own blood and fell again. Gunnar shouted, "Just go. Get out, go!" But she didn't. Instead Macie hooked Gunnar by the armpits and dragged him back behind the demo counter. "OK, fine, now run." Still she stayed. "Idiot," he muttered. Blood flowed from his wound, a deep graze across the meaty part of his calf. Macie handed him a dish towel to press over it. She found cheesecloth on the rack beside the towels and she looped some around his calf to make a tourniquet.

"Think you can make the door?" she asked. Before he could answer, the sound of metal gouging linoleum and spatulas clanging told them what was happening on the next aisle. They both slumped down behind their barrier, not to wait, but to figure out what to do. She looked to Gunnar for an idea and saw eyes glazed by shock. Macie's training as an attorney had not prepared her for this. But a lifetime of drive had.

She reached into the litter of cook tools around them and picked up an ice pick. "Don't tell me you're going to try to stab him with that," Gunnar muttered. Too busy to reply, Wild crawled to the crème brûlée torch display behind them and came back with a six-pack of butane refills bound in cellophane. Just yards away on the next aisle, they heard a heavy sigh and feet kicking pie weights aside.

"Open one of those cheesecloths," she said to Gunnar. Then she darted to the end of the aisle where Borodin had approached them before. Using the ice pick, she poked a hole in each of the butane canisters and left them there on the floor, leaking slowly.

When she returned, Gunnar had extracted a wad of cheesecloth from its packaging and handed it to her. "What now?" It was a curious reversal for her to be in charge of this sort of thing instead of him.

"Pray," she said. Displayed with the fondue pots she found a plastic bottle of Swissmar Fire Gel. Basically gourmet Sterno used for heating chafing dishes. Wild had another use in mind. She squeezed the gel onto the ball of cheesecloth and had almost saturated it with the entire bottle when they heard groans and heavy exhales around the corner. After that, an ominous beat of silence broken by the spinning of the Anaconda's cylinder. Their gunman was filling his loads.

Macie lit the gas burner on the range and set it to low. In the dim light, they made out the shadowy top of a head about to round the display to their left. Wild hauled herself up, steadied, waited, lit her gel-soaked wad, and let it fly. The flaming ethanol packet smacked Borodin high on the chest just as he came around the corner and it plopped on the floor at his feet. Immediately there came a loud *whoooomph* as the burning gel met the butane leak.

The lightning-bright flash of fire that followed engulfed the entire front of his body. The Russian screamed a native curse that mixed with the popping of the six cans as the remnants of their compressed gas exploded the cylinders. The shelving crash must have messed up his left arm because it hung limp at his side. In his frenzied dance to beat out the flames on his chest with his right, he dropped his revolver. Macie bolted for the gun, but he dove on top of it.

Wild delivered a hard kick to the side of his head. He hollered but went fetal, smothering the gun under him. As he brought his good hand up to grab it, she delivered another goal kick, this one to his injured arm. He howled so she gave it another and another. The Colt came out from his chest, a gleam of silver catching the blue tint of the dying flames licking his shirt. Just short of Gunnar's arrival Borodin used his leg to sweep at his wounded calf. It took Gunnar down hard. Macie rolled on the thug, trying to get the gun away but, injured though he was, this man possessed massive strength. All she could manage was to keep the Anaconda pointed away, and just barely. So she stiff-armed his gun wrist with one hand and used the elbow of her free arm to deliver blows to his face. Powered by pure survival instinct, Macie hammered his nose in a rapid succession of back jabs. Yet Borodin's hand, rough as a cinder block, began gradually to force the muzzle of the Colt toward her. Wild dug deep, fracking adrenaline from her life's pent-up rage—primal fury over the violation this animal had brought to her, the TENS torture, the murder of her brother, the failure of the DA to nail his killer, the estrangement of her parents, her ex's abuse in Paris—all of it. Octane fueled, she delivered harsh blow after blow. Soon came the wet crunch of bone, then a spray of blood peppered the nearby wall. His grip slacked. She brought both hands together with all her force and snatched away the revolver. Soon as she had it, Wild rolled off and stood above him, pointing the gun at him, panting.

"Stay down," said Cody, sliding on his butt back toward Borodin.

The killer stayed on the floor but not flat. He sat up, hanging his head between his raised knees, plucking at the bloody tatters of his shirt, then dropping his good hand to his side. "Too bad I didn't get you in my trunk that night," he said in a drooly slur.

"Shut up," she said, still gasping coarse breaths.

Gunnar leaned back against the counter. "Macie, this is your shot. You want to take it, I'm all-in."

"If I did, *pizda*, I'd still be fucking you."

"I said shut up." Macie's voice broke in a choking sob and she brandished the Anaconda at his face.

"Taking you up the ass, and you'd like it. *Ach! Ow. Oo-oo-oo!*" He smiled a devil's grin, blood coating every tooth.

Quietly, evenly, Gunnar said, "Just us, Mace."

Wild blew an audible exhale. "No. Not how it works. Not for me." She looked at Gunnar to finish the thought, to find the way to say what lived in her heart without sounding corny. The instant she turned, Borodin went for his ankle and drew a back-up gun.

It never got as high as his shin. Macie caught the movement and fired. The Anaconda's recoil nearly launched the gun right out of her hand. Luka Fyodor Borodin's left eye took the slug. He sat there, upright, a full two seconds, even though the exit wound had taken off the back of his skull. The pocket pistol fell from his hand and hit the deck right before he pitched backward on the linoleum, spilling brain.

It was just after four thirty the next morning when Gunnar's cell phone came alive with insistent text messages from Channel 2 dispatching him to Edie's Gourmet on East Seventh where an unidentified body had been found in the culinary store. He texted back to decline and handed his iPhone to Macie. "Hold still, Mr. Cody, would you please," said Dr. Patel. "It is difficult to suture unless you remain still."

Wild sunk into the chair at the foot of the exam table and closed her eyes. They stung from tears and fatigue, and the fluorescents didn't help. What she needed was a month in a tropical all-inclusive to beach-veg and to let the emotional toxins evaporate. After the death match with Borodin, she should have felt relief, even requital, but there was no satisfaction in killing the man who had likely murdered Rúben Pinto and, more likely, a score of others over time. Macie felt only numbness. If she tried for anything beyond that the bile would rise and the sobbing would return. And the guilt.

Guilt over the taking of a life. Guilt over what came after.

Macie had wanted to look for a phone in the back office of the store to call the police. Gunnar wanted to get out of there before the gunshots brought the police to them. The crisis had taken them to their essential poles. Wild told him that, for the same reason she couldn't shoot Borodin in payback, she had to stay and report. She not only had a moral obligation, but had a sworn duty as an officer of the court to—

Gunnar yaddah-yaddah-ed her. Actually interrupted with, "Yaddah yaddah." He told her, fine, reporting might clear her conscience but not the books. There were still numerous dicey questions upstream. Questions about having knowledge of Jackson Hall's hideout and not sharing that with the DA. Removing material evidence of a crime from Hall's secret storage locker instead of calling in the crime scene unit. Illegally having, then losing, custody of her defendant. By then, he had gotten under her skin and it flared into a full-blown shouting match. "Yeah, Hall's out there again," she snapped, "only now he's armed. And whose fault is that?"

"Right, glad you brought that up. Because guess what? Your sanctimony is going to pull me into the shitter with you."

They didn't have time for this. Not standing over a fresh corpse.

But Gunnar had gotten to her enough, and when he calmed and offered a way out, she took it. He convinced her that he was in bad shape and that they should get him medical help immediately as her plausible reason to depart the crime scene, then they could reassess. "You can always opt to report this in the morning. And drag in my sorry ass."

His need for immediate emergency medical aid was all the rationale she needed, even though he was sufficiently nonemergent to delay their exit until he completed some tasks. He put Borodin's Anaconda in his Timbuk2. Her prints were on it. Then he searched the dead man's pockets, taking his wallet and his cell phone. "This will buy some time before they can ID him. No sense getting word out about his shitty luck too quickly."

Macie helped Gunnar back to the van where they found their phones and his Sig Sauer, which was wedged under the driver's seat. After grinding the E-350 on three tires into a loading zone, Gunnar woke up his mechanic to come tow it before the police detectives started to work the block for clues, tossed his NYPD courtesy placard on the dash, and got in the Uber Macie had gotten them. She told the driver Bellevue. Gunnar scotched that and gave an address in Queens. An ER visit for a gunshot would mean mandatory notification of NYPD. "But you need a doctor."

"I know a guy."

"Of course you do." Which was how they ended up in the finished basement of Raj Patel, an MD who was part of the New York subculture of foreign-trained, but unlicensed, immigrant physicians. Legions of these docs from the block made ends meet delivering dry cleaning or hack driving, but serviced their communities with off-the-books medical help, including the occasional criminal who didn't want an emergency room visit to light up the radar.

◇ ◇ ◇

Macie unslung Gunnar's bag and looped it on the hook inside the door as she helped him into his apartment. The .44 hadn't broken any bone so he was able to bear weight, but the local was wearing off, and he steadied himself on her to ease the pain as he hobbled in. Dr. Patel said he was fortunate the slug hadn't struck an artery, or he'd be in the OCME's basement instead of his. Even so the wound took a lot of stitches and would leave a trench of scar tissue after it healed. Gunnar bore up without complaint; he was just wasted and on the weak side. Wild delivered him to his bed and lifted his wounded leg up by the heel to help him swing it on the blanket where he stretched out with a deep sigh.

In the kitchen she found a sleeve of English muffins and spread a half with peanut butter to boost his protein. But when she came back to the bedroom, he was drawing guttural lion breaths, just this side of snoring. From the great room, she texted Tiger to let him know that she would be working out of the office that day, and not to expect her. A scan of her e-mails showed nothing pressing. Since a resort getaway was nowhere in the foreseeable, Macie did the next best thing and tiptoed through the bedroom to take a shower.

The cascading water felt luxuriously hot. Wild became an environmentalist's nightmare, standing a quarter of an hour under the jet, washing off the night. As it lost temp, she kicked it up a notch and let the heat loosen the aching muscles in her back and neck. The tops of her toes stung where skin had chafed in the ferocious kicking she had delivered to Borodin. Borodin. A wave of deep sobs started to erupt again. Wild angled her face to the shower head and let it come.

Languid but refreshed, she opened the bathroom door to peek out at Gunnar. He was still asleep. Macie turned back to dry her hair some more, but without a thought—or ceremony—she dropped the towel and got on the bed to lie down naked beside him. She nestled against his body, feeling natural and warm. She tried to doze, too, but instead got up on one elbow to study Gunnar's face in its relaxed innocence. Impulsively, but, in the end, deliberately, she lowered her head and lightly kissed his stubbled cheek. His lids drifted open and she withdrew, but only inches. They remained like that, sharing a long minute of silent eye contact. What had happened? Something unspoken had either bonded them or made the obstacles not matter. Macie couldn't articulate it and didn't want to try. Not right then. Enough thinking and examination. A feeling drove her, as strong and unbidden as the emotional wave in the shower. The warmth she felt beside him spread inside her. Still holding his gaze, she let her hand cradle his jaw, then traced her fingertips down his neck to his chest and across the hard flat of his stomach to his belt buckle. Wild lingered but not for long. She gently cupped him through his jeans. He responded and Macie firmed her grip as he grew. Gunnar shifted toward her and winced. "Sh, sh," she whispered. "Stay just like that." He reached for his protection in the nightstand and settled back, lifting his hips as she undid his belt and slid down his pants, careful to keep them above where the doctor had slit them to get at his wound. Wild swung a leg over him and hovered above him on her knees, balancing herself with a palm beside each of his shoulders. They stared into each other some more. There was a moment of teasing but not of decision. Wild lowered her mouth onto his as he rose to meet it.

They tasted each other hungrily, and, as they kissed, every shared breath became fuel to devour the next one. Macie felt the vast store of suppressed emotions that ushered her to this moment bloom into need. As his hands caressed her, she pressed them to her skin, welcoming every touch. When he found her, and she fell upon him, swept into a frenzy matching his, they hurtled to a place where there were no words, no debates, only fire. And for a shining moment, carefree timelessness with no secrets.

Her cell phone vibrated in her bag across the room and woke them in a stream of morning sun an hour later. "You need to get that?" His breath tickled the soft well of her neck as he spoke.

"Eventually," she said, not wanting to move, but to hold onto him—and all this—as long as she could.

"Just so you know? We're not even."

"Explain, please."

Gunnar angled his head so he could see her profile on the pillow. "Last night, when you dragged me out of the line of fire and then stayed?"

"You mean when I saved your life?"

"Yes. That's one." He paused. "Against my two."

"You're welcome."

When Macie and Gunnar finished laughing they made love again.

The phone message was from Jonathan Monheit, sounding very high strung, inserting two call me's in the same voice mail. "What have you got, Jonathan?"

"News about The Ajax."

She reached for a pen. "Let's hear it."

Gunnar limped out of the bedroom, shaved and changed, and read her expression as she ended the call. "Tell me."

"That was Jonathan. He kept digging into Trifonov's LLC, doing a search of public records to see what shook loose. Ready for this? He uncovered a construction company lien for unpaid renovations that names the prior owner of The Ajax penthouse."

"Interesting, but that's the old owner. Unless it names Trifonov, how does it help?"

"You tell me. The document was later redacted but Monheit drilled down and found the name in the original filing. The lien was against a Jerónimo Teixeira."

Gunnar clapped his hands once. "Jonny Midnight, sticking the landing!" For once, he wasn't being snide. They both felt the impact of this information. It was concussive.

"So follow along, kids." Wild stepped to him and traced the points of a triangle in the air with each name. "Your bad-boy prince, whose bodyguard was Luka Fyodor Borodin, sold The Ajax condo to Pyotr Trifonov. Coincidence?"

"Hate that word."

The connection had finally been established, but the meaning still eluded them. Like with any puzzle they both knew there was a solution, but without more information, they had to resort to imagination to try to bring it all together. "Damn," she said. "It feels this close. The one thing that absolutely links up now is the Russian connection, Borodin to Trifonov."

"I think we both know there's another thread here."

Without speaking it, Wild said. "Yes, but we don't do circumstantial, do we."

Luka Borodin's death was by no means the end of this. They had severed an arm of the beast but not the head. One thing Wild did know for sure was that she still needed to unwind the mystery of Pyotr Trifonov if she had any hope of clearing Jackson Hall. Macie and Gunnar continued their conjecture, replete with dead ends, half-finished sentences, and whack conspiracy theories. Macie studied the JPEG she'd made of the Case Board, looking for loose ends or unexplored threads concerning Trifonov. A nugget from Monheit's lecture on the oligarch struck a chord and she called Monheit back and told him to enlist Tiger and Chip to help him gather everything they could find on Pyotr Arkady Trifonov during the time of his African mining stint. Then she rolled the call to Soledad, asking her to get back in touch with Jackson Hall's girlfriend. "Tell him to make contact with me ASAP. Have Pilar tell him exactly this. Say that Borodin is no longer a factor."

"Cryptic," said the social worker. "Do you know how cryptic you've been lately?"

"All the better to help you keep your license." Wild knew her friend would leave it there.

Gunnar put in a call to CyberG to ask his black hat how he was coming with Orem Diner's server. He covered the phone and turned to Macie. "The Gauchito got inside it last night." He instructed his hacker to focus all attention on financial records. "Especially related to The Ajax purchase, Jerónimo Teixeira, or any other transactions linking to Exurb Partners LLC. Bank accounts, lines of credit, you get the idea."

The callback came an hour later. "This could move the needle," said CyberG. "I was running scans for the financials, like you asked, and found an active credit card that is billed to one of Pyotr Trifonov's smaller companies. Most of the purchases are day-to-day. Liquor, restaurants, florist."

"Sounds like a personal card."

"Here's the BFD. There's a line of credit currently open at the Hotel Cornwell. Premium movies, dry cleaning, and lots of room service charges, morning, noon, and night. If that's your boy Trifonov—"

"Shit, he could be there right now." In his excitement, Gunnar bolted to his feet, then cringed in pain.

CHAPTER 37

The Hotel Cornwell is one of those unabashedly old-line landmarks you find in every great city of the world where traveling diplomats, publishing titans, and Fortune 500 big shots over fifty cheerfully part with their USDs for quiet luxury, first-rate service, and, above all, privacy. Macie Wild and Gunnar Cody knew it would be near impossible to bluff their way past the layers of hospitality staff and career security to locate, let alone access, their Russian, so when they arrived, they came with a plan. Actually it was a credit card. "We called about reserving a standard king for one night," said Gunnar, snapping his runandgunn.com business Amex down on the black marble counter. Some of the best plans are simple. And expensive.

The host took his card and ID then dipped his chin to acknowledge the wolf's head cane Gunnar was leaning on, the walking stick Macie had just bought from the second-hand boutique on his NoLIta street. "Mr. Cody, if you'd be more comfortable with a seat in our library, I can bring you your keys after I check you in." He indicated the clubby alcove in the corner of the lobby, an oasis of soft lighting, burgundy wing chairs, and complimentary Fiji Water.

"That would be lovely," said Wild, answering for him.

"I'm fine, really," he said to her when they sat.

"It's not about being fine. It's about acting like we belong by accepting the service. Are you bleeding?"

"No, but later I may need a naughty nurse. Just planting the thought."

Upstairs in their room, while Gunnar fished small electronics and fresh batteries out of his weekender, she opened her iPad and studied the research she had requested from Monheit on Pyotr Trifonov's mining activities. The top of the attachment included some Internet photos taken of the oligarch over the years. When Macie had glimpsed him two weeks before, Trifonov still sported his Fab-Four-meets-Dudley-Moore haircut, but it was salt and pepper, not jet black like the 1994 shot of him with the other *nomenklatura* smiling behind Putin. A more recent image was from a *Financial Times* clipping about Canada denying the klepto-crat's immigration request due to laundering plundered money through crony banks. But the picture that she lingered on was a 2010 shot of Tri-fonov in a khaki bush jacket outside his copper mine in West Africa. It was pure PR optics: a benevolent Russian patrician, posed with a black teen, pointing to the young African's own country, as if to say, "Someday this will all be yours." When she had finished, Wild slid her tablet back in her bag. Gunnar hoisted himself by the arms of his easy chair and picked up his bag. "Ready?"

"Soon as I make the call," she said. Macie tapped in the number from the business card and waited. While it rang, a knot formed in her di-aphragm. Borodin may be dead, same as Pipe Wrench and his partner, but even with the immediate threat of those men gone, Wild's common sense told her there were plenty more where they came from—hired killers enlisted by some larger operation she had not yet fathomed. She and Gunnar were hoping to find some answers to that in minutes, four floors above them, and it gnawed at her that she had no idea what they'd be walking into.

"It'll go fine," said Gunnar, reading her.

She smiled. "You think so?"

Instead of answering, he chambered a round in his Sig Sauer then limped to the door.

The qualms Macie had expressed to Gunnar still nipped little bites off her insides. Mainly, shouldn't they just let the police take it from here? All he needed was the short elevator ride up to rationalize his no: that they would then expose their credit card hack that led them to this ho-tel; that they would get cut out of their own case, same as the DA had refused to share evidence; that they had no idea who else was involved in this crime and, if that sounded paranoid, all she needed to ask herself was if she ever knew anyone to walk out of the Bellevue jail ward with-out insider help. "You sure you're not a lawyer?" she asked.

"Don't insult me," he said as the doors parted on seven.

Wild and Cody took their places on opposite sides of Room 716 and leaned against the jamb to listen. They had the hallway to themselves and the only sound was the comforting hum of a housekeeper's vacuum far up the corridor and around the bend. Gunnar leaned his cane quietly against the wall, knocked twice, then cued her. "Minibar service," she called in a pleasant sing-song. He had suggested during their planning that a female voice would raise less suspicion. They pressed their ears to the wood. No reply. No sound at all. Not a footfall, a shower, nor a TV. This time she knocked and sang the same greeting. Still nothing.

Macie watched him get out his cell phone, tap his Voice Memo app, then slip a Dry Erase from his bag. Gunnar, the self-professed gear head, had learned to modify these markers for his TARU squad by removing the innards of the Expo, popping in a barrel jack where the felt tip had once protruded, then stuffing a mini Arduino circuit board into the hollow pen body. Gunnar felt underneath the hotel door's lock hardware for the power receptacle, which doubled as a one-wire communications port, and inserted the barrel tip into the jack. It fit perfectly. In a quarter of a second there came a soft chirp and the whir of a servo motor as the tumblers of the lock disarmed. He turned the handle and opened the door a few inches, cueing her again. "Good morning, minibar service." Gunnar entered ahead of her, quickly, in spite of his limp.

He angled himself to present the narrowest target. She grabbed his cane before following and made out the soft glint of stainless steel from the P220 pressed against Gunnar's thigh before he drew it up in a shooting stance as he cleared the foyer. "Freeze," he said, and her heart thudded.

Wild hung back in the safety of the entryway but made out the man Gunnar was aiming at in the reflection from a wall mirror. He was on the bed, lying back on a stack of pillows against the headboard with his right hand on a revolver hovering an inch over the comforter beside him. The man's arm quaked. His breathing sounded labored. With heavy lids raised slightly, his gaze tracked sadly from the gun to Gunnar before he let the weapon fall onto the bed. Gunnar darted forward and removed the revolver. "Keep them where I can see them," he said softly. With one eye on the man on the bed, he checked the closet and the bathroom and gave her the all clear.

Advancing into the mini suite, her first thought was, where's Trifonov? Then it struck her. This *was* Trifonov. Or his ghost. Never mind the Beatle cut, he was entirely bald. A man in his early sixties, Pyotr Trifonov now wore twenty more years than a week ago when he fell ill inside that revolving door. Emaciated and feeble, the front of his white undershirt bore peach-colored stains from watery vomit that had dribbled and dried. The heat was on high in the room, yet he had long flannel bottoms which bore the unmistakable scent of intestinal distress. A room service tray of untouched food sat on a rolling cart done up with a white tablecloth, silver service, and a single peony in a vase. A bottle of Saratoga water lay on its side where he had knocked it over and its contents spilled.

She handed Gunnar his cane, and he asked her to check under the bed. She got on her knees for a peek and shook no. "Any other weapons?" he asked.

Pyotr Trifonov swallowed, then spoke for the first time. In a Russian accent that was more continental than Volga boatman, he said, "My gun, it was . . ."—he hitched in a breath so he could finish the sentence— "it was too heavy."

"Any other weapons?" repeated Gunnar.

The Russian wagged no on his mountain of pillows. "You. You are not from Baltik-Eskort, no?"

Feigning ignorance, Gunnar asked, "What is Baltik-Eskort?"

"Not sent from *siloviki*? FSB?" he asked, referring to the rebranded KGB.

"We're not from them," said Wild.

"I thought as much. You are police? Homeland Security? No, not you," he said of her. Then he appraised Gunnar. "You, perhaps."

"I'm a journalist."

"Journalist. With a gun."

"Oligarch. With a gun," replied Cody.

Trifonov's mouth narrowed in amusement at his pushback. "Is for protection."

"From what?" Macie asked. When he didn't answer, she pressed. "Mr. Trifonov, Mr. Cody is indeed a journalist, and I am an attorney." When Trifonov turned away from her, she positioned herself back in his view. "My client is accused of a murder he didn't commit, but somehow got mixed up in whatever it is that—well, you seem to be part of. I personally have experienced three attempts on my life since I got involved, plus one on my friend's here. We went to a lot of trouble to track you down, and now I demand that you tell me what the hell you know about this."

The man let his eyes close a moment then he opened them in a squint of sly deliberation. Whatever illness had leveled Pyotr Trifonov, it appeared the shrewd opportunist in him would be last to wither. At last, he spoke, as much to himself as to them. "All right, very well. Maybe . . . maybe this is for the best, after all." He elbowed himself higher on his pillows, showing a surge of strength and resolve. "I will tell you. I especially wish to tell this journalist. But sit, please, so I don't have to look up so much." Gunnar holstered his Sig then unloaded Trifonov's piece, dropping the bullets in his coat pocket before placing it in the dresser under the flat screen. When they sat, the Russian strained to reach for a composition book on his nightstand. "You are not taking notes?" he asked of Gunnar.

"Already am." He slid his iPhone out of the breast pocket of his sport coat and set it on the corner of the bed. The Voice Memo app had been rolling and recording everything since their entrance.

"Sneaky journalist."

You have no idea, thought Macie.

Trifonov's body shuddered with a barking cough. When he finished, he drew long breaths to settle himself then said in broken English, "I am dying. I am dying man because I have been murdered, poisoned by fucking cowards, and I have no choice but to be waiting for my death sentence to come." He let the words sink in and drew more oxygen while they did. "You ever hear of Alexander Litvinenko?"

They both nodded, but Gunnar answered. "Sure, the Russian agent who blew the whistle on Putin. Back in '06 or '07 it was all over the news when he . . ." Awkward. Gunnar let it drop there, but Trifonov finished for him.

"When he got poisoned in London. And it was 2006. I know the date because I Googled it up. Poisoned by polonium-210 on 1 November. Dead from acute radiation syndrome, 23 November. Three weeks, and gone. The fucking bastards got him, and now they got me."

"And there's no cure?"

"Fuck no, lady. And I do not apologize for my language!" He pointed two fingers at his forehead. "They could have shot me, bang dead, but no. Same as Litvinenko, they want to make me example. So I get invited to meeting with two traveling friends from home. You know, in Kremlin we were the *nomenklatura*, Volodya's elites," he said, using one of Putin's nicknames. "I had this problem, an incident, here in New York City, and they said they wanted to hear my side and to say no worrying, Petya, will all be fine. We had nice tea in one of their hotel rooms. I had tea. They had Coca Cola. From bottle. I leave, and they say, 'Pyotr Arkady, *komarik*, don't you worry, your worries are over.' That night, all night long, I vomit and shit the bathroom floor like crazy. I will not bother to tell you the tests and tests, and finally, the lab says I have radiation poisoning from the polonium. Do you know how little it takes for lethal dose?" He held up his fingers in a pinch. "The size of one grain of pepper will kill." He must have read their reactions. "Relax, it must be ingested. It is alpha waves, and can't pass through skin. I am expert now. It was in my fucking tea, I believe this."

He struggled higher on the pillows. "So I do the chelation therapy. No good, I get worse. The doctor, he gives me the Dimercaprol. My lymphocyte count continues to fall and he says, 'Pyotr, come to hospice and get affairs in order.' I do not go to hospice. I come here to get my affairs in order." He brandished the orange composition book. "My affairs. All in here. I come here to this hotel to hide and write diary of all the bad shit. I record in here all the secret bank numbers with the dark money I helped loot under Putin's *bespredel* from state treasuries and industry ventures. In here are the fake banks I set up in Moldova, the hidden Irish accounts, the money laundered through my mining in Africa, the millions scooped out of PetroMed that built Vladimir's palace in Sochi . . ." He was riding a wave of energy and fanned the pages, the entire Rhodia, densely filled with his notations and numbers. "Is smoking gun, yes? Ha.

Yes. I sent a fuck-you e-mail to those bastards before I disappear. I say to them, 'You want to take little *komarik* down? You go down with me."

Even though Trifonov was a willing talker, driven by his own agenda, Wild had hers too. Together Macie and Gunnar had painstakingly assessed the bits of solid information they had, including that lien against the previous Ajax owner, the research Monheit put together on the oligarch's mining activities, and, of course, the zip pouch Rúben Pinto had skimmed from the safe in Trifonov's penthouse burglary. What they needed now was the connective tissue. So she decided to keep Pyotr talking by feeding his sense of betrayal. "That's outrageous," she said. "Litvinenko publicly outed Vladimir Putin, accusing him of corruption and sanctioning murders. I've read about you. Weren't you loyal to him?"

"Always! This is—yes, as you said—my outrage!"

"Then why the polonium?" asked Gunnar, falling right in step with her, feeding the indignation to beckon him onward.

"Because in Russia now, money is more important than loyalty after all."

Wild said, "Help me understand, Mr. Trifonov. You were loyal and you helped make—and, as you just admitted—hide money too. Killing you . . . Why?" He pulled a face and his long pause made her suddenly worry she had pushed things too eagerly. But then came his reply. And it was big.

"They kill me this way and make me an example to all because I fucked up. Oh, yes, I do well for the, ah, consortium, for years, make profitable doing the business, doing the laundering, doing it all. Life is champagne and thumbs-up, right? But then a single theft jeopardized our whole enterprise. I was blameless. But they called me careless. No matter, the impact was costly. Enormously so. Someone had to pay. To show the others. And, I am consortium's revenge."

Macie recalled the Putin credo about reward and punishment. Trifonov had lived the friend side of that equation. Now something had made him an enemy. She played again to his sense of indignation. "It's unbelievable to me. How could something like a small theft create such an injustice?"

"Because it was not small! Did I say it was small? Look what they did to me. Does this look small?" Some drool trickled onto his undershirt, creating an amber pond. "They broke into my apartment, thieves in the night. Most of what they took was meaningless. Duplicate copies of public documents, my immigration papers, business and trade proposals, some cash, about $600,000, nothing much. But they stole the one thing that is explosive. Was worth killing me." He held up his orange notebook. "All this in here? Damning, yet nothing compared to that one item taken from that safe. That is devastating."

"Tell us," urged Gunnar.

"Yes, please," added Macie, leaning forward to make him feel even more the star.

"A pouch. Such a small thing, really. But inside . . ." The Russian cast his eyes down in shame. "They told me I should have used the embassy vault. But I wanted it kept physically separate from government to keep it clean. So that apartment safe was where I kept the banking instruments." He looked up to explain. "I was the keeper of the official government stamps and seals that we used to illegally validate our stolen currency transfers. You see, you can't just take money out of the country. It has a trail, a provenance. So my task was to create false, yet legitimate-looking, documents that allowed the billions and billions to flow from Russia, Ukraine, what have you, to the crony banks I set up. Mostly in Moldova."

"Crony banks?" asked Gunnar.

"Where we own the bank and we are its only customer. Dirty money in, we validate with stamps and seals on the documentation, clean money out. From there it goes to secret offshore accounts or gets laundered again through various means." Wild had something to say about one of those means but held it for now. Satisfied that she had all she needed for the moment, Macie gave the sign to Gunnar, and he pulled a cell phone out of his backpack. But it wasn't his phone. It was the one he had taken off Borodin's body.

Earlier that morning, Gunnar had examined the cell to see what he could find in Borodin's Recents and Messages. It didn't require much effort. This device had only communicated with one other number, and that was by text. There were no e-mails, in, out, or saved. The text messages themselves had been deleted, but the phone number—without a name—resided atop the blank window when he opened the Messages app. The area code was listed to Montana. Unless Borodin had a pal who was a fly fisherman, Gunnar assumed it to be a burner.

He thumbed-in the message he and Wild had agreed on.

> Found Hall. Tracked him to Hotel Cornwell.
> Hall has the pouch and tried to make deal
> with fucking Trifonov. Holding both. Rm 716.
> Will tell front desk OK to send you up.

At the send whoosh Macie moved beside Gunnar to monitor the screen with him. Trifonov had spent a lot of energy, and his chest rose and fell in dozy oblivion. After half a minute, she whispered, "Shouldn't we get an answer by now?"

"Would be nice," he said just as the incoming text chimed.

> K. 30 mins.

Even though the digital time was right there on the phone, they both checked their watches. "So. By noon," she said.

"Unless word leaks out that Borodin bought it. If so, our plan's pretty much screwed."

"Happy thoughts, happy thoughts."

Gunnar sat and checked his gun again. "Happy now." Then they went to work preparing the room.

Twenty minutes later there was a knock at the door. They didn't answer it. Gunnar had stationed Macie inside the bathroom with Luka Borodin's pocket pistol in her trembling hand, armed for the worst-case scenario. The ex-cop had positioned himself just out of sight, hugging the corner where the entry hall met the bedroom. The blackout drapes were drawn and all the lights were out except the reading lamp on the nightstand beside the sleeping Russian. Gunnar's stage setting was all about tactical shadows and illumination that drew the eye away from him. He had wedged the door ajar by swinging the hinged security bar between it and the jamb so it wouldn't close. Macie heard the door push open. Corridor light fanned across the entry floor. The wall switch snapped on then off uselessly. She had removed the overhead bulbs. "Borodin?"

Cody grunted in a whisper laced with Luchik's accent. "Yuh."

The door swept closed, bounced once on the metal swing bar, and the entry was cast again in darkness. Footsteps, muffled by the deep carpeting, approached slowly. In silhouette, she made out Gunnar bringing his Sig up in a two-handed brace. Wild couldn't see around him but wasn't too surprised when she heard Gunnar say, "Hands in the clear, counselor." But when she emerged from behind Gunnar and saw who it was, Macie had to steady herself against the wall.

Because the counselor being held at gunpoint was her father.

CHAPTER 38

"Oh, good Lord, no," she moaned. Beyond stunned, Wild's gun felt stupid and heavy, and she lowered it to her side.

Jansen Wild's dumbstruck gaze drifted from his daughter to the bore of the .45 Gunnar was aiming at him then back to Macie. Her father gulped some air, a goldfish out of his bowl, and then he spoke. "What the hell is this?"

"No—Dad—let me ask you," said Macie, who was still reeling. "What the hell?" Mr. Wild said nothing. Gunnar switched on the table lamps then limped into the entryway to stow the security bar and close the door. Jansen seemed annoyed by that. "This is false imprisonment, you know." But the ex-cop, unfazed, began patting him down.

"Gunnar," said Macie. "Is that necessary?" No sooner had she asked than he removed a Walther CCP from the outer pocket of her father's suit coat. Yet another blow to absorb. She dropped her chin to her chest and ditched her own weapon into the pocket of her blazer.

Without comment, Gunnar dropped her father's pocket pistol in the dresser drawer where he had moved Trifonov's piece. "Have a seat."

Jansen followed the sweep of Gunnar's hand to the armchair and complied. "I'll say it once more: This is false imprisonment. I wish to leave. Macie, even if this miscreant doesn't, I know you respect the law. There's been some mistake, some misunderstanding."

"Jansen?" came the weak voice from the pillows. The silence that followed hearing his name undid any pretense of a mix-up.

Clinging to quiet indignation, Mr. Wild said to Gunnar, "I have no idea what this is about, but you hold the gun, so I'll just have to sit here and wait."

Macie caught Gunnar's eye then trailed her gaze to the Sig Sauer. He hesitated briefly, but holstered his pistol. Gaining a small amount of equilibrium, she sat on the corner of the bed to face her dad. "I'm very afraid. Afraid of what we're going to have to talk about."

"Are you pulling some good-cop angle on me? My own daughter?"

The shock of his involvement made something deep inside her crack. Small fissures began hatching anger the more he acted like a goddamned lawyer. She could only guess how many therapy sessions she would have over this. But for now, Macie stuffed all that down and pushed back. "We are going to get into this, Dad. And I want—no, I demand—the truth from you."

"Mace, I'm sorry I—"

"No. Do not sorry me." She steamrolled ahead before her broken heart weakened her resolve. "I'm going to give you a chance to tell me—honestly—what are you doing here? And with a gun?"

"Mr. Trifonov is a client. I was concerned for his well-being."

"Oh, you *are* so pissing me off. Trifonov is a client of Orem Diner's."

"Are you actually asking me to violate privilege?"

"I will tell you," said Trifonov.

"Pyotr, be quiet," called Jansen to the man in the bed.

"Yes, Orem Diner is my attorney—for most things."

"Pyotr, please."

"But Jansen Wild, he arranged for The Ajax."

"Will you shut up?"

Trifonov suppressed a wheezing cough. "Is all in the diary."

Feeling Macie's glare, her father said, "I never figured you to stoop to entrapment."

"I never figured you to be a criminal."

"Why, because I helped someone set up a legal shell corporation?"

She pointed to the bed. "So he could illegally launder millions plundered from Russia." Macie's head was still spinning but, sorting through the maelstrom, she managed to pull out a recollection. "Remember at lunch when you schooled me on LLCs, you said that you caught overflow from Orem Diner? It makes sense now. Diner already handled the previous owner of The Ajax penthouse. So your pal farmed out Mr. Trifonov's LLC setup to you so he'd be the seller and you'd be the buyer. Just a little camouflage for nosy investigators."

"Come on, Mace, even a public defender should know there's no law against helping wealthy clients broker real estate deals. Manhattan would still be a bunch of thatched roofs otherwise."

"But it wasn't between two clients," said Gunnar. "It was between one client and himself."

Mr. Wild's blink rate increased. Trifonov croaked out from the bed, "Jansen, they know."

"My client is delusional." He was starting to crumble, which ate at Macie's heart. But it was this man before her who had given her the gene to stand for the truth. And she would get it.

She picked up her iPad. "The prior owner, as recorded on a property lien, is named Jerónimo Teixeira." Wild swiped to open a doc. "My investigator checked Mr. Teixeira's worth. He has an allowance through his mother, but nowhere near the $30 million cash he paid for that condo. She repeated the sale price for emphasis. "Thirty million. In cash. That money came from Jerónimo Teixeira's father." Macie indicated the bed. "Pyotr Trifonov." There came a loud sniff from the mattress. Jansen Wild, meanwhile, swallowed hard and licked his lips with a stale tongue. She continued.

"When Mr. Trifonov invested his plundered funds from Russian banks and corporations, one of his laundering ventures was a mining operation in Africa. Specifically, Angola."

"The Internet is a stubborn thing," said Gunnar. "All those nasty little stories get posted and then stick like burrs to your socks."

Macie tapped open the 1990s article from the European tabloid that Tiger had dug up. " 'Russian Mining Boss Digs Local Woman,' " she said, reciting the headline. "You don't need me to read it, do you? You know the story. A scandal over an illegitimate son. Then a fat hush money payoff to make it go away. The mother gets rich, and gets amnesia." Macie walked the iPad over to Trifonov and showed him the picture from the old newspaper of himself and the Angolan teen observing the mining operation. "This would be your boy, wouldn't it?"

"Jerónimo," he sighed, a lifetime criminal making peace with truth in increments.

She moved back to show the screen to her dad. "I just learned that, two years ago, Mr. Trifonov's mining firm paid a one-time consulting fee of $30 million to Jerónimo Teixeira. Really? An eighteen-year-old college student, as a consultant in what?"

"Lap dances?" asked Gunnar.

Macie pressed her case. "I'm going to say that the thirty mil from Mr. Trifonov was funneled directly into purchasing that penthouse condo at The Ajax. The very condo that your client then bought from his own son at a cash price of $40 million through the LLC you set up for him."

"Kinda like robbing Pyotr to pay . . . well, Pyotr," said Gunnar. "Clever, but it's still laundering $70 million of Mother Russia's illegal money."

He snapped at Cody. "You have balls lecturing me on ethics." It was a flash of bravado, but her father began to fidget. Sweat glistened on his upper lip.

"Dad, you are so past ethics."

"You can just stop."

But she didn't. "This is criminal activity."

"Enough!"

"And conspiracy."

"Oh, now it's conspiracy too?" He broke eye contact, couldn't look at his daughter. But Macie was swept up in a current and couldn't hold back.

"These past weeks you kept saying you were so concerned about my safety. And all the time, you were working with Luka Borodin. I'm not sure whether you were working for him or he was working for you, but I do know you were in deep." When he dropped his head and studied his hands, she shouted, "Look at me! I'm talking about the same man who tried to kidnap me. And I am certain that he killed Pinto."

"What makes you think I'm connected with this man? What's his name? Borden?"

"Borodin," Gunnar repeated with emphasis. "I'm surprised, sir, because how do you think we got you to come here?" He held up the phone. "I used Borodin's cell to text you. And you responded. And here you are." The attorney stared at the cell phone and sighed.

Whatever small amount of restraint Macie clung to shattered. "God-damn it, how can you just sit there like this?" She came off the corner of the bed and threw herself at her father, shaking him by the shoulders. He raised up his arms in defense and she swatted them down. He shoved her away and stood. Macie came back on him. This time she hurled curses and shook him again, hard. Gunnar waded in to pull her off. He got his arms around her, but his leg kept him from getting the leverage he needed. When he was finally able to draw her away, they both froze.

Jansen Wild was holding Gunnar's .45 on them.

"OK, let's clamp a lid on this right now," said Gunnar. His voice carried the strain of reproof for letting his holster get stripped. He extended an open palm. Jansen Wild ignored it and stiff armed the Sig. He took a tentative step back toward the entryway.

"You're not leaving." Her father turned his attention from Gunnar to find Macie two-handing the Ruger she had fished from her pocket.

Mr. Wild's eyes blinked rapidly behind his glasses. Gunnar lowered his tone, trying to instill calm. "Everybody just hold. Don't anyone do anything."

"Macie . . ."

She disengaged the safety of the LC9s the way Gunnar had instructed her earlier. "Sit back down." He didn't move. Neither did she. Father and daughter stood mere yards apart in a lethal standoff.

"What are you doing with that?" he asked.

"I got it from your man Borodin," said Macie. "Right after I killed him."

Was it the news that Borodin was dead? Or was it the flat stare in the eyes of his own daughter that made the Sig Sauer waver in Jansen Wild's hand. "You . . . did that?"

"I had to."

His lower lip developed a tremor to match his arm's. "You what . . . ? Because of me— Oh, God, Macie . . ." Tears fell down both cheeks and his glasses started to fog. "I never meant for this to go so far." Yet he still held out his gun, and she, hers. But then emotion overwhelmed him. "Forgive me." His breath shuddered and he started to bring the gun up off her toward himself.

"No, Dad!"

Gunnar threw himself at him and batted the pistol away before he got it under his chin. The Sig flew from his hand onto the carpet. Jansen lost his legs and started to crumble. Gunnar caught him and spun him to the chair where he bent forward, folded over his own lap, gagging with sobs. Macie started toward him. Gunnar relieved her of Borodin's Ruger and she fell on her knees beside her father, trying not to cry herself for fear she would never stop.

After he was spent, he brought himself upright in the chair. "Macie, I never meant any harm to you. I tried to get you out of this—multiple times. I kept pushing to get you to give up the case and steer you clear of all this, but you wouldn't do it." She thought about his warnings—even about his urging her to go away to Germany—and did believe him. With bankrupt eyes, he studied his daughter. "And now you killed a man . . ."

"Because of you," she couldn't help saying. "Did you send Borodin to Rúben Pinto?"

"Let's say Pyotr fell from grace and I got a clear message I had better help clean things up."

"Who gave you this message?"

Her father ignored the question and sniffed. "I didn't think Borodin would kill Pinto. But Pinto started playing games. Macie, that little asshole stole something. Something more valuable than you can imagine. He called. I showed up to pay the ransom. I get there, and he tried to jack the price. He didn't even bring the package with him."

"So you sent Borodin," she said, staying on point.

From the bed came a moan. "Borodin . . ." Then a papery mutter, "Luka Borodin, he was there when I got poisoned." Confirmation that Luchik was no mere repo thug from Long Island. Her tacit assumption, because they were both Russian, had been that Trifonov and Borodin were working together. Now it looked like the opposite: Like Borodin was a contractor for Baltik-Eskort hunting down Trifonov. So was Pipe Wrench. During her rendition, when he kept asking where the Russian was, she thought he meant Borodin when he meant the dying man before her. Pyotr's fuck-you-e-mail threat obviously had changed the game after his poisoning; they were no longer content to let him go off and die as an example. They needed him found and silenced.

"So your man from Baltik-Eskort beat it out of Pinto," said Gunnar.

"Or tried to. Until Rúben died on him. All for this." He reached in his backpack and pulled out the zipper pouch.

Both men reacted at the sight of the package, Trifonov most strongly. He smacked both hands over his face. "I fucking die for this! Those *mudaks* kill me for losing!"

While the Russian wailed in heart wrenching despair, and her father slumped back in silent agony, Wild capped the most traumatic day since the murder of her brother by sending a one-word text from her phone: "Now."

No longer than it took for Gunnar to pick up and reholster his Sig Sauer, the lock chirped and the hallway door opened. "FBI," said Special Agent Stack as he and Special Agent Nemec entered.

The management and guests of the Hotel Cornwell could not have been too pleased with the activity at the decorous East Side retreat, including a cordoned-off seventh floor, one of its two elevators commandeered by law enforcement, plus a small convoy of inelegant government vehicles double-parked out front, but, with any luck, the operation would be over by afternoon check-in. That was the least of priorities in Room 716. Directed by SA Stack, the six other FBI agents who had swarmed into the junior suite behind him went to work in quick order, all at once searching Jansen Wild and Pyotr Trifonov for weapons and escorting Borodin's Ruger to the hallway in an evidence bag. With gloved hands, they opened the dresser drawer where Gunnar had deposited Trifonov's revolver, Jansen Wild's Walther, and the most smoking gun of all: the orange Rhodia comp book with Trifonov's holistic confession, including the orchestration of laundering all those Russian millions through Manhattan real estate.

The feds not only had the time to coordinate deployment but to arrive with warrants, thanks to the heads-up call Macie had placed to Stack before she and Gunnar made their move on Trifonov's suite. The Evidence Response Team, the FBI's Crime Scene Unit, took possession of the weapons, the diary, the burner phones, and the zippered pouch holding its damning collection of stamps and seals. They carefully placed each in its own container, all labeled and signed-for, creating the chain-of-evidence paper trail. There would be no screw-ups on the road to this trial, certainly not by the bureau.

Paramedics arrived and administered to Trifonov. Gunnar briefed them on his polonium-210 poisoning, not so much to do the doomed man any good, but to aid the safety of the medics. When they gurneyed him from the room, he had withered, singing a children's song to himself in Russian on the way out.

Macie and Gunnar gave statements out in the hallway. The agents took it all down, and without needing too much reflection, Stack said that Trifonov's diary would be a bonus, but the stamps and seals were the prize and had been long sought. They were the only proof they needed to crack open the laundering operation. It also was the only evidence sufficient to enable them to freeze illegal Russian bank accounts. "That's why Trifonov had to be made an example of for his fuck-up. This is not going to be a happy day for Vladimir Putin," said the agent. "Let's just say, if you saw him shirtless, those nipples would not be hard."

Hearing the FBI say that they had been after those stamps and seals a long time knocked a loose thought free in Macie. "Jeffrey Stamitz. I hear the crew chief was a confidential informant for you guys. Did you give him a shopping list for The Ajax?"

Special Agents Stack and Nemec exchanged glances. Stack maintained a poker face. "I don't know the source of your information, but I am sure I would not comment on that."

"I think you just did," said Gunnar.

Downstairs Macie and Gunnar watched agents from the Evidence Response Team load Pyotr Trifonov's luggage and some bankers boxes that they had brought down from his suite into an unmarked van. "Tell me the truth," said Gunnar. "Were you expecting Orem Diner?"

"I would have preferred," she said. That was her truth.

"Do you think Diner is dirty?"

Macie shrugged. "I think he's a lawyer."

The evidence team returned for another load, lagging briefly at the lobby doors to let out Stack and Nemec, who were escorting Jansen Wild in handcuffs. Macie's vision fluttered slightly upon taking in the tableau she never would have imagined seeing in her life: her father in custody.

Upstairs she had asked to have a private word with him before they left, and Special Agent Stack gave her the nod and looked the other way as soon as they had buckled him in the back seat of their SUV. Macie stood in the open door and looked in at him. His face was swollen and mottled from crying. "I am so sorry for what I have put you through," he said hoarsely, the voice of all broken spirits.

"I have to know something, Dad. I need to know why." When he didn't answer, just cast his gaze downward, she said, "Do you think you can tell me that?"

When he brought his eyes to meet hers they were rimmed with water again. "I knew it was wrong. I never knew it would get to this, but I knew it wasn't right."

"Then why?"

He cleared his throat. "It was Walter." Macie's own eyes started to fill at her brother's name. "When he got taken. So violent. So stupid. It just . . . I lost every . . . I lost my soul, Macie."

"It hurt us all, Dad."

"I lost my soul," he repeated, but louder, a plea to be heard. "My marriage, my work, everything. Meant. Nothing." After the sourness of that, the corners of his mouth twitched, a failed attempt at a smile. "Except for you. You were—you were my Mace. But. When it's all shit?" He tilted his head back to blink the tears away before he resumed. "I said, fuck it." He looked around the FBI vehicle then to her. "And I guess I did." Agent Nemec opened the shotgun door and got in. Stack sidled up beside Macie and rested his hand on the door frame. "Can you forgive me?" asked her father.

"I'll come see you, and we'll talk some more." She wanted to take his hand, but it was cuffed behind him. So she leaned in and kissed his cheek. Macie and Gunnar stood in the driveway of the Cornwell and watched the SUV depart with its prisoner. She couldn't see through the tinted windows and started to give a wave as it left, but she never did.

Macie did move to the sidewalk, though, so she could watch it go until it disappeared in traffic.

The hotel doorman got them a taxi that made two stops: University Place to drop Wild at her apartment, then onward to deliver Gunnar to his loft in NoLIta so he could get off his leg and take a recuperative nap. Macie's plan was to make a quick change and then head off to the Manhattan Center for Public Defense. It was an insane form of denial, Gunnar had warned her. The serial traumas of the past twenty-four hours alone would have put the most hardy soul in a psych ward. Wild couldn't drop everything, but compromised, deciding she would handle the essentials only, and from home.

After a phone call to her mother in Germany and the anguish that came with it, Macie acknowledged Gunnar's emotional intelligence and was glad she had decided not to go in. It wasn't her mom's upset that distressed her, but the lack of it. Dr. Wild took the news of her father's arrest stoically, you could even say, clinically. Although she said she would come home on the first available flight, for Macie, her mother's arid response signaled the true ending of the Wilds as a family.

In defiance of her fragility, Macie set about knocking off her workload via e-mail. In sanitized bullet points, she updated her team on the disposition of the case, omitting the juicy (translation: self-incriminating) parts of her experiences, such as Luka Fyodor Borodin's death—which Gunnar had insisted would never blow back on them, same as Pipe Wrench and his pal in the Bronx. Too many law enforcement entities would prefer not to draw attention to their ineptitude or secret involvement. "Some conspiracies aren't just theories," he'd said. "This time it breaks our way."

"That doesn't make it disappear."

"Trust me, it's in their interest to sweep this under a rug. And they have a very big rug." Macie reflected on his absolute certainty of that. Was Gunnar sending her an oblique message, a hint to her about his own sealed records? Having suffered enough discord for a lifetime, she had decided not to touch that nerve, and let it go.

Macie was mind-mapping on a legal pad to brainstorm an approach to deal with Jackson Hall's charges when Gunnar called. He spoke to her over a wall of noise: the safety doop-doop-doop of a vehicle backing up and dispatcher calls amplified over radios. "You don't sound much like you're napping."

"I'm up in Jerome Park near the reservoir. Channel 2 called with a gig."

"You should be resting."

"Yeah, well, I was going to turn it down until I heard what it was." A throaty horn sounded, unmistakably from a fire engine. "Hang on, moving out of the way. Shit. You still there?"

"Here."

"The call was for a vehicle fire, fully involved. Mace, it was the FBI evidence van. Some heavily armed guys in masks jacked it at a light on its way downtown. They kicked out the driver and took off. It's been torched. I mean completely torched. They left it here in the park. All that evidence, including Trifonov's diary, is either gone or up in flames."

The lone figure on the end of the East Harlem Fishing Pier cast straight out and watched his bait sail sideways on a sudden gust before it plunked into the whitecaps. In the distant miles ahead of him, bruised clouds shot strobes of lightning over Long Island as an early season storm fired up to the east. A metallic click behind him made the man turn. Jackson Hall regarded the tip of Gunnar Cody's cane on the concrete. "Not going to sneak up on anybody like that." He gave a nod and a hello to Macie then excused himself to reel in his hook. "If you don't mind another cast, it may be awhile before I get another fishing day in."

"Go for it," she said. This time he anticipated the wind and gained more distance. While he slowly rewound his reel, Hall toed a White Castle bag on the deck next to his bait pail. "Mr. Cody. Something for you there." Macie picked it up and handed it to him. Under the burger wrappers rested his Beretta Jetfire. "Slugs are in the bottom of the sack. It's unloaded." Then he added for good measure, "And unused."

"Appreciate it," said Gunnar. "By the way, is this the same bag you left me holding when you took off with my gun?"

"Would it help if I apologized?"

"Not much," Gunnar replied. But he'd had his say, and that seemed enough for now.

Macie looked off in the direction of Rikers Island, not visible from where she stood, but she pictured it somewhere past the crescent arch of the Hell Gate Bridge. Jackson Hall would be back there by supper, commencing the eighteen months for burglary Wild had pled down from the six years Fontanelli wanted. Whether it was the public defender's threat to go for a media-splash jury trial after her client had first been falsely accused of murder then strung up in jail, or the bigfoot call from Special Agent Stack of the Federal Bureau of Investigation, WTF, literally, said the words, "What the fuck," and caved to Wild's deal.

Her client was good with it too. When Soledad arranged a call from him to hear the terms, his immediate reply had been, "Whatever you say's good for me, Ms. Wild. That's why I asked for you at the jump."

She watched him now, giving his rod a small jerk as if he had a bite, then he shrugged and reeled it in again. "Mind if I . . . ?" He pointed to the river.

"When you're ready," she said.

"Not ever going to be ready. You tell me when." He prepared another cast. Before he did, Jackson Hall turned back to face them. "Thank you. Thank both of you."

Macie and Gunnar backed away and sat on a park bench under the pavilion to let him make a few more casts before they took him in.

Happy hour was anything but for Macie, but she agreed to go with Gunnar to Tortaria, a Mexican joint in her neighborhood with authentic food and a killer bar. They were both running on fumes after the marathon they had been through, and were both nursing wounds: his physical, hers emotional. So much so that she'd almost declined. But Wild desperately craved some tequila-aided downtime. And she wanted to be close with this man.

It was hardly downtime though. After what they'd been through, all they could talk about was what they'd been through. Neither could get past the FBI vehicle blaze. He said, "You have got to ask yourself this: not just who has the balls to jack an FBI vehicle? Who has the wherewithal to jack an FBI vehicle, and get away with it?"

"As with anything," she said, "it's not just the how, it's the why."

"To kill the evidence obviously."

"Russia, then?" she asked, but wasn't asking, really.

"Losing $70 million is nothing to them. This is about the whole laundering operation, counted in billions not millions." He took a sip of his margarita. "Look at the lengths these assholes went to just to get their hands on those stamps and seals. Who knows if they were even aware that Trifonov's diary was in there? But could you imagine the impact of that bundle? We're talking one jumbo kick in the nuts to the *nomenklatura*."

"Impressive."

He repeated it. "*Nomenklatura*. Just don't ask me to spell it. Of course they torched the evidence."

"And Trifonov's not doing any more talking. When I asked Special Agent Stack to help me out with the DA, he told me the hospital put him on heavy palliative therapy. They give him a day, at most." She studied the candle flame, lost in a pensive stare.

"But on the upside, it does make the case tougher against your father. All the evidence against him is circumstantial."

"Well . . . he did confess to us." She made a confidentiality check and leaned closer, speaking in a hushed tone. "And you recorded it."

They both considered that gravely. Gunnar said, "That's true. I was rolling audio the whole time in that hotel room. I got Trifonov's confession and your father's." While he got out his phone Macie quickly tossed the moral—and legal—implications over what to do with this audio. On the one hand, it was valuable evidence. It damned her father, but it also made the case against the Russians for their laundering. On the other hand, nobody but the two of them knew it had been recorded. While she weighed the brutal ethical choice, Gunnar's face clouded. He looked up from his phone. "It's gone."

"Gone how?"

"Gone, as in not here anymore." He held up his screen for her to inspect. The white field was blank except for two words: "No recordings."

When they got to his loft, Gunnar didn't bother switching on lights; he hobbled in, clacking his cane across the hardwood on a wincing beeline to the editing bay. Wild lit some lamps and found him seated before a keyboard typing in a password to access the backup he'd uploaded. Gunnar maintained his usual cool, but she had gotten to know him enough to read his darting eyes as they flashed reflected light from the monitor. He double-tapped the track pad, opening one cloud storage file, then another, silently shaking his head with each. Finally, he creaked back in his chair. "I don't get it. . . .Gone." He turned to her. "It's just gone."

"You sure you—"

"I am damn sure." He snatched up his phone and reached the CyberGauchito on the first ring. "G-man. Got a situation here." Gunnar sighed repeatedly as he clicked and scrolled through his hard drive. "How bad?" he said into the phone. "Catas-fucking-trophic."

The cyberattack on Gunnar Cody ran deep and ugly. The Gauchito himself confirmed the worst of it when he arrived minutes later to work the rig, as he called Gunnar's computer system. "They took everything," said Gunnar. "The VICE material, all my footage of Borodin, Teixeira, the gait analysis video of Trifonov . . ."

Wild said, "I think I can guess, but who would do this?"

"Personally," said CyberG, "I'd go with state sponsored. Or, at least, farmed out to cronies. And I definitely recognize some of the digital fingerprints I found."

"We're back to Russia," she said.

The *porteño* nodded. "The bear has hacked the anti-doping results from Rio, the DNC, and turned off the fucking power grid to Kiev. Why should your computer present a challenge?"

"They got me through the Internet, but guess what?"

"You do external back up." CyberG extended a fist to bump. "Dude! Data hygiene!"

Gunnar rose from his chair. Favoring his tender calf, he hopped to the built-in where he stored his hard drives. He swung open both doors of the cabinet. Then turned to face both of them in disbelief. "Fuckers stole my hard drives too." He surveyed the edit bay, then hopped on one foot to peer into the great room. "They were in here. Today."

To spare Gunnar the walk, Macie and the CyberGauchito made the trip down to the basement to retrieve the hard drive from his building's security cam system. Gauch plugged the Seagate into his laptop and scrubbed the lobby comings and goings from that morning. "Got 'em," he called. Macie drew Gunnar against her to support him while they surfed CyberG's screen. He rolled the video back to where a pair of workmen in coveralls entered. One watched the glass door while the other used a key to pop the elevator.

"Freeze it there," said Gunnar. The image stilled with both men's faces open to the camera.

Macie said, "Gunnar, I've seen these two before."

The three of them piled into the Gauchito's Kia Soul and headed down to the Manhattan Center for Public Defense. Macie and Gunnar watched as CyberG stood on her desktop, loosening the ventilation grate in the ceiling. "It was the hairy eyebrows on the one guy that I remember. About a week and a half ago I came in early, and passed these two coming out. They had a ladder, but they left footprints on my desk, and when I griped to my paralegal he said maintenance was cleaning my AC vent for summer."

"And leaving you this," said the G-man. "Testing one, two, three." He tossed a small plastic box to Gunnar. He pried it open and showed her the insides: a lipstick camera and condenser mic connected to a circuit board with a blinking light.

"Sound, picture, transmitter," he said, disconnecting each. It resembled the fake rat trap he had planted in the Bowery flophouse. "Congratulations, everything in this office has been on camera."

CyberG gave them a lift to Macie's apartment. She set up Gunnar to lounge with his leg elevated on her sofa then poured them each a glass of wine. "I can think of one pick-up they captured, for sure," she said, taking a seat on the rug beside the couch. "You and I sat there in my office on the speaker phone when Soledad told us where Jackson Hall was hiding out in Harlem. No surprise, then, how Borodin knew how to tail us on his Ducati."

"That cam could definitely pick up your keyboard and surf your passwords too. Assume all your e-mails and files have been read." Macie rocked her head back onto his lap and closed her eyes. He added, "It's like you said in the van that night."

"What's that?" she asked.

"Nothing is sacred."

She twisted around to study him. "Is this you, coming around?"

"Let's just say you see the world differently when you've been hacked down to your skivvies."

She squeezed onto the cushion beside him and the two of them drifted half awake, half asleep, in contemplative silence. Needing this closeness, Macie was too fragile to do more about it than take his warmth and contact. Her phone vibrated on the coffee table, and she picked it up. The caller ID said it was Len Asher. "My boss," she said.

"Take it," he said.

"Hey, Len." Then Macie gasped and bolted to her feet and wailed, "No!"

Wild experienced the ensuing two weeks in a netherworld of blackout and blur. Left to handle her father's funeral arrangements until her mother returned from Munich, Macie felt every bit an orphan. But soon her friends and colleagues rallied in support. Bunny Liuizzi found her starch and became her chief of staff, taking on all the logistical details after gleaning Macie's desires or guessing at her father's wishes. Soledad staved off all but her most acute social worker clients and stayed close, providing what comfort she could and functioning as her friend's emotional buttress. Tiger kept the office running, making minimal contact.

Every decision flailed away a chunk of her heart: closed casket, due to severe facial disfigurement at the time of his death; yes to burial in the plot beside her brother; in lieu of flowers, donations to The Father Walt Foundation to Aid Indigent Families. Every item on the checklist segued to another personal loss like an infinite loop of Satan's mixtape. Tears, then no tears, then spontaneous waves of tears punctuated her days and, especially the nights of broken sleep in her childhood bed in Rye. After her mom returned, the two women held each other and sat up too late, drinking too much, and trying to find sense in what he did and what each of them was to be from there.

Jansen Wild's funeral was delayed those weeks because of the thoroughness of the government's toxicity report and the internal investigation at the federal lockup in Manhattan where he had been held to await arraignment. The fatal diagnosis was confirmed as poisoning through the oral ingestion of tetrodotoxin, a potent neurotoxin found commonly in pufferfish. In this case, it had been introduced into a turkey sandwich on a tray delivered to her father's holding cell. The medical examiner's report said his death came from the immediate and total shutdown of his respiratory system, leading to tremors, paralysis of the diaphragm, and suffocation within minutes. The source of the poison, and who was responsible for getting it to him, was still under investigation with no leads. Macie and Gunnar both knew it was unlikely any would surface.

The day of the funeral Mass, the nave filled only to one-third capacity. All the dignitaries who had been so much a part of his life distanced themselves in his death. Jansen Wild had died in federal custody with the kind of rumored activities that meant that no governor, mayor, judge, Wall Street CEO, or even town selectman could brook an association. However most of Macie's colleagues, coworkers, friends, and childhood pals from the neighborhood, along with her mother's circle, did come. Most startling and moving to Wild was the unexpected procession of more than fifty priests and nuns, turning out in honor of the father of her beloved late brother. They streamed up the center aisle then formed a semicircle, three-deep, rimming the back wall of the chancel. Macie came forward at the appointed time to read her eulogy, stumbling and thrashing through it, unable to take her eyes off the oblong box before her. She tried to talk convincingly about doing him justice when justice was what he had raised her to live for.

At home after the burial the mourners ate catered food and shared memories and well-wishes that comforted her, at first, then (God help her), bored the piss out of her. Orem Diner showed his respects but kept a distance, only exchanging nods with her the way the keepers of secrets acknowledge nothing. She wondered if he was one misstep from a turkey sandwich himself.

Macie broke free of the reception and crossed the sunny acre of lawn to Gunnar Cody. His cane lay in the grass, and he sat in the chair swing hanging from the branch of her family's old elm. She settled into the seat beside him. "Nice eulogy."

"Poorly delivered," she said.

"I liked the message."

"On the subject of justice? Monheit just told me the feds busted Gregory Eichenthal for insurance fraud. He was hiding that Chagall he claimed got stolen."

"Interesting."

"Apparently they used an RFD receiver to find it in his attic in Amelia Island."

"It's RFID," he said, correcting her. When she fixed her lawyer's gaze on him he added, "OK, remember that alphanumeric code CSU found in Stamitz's medicine cabinet? It was in an Advil bottle?" She thought back to that night in the surveillance van and nodded. "Since Stamitz was an informant, I thought, for laughs, I'd try using the code as a pass-word on one of the FBI servers. I got in. It's apparently a secure e-mail drop where informants, well . . . inform."

"You dimed the pharma CEO? Why?"

"Because he was mean to you." Wild searched him, looking for irony. But the earnest face Gunnar gave back told her he meant it. The sim-plicity of that warmed her. With his good foot, he gave a push. The limb groaned, and they rocked together in the swing. "Think it will hold?" he asked.

She put a hand on his thigh and said, "Depends on what you have in mind." He arched a brow in surprise. It was the first time in fourteen days she had joked about anything.

Whether he took hers or she his, they held hands in the shade on the steamy day in Rye. As they gently swayed, Macie Wild thought about the life she had begun, and lived, on that property. The cookouts, the volleyball, even reading *To Kill a Mockingbird* on that very swing until it got too dark to see the print. It was in that house that her father had declared they should embrace their Kennedy gene. From the murder of her brother to the burial of her father she had learned some hard truths about accepting that marker. It not only meant public service, it carried the same DNA for tragedy. She decided when you compare yourself to a Kennedy, you'd better own a black suit.

The screen door slammed and guests started drifting outside. "Let's get lost," she said. "Can you walk? I mean that far?" Macie chinned in the direction of the woods.

She led him to a secret trail, and they took it slowly, although he seemed to need the cane much less than before. Surrounded by shady forest, and alone, but for the blue jays, Macie guided Gunnar by the hand off the path into a small clearing that formed a cove surrounded by thick brush overlooking a brook. She twirled in front of him and raised her face to his, and they kissed. He let the cane drop and freed both hands to hold her, then to feel her as she was feeling him. Macie thrust her pelvis against him. He pressed right back but then drew away from her.

"What? Trust me, we're alone."

"I know that, I just . . . Look, I have wanted you like crazy. Ever since our first. But take a breath. Look at what went on here today. Not to mention over the past few weeks. This has been a rough time for you emotionally, and your judgment might be clouded. What I'm saying is that I want this, I do, but— Mace, you're vulnerable now. I don't want to take advantage of that just for some impulsive sex."

"Now who's the buzz killer?" she said. Then Wild cupped both hands on his ass and drew him back to her.

ACKNOWLEDGMENTS

My first acknowledgment is to you for the honor of reading this novel. There's not much I love more than taking your hand and leading you into the misty alleyways of a made-up adventure. But we both know the imaginary stuff craters if it's not built on what's real. And for that I'd like to recognize some experts who provided valuable expertise.

Two retired detectives from the NYPD's Technical Assistance Response Unit, Sam Panchal and Dave Fitzpatrick, gave up hours to listen to my questions. Both generously shared logistics and color from their TARU days. I thank them for their heroic service and for contributing to my knowledge of their important work.

Most of what I knew about public defenders came from TV, and that got put right by respected leaders in the field. I am in the debt of Michael Coleman, then Executive Director of New York County Defender Services as well as Lisa Schreibersdorf, Executive Director of Brooklyn Defender Services. Jerome E. McElroy, Executive Director of the New York City Criminal Justice Agency gave me a master class in how the arraignment and bail systems work.

Thanks to the New York Public Library's Carolyn Broomhead, Ph.D., and Melanie Locay, MLIS, for my research fellowship and a base in Gotham with access to the unparalleled collection at the NYPL's Stephen A. Schwarzman Building.

In my research I studied countless nonfiction sources but none impressed me more than *Putin's Kleptocracy – Who Owns Russia* by Karen Dawisha. Allow me to plug another author and recommend it wholeheartedly.

Thanks go to my book agent, Sloan Harris of ICM Partners, as well as Heather Karpas for their encouragement and belief. Nancy Josephson at WME remains a beacon in my career. Roger Arar of Loeb & Loeb keeps me on the legal rails and is nothing like the types you met herein.

Making a book is nothing you do alone, and I had the best support from cover designer Steve Cooley, copyeditor Barbara Anderson, Jaye Manus who beautifully designed the interior, and publicists Jason

Hargett and Nick Courage. Huge thanks to the legendary Jill Krementz whose camera didn't break after all when she generously took my author photo.

So many people I revere in the creative community lent support, advice, and encouragement. Gotta start with Lawrence Block whose insights on everything from writing to publishing tips were pure gold. For over two decades Clyde Phillips has been a collaborator, a writing partner, and a friend. I thank him for his generous assistance with this book and the model of professionalism and humanity he brings to everything. As always, my pal Ken Levine reminded me that a murder was a good place to start a murder mystery, advice that still seems to hold. Alton Brown consented to make another cameo in my pages, where he is always a welcome presence. A big tip of the brim to Jack Rapke and Jackie Levine at Robert Zemeckis's ImageMovers who read my early chapters and whose response gave me rocket fuel. Fellow members of the Mystery Writers of America I'd like to thank for help are Charles Ardai and Chris Knopf. Same to John and Miranda Dunne Parry for their perspective and their cherished friendship. In publishing, I give a smart nod to Will Balliett for that big start and all the nudges with every book since. Same for Gretchen Young, editor extraordinaire, who became my friend, advisor, and chief encourager.

From *Castle*, warmest thanks go to Andrew W. Marlowe and Terri Edda Miller. Both humble me with their faith and inspiration. Not to mention the fact that our collaboration changed my life.

In my family, I had better acknowledge my mom, who kept saying, "Finish it!" Also Kelly, Andrew, and Chris, who are old enough now to give unsparing feedback on everything from concept to cover. And did they ever.

Saving the best for the coda, the greatest appreciation is for my bride, Jennifer Allen, who inspires me to dream—and then dreams with me. May it always be thus.

Tom Straw
Connecticut,
September 2017

TOM STRAW published his first mystery novel, *The Trigger Episode*, in 2007. Writing as Richard Castle, he subsequently authored seven more crime novels, originating the Nikki Heat series, all of which became *New York Times* Bestsellers. He is also an Emmy- and Writer's Guild of America-nominated TV writer and producer as well as a former board member of the Mystery Writers of America, New York Chapter. He lives in Connecticut, where his home is his castle.

Author photo © Jill Krementz

Made in United States
Orlando, FL
28 December 2022